"Again and again, Ms. Barclay proves that she is one of the best authors today in historical romance!"
—*The Literary Times*

"...richly detailed, completely believable and totally satisfying..."
—*The Gannett News Service*

"...page-turning adventure...seduces your senses and lays siege to your heart."
—Author Theresa Michaels

"A rare treasure!"
—*Rendezvous*

"...a great superstar."
—*Affaire de Coeur*

"...a magician with words..."
—*Romantic Times*

"...pure magic...a glorious tapestry of love and redemption."
—*Old Book Barn Gazette*

**Discover the magic.
Read Suzanne Barclay today!**

Dear Reader,

If your mother didn't tell *you* about Harlequin Historical, this Mother's Day might be a good time to let *her* in on the secret. The gift of romance can enhance anyone's life, and our May list promises to be a spectacular introduction. Award-winning author Suzanne Barclay returns this month with *Lion's Lady,* the fourth title in her highly acclaimed SUTHERLAND SERIES. Intrigue, betrayal and passion abound in this medieval tale of a newly widowed noblewoman who travels to Blantyre Castle to secure her son's inheritance and is shockingly reunited with the valiant warrior who is her child's natural father.

A feisty young adventuress with dreams of the West heals the haunted soul of a handsome wagon train leader in *Jeb Hunter's Bride,* the newest title from the versatile Ana Seymour. And in *The Wilder Wedding,* a compelling Victorian by Lyn Stone, a young heiress who believes she is dying proposes to a jaded but irresistible private investigator she's only just met.

Rae Muir's *Twice a Bride* is the second book of her captivating WEDDING TRAIL series about four friends who find love on the road to California. In this Western, a trail scout's daughter marries a rugged hunter to fulfill her father's dying wish—only her father doesn't die....

Whatever your tastes in reading, you'll be sure to find a romantic journey back to the past between the covers of a Harlequin Historical. Happy Mother's Day!

Sincerely,

Tracy Farrell
Senior Editor

Please address questions and book requests to:
Silhouette Reader Service
U.S.: 3010 Walden Ave., P.O. Box 1325, Buffalo, NY 14269
Canadian: P.O. Box 609, Fort Erie, Ont. L2A 5X3

SUZANNE BARCLAY
LION'S LADY

Harlequin Books

TORONTO • NEW YORK • LONDON
AMSTERDAM • PARIS • SYDNEY • HAMBURG
STOCKHOLM • ATHENS • TOKYO • MILAN
MADRID • WARSAW • BUDAPEST • AUCKLAND

ISBN 0-373-29011-X

LION'S LADY

Copyright © 1998 by Carol Suzanne Backus

All rights reserved. Except for use in any review, the reproduction or utilization of this work in whole or in part in any form by any electronic, mechanical or other means, now known or hereafter invented, including xerography, photocopying and recording, or in any information storage or retrieval system, is forbidden without the written permission of the publisher, Harlequin Enterprises Limited, 225 Duncan Mill Road, Don Mills, Ontario, Canada M3B 3K9.

All characters in this book have no existence outside the imagination of the author and have no relation whatsoever to anyone bearing the same name or names. They are not even distantly inspired by any individual known or unknown to the author, and all incidents are pure invention.

This edition published by arrangement with Harlequin Books S.A.

® and TM are trademarks of the publisher. Trademarks indicated with ® are registered in the United States Patent and Trademark Office, the Canadian Trade Marks Office and in other countries.

Printed in U.S.A.

Books by Suzanne Barclay

SUZANNE BARCLAY

has been an avid history buff all her life and an inveterate dreamer since she was very young. "There is no better way to combine the two than by writing historical romances," she claims. "What other career allows you to journey back to the time when knights were bold and damsels distressed without leaving behind the comforts of central heating and indoor plumbing?" She and her husband of twenty-one years recently moved into a new house with a separate office where Suzanne can dream in blissful peace…when not indulging her passion for gourmet cooking or walking their two dogs, Max and Duffy.

Suzanne has prepared a comprehensive Sutherland family tree, detailing the marriages and progeny of all the Sutherlands, even those who did not star in their own stories. To receive a copy, send a large SASE to: Suzanne Barclay, P.O. Box 92054, Rochester, NY 14692.

Prologue

Highlands, July, 1384

He wasn't coming.

Rowena MacBean closed her eyes, her head bowed by a pain so sharp it was physical. Her hand fell reflexively to her belly. Flat still, it was, but if old Meg was right about what she'd told Rowena this morn—and the midwife usually was about such matters—it would not be flat much longer.

Rowena was pregnant with Lion Sutherland's baby.

The joy she'd felt on hearing the news had faded to fear and finally gnawing panic as the hours waned and Lion didn't arrive. A shudder worked its way through her as she imagined the confrontation to come when she returned home.

"Fool," her mother would cry. "What were ye thinking, carrying on with the likes of him? He'll not wed ye, ye know. When he takes a wife, the heir to the high-and-mighty Sutherland clan will wed a lass as wealthy and noble as himself, not a lowly MacBean. And why should he, since ye're willing to give it away free?"

Rowena would likely get her ears boxed for good mea-

sure and have to endure the pain in her older brother's eyes
and the sneers of the lads she'd snubbed.

"Lion isn't like that, Mama," she whispered now, pressing her back against the aging pine for support. For two
months—ever since their meeting at the clan gathering in
May—they'd secretly trysted here, in the woods halfway
between Tarbert Keep and the Sutherlands' fine castle at
Kinduin.

He'd come. Lion always came. Though born into wealth
and privilege, he was a man who put honor before all
things. He'd said he loved her. He'd promised to wed her
in three years when he returned from France with the education his father insisted upon. "You'll be ten and eight
then," Lion had said, holding her close to his naked body
as their racing hearts slowed. "Together we'll rule my wee
tower at Glenshee."

The memory of their loving warmed her chilled blood,
gave her heavy spirit a glimmer of hope.

Lion loved her. He would come. He was just late.

He had never been late. Not once in two months. More
often than not, he'd met her just out of sight of Tarbert,
being so anxious he'd come all the way instead of half.
He'd have come to her front gate if she'd allowed it, but
fearing her mother's wrath, Rowena had insisted they meet
in secret.

Preparations for the journey to France must have delayed
him, for he was due to depart in a fortnight.

What would her announcement do to his plans?

Her faith faltered, then steadied as she recalled Lion's
face when he kissed her, his mouth curved in a heart-
stopping smile, his brilliant amber eyes warm with love.
He'd not fail her, her rugged, black-maned Lion. He would
convince his parents to let them wed. He'd take her with
him to France. The court would surely be grander even than
Kinduin's fine hall, but with Lion beside her, she'd brave
the stares of the foreign nobles. She'd sew herself velvet
gowns of the sort worn by Lady Elspeth, Lion's mother.

Rowena would even tame her unruly blond hair beneath a stiff headdress such as fine noble women wore. She'd work hard to become a lady so she would not shame her Lion.

Her Lion.

Aye, he was that. Recklessly brave, hot of temper, quick to anger, quicker to forgive. Yet so incredibly gentle and tender with her. The memory perked up her spirits. He loved her.

Rowena pulled her cloak a little tighter and watched the trail. An hour passed. And then another. Her shoulders slumped. Four hours she'd been waiting. Soon it would be nightfall. If she didn't leave soon, she'd be riding home in the dark.

As the sun sank slowly behind the majestic mountains, Rowena untied her pony's reins from the branch and mounted. She felt as creaky and stiff as an old woman, as though someone had been beating her. Well, she'd get that beating soon enough, when her mother found out she was carrying a bastard child.

It was fully dark by the time she approached the wooden gates of Tarbert. Toothless Will poked his head over the wall and scowled down at her.

"Out late ye are, lass."

"Aye." She was so cold it seemed her feet were made of ice as she dismounted in the courtyard. Tarbert Tower glowered down at her in the gloom, stern and disapproving. Light shone from the narrow arrow slits in the great hall a story above. Her kinfolk were at supper. Her stomach rumbled, but she couldn't face them. Instead, she sneaked in through the kitchens and up the back stairs to her small wall chamber.

Shivering, she undressed in the dark and crawled under the scratchy blanket. Then and only then did she let fall the tears that burned the back of her eyes. She wept as she hadn't in years. When the storm had passed, she dozed, awakening at first light.

What was she going to do? Huddled under the covers,

she devised and discarded a dozen plans. Only one course made sense. She must ride to Kinduin and see Lion. Only then could she decide what must be done.

Though it was summer, the room was icy cold as she washed and dressed quickly in her feast-day best. She took extra pains with her hair, brushing out the snarls, then braiding it. Her hands shook as she pinned the braids atop her head, as she'd seen the fine ladies do. The only piece of jewelry she possessed was a broach in the shape of a swan, which her father had given her the year she turned thirteen. She used it to fasten her cloak, then crept from the room.

No one was about when she saddled her pony. To the guard at the gate, she lied about having an errand in the village. The five-mile ride to Kinduin passed too quickly and too slowly, with her stomach in knots, her nerves ajangle. By the time she reached Kinduin's gates, she was dizzy with dread. Her voice shook as she gave her name to the guard in the gatehouse. After a long wait, the small door set in the drawbridge opened, and a soldier in dark Sutherland plaid motioned her forward.

"What do you want?" the man inquired warily.

"I—I've come to see L-Lion Sutherland."

"Alone?" He scowled and looked about, as though expecting men to sprout from the rocks at her back.

"A-aye. Could—could I speak with him?"

"He's not here."

"Not here? Where...?"

"France," the soldier snapped. "He's gone to France."

"But—but he was not supposed to leave for a fortnight."

"Plans changed."

Nay. He can't have gone...not without a word. Stunned, Rowena swayed in the saddle. "Why?" she whispered.

The man's eyes narrowed. "Who are you?"

"R-Rowena MacBean. I—"

"MacBean!" His eyes narrowed. He stepped closer, shoving his scruffy face into hers. "Now what would a worthless MacBean be doing asking after our Lion? Did ye think to lure him into yer bed and trap yerself a rich husband? Get ye gone before I drive ye away with the point of my sword."

Rowena wheeled her horse and sent it careening down the steep trail, more to outrun the terrible pain than to escape the man's threats. At the bottom of the hill she gave the pony its head, but the rush of wind in her face did not scour away the anguish in her heart. He'd left. He'd left her without a word. The dreadful finality seemed to pound in her head in cadence with the pony's hoofbeats. By the time she reached Tarbert, the pain had hardened to anger.

She'd never been one to trust easily. With a lethal combination of intelligence, gentleness and sensual seduction, Lion had cajoled her into trusting him. How he must have crowed over his triumph when she finally surrendered her innocence. Angry as she was with him, she was furious with herself. She should have known better.

Worthless MacBeans, the guard had called them, and Tarbert was certainly not much to look at—a huddle of dilapidated buildings, a few scruffy cattle. For generations, the MacBeans had earned what they could training other men's horses. It put food on the table, clothes on their backs, but not much more. Still, the keep was clean, her kinfolk honest. Which was more than could be said for the Sutherland heir, she thought.

The MacBeans were at the noon meal when she cantered into the courtyard. No one came to take her pony, so she led it into the stables herself. She unbuckled the girth, then braced to slide the heavy saddle off.

"Let me," commanded a gravelly voice.

Rowena squeaked and turned. "Oh, 'tis you, Laird Padruig." She inclined her head in greeting to him, a customer come to pick up the ponies her brother, John, had broken to saddle.

"Where've ye been?" he demanded. The gloom in the stables emphasized the lines in his weathered face and the harshness of his features. His eyes were hard; his mouth never smiled.

"R-riding." The last thing she wanted now was company. "I should get inside."

"A moment." He plucked the saddle from the pony's back as though it weighed nothing and set it in the straw. "The stable lad can see to her when he's finished eating." He took Rowena's arm and escorted her from the barn. But when she started toward the tower, he steered her around the stark stone edifice and into the kitchen garden.

"Laird Padruig?" She was not frightened, for he'd been a frequent visitor to her father, then her brother.

"I've been waiting on ye."

"Why?" Rowena stopped, fear clutching at her battered nerves. "Is it Mama? John?"

"Yer mother and brother are well, far's I ken." He stopped in the shadow of the huge rowan bush by the back door, yet still kept hold of her arm, as though fearing she'd run off.

"What is it, then?"

"Ye'll not have noticed, but I've had me eye on ye."

"I—I had not." She'd been too caught up in her feelings for Lion and in making the most of the time they had. "Why?"

"I'm in need of a wife," he said bluntly.

Rowena blinked. Padruig held the Highland record for most handfasts, having contracted himself to no fewer than fifteen women over the years. None of the unions had lasted more than the prescribed year and a day, for none had produced what Padruig needed more than anything—an heir to rule the Gunns after him. She recalled John saying it had something to do with Padruig's mistrust of his half brother, Eneas, who would be the next chief if Padruig failed to get a son.

"Why are you telling me this?" she asked warily.

"Because I need a wife, and I think ye need a husband." He looked at her belly, and she fancied those muddy brown eyes of his could see through her gown and shift to her womb.

Rowena shifted uncomfortably. "I do not know what you—"

"Aye, ye do. And ye're a clever lass and sensible...for the most part. Ye'll not be wanting to tell yer family ye're breeding and no husband in the offing."

"How can you know?" she demanded.

"Over the years, I've watched other men's wives and sweethearts swell with child. Watched and envied. Ye've the glow of a lass who's well and truly caught." A hint of a smile tilted his lips. "And I chanced to overhear yer conversation with old Meg the other morning."

"Oh." Rowena wanted desperately to sit down.

"Here." Padruig grabbed her arm and led her to a wooden bench. "Can't have ye tiring yerself and risking my babe."

"You—you'd claim another's child as your own?"

"Aye, I would, and if ye've listened to half the gossip that goes around, ye know why."

"But the child has no Gunn blood."

"It comes of good stock. Ye're a fine lass, gentle and clever...if a bit foolish about love. But then, most lasses are. And the father..." Padruig Gunn gritted his teeth. "'Tis better if his name is never spoken between us, lest we be heard, but I've learned good things about him. Courageous in battle, dedicated to his clan and honorable... I could die easy knowing a lad with those qualities would inherit and safeguard all I'd worked so hard to build." His expression turned as stark as the mountains beyond Tarbert's walls. "I'd do almost anything to keep Eneas from becoming chief after me. He's ruthless and so hungry for power he'd drag our clan into hell with him."

Torn, Rowena studied her hands.

"Ye're thinking mayhap that he might change his mind and come back for ye."

"How do you know he's gone away?"

"I made it my business to know everything about him. His father has great plans for him. He's to be educated in France, trained and groomed as befits Highland nobility. They'll marry him off to a great heiress. What with the way the English killed off the French nobles, there are wealthy, titled daughters and widows aplenty over the narrow sea for him to choose from."

Rowena sighed and hung her head. His words mirrored the fears she'd had when Lion had first taken an interest in her. If only she'd listened to her inbred caution and ignored the attraction that had leaped between them from the instant their eyes had met. "What if the babe is a girl?"

"I'll take that chance, raise her to be strong and wed her to a man of my choosing. It's settled, then?"

Nay, her heart cried out. But for the first time in two months, she listened instead to her mind. "Aye."

Chapter One

Highlands, May, 1390

The night was as wild and unruly as the times. A bank of clouds hid the moon and deepened the natural shadows in the little wooded glen where Lionel Sutherland lurked. The wind blew briskly from the west, whipping the pines and barely budded oaks into a rustling frenzy.

How much he missed this, the raw land, the damp weather, the sweet, sweet smell of home. As he lifted his head to sample the air, the wind tugged at his shoulder-length hair like an impatient lover.

Aye, 'twas a perfect night for the things Highlanders did best—for skulking about in the brush, for executing a raid or meeting in secret. And Lion was about all three. Appreciating the irony of the situation, he smiled. The twinkle in his pale eyes and the dimple that softened his lean face had earned him the undying devotion of more than a few lasses. But not the one he'd wanted most.

Lion's smile dimmed. How ironic that he had braved the spring storm to try and save the life of the man he hated above all others. If he did nothing and Padruig Gunn died, Rowena would be free... Nay, he'd not be able to live with the guilt.

Sensing his restlessness, Turval pawed the ground.

"Steady, lad. It'll not be long now." They'd left Blantyre Castle well ahead of his quarry, and Padruig had to take this trail on his homeward journey. He'd be along any moment; Lion would do his duty, then ride off.

His horse started, long ears pricking forward.

"Is he come?" Gathering the reins to steady his mount, Lion leaned low and peeked between the branches of a sheltering pine. Sure enough, a single man guided his horse along the rocky banks of the creek swollen with late spring runoff.

"Jesu, he's daft, riding in the open as though he hadn't a care in the world," Lion grumbled. He should leave him to his own devices, but his sense of justice wouldn't let him.

As Padruig rode abreast of his hiding place, Lion urged his horse out from cover.

"What the...?" Pale light shimmered on deadly steel as Padruig lifted the sword from across his thighs. "Who are ye?"

"A friend." Lion held both empty hands aloft.

"Friends dinna creep up on a man in the dark." Padruig was a big, rawboned man of some five and forty years, with thinning hair and a warrior's scarred face. How could Rowena have wed him? It hurt thinking of him with his Rowena, kissing her, lying with her, getting her with child.

"You left Blantyre in rather a hurry. And given the delicacy of my mission, it seemed best to meet you here."

"Step into the open where I can see ye."

Lion edged his horse out from under the canopy of branches.

Padruig's widened as they focused on Lion's face. "Lion Sutherland." A brittle note underscored his surprise.

"Aye." They had not been introduced during the brief hours Padruig had spent at Blantyre, come in answer to the summons of Lion's current overlord, Alexander Stewart, Earl of Buchan. "How is it you know me?"

Padruig shrugged. "I'd reason enough to learn yer name."

Had Rowena spoken of him? Had she told her husband that because of Lion she'd come to him no maid? It gave Lion savage satisfaction to know he'd been the first to taste her sweetness. It was not nearly enough, but it was all he had to ease the ache of yearning and regret. "I see," Lion said edgily, wondering if he faced a jealous husband. It would be his first time for that, for he was no poacher.

"I doubt ye do. Then again..." Padruig's thin mouth lifted in what could have been a smile or a grimace. "Have ye come to kill me over it?"

Lion frowned. Although he seemed a blunt, uncomplicated man, there were unnerving layers of meaning in Padruig Gunn's speech. Mysteries Lion had no time to unravel. "You rejected the earl's request for men to help him subdue the outlaws that plague the Highlands," he said, returning to the business at hand.

"Subdue outlaws?" Padruig cursed and spat. "'Tis an excuse to curb our independence and strip us of our property. Alexander Stewart'll wipe out those clans that oppose him and take over their lands. He'll make himself king of the Highlands, mark my words."

Lion was amazed at how well Padruig understood the situation. Most of the clan leaders who had agreed to follow Alexander had either been fooled by his high-sounding mission or thought to gain power themselves. Those who had not joined him were of two groups—the lawless ones who did, indeed, need to be controlled and a few clans like the Sutherlands who guessed the earl's darker purpose and wanted to stop him.

It was a dangerous, mayhap impossible task. One that had cast Lion in the role of spy in Alexander's court. "If Alexander is as ambitions and ruthless as you say—" and Lion knew firsthand that he was "—then you were a fool to defy him so openly."

"Bah. He'll not miss the few Gunns I could have brought to his army. We're a small, isolated clan."

"He's not a man who takes kindly to being told nay."

Padruig snarled a curse.

Lion sighed. He couldn't imagine his young, sunny Rowena wed to this cold, gruff man. Trying to do so hurt. "It would have been better to pretend to fall in with his plans."

"Lie?"

"What harm in a lie that saves lives and buys us time?"

"Time to do what?"

"Find a way out of this damnable situation," Lion replied.

"By agreeing to side with a rogue and murderer? Wolf, I've heard men call him behind his back. And it seems most apt, given the relish with which he raids and murders."

Lion admired his convictions, if not his stubbornness. "Have you no care for your clan? For your…your *wife?*" The word stuck in his throat.

"Ah, my wife." Padruig's searing gaze raked Lion from his bare head to his leather boots, then back up. "I've a care for her—and for the lands I'd leave my son. Which is why I'll not dirty myself by associating with that bastard. But I thank ye for the warning. Were our positions reversed, I wonder if I'd do the same." He tugged on his horse's reins and urged the beast into motion.

Lion sat scowling as he watched Padruig pick his way up the glen. When he passed from sight, Lion reluctantly moved off to the left, up the little-used trail he himself had taken. At the lip of the ridge, he paused long enough to ascertain he was alone, then set off to get his men. They had miles to go for his meeting with Fergie Ross.

Another hard, crusty old man with a stubborn streak who would rather defy the earl than harken to Lion's plans.

He'd gone scarce a quarter mile when he heard it—a hoarse scream that tore across the quiet land. "Bloody hell." Wrenching his horse around, he raced along the rim of the glen, calculating how far the Gunn might have gotten in the few minutes since they'd parted. When he reached the cut in the land where a stream poured down to join the creek in the glen, he dismounted, hobbled his horse and crept down on foot.

He was nearly to the bottom when a troop of men galloped past. A score or more, he judged by the sounds of their horses. Though he could not see them for the brush, he caught a flash of red and blue. MacPhersons? Aye, it made sense. Alexander often sent Georas MacPherson to do his dirty work.

Blade drawn, Lion crept through the underbrush. The sight of Padruig sprawled beside the stream in a pool of blood stopped him. He moved forward to feel for signs of life, but found none.

Damn. Damn. He should have gone with Padruig. Followed him at least. And died with him? Sobering thought, but Lion's guilt didn't ease. "Jesu, Rowena, I'm sorry. So sorry."

The clatter of hooves on stone sent him scrambling for cover. It was not Padruig's murderers come back, but his own men who burst onto the scene.

"We heard a cry," Bryce explained, controlling his nervous mount as he surveyed Lion. "Are you hurt?"

"Nay, but Padruig Gunn is dead."

"Alexander's men?"

"Likely. They were MacPhersons, I think." Lion knelt again by the body. "And it wasn't robbery, for his purse is still here."

"Damn, if only we'd realized the earl would stoop to this."

Lion stood. "He grows desperate indeed if he will murder a man over a few troops for his damned army. I should have tried harder to convince the Gunn he was in danger."

"What now? Will you take the body to his people?"

Lion debated only a moment before shaking his head. "I'm overdue to meet with Fergus. If I do not show up, God alone knows what foolishness he'll undertake." He looked down at Padruig again. "And the Gunns are bound to ask who did this, mayhap seek revenge against Alexander, and die in turn." He exhaled. "Red Will, take three of the lads and carry Padruig Gunn near to home. Leave him at the side of the road..." Like refuse. Lion cringed, but couldn't waver. "Make it look as though he'd been attacked and robbed." Fewer questions that way.

Even by Highland standards, Padruig Gunn's funeral was a wild and raucous affair. The Gunns come to mourn their fallen chief cavorted about Hillbrae Tower's great hall like revelers on a feast day. Shouted songs and laughter vied with sobs of regret at his passing.

But then, the Gunns did everything to excess, thought Rowena as she surveyed the mess and swiftly calculated the cost in food, drink and broken furniture.

"'Tis a grand send-off we're giving him, eh?" Finlay Gunn shouted above the din. "Cousin Padruig would have loved this."

Seated beside the old warrior at the head table, Rowena, widowed four days and terrified at what lay before her, let loose her temper. "He'd have enjoyed it a bit more had he been alive to do so. Damn him," she snapped. "Where had he gone? Why was he riding about alone?"

"Clan business," said Finlay, who was the only one Padruig had ever confided in. "Ye know what store he set by duty,"

"Duty!" She spat the word out like a curse. "Men wave that banner about as though it was handed down from God, but 'tis only an excuse to go adventuring." The memory of Lion's long-ago desertion twisted sharp as a knife in her chest. Though she would never forgive Lion Sutherland, she'd tried hard to forget him. Padruig's death, *his* desertion, had brought it all back: the pain, the fear and, aye, the anger. They roiled inside her, stinging like salt in a fresh wound. "'Tis the women and children who pay the price while you men go off to pursue your duty."

"Easy, lass." Finlay laid a scarred hand on her arm. "I ken ye're grieving for Padruig and worried about what the next years will bring, but there's no need to carry on so."

Oh, but there was. Shivering, Rowena sagged against the high-backed chair, a smaller version of Padruig's mammoth one to her right. She cast a sidelong glance at the chair's occupant—the new chief of Clan Gunn. Paddy, her five-year-old son.

The red head of hair that seemed to mark him as a Gunn was bent over his plate as he toyed with an oatcake. His sweet face was in profile to her—rounded cheeks, a stubborn jaw and a nose he'd need to grow into. The nose handed down from Lucais Sutherland to Lion and thence to Paddy.

He was so young, so precious, so vulnerable. She'd do anything to protect him. Anything.

Her gaze shifted to the man on Paddy's other side.

Eneas's face was also in profile—harsh, lean and predatory. Padruig had warned her often of his brother's ambitions to rule the clan. Now the only thing that stood between Eneas and his goal was her Paddy. Suddenly Rowena was afraid, more afraid than she'd been in years. What if Padruig had not been set upon and murdered by thieves? What if Eneas had killed him? What if he planned to eliminate her son as well?

A crockery cup flew past her nose and smashed against the floor inches from Padruig's bier, drawing her attention from the past to the dangerous present. Even in death, Padruig looked harsh and indomitable, his craggy features set in disapproval, his red-gray brows bunched in a frown over his broad nose. She had not loved him. She could never love anyone again, but Padruig had sheltered and protected her. Till now...

"I have to keep Paddy safe," she said under her breath.

"Aye, and I'll help ye," Finlay whispered. Older than Padruig by three years, a seasoned warrior sidelined from the battlefield by a knee injury, he was kinder, more compassionate than her husband. Finlay had been the first to welcome her when she'd come here as a frightened bride. She was frightened now, longed to take Paddy and run home to the MacBeans. But she'd given up her right to leave when she'd wed Padruig and accepted his bargain. For the sake of that vow and Paddy's future, she was bound to the Gunns of Hillbrae till the day she died.

"I'm sorry to tear at you, Finlay. 'Tis just that I'm worried." The knot in her belly tightened. Padruig had been a cold and indifferent husband, preferring his mistress's bed to hers, thankfully. But he'd been Rowena's bulwark, her protector.

Finlay smiled faintly. "Dinna fret. Before he went off, Padruig bade me take care of ye and the lad. I'll see he's raised right, taught what he needs to know. He's been declared Padruig's heir, and the men will honor that. Paddy will rule Clan Gunn when he's old enough."

'Twas what she'd schemed, sacrificed and, aye, even lied to ensure. Paddy's future. Everything she'd done these six years had been for her son. "You're a fine man, Finlay Gunn. I know you'll do your best by us," she said softly, her expression carefully controlled again. "But 'twill be ten years at least till he can fight for himself. Years filled with peril."

Finlay nodded, his brown eyes sober. "I'll watch over him till then, see that he's strong and capable."

"But you do not know what Eneas has planned," Rowena murmured, giving voice to her fears at last, even though it meant embroiling Finlay in more danger. "An hour ago, I passed by Padruig's counting room and heard Eneas speaking with Clem."

"Go on," the old man urged.

She hesitated. But where else could she could turn? Few of the Gunns would believe Eneas capable of harming his own nephew. Her father was dead, and her brother was not strong enough to face down Eneas Gunn. *Lion was,* whispered a traitorous voice.

She had a brief, vivid image of Lion wielding his heavy claymore, muscles rippling beneath his saffron shirt as he fought to drive off two men who had attacked her at that first clan gathering. His opponents had been grown men, Lion a youth of ten and eight, but he'd bested them to save her life.

Lion, the champion of her youth.

Lion, the nemesis of her darkest nightmares. After what he'd done, she'd not accept a cup of water from him if she were dying of thirst. If there was any justice in the world, Lion Sutherland was dead of the plague.

"Come, lass, a burden shared is lighter," Finlay said.

Rowena sighed and leaned closer, glad of the noise in the hall. "On the morrow, Eneas rides to Blantyre Castle to meet with the Earl of Buchan."

"What? But—but that is where Padruig had gone, in answer to the earl's summons."

"Why? Who is this earl?"

"He's the king's brother, sent here to subdue the clans that have been reiving and murdering. To do it, he must raise an army, and he wanted Padruig to provide some men."

"Oh. It sounds a grand scheme," Rowena said absently, her own troubles more immediate. "Eneas plans to tell the earl of Padruig's passing and swear fealty to him on Paddy's behalf."

"Fealty? Some of the Lowland clans follow that English custom of swearing allegiance to the king, but we Highlanders do not need to seek anyone's approval of what we do. Especially when the king's as weak a vessel as Robert. What does Eneas hope to gain by groveling at the earl's feet?"

"Eneas told Clem he'd ask the earl to declare himself Paddy's guardian," she said faintly.

"But Padruig intended for you, Father Cerdic and myself to have the raising of the lad. He said so before all the clan and made every man swear to support Paddy as his heir."

"Clem reminded Eneas of that, but Eneas said that the earl would not know of this—this unnatural notion of Padruig's." She twisted the linen napkin in her lap, the burning in her belly intensifying. "Eneas says that task should fall to Padruig's only brother, and he's certain the earl will agree."

"No Gunn will care what this earl says."

"But they may." She took hold of Finlay's arm. "Much as they loved Padruig and do love Paddy, also, there are many in the clan who will not love being ruled by a woman, a priest and a—a..." She could not bring herself to call Finlay a cripple, as Eneas had when making his point. "The young men especially want a vigorous chief who can hunt with them and lead them into battle. They will not see the danger to Paddy. They will not see that once Eneas is Paddy's guardian, he could take my son away from us and...and mayhap kill him."

"Eneas would not harm his own nephew."

"Life in the Highlands is hard and chancy. Accidents do happen, even to a grown warrior like Padruig," she added pointedly. "I mean to see that none befall my son till he's old enough and strong enough to fend for himself."

"I will speak with Eneas and make him see that we will not stand for any mucking about with Padruig's wishes."

"He will not listen."

"Then I will ride to Blantyre and inform this earl of Padruig's desires."

"Thank you," Rowena murmured. But she knew that even a few minutes in the saddle were torture for Finlay's bad leg. "We will think of something, I am sure."

"Now what are you whispering about, Rowena?" inquired a voice as cold and sibilant as a snake's hiss.

Rowena gathered her courage, then slowly looked over her son's red head to the glittering eyes of her adversary. Eneas had disliked her from the moment of their first meeting, the young wife of his childless brother, bringing with her the promise of an heir to displace Eneas. When she'd fulfilled that promise and birthed Paddy, Eneas's animosity had ripened to a hatred that burned bright in his dark eyes.

Even in the crowded hall, with Finlay beside her, she felt vulnerable. Eneas had always unnerved her, his malevolent stare seeming to strip away her lies and pretexts. She resisted the urge to squirm. One sign of weakness and he'd strike like the hawk he so resembled. Before, she'd had Padruig's support. Now she was on her own, her wits her only defense. Digging deep into the well of strength some say came to all mothers when their young were threatened, she prepared to do battle for her son's future, his very life. "We were discussing the order of march to the gravesite." She was pleased by her level voice.

"Indeed?" Eneas's hard gaze narrowed. He was a large, lean man, with sharp features and thin lips set in a permanent sneer. Younger than Padruig by ten years, he had his half brother's strength and determination, with none of Padruig's sense of honor. "Father Cerdic first, then myself and Paddy."

"He's too young to walk so far."

Between them, Paddy left off crumbling his oatcake and tipped his head back to look at her. His round face was unusually pale. Mauve shadows bruised the hollows below expressive, whiskey-colored eyes the same shape as his father's. In them, she saw fatigue and confusion. He liked his uncle Eneas no better than she did. Her fault, but better wary than too trusting. "Mama, can I get down now? My bum's gone to sleep."

Poor lamb. He'd been through so much. The shock of losing his stern, remote father, the tensions sparking between the remaining adults in his life, the excitement of the funeral...

"Aye, love, I'll have Jennie take you up—"

"He stays," Eneas said flatly.

Rowena's head snapped up. She felt her face heat, and struggled with her temper. "He's exhausted from kneeling by his father's bier all night." *At your insistence.*

"We all sat vigil. 'Tis expected. As laird, Paddy must look beyond his own comforts," Eneas said with obvious relish.

"He's just a lad."

"Aye, he is." *And I'm a man grown. More than capable of ruling if I can find a way,* his eyes warned. "But he must grow up quickly." He smiled thinly. "I'd be remiss in my obligations as Paddy's uncle and teacher if I let him shirk his duties."

There was that hated word again. And with it came the opening shots in what promised to be a long, deadly war. Damn Eneas for making it seem he wanted the best for Paddy when she knew he didn't. Despite the suffocating heat in the crowded hall, a chill slithered down her spine. What to do? Should she fight Eneas on this and look disrespectful to Padruig's memory? Or give in and risk appearing weak?

"'Tis all right, Mama." Paddy put his hand on her arm, his small fingers warm and as reassuring as the light squeeze he gave her. His face was childishly round, his eyes so like his father's, sharp and wise beyond his few years. "I want to be there when they bury Father, so I can mark the spot. I'm going to raise a cairn there the way they do for the heroes in the tales you've told me. 'Twill likely take awhile and the stones will be small, but I'll carry larger ones when I'm bigger."

Now it was tears she battled. Paddy, her wee Paddy, was protecting her, just as his father had done so long ago.

"Well put, Paddy," Finlay said a trifle too heartily. "He has the makings of a fine chief."

"With the proper guidance," Eneas said pointedly.

"You'd be just the man to teach him," shouted a voice Rowena knew right well.

She glanced at the nearest table, where Clem sat smiling at Eneas. A huge lout, Clem was a veritable devil with claymore, dirk or his bare fists, and the most dangerous of Eneas's thugs. There were other men in the crowd, men

who were more honorable and less greedy for power than
Eneas and his cronies, but if Eneas insisted on being named
Paddy's guardian, they'd side with him over her—an out-
sider and, worse, a woman.

Rowena knew then what she must do—go to Blantyre
and convince the earl to uphold Padruig's will. Eneas
would not like it, would try to prevent her from making the
journey, if she asked his permission. So she wouldn't ask,
she'd strike now, in the presence of these witnesses—and
quickly, before they were too drunk to care.

Rising, she shouted above the din, "Silence, please. I
need a moment of your time on urgent clan business."

The Gunns stopped talking and stared at her as though
she'd suddenly sprouted wings. Small wonder they were
shocked by her outburst. In all her years at Hillbrae, she'd
never raised her voice in the hall. While Padruig had given
her the running of the keep, the management of the clan
was men's business, so she'd stayed quietly in the back-
ground, reading her few precious books, sewing her husband's clothes and raising her son.

"First, I want to thank you for coming to honor Padruig.
I know he would be pleased." Conscious of the incredulous
stares, she hurried on. "Last night while I kept vigil beside
Padruig's bier, I recalled his fears that should something
happen to him before Paddy was grown, some other clan
might think us leaderless and try to snatch up our hold-
ings."

"Think you I cannot defend what is ours?" Eneas
snarled.

Rowena smiled. "I know you would fight valiantly to do
that, but our losses might be heavy. Why risk a fight when
Padruig himself had a plan that would avoid bloodshed?"

"He did?" asked Finlay.

"He did," Rowena lied without compunction. "The king
has sent his brother, the Earl of Buchan, to subdue the more
warlike clans and bring peace to the Highlands. I will go

to the earl, tell him of Padruig's passing and swear fealty
to the crown on Paddy's behalf.''

"You!" Eneas shouted. "Why would you go?"

"Because Padruig named me as Paddy's guardian, along
with Father Cerdic and Finlay," Rowena said sweetly.

Her statement was greeted by murmurs of ascent from
some in the crowd and a low curse from Eneas.

"With the leadership of Clan Gunn thus confirmed by
the king's representative, no clan would attack us without
running afoul of the earl and risk being declared outlaw by
him," Rowena said in a calm, firm voice, rather pleased
with her reasoning.

The grinding of Eneas's teeth was so loud Rowena could
hear it over the nervous pounding of her heart. Her palms
were wet, her stomach in knots, but she knew she'd won.
Eneas could not decry the scheme and then set out on the
same errand himself.

"I will, of course, go with you," he growled. "To make
certain no harm befalls my brother's widow."

"How kind you are."

Eneas glared at her, his eyes lethal weapons. "The journey will be hard and dangerous."

"I look to you to see us safely to Blantyre."

Eneas cursed under his breath, then motioned the steward
over to him. "Wat, pass the word, 'tis time for the lifting."
Spearing her with another scathing look, he shoved back
his chair and stomped away toward his underlings.

Finlay stood also. "That was well done Rowena, but I
will go with you to make certain Eneas minds his manners."

"I can look out for myself, Finlay. I need you to remain
here to make certain Paddy is safe."

"For all he's a hard man, Eneas loved Padruig. He'll not
harm his brother's son," Finlay repeated.

The icy fist around Rowena's heart tightened. If Eneas
learned that Paddy was not Padruig's son, he'd have no
compunction about killing him.

Paddy's giggle cut across her dark thoughts. "I dinna think most of the men will get themselves up the hill, much less lift Father," he said lightly.

Squinting against the smoky pall, she watched the Gunns attempt to rally themselves for the trip to the kirkyard. Drunk as they were, most of the men and some of the women were literally falling down. "Not surprising. Ten kegs of ale emptied since dawn."

"Aye. But ye did him proud." Finlay grinned as he helped her to her feet. "For all he was spare with his words and not one to share his feelings, Padruig respected ye lass."

Rowena nodded glumly, looking back on her cold, love-less marriage and ahead to her bleak, dangerous future. "That is something, I suppose."

"Make way," Wat the Steward cried, elbowing people aside as he cleared a path for the fallen laird's nearest and dearest.

Jennie met Rowena at the outer door. "I've brought your fur-lined cloak and the young laird's, too." She handed Finlay Paddy's cape, then drew Rowena aside to assist her in dressing. Three years Rowena's senior, the maid was plump and pretty, with red hair and freckles as numerous as her suitors. A capable maid and trustworthy friend, she had left Tarbert to live among the Gunns with her mistress. If not for her support, Rowena wouldn't have lasted a fort-night as Padruig's bride. "You're pale as new snow," Jen-nie scolded.

"Small wonder." Rowena pressed a hand to her head, hoping to still the grinding ache.

"What has Eneas done to hurt you now?"

"Jennie…"

"Eneas knows I hate him."

"Aye, but that was before." Rowena glanced ahead.

Someone had opened the door, letting in a swirl of bless-edly fresh spring air. Eneas stood in the entryway, his big body blocking the light. A symbol, surely, for he'd like to blot her and Paddy out...permanently.

"From now on, I want you to keep that sharp tongue between your teeth, Jennie MacBean," Rowena said in a rush. "With Padruig gone, we must all watch our step."

"And our backs."

"Aye." Rowena shivered and turned, her heart quieting when she saw Finlay kneeling to fasten Paddy's cloak with the heavy broach, the symbol of his lairdship. *God keep him safe.*

"Mama?" Paddy tugged on her hand. "If I build Father's cairn very high, do you think he'll like me better?"

"Your father loved you," Rowena said.

Paddy looked down and traced a circle on the stone floor with the toe of his boot. "He never said so. Sometimes he looked at me..." his thin shoulders moved restlessly beneath the heavy cloak "...as though I'd turned into a bowl of boiled kale." Paddy's least favorite food.

Rowena sighed, aching for her small son but knowing no words to explain. "He had much on his mind, love. If he grimaced and glowered, 'twas not at you. You were very, very important to him. Come, the others will be waiting. Let us walk up together and bid your father farewell."

His hand, though small, was reassuringly warm in hers. She wondered who was helping whom as they began the long trek up the slope to the kirk. It had rained last night, and the ground steamed mist into the chilly air, giving the scene an otherworldly quality. If only this was a dream and she'd awaken to find Padruig alive, her life unchanged. While she was about it, why not wish she could awaken and find these past six years had been a nightmare and she was still Rowena MacBean, young, carefree and in love with Lion Sutherland?

Nay, for then she'd not have Paddy.

As they followed the line of mourners up the hill, Rowena vowed on Padruig's soul that she'd find a way to keep Paddy safe, no matter what she had to do.

Chapter Two

The journey to Blantyre was every bit as horrible as Finlay had warned her it would be. Rain turned the roads into mud-clogged trails, slowing their progress through the mountain passes. A two-day journey dragged into five interminable ones, riding at the mercy of the wind-driven rain and Eneas's equally foul temper. Each night, he'd insisted on camping in the woods, with only their plaids and the oiled cloth Wat had sent along for protection from the elements.

Just to spite her, Rowena was certain. Wet, exhausted and miserable as she was, she refused to give Eneas the satisfaction of showing it. She rode behind him, shoulders square, with only the heat of her determination to keep the cold at bay.

"When do you think we'll reach Blantyre?" grumbled Harry Gunn, the young soldier Finlay had sent along as her squire.

"Ye've got to have someone to do yer bidding and watch out for ye," Finlay had muttered. "Seeing as how ye've refused to take along one of the maids."

"I must leave Jennie here to care for Paddy. Bad enough he's lost his father. Now his mother is riding away. He needs someone to cosset him and reassure him. And the other maids are either too old to withstand the ride or too flighty.''

"The earl's court is likely to be a rough place."

"I've lived among rough men all my life," she'd said with a toss of her head, rather enjoying the freedom to decide things for herself after so many years under Padruig's thumb.

"I heard Eneas tell Clem we should reach Blantyre sometime today," Rowena said now to her freckle-faced escort.

"Not a moment too soon." Harry grimaced as he shifted. "Me bum's permanently flattened, I'll wager."

Rowena smiled and blew a drop of rain off the end of her nose. "I know just what you mean."

"Will it be a grand place, do ye think?"

"I shouldn't wonder, for Finlay tells me it is the ancient seat of Clan Shaw, and they a wealthy house." Oh, she did so want to make a good impression on the mighty earl who'd taken up residence there. She had a moment's qualm, thinking of the woolen gown carefully folded into her saddle pouch. It was the finest thing she'd ever owned, and Jennie had assured her that the deep blue color was vastly becoming. Yet Rowena feared the noble courtiers would see through the bright plumage to her drab MacBean roots.

"Do ye think there'll be lassies there, and all?"

"For shame, Harry," she said. "You are supposed to be guarding me, not chasing after a flock of light skirts."

"My lady! I—I assure ye I didn't mean it, I—"

"I was teasing, Harry."

He glanced sidelong at her, dark eyes wide under a tangle of dripping red hair. "I've never heard ye jest before, my lady. Ye were always a most serious and proper sort."

"I suppose that's true." But there had been a time, a brief time, during that wild, glorious summer with Lion, when she'd been gay and happy and loved. The memory brought with it a pang of longing so sharp she could smell the heather that had grown in the fields. Six years it had been since she'd been held or kissed. Six long, lonely years.

"Lady Rowena?"

She started. "Aye, Harry."

"Look up ahead. Eneas's scouts have ridden in with word we're within a league of Blantyre Castle."

"Praise be," Rowena said. "Can we pause that I might change into fresh clothes and try to get a comb through my hair?"

"I doubt Eneas'll stop, and I'd not want to linger alone in these woods."

Rowena followed his wary gaze into the dark, dripping forest, which seemed to close in on them. Steam rose from the black boulders crowding the edge of the trail. It mingled with the mist in the trees, forming a dense fog within whose depths all manner of evil might lurk. Somewhere nearby a hawk's lonely cry split the silence, sending a shiver down Rowena's spine. "I suppose you are right. Hopefully the earl will understand."

"Ye look fine as ye are, in any case, my lady. Except for the bit of mud on yer cheek."

Rowena hastily scrubbed at her face. "Oh dear, it is vitally important that the earl look kindly on me."

"We must hurry along," Harry urged. "Eneas and his men have reached yon bend in the road, and we'll lose sight of them."

Rowena lifted her head to find Eneas glancing back over his shoulder, watching her from the head of the column. The hatred in his eyes settled the question. He'd like naught better than to lose her...or see her fall prey to some lethal accident. "You are right, Harry. Let us make haste."

The words had scarcely left Rowena's mouth when the thud of muffled hoofbeats came from behind them, mingled with the low rumble of male voices.

"Mayhap 'tis scouts from Blantyre come to welcome us," Rowena whispered.

"Nay, they come too fast." Harry freed his sword. "Quickly, make for Eneas and the others," he urged.

Too late. Mounted men erupted from the trees behind them, brandishing swords and screaming fit to curdle the blood.

Eneas showed his true mettle. Or rather, his back. He fled ahead of the attacking horde without a backward glance, his men scrambling after him like a pack of terrified rabbits.

"Sweet Mary, we are lost," Rowena cried.

Harry wheeled to face the oncoming men. "Ride, my lady," he shouted. "Dinna stop till ye reach Blantyre."

There was no time to argue, no time to thank Harry. Digging her heels into her horse's ribs, Rowena sped along the track Eneas had taken. Branches slapped at her face; briars tore at her clothes. Behind her, she heard the grate of steel on steel, followed by an ominous cry.

Harry.

There was no time to mourn, no time for pain and regret. Rowena focused all her energies on staying in the saddle and keeping her mount moving on the track. A minute they rode, maybe two, before she heard the pounding beat of hot pursuit.

"Faster! Faster!" Rowena urged, giving her mare its head. Her heart flew into her throat as the beast stumbled. "Nay." She pulled back on the reins, fighting for balance, praying for a miracle. It was not granted. With a sharp equine squeal of protest, the horse went down, throwing Rowena off over its head.

She hit the ground with a teeth-jarring thump. The world went black, then misty gray. Stars danced before her eyes. She tasted blood and dirt.

"Chase down the others, I'll see to the wench," shouted a coarse voice.

Rowena clawed at the dirt, trying to rise, to crawl into the concealing foliage a foot away. Hard hands grabbed her by the shoulders and wrenched her up. There she dangled, like a fish on a hook, feet milling in the air, her head muzzy as a drunk's.

"Well, well..." Even seen through a misty haze, her captor's face was terrifying, with blunt, brutish features weathered by sun and wind, close-set black eyes and a tangle of inky hair. "She's a mite dirty at the moment, but she may clean up fine."

"I dinna want to wait," snarled a sullen voice. The speaker was smaller than his hulking companion and better looking, if you discounted the meanness in his pale eyes.

Terror chased the cobwebs from Rowena's aching head. Mustering what courage she could, she said, "Release me this instant," in her most imperious voice. The effect was ruined by her position.

The brute laughed. "Why, 'tis no serving wench we've caught, Dickie me lad, but a fine lady."

"She don't look so fine...and it don't make a damn bit of difference to me who she is." Dickie reached for the laces on the front of her gown.

"Wait!" Rowena said, hating the quaver in her voice. "I am Lady Rowena Gunn, come with my kinsmen on important business with the Earl of Buchan. If you will take me—unharmed—to Blantyre Castle, my brother will reward you richly."

The brute's eyes narrowed assessingly. "Dickie and me, we've no need of gold, but a fresh wench..." He cocked his head, a merciless grin splitting his ugly face. "Now that's a reward a man'd have to be dead to pass up."

"Dead is what you'll be if you don't release the lady," said a low, soft voice. The man who stood behind the brute was leaner but taller than her attacker. A helmet shadowed his face. From beneath it, black hair flowed over massive shoulders. With his sword held before him and his dark cape fluttering out in the wind, he resembled an avenging angel.

"'Tis Glenshee," Dickie exclaimed.

Cursing, the brute cast Rowena into the bracken and

drew his sword as he turned to face the newcomer. "Ye're alone." A savage smile split his ugly face.

"I have Avenger." The knight hefted his claymore with one hand, letting the half-light play on the runes carved into the gleaming blade. "That's enough to deal with the likes of you, Georas MacPherson."

Georas's laughter was coarse and mean, his attack lightning quick. His sword slashed down. Metal screamed on metal as the dark knight countered the stroke, driving Georas back. Face red with fury, MacPherson lunged, shouting for Dickie, who came in swinging his own blade. The blow fell on the leather-and-metal targe the knight held over his left arm. Before Dickie could disengage, Glenshee twisted the shield, scoring Dickie's arm with the metal point at its center.

Dickie cursed and drew back, then resumed the attack, raining a flurry of blows on the targe.

"That's it! Give no quarter!" Georas roared. He slashed with more fury than finesse, but the air resounded with the grating of steel on steel.

Rowena scrambled up from the dirt, back braced against an oak as she watched the struggle. Surely Glenshee could not prevail against these two. Should she call for help? Oh, that was rich. Whom did she expect would come?

While she debated, the dark knight sent his blade sliding down Georas's. With a flick of his muscled arm, he sent his opponent's sword arcing into the brush.

"What the...?" Eyes wide, Georas backed up, rubbing at the small, bloody slice on his wrist. "Get him, Dickie."

"By all means, Dickie. Come and get me," Glenshee taunted. The deadly tip of his blade swung back and forth between the two, keeping them at bay.

"The hell with this." Dickie backed up a step, then turned and ran to his horse. "No wench is worth this much trouble."

Georas glared at the knight. "We'll finish this another day, Glenshee."

"Name the time and the place."

Georas growled a low curse and backed toward his horse. He sprang into the saddle, sent a last, scathing glance at her rescuer, then spurred away into the mist.

Rowena released the breath she'd been holding and sagged against the tall oak, scarcely feeling the damp. As her breathing quieted and her heart settled, she became aware of the hushed silence all around them. The trees stood motionless; expectancy hung heavy as fog in the air.

Her rescuer stood a few feet away, staring after the MacPhersons, his face hidden in shadows. His sword, held still in his right hand, gleamed evilly in the pale light.

Suddenly the lump was back in Rowena's throat. Had she traded one thug for another? "Thank you, sir, I—I am in your debt. I do not know what would have happened had you not come."

"I do, I am afraid. Georas MacPherson and his brother are old hands at picking on things that are small and fragile."

Was that how he saw her? Defenseless? Vulnerable? She tried to step back, found the way blocked by the oak.

"Pray do not be alarmed." He sheathed the sword and extended his large, lean hands, callused palms up. "You are quite safe with me, lass."

A sense of déjà vu swept through her, taking her back to another time and another man—a lad, really—who'd saved her from a band of bullies at a clan gathering. Lion Sutherland. Friend, lover, enemy. She stared at him, eyes aching as she tried to pierce the gloom. There was something in the timbre of his voice, in the way he held himself, so straight, assured and proud, that made her tremble. "Who are you?" she whispered.

He cocked his head, considering. A smile flashed briefly. "How remiss of me." Sweeping off his helmet, he bowed low, courtier to lady. "I am Lionel Sutherland of Glenshee."

"Sweet saints above." Rowena swayed, praying for the ground to swallow her up. "It cannot be you."

"Rowena?" He closed in on her, his hand warm and hard as it seized her chin and tilted it up. "*Dieu.* 'Tis you." His grip tightened. "Bloody hell. If I'd known, I'd have run Georas and Dickie through for daring to touch you." His thumb whisked over her jaw. "Are you all right?"

"Aye," she murmured, dazed by the unexpected turn of events. It was horrible, yet thrilling to see him again, to stand so close after so long. His hair was shorter, the dark mane just brushing his shoulders, its red lights dulled by the gloom. Nothing could dampen the glow in those amber eyes, though, eyes that could freeze or burn. Eyes that studied her with searing intensity. Aye, he was still a magnificent man, with the body of a warrior and the face of a poet. A man other men followed into battle, a man women sighed over and burned over. She'd sighed and burned. Oh, how she'd burned.

Oh, how she'd grieved when it was over.

The memory of his leaving broke through her dazed state. Shivering with emotion, she tried to draw back.

"Shh. No need to fear, I've got you safe." He drew her into his embrace. The feel of his arms was so familiar, so welcome after six long years of drought, that she shivered again. "Easy." He stroked her back, as he'd done so often in the past, holding her as she drifted down from the heights of passion into blissful contentment.

Angered by her own weakness, she tried to twist free, but he held her fast. Clearly, whatever he'd been doing in France these six years had built up his strength, not depleted it. "You are hurting me," she said, knowing his one weakness.

His grip eased, but he didn't let her go. "I know I hurt you," he said, his voice low and tight, and she knew it was not the present of which he spoke, but the past.

"I do not want to talk about it."

"I understand, but—"

"Oh, you do?" The temper Rowena had held in check all the while she'd lived with the Gunns suddenly threatened to explode. Shaking free of his grip, she shouted, "Well, understand this, I loved you. With all my heart. When you left, you broke it. You nearly broke me. Do not," she added, when he reached for her again.

"You have every right to be hurt and upset, but there are things I need to tell you."

"Well, I don't want to hear them."

He sighed and raked a hand through his hair, a sure sign he was agitated and trying to work through a problem. Good. She hoped it plagued him into the early grave he so richly deserved.

"At least listen to what I have to say," he argued. "You owe me that much."

"I owe you?" Rowena's simmering fury boiled over. She buried her elbow in his rock-hard midsection, ignoring the shaft of pain that traveled up her arm. His grunt of surprise as he bent over was satisfying, but not half as much as the sharp oath she wrang from him when her knee caught him under the chin.

The earth shook as he hit the ground. "Damn." He dragged the hair from his eyes with an angry swipe. "Where the hell did you learn such low tricks?" he gasped.

"From you. You said a lass should be able to protect herself." Rowena stood over him, hands on her hips, wounded spirits soaring. Seeing him lying at her feet almost made up for the past. Almost. "And I could not agree more." Dusting off her hands, she spun around to look for her horse.

But she'd forgotten how quick he'd always been to retaliate. Grabbing hold of her ankle, he jerked her down on top of him. Before she could wriggle upright, he rolled, pinning her to the soggy ground with one heavy thigh. His elbows were planted just above her shoulders, caging her, yet sparing her the brunt of his weight. Eyes bright with anger and something even more dangerous, he smiled down at her. "Even better."

The feel of his warm, solid body pressing into hers, the scent of his skin, the quick hammer of his heart against hers were so achingly familiar that for a moment her mind emptied of everything but this. She'd thought herself dead to all emotion save her love for Paddy. 'Twas the worst irony to find that even after six years of hating him, with one touch Lion could still make her yearn and burn.

"Ah, Ro. Jesu, but I've missed you." He lowered his head, his breath warm on her mouth.

Buffeted by memories, she waited, wanting his kiss, craving the taste of him. And then what? She'd been down that path before. It promised paradise, but lead to hell. "Nay!" She turned her head aside, shivering as his lips grazed her ear.

"You cannot avoid the inevitable," he whispered, nibbling his way across her cheek.

She had to. Desperate, Rowena fought back the only way she could. When his lips grazed hers, she bit him. Hard.

"Hell!" Lion reared back, eyes shocked, blood welling from a neat set of marks in his lower lip.

Rowena was so furious with him, with herself, that she shook all over. Nay, 'twas the ground that shook. She looked up, past Lion's shoulder, to see a troop of mounted men galloping toward them.

"Lion!" called one of them. "I thought you were rescuing the lady, not debauching her."

Lion rose lithely. "Save your pity, Bryce. I'm the one with bruised ribs and a bloody lip. Any losses?"

"Nay, we chased the MacPhersons off before they could do more than frighten these folk. And the lady?"

"Is just fine, thank you," Rowena said briskly. She dusted off her hands and searched the crowd of milling men, finding the Gunns knotted together in the throng. Eneas's disappointment at finding her alive was apparent. Some of the others looked shame-faced. And well they should, riding off and leaving a lady and a lad to face a horde of— "Oh, my guardsman," she exclaimed, starting back down the road. "He was injured."

"I will find him," Lion said, trotting alongside her.

Rowena turned on him. "I do not want your help."

He had the nerve to look hurt. "Bryce," he called over his shoulder. "Would you assist the lady Rowena in finding her man?"

Rowena marched down the muddy track, the knowledge that Lion watched her sending an odd thrill down her spine. Seeing him again after all this time was...

Terrible. Horrible.

And exciting.

Dangerously exciting.

That was what frightened her the most.

Bryce Sutherland waited till the little cavalcade, with himself and Lion at its head, had gotten underway before he broached a delicate subject. "How does it seem, seeing the lady Rowena after all this time?" he asked of his cousin.

"I am not sure," Lion replied.

This from the man who was always confident, always knew which way to jump, no matter how perilous the situation? "'Twas a shock," Bryce said. Ten years Lion's senior, he was as much mentor as captain of the elite force that had fought under the Sutherland banner during their years in France.

"Aye. When I realized the lass I'd saved from the MacPherson was Rowena, I damn near fell over." A muscle in Lion's cheek jumped as he flexed his jaw. "She is not well pleased to see me," he said in a low, troubled voice. "And who can blame her, for she thinks I left her without a care or a qualm."

"Did you not explain what happened that night?"

"She would not speak of it." Lion exhaled, his eyes bleak in the sockets of his helmet.

"Mmm. Mayhap she will when she is over the shock of the MacPhersons' attack and her guard's wounding." Bryce deftly changed the subject. "Did she say what they were doing here?"

Lion shifted in the saddle, barely resisting the urge to look back at the object of his turbulent thoughts. She'd refused any further help from him. That had hurt. "I did not think to ask."

"Aye. You were a trifle *busy* when we arrived."

Lion flushed. "Appearance to the contrary, I was not trying to seduce her." Though he'd wanted to. Still did, if the truth be known. He'd gorged himself on women when he'd learned his Rowena had wed another, but none of them had captured his heart or satisfied his soul the way she could.

"Have your feelings for her changed, then?"

"Nay." His heart had soared when he'd recognized her. "But she made her hatred of me plain enough."

"She is only recently widowed."

Lion nodded, gut tightening with guilt.

"According to Eneas Gunn, Padruig's brother and the leader of this band, they believe Padruig was killed by thieves."

Did she mourn him? Had she loved him? "Eneas is the wretch who ran off and left her to MacPherson?"

"The same. I'd say there is little love lost 'twixt him and Rowena, for when we'd routed the MacPhersons, he was not anxious to go back and find his brother's widow."

"Bastard. I'll see she's kept safe," Lion murmured. "Whether she wants my help or not."

"I still cannot believe Alexander had Padruig killed simply because he would not bring his few men to Blantyre."

"The Wolf grows more and more unstable in his thinking." Silently Lion cursed the earl for wreaking havoc in the Highlands. 'Twas not peace Alexander wanted, but power. Under the guise of curbing lawlessness, he planned to gather about him a huge Highland army. With it, he'd wrest the throne from his weak, ineffectual brother, Robert. "If only we could find proof of Alexander's true intentions."

"Mad he may be, but Alexander is clever, too clever to leave evidence lying about."

"But we know he has designs on the crown. He has promised that when he's king, he'll grant land and other favors to some of the more powerful clans, the ones he cannot now sway to his side with gold or intimidation. Rory Campbell saw the document Alexander sent to Archie, chief of the Campbells."

Alarmed, Rory had ridden to Lion's family at Kinduin, where he'd been fostered as a lad. Lion had only just returned from France when Rory burst in with his tale of treachery and intrigue. They'd agreed that Lucais, Lion's father, would go to Edinburgh to try and convince the king to recall Alexander from the Highlands. Rory would return to Blantyre and secure the promissory note. But Rory had been ambushed and killed. The murder of his friend had launched Lion into a desperate scheme of his own to infiltrate Alexander's ranks. He'd been right successful, too. The earl trusted him...as much as the wily wolf trusted anyone.

"We've had Alexander's things searched and found naught," Bryce glumly reminded him.

It had not been easy getting a Sutherland, disguised as a servant, into the chamber Alexander used at Blantyre. "Naill could not get into the locked strongbox. 'Tis the most likely place for the earl to store such damaging evidence."

"We must somehow get inside that chest, no matter how dangerous," Bryce murmured. Searching the personal belongings of a man as powerful and ruthless as Alexander Stewart would be akin to walking bare naked through a room full of vipers. One false step and they'd all be dead. "Mayhap we might slip a sleeping potion into his wine and take the key from around his neck while he is unconscious.''

Lion shook his head. "If he suspected that he'd been drugged, he'd kill every servant in the place...and mayhap even harm Lady Glenda." Lion liked the woman, who was chatelaine of Clan Shaw's stronghold Blantyre Castle. Three months ago, Alexander had decided the large, strategically placed fortress would make the perfect headquarters from which to conduct his "pacification" of the Highlands. He'd presented himself at the castle gates, and when Lady Glenda had balked, had proceeded to seduce the homely, middle-aged woman. Lately, however, there'd been signs the earl wearied of his mistress.

"We must come up with something," Lion said grimly. And while he was on the subject of problems, he added, "I will think on it whilst I escort Rowena to wherever she is bound."

"Eneas said they were destined for Blantyre Castle."

Lion gasped and whirled to stare at the woman whose image had haunted him—waking and sleeping—during his years in France. She was looking down at the injured man his lads carried in a litter. Harry had received a grave wound to the side trying to defend her. His sacrifice had given Lion the time to reach her. Harry was unlikely to live, but that hadn't discouraged Rowena from tearing up her own shift to fashion a bandage for him. She'd always had a soft spot for hurt things.

"Why are they going there?" Lion asked.

"Clan business, Eneas told me. Nastily, I might add, as though I had no right to inquire into his affairs."

"Any man who leaves a woman in distress is no man at all." He looked back again, studying the delicate line of her face. "And Blantyre is no place for a gentle lass like Rowena." The vain, shallow women who hung about the earl's court would slash her to ribbons with their vicious tongues. And the men... Lion's gut roiled at the thought of his fragile Rowena pursued by Georas MacPherson and his ilk.

As though sensing his scrutiny, Rowena looked up. Their gazes met, locked. Her eyes were as dark as peat smoke and just as mysterious, her pale, dirt-streaked features coolly blank. When had she learned to guard her thoughts like that? Lion wondered, remembering the lass whose every notion he'd been able to read from the first.

Staring into her closed face, he knew exactly what he wanted. To win her back. But would she give him the chance? Not willingly, if her steely gaze and set jaw were any indication. They were all the spur his competitive spirit needed. She'd been a cautious, wounded thing when he'd first met her. He'd gentled her and won her then. He'd do it again.

Lion grinned, flashing her fair warning with a look. His smile widened when she stiffened, outrage painting red flags on her colorless cheeks. 'Twould be an interesting contest.

Chapter Three

Though she rode with one eye on poor Harry, Rowena's thoughts were on the man who led them through the misty forest.

She'd never expected to see him again. In the early days following her marriage, consumed by pain and bitterness, she'd wished for Lion to die of some withering disease. Surely her life must be cursed, for not only was he hale, hearty and twice as handsome now, she was also in his debt. Oh, how that galled.

"Lawd, that must be Blantyre Castle," Clem Gunn said from the pack of clansmen who rode behind her. "Is it not the grandest place ye've ever seen?"

Rowena looked ahead, her eyes widening. Blantyre rose out of the fog, spires pricking the sullen sky from behind tall, stout walls. The lights shining from the square towers beckoned, offering warmth and comfort. Like a stalwart gray sentinel, the edifice seemed to offer sanctuary. Or was it only her need for a haven that made her fancy she'd find one here?

The gatehouse bristled with armed men, but Lion was instantly recognized and the drawbridge lowered. Over the narrow causeway they rode, and into the spacious outer bailey. The grassy field was crammed with tents of all description, from fine canvas ones to drab bits of oiled cloth.

'Twas like a miniature city, really, with stables, a blacksmith and even an ale tent set up by an enterprising merchant.

"Who are these men?" Clem asked.

"Likely the men come to help the earl subdue the outlaws," Eneas replied. "Large as it is, there would not be room for so many inside Blantyre. The most important of the clan leaders would have chambers inside the castle. And those of lesser rank might sleep six and eight to a room in pallets on the floor."

"Where will we sleep?" Rowena asked faintly.

"I'd wager that Lord Lion will find a cozy spot for you...in his room," Eneas said nastily.

He would not dare. Would he? "I will seek out the steward and ask if I may have a pallet in the serving maids' garret," she said firmly. Yet her trepidation grew as they rode under the sharp teeth of the portcullis into the inner bailey.

The cobbled courtyard was bounded on all four sides by stark gray walls, the great tower of the castle rising five stories above them like a stone giant. The area teemed with activity like a disorderly hive. Some men practiced with dirk and sword, their curses and grunts ringing off the stone walls, their flailing weapons imperiling those who chanced to walk too close. Other men sat about drinking or dicing.

"See what Lion's brought us," shouted a coarse voice. "A fresh, winsome lassie."

All activity stopped. Men lowered their swords and stared. Others left off their gaming and watched goggle-eyed as Lion led his band to the foot of the main stairway. Then they surged forward, an unkempt tide of shouting males.

Rowena gasped and recoiled in the saddle.

"Back!" Lion roared. "All of you." His command was reinforced by a solid wall of Sutherland targes and swords. "These people are my guests." Lion's hard, censorious gaze wandered over the crowd. One after another, the men shrugged and turned back to what they'd been doing.

Lion appeared beside her. "Rowena, I apologize for these men. They are not under my command and—"

"They seemed to obey you." Evading the hands he extended to lift her down, she slid to the ground on her own.

"Listen to me." He placed his hands on the saddle, caging her between the horse and himself. "Blantyre is not a safe place. Be on your guard," he added, thrusting his face close to hers, "lest you find yourself cornered by one of these lechers."

"*You* are the only lecher who impugns me." She drew in a sharp breath and with it the scent that was uniquely Lion's. It taunted her, brought her senses vividly alive. The small space between them seemed charged with a life of its own. He felt it, too, his long-lashed eyes going wide, his nostrils flaring. Nay. She did not want this. What had been between them was dead, killed by his desertion. "Let me pass," she said, wishing she sounded firmer, less desperate.

"Lion! Lord Lion!" shouted a high, panicked voice.

Lion turned his head. "Here is Donald Shaw, the steward. Blantyre is crowded, but I will see if I can get him to—"

"We will make our own arrangements," Rowena said regally, ducking under Lion's arm.

"There's no room," Donald exclaimed as he waddled down the main stairway. His round belly heaved before him like a bag full of fighting cats. "No room at all. Neither in the castle nor the outer bailey." He stopped beside Eneas Gunn, apparently having picked him out as the leader of these newcomers. "Ye'll have to pitch a tent outside the walls."

"The hell you say." Eneas leaped from the saddle and glowered down at Donald from his considerable height advantage. "I'm Eneas Gunn, and I've important business with the earl."

Donald crossed his arms over his fine woolen tunic. "Lady Glenda, chatelaine of Blantyre, has graciously allowed the earl to use the castle as his headquarters, but my lady has the running of the castle." He glared up at Eneas. "I say it would not matter if ye were the king's own brother. There are no beds to be had. Not even a pallet on the—"

Eneas grabbed hold of Donald's tunic and shook him so the poor man's chins quivered. "Now listen here, you little—"

"Release him," Lion said, seizing Eneas's upper arm.

Swearing loudly, Eneas let go of Donald and tried to shake off the offending hand. "How dare you presume to touch—"

"Be glad I don't break your arm for leaving your brother's wife to the MacPhersons." Lion's voice was low, yet dangerously tight, his eyes nearly black with anger. "Or beat you bloody for abusing Donald, who is only doing his duty."

Rowena, who had witnessed a few of Lion's more passionate outbursts of temper years ago, marveled at this newfound control. Combined with his size and strength, it would make him a formidable opponent.

Eneas, however, was either too blind or too enraged to sense the danger. Curling his lip, he jerked free to address the nearest man. "Where is the earl?"

"Out riding."

"We will wait, then, to pay our respects and hear what the earl has to say about our accommodations." Eneas whirled on his own men. "Dismount and stay here." With a last malevolent glance at Lion, he stomped up the stairs and into the castle.

The name Donald called Eneas under his breath made Lion chuckle. "I know you're a mite pressed for space, but we've an injured man." He gestured toward the litter his men had set on the ground.

"I'd gladly give up my tiny chamber to show my

thanks," Donald said heartily. "But Felis, the herb woman, has a small chamber where she treats the sick."

Lion nodded and gave the order to bring Harry. He frowned when Rowena stepped along beside the litter. "There's no need for you to go. Felis is very skilled."

Rowena froze him with a glare. "Harry is one of mine. Even had he not been wounded protecting me, I'd still see to him." Head high, she marched behind in the wake of the litter. Donald led them through a maze of well-lit corridors to a narrow wall chamber.

The herb woman answered the door and ordered the bearers to place Harry on a pallet by the small fire. "'Tis a mortal wound he's taken, my lady," she said ominously.

Rowena looked at the blood-soaked pad and grimaced. "Aye, it is severe, but mayhap if it's stitched shut and a tight compress applied, the bleeding will stop."

The old woman nodded. "I think 'tis a waste of time, but feel free to use whatever you need." She gestured to the chest of medicines in the corner. "I've been summoned to the village to help with a birthing. The mother lost her last one, poor thing, so I cannot tarry."

"That is all right. I've some skill in such things. Thank you again for the use of this room and your supplies."

"Aye." Felis drew on her cloak. "Any friend of Lion's is deserving of my help," she said before she left.

Rowena scowled at him.

"Is there anything I can do?" Lion asked hopefully.

"Nay. I need nothing from you."

"I've a bit of experience with wounds, and I know the sight of blood always made you queasy. I could——"

"I have overcome my aversion to blood," she said flatly.

Lion's mouth thinned. "I will stay nonetheless."

"I would prefer you did not, but doubt that will sway you."

"Nay, it will not. For as long as you are in Blantyre, you must be under my protection."

"I do not believe I am in any danger. I think you just

want an excuse to—to annoy me,'' she finished, unwilling to give voice to the tension that simmered between them.

''Many of the men who've answered the earl's summons are of the worst sort, the dregs of the Highlands. They are without honor or conscience. Pray forgive me for not wanting you to fall into the clutches of others like the Mac-Phersons.''

Rowena stifled a shudder at the reminder of what he'd saved her from. But forgiveness didn't come easy. ''I've not the time to argue.'' She turned her attention back to Harry. ''He has lost a great deal of blood, so I must act quickly.'' She peered into the pot beside the fire and found it empty.

''I sent my squire for hot water and whiskey,'' Lion said.

Rowena gritted her teeth. ''I must cut his tunic away from his body.''

Kneeling, Lion proffered his own dirk to her. '''Tis sharp, so mind what you're doing, lass.''

''Around you, always.''

A fair-haired lad stuck his head into the room. ''I've got the things you asked for, milord.''

''Bring them in, Sim. Set the pot on the coals to keep warm and put the whiskey there, beside Lady Rowena.''

Sim did as he was bid, paling a bit when he glanced at the injured man. ''I'll wait outside in case you need anything else.''

When she'd sliced away Harry's shirt, Rowena lifted the bandage she'd put over his wound, and her heart quailed. The slash was a long one, extending from under Harry's left arm across his chest to his waist, laying bare two rib bones. It would be a miracle if he lived.

''Let me keep pressure on this while you ready the needle and thread,'' Lion offered.

''All right.'' Opening the medicine chest, she rummaged through it, bringing out a needle, stout silk thread and several packets of herbs. She dipped both thread and needle into the whiskey Sim had brought. Her hand trembled slightly as she prepared to dig into Harry's ruined flesh.

At the touch of her needle, Harry roused. "My lady!" he cried, sitting up with no warning.

"Harry! Lie still!" Rowena reached for him, but he pushed her aside with surprising strength.

"Have to save her," he cried, his eyes wild and unfocused.

"Easy, lad." Lion grabbed hold of Harry's shoulders and forced the boy to look at him. "She's safe, do you hear? We got to her in time. She came to no harm."

"Praise God." Harry sagged in Lion's grip, shivering as he was laid back down on the pallet. "So afraid for her."

"As was I." Lion lifted a cup of whiskey to Harry's lips. "Drink deep, lad. You've a bit of a cut on your side that wants stitching. It'll go a mite easier with this in your belly."

Harry drained the cup, then sighed. His eyes closed; his breathing eased.

"Best begin," Lion said softly. "I'll just steady him for you, least he rouse and cause more damage."

She looked up at him, too weary in body and soul to fight against his help. "Thank you," she murmured. Curiously, the words did not stick in her throat. With steely determination, she began to ply her needle.

It was nearly nightfall by the time Rowena left Harry's bedside. She was stiff from crouching over her patient, and so tired she could have curled up on the bare floor and slept. Felis had returned from a successful birthing, however, and insisted she would sit with Harry a spell.

As Rowena stepped from the sickroom, Lion came away from the wall he'd been leaning against. "Harry?" he asked.

Rowena tensed. "He yet lives. Why are you here?"

"I told you I'd be nearby."

"And I told you to leave hours ago."

"I quit the room, for my presence made you nervous. But I am not about to leave you undefended." Before she could stop him, he seized a stray curl and tucked it behind her ear.

Rowena jumped back, uncomfortable with the thought that he'd been near all this time. "I do not require a guard."

His grin was mocking. "You say that only because you do not know the men gathered at Blantyre as well as I do. Some of them have the manners and morals of pigs."

He was protecting her. The notion was both comforting and frightening. "I can look after myself." She started down the corridor away from him.

"Really? What business have you in the guards' quarters?"

She stopped and turned. "What?"

"That is where you are headed."

"I see." She changed direction, brushing past him without touching him, yet the heat from his body singed her. Down the hall she went, conscious that he kept pace behind her though she could not hear his footsteps. At an intersection, she paused.

"The great hall is to the left."

Rowena sniffed and turned toward the hall in search of Eneas. Loath as she was to see that turn-tail lout, she had to learn what plans he'd made for their accommodations. With any luck, he'd already spoken with the earl and arranged for the swearing to take place on the morrow. Pray God they could leave soon, for being in Lion's presence was painful beyond bearing.

"Why have you come to Blantyre?" he asked.

"I have business with the earl." Rowena quickened her pace. As she turned the next corner, she was assaulted by such noise: shouts and bellows, laughter and...was that the crack of breaking wood? It came from behind a double set of metal-banded doors at the far end of the corridor. "The great hall?" she asked weakly.

"The very same." Lion moved up beside her, his grin

flashing in the torchlight. "We could sup in my chamber instead."

"Certainly not. I've no wish to be private with you. I must see my kinsman." Ugh. To call Eneas that grated. "And pay my respects to the earl."

"Mayhap you'd like to wait till you've bathed and changed."

Rowena stopped and looked down at her gown. To say that it was the worse for wear after five days in the saddle and another spent crouched on the floor was an understatement. "Somewhere I have a pack with a clean gown."

"Why not wait till the morrow? Alexander is likely deep in his cups by now and—"

"Nay. I would conclude my business quickly. I do not want to spend a minute more at Blantyre than I have to."

"A wise decision. The men here are barbarous."

Steeling herself, she met Lion's amber gaze squarely. "You keep saying that. Have you become a barbarian?"

"I hope not." His smile was as compelling as ever.

"Why are you at Blantyre?"

"Like you, I have business here."

She sensed evasion. He'd always been clever with words, able to wriggle out of a question quicker than the river salmon they'd fished for that long-ago summer could escape from a net. "I see. Well, I hope to conclude mine the quicker, for then I can be the one to ride away from *you*." When pain darkened his beautiful eyes, the heart she'd thought fortified against him tripped. *Why? Why did you leave me without a word?* Nay, she did not want to know, could not afford to care why. She lifted her chin. "Do we enter the hall or stand here trading barbs?"

"The slings and arrows of outrage are all yours, lass," he said quietly. "I would have peace between us."

"That can never be." Rowena moved past him and flung open the right-hand door. The wash of light and noise stopped her in her tracks. Blinking, she surveyed the great hall.

It was several times the size of Hillbrae's. Into it were crammed more people than she'd seen in one place before—beautiful women and burly knights. They laughed and shouted, sang and danced, cavorting about to the riotous wail of a pair of pipers. Torchlight played on formfitting silken gowns in a dozen brilliant colors. Gemstones glittered at the women's necks and on their fingers. Like fairy princesses they were, bonny and ever so polished.

Rowena hung back, hands clenching in her rumpled skirts. "I must look a sight," she murmured.

"The offer of my chamber is still open."

"I am still not interested. Ever," Rowena said, turning on him.

"Ah, well, can't blame a man for trying." He grinned and waggled his eyebrows. "At least let's clean you up a bit before you must face the harpies." He seized her chin before she could move away, whisked a square of linen from inside his tunic, moistened it with his tongue and dabbed at her cheek. "Hold still," he admonished when she squirmed. "Well, you still look like a wee lassie who's been playing in the mud, but you'll have to do," he said cheerfully after a moment.

"Thank you so much." Rowena flung his hand aside, turned and plunged into the hall, too angry with him to mind the surprised looks cast her way. Belatedly, she realized he'd probably meant to make her angry so she'd forget about being ashamed or intimidated. Why couldn't he just leave her alone?

Two men suddenly leaped in front of her, their hands around each other's necks. "Take that back," one screamed, shaking the other so his teeth clicked.

"Will not." His opponent sent a fist flying. It glanced off the first man's jaw and headed for Rowena.

She gasped and braced for a collision.

Lion whirled her clear of the two combatants. "Mind where you go." He swept her over to a table near the hearth. Pulling out a bench, he gallantly seated her, then himself.

"I suppose I should thank you."

"Only if the gratitude is sincere. If it's not, it'll be sure to curdle your belly. Hungry?" he asked. Chin propped in his hand, he regarded her with a friendly smile.

Rowena shrugged and looked out at the revelers, seeing a sinister side to the merriment. The two men who'd nearly felled her were themselves rolling on the floor. She caught the glint of a dirk in one man's hand, but none of those nearby made any attempt to intervene. Mayhap because many of them were drunk, too. A few had passed out on the tables. One man lay retching beneath a bench. No one paid any attention.

She looked away, just in time to see a large man grab one of the serving maids, sling her over his shoulder and stride from the hall. "Why does someone not stop him?"

"'Twould be one against a hundred, and most of them so drunk they'd not listen to reason."

"Where are your men?"

"Out and about. We none of us care for the entertainments to be had at Blantyre these days."

"But…" Rowena began, then she sighed and looked down at her hands. She'd fought this same battle when she'd first come to Hillbrae, for the Gunns were a wild and unruly bunch. Padruig alone could control them, except when they were gone with drink. Rowena had learned to lock the maids in her solar when the men were in a festive mood. These men were meaner than the Gunns, she decided. Her gaze strayed to the pair of fighters. One of them lay bleeding on the floor. Seeing the other calmly going through his victim's money pouch, she shivered.

"This is no place for you, lass. Let me provide an escort to see you home on the morrow."

Much as she wanted to go, Rowena shook her head. "I cannot leave till my purpose is accomplished."

"Milord." A plump, homely maid approached the table

and set down a cloth-covered tray. "Here's the food ye asked cook to keep by for ye and the lady."

"My thanks, Mairi, and to cook, also." His smile would have charmed the birds from the trees.

"Always a pleasure to serve ye." Mairi cast an envious glance at Rowena, then hurried away, evading a dozen groping hands with skillful swats.

"You have many friends among the serving staff."

"The best kind...if a man plans to eat well." He whisked the cover off the tray and sniffed. "Cook makes the best meat pies." He lifted one and juggled it, wincing. "Hot, too. Better let me hold it, or you'll burn your fingers.

Dazzled by the smell, Rowena did as he bid, leaning forward and taking a big bite. It was delicious, the crust flaky, the meat juicy. It wasn't till she'd taken her third bite that she realized Lion had her eating out of his hand. Sitting back, she scowled at him. "You think you are clever, don't you?"

"Time will tell if I'm clever enough," he said lightly.

To do what? Seduce her? Likely he'd try, and yet... Rowena frowned, struck by the hidden meaning in his words. She'd known him as a canny lad of eight and ten, yet sensed that the time away had broadened his intelligence. What had he done in France?

"Lion!" A voice boomed out over the din in the hall, silencing the laughter and even the wail of the pipes.

Everyone, Rowena included, looked to the doorway. There stood a tall, dark-haired man, his muscular body draped in velvet and gold chains. The princely tilt of his head as he arrogantly surveyed the hall confirmed his identity.

"The earl," Rowena breathed.

"True, unfortunately," Lion said just as softly.

Alexander Stewart's piercing gaze pounced on their quarry. "Lion! I have need of you."

Lion sighed and stood. "I regret that I must leave you." He took her hand, his lips lingering a moment in a gentle kiss, his eyes locked on hers. "I will have one of my men stay with you."

"C-could you not introduce me to the earl?" she asked. "Lion!"

"In his present mood, 'twould do more harm than good." Lion bowed formally, then strode over to meet the royal prince, who whisked him from the hall.

Of all the times for Alexander to choose for a meeting, Lion thought as he grimly followed the earl across the courtyard and into the ancient tower, built by the Shaws a century ago. Up the winding stairs they went, to the old hall where once the Shaw chiefs had ruled. Here Alexander's inner circle of followers met to drink and talk strategy.

A fire struggled in the central hearth, but a dozen or so torches burned brightly in sconces set the length of the long, narrow room. Alexander did not like dark corners where assassins might lie in wait. Ten Stewart clansmen, the earl's personal bodyguards, sat gaming and drinking at one of the trestle tables. The other tables were occupied by leaders of the clans who'd thus far come to serve Alexander: the Keiths, Chisholms, Mackintoshes, Cummings and, of course, the MacPhersons.

As Lion entered beside the earl, Georas MacPherson jumped up, toppling the bench on which he'd been sitting. "Glenshee!" His hand fell to his sword hilt. "I demand satisfaction."

"Name the time and place," Lion said coolly.

"What is the meaning of this?" Alexander exclaimed.

Georas snarled, "He attacked me on the trail."

"Not without provocation."

"The hell you say. I'd done naught to you," Georas roared.

"To me, nay, but to the lady—"

"I saw the wench first. You had no right to interfere."

"What is this? Two of my best men fighting over a wench?" the earl grumbled.

"Not a wench, a lady," Lion said grimly. "And you are wrong, Georas. I had every right to stop you. The lady Rowena grew up five leagues from my home at Kinduin. I have known her for years. I'd not stand aside and see *any* lady mistreated, much less one I—"

"Mistreated!" Georas MacPherson's face turned scarlet. "She wanted me. I could tell. She just needed a bit of persuading, same as most females do."

"Persuading, is it?" Lion asked with a softness his men would have recognized as more dangerous than another's shouts.

"Aye, and I demand a piece of yer hide to replace the one ye ripped from my hand."

"Easy, Georas. You've forgotten our Lion is more chivalrous than most," the earl said, clearly hoping to ease things.

Lion knew that Alexander would not discipline Georas, who commanded one hundred of the most ruthless fighters in the Highlands. While others might quibble over being asked to commit murder and wreak havoc, the MacPhersons thrived on it. Likely Georas himself had killed Padruig. Nay, the earl could not afford to alienate the MacPherson chief. But neither would he want to lose the Sutherlands, Lion mused.

His clan was large and prosperous with strategically located land. Alexander had tried without success to woo Lucais, Lion's father, to his cause. He'd been delighted when the heir to Kinduin had showed up in his camp, never guessing he was welcoming a spy.

"A pox on his damned chivalry," Georas muttered.

"Nay, nay, Georas, we could learn much from our old friends in France. 'Tis pleased I am we've someone who's spent time in the French court." The earl winked at Lion.

Coarse himself, Alexander made much of Lion's courtier ways and was anxious to acquire some himself. Thus Lion spent an hour each day in the hopeless task of trying to coax lyrical French phrases from the earl's wide Scots mouth. He'd had better luck teaching Alexander and his men to wield the lighter-weight Spanish swords and fight in the manner popular on the Continent.

Georas uttered a crude oath regarding Lion's parentage and the origins of the French king.

Lion's face heated. The urge to teach Georas a much-needed lesson, burned hot in his veins. It was his Carmichael blood, the cursed temper inherited from the grandsire for whom he'd been named. Lion cooled it with Sutherland logic. A brawl would ruin his plans. "Name the time," he repeated calmly.

"We'll have none of that," the earl snapped. "I've not enough men that I can afford to lose two of the best. Georas, you'll respect Lion's right to defend his friends. Lion, you'll overlook Georas's rashness. 'Tis just high spirits," he added, signaling his squire to pour ale for all. "Nigh five hundred fighting men have answered my summons, and here they sit, with naught to do till we're strong enough to begin."

On that, Lion could not disagree. Battle-trained men with too much time on their hands were always a liability. He'd seen the same in France. There the leaders had kept their men busy with constant patrols and with jousts. Unfortunately, the patrols here led to just the sort of thing that had happened to Rowena. Innocent farmers and merchants were often attacked by bored warriors out for sport and plunder.

What of jousts? The idea of two bands of Highlanders conducting themselves as did tourney knights was laughable. There were no lances, no trained mounts, but...

"Football," Lion said.

"Football?" the earl repeated, frowning.

"Aye, well, it does not have to be that. Any sport will do, so long as it'll let the lads test their strength against one another and, mayhap, win a prize or two."

Alexander's dark eyes sparkled with understanding.

"Aye, that is a grand notion. And it'll make a suitable display when the MacNabs come calling." He added, "Aedh MacNab is sending his heir, Robert, to talk about joining us."

Lion smiled, but his mind was racing. He knew Aedh and Robbie. Neither were the sort to fall in with the earl's schemes. He had to meet with Robbie before he reached Blantyre, and try to convince him to see this Lion's way.

Dickie MacPherson ambled into the room, cast a malicious glance in Lion's direction, then went to whisper in Georas's ear. Their furtiveness made Lion apprehensive.

Georas grinned, clapped Dickie on the shoulder and approached Alexander. The smugness of his expression made the hair on Lion's nape prickle.

"Gunn!" the earl roared. "She's Padruig Gunn's widow?"

"Aye." Georas's smile turned feral. "That she is."

"Why is she here?" Alexander demanded, spearing first Lion, then Georas with an enraged gaze.

"I do not know," Lion was forced to admit.

"Yer childhood friend has not confided in ye?" Georas taunted. He must not know why, either.

"There was no time," Lion said stiffly, alarmed by Alexander's anger. The earl had an unpredictable temperament, being generous and friendly one moment, petty and vicious the next. Too often of late he would fly into a rage over a small thing. "But rest assured, Your Grace, I will know by morn."

Alexander muttered a curse and drained his cup.

"It is possible they have come to join you," Lion added.

"A woman?" Alexander's black brows rose. "Much as I need men, I'd not take any who'd follow a woman," he scoffed. His gaze went to Lady Glenda, a woman of great wealth. Kindly but homely, with a long, horsy face and mud-brown hair, she sat at a distant table playing at draughts with Selena MacPherson.

Lady Glenda looked up, caught the earl's glance and

immediately abandoned her game to join him. "You wanted me, my lord?" she said in her soft, lisping voice.

"Nay," Alexander said absently, oblivious to the lady's hurt expression. He'd seduced her, played court to her in order to gain the use of her castle. His interest in her was obviously waning, for he treated her with less respect every day.

"What of you, Lord Lion?" Selena inquired archly. "Is there aught you desire?" The seductive gleam in her pale blue eyes left him in no doubt she'd satisfy any craving he might have. She was breathtaking, her red hair a perfect foil for her porcelain-pale skin. Selena was newly arrived at Blantyre, but rumor had it she was a talented and inventive bedmate. Had she approached him the day before, Lion would have been tempted. As it was, he felt scant interest in the lush curves she pressed close to him or in the sensual promises glittering in her eyes.

Lion smiled coolly. "Alas, my lady, I must be about the earl's business this evening." With that, he bowed to Selena and took the unhappy Lady Glenda aside. "If your sister's chamber is yet unoccupied, could my lady Rowena use it while she is here?"

"Well...I do not mean to seem miserly, 'tis just that Annie values her things greatly and—"

"You'd just as soon not see them misused by some careless trollop." He looked pointedly at Lady Selena, who leaned close to the earl as she refilled his ale cup. "Rowena is my lady, and has no designs whatsoever on any other man."

"I would be pleased to have her use the room, then."

"She is in the great hall, if I could send word—"

"I'll go myself." Lady Glenda glanced at Alexander, her expression filled with pitiful longing, then left the room.

Lion bowed to the earl. "Until the morrow, Your Grace," he said before exiting the room. Every step of the way, he was aware of Georas's hate-filled gaze.

As he stepped into the gloomy corridor, Lion nearly fell over Bryce.

"What has he done to upset Lady Glenda?" Bryce said, staring after the lady's retreating back.

"He ignores her now that he has what he wanted—the run of Blantyre and her Shaws to ride under his banner."

"Yet she pines for him, dotes on his every word and whim. Can she not see what worthless slime he is?" Bryce snarled.

"Easy, my friend, I know you sympathize with her." More than that, he feared Bryce was smitten with the earl's lady. "But we've more pressing problems just now." As they walked down the stairs of the old tower, Lion told his cousin about the imminent arrival of the MacNabs and the threat to Rowena. "I've asked Lady Glenda to give her Lady Annie's chamber. 'Tis all I can do for tonight—that and post two men outside her door. Tomorrow I must persuade her to leave."

"And the MacNabs?"

"That is the rest of tonight's problem."

Chapter Four

Rowena finished her ale and set the cup aside.

"More?" Sim inquired, standing behind her, ready to serve.

"Nay, I could not eat or drink another morsel." She eyed the remaining scraps of meat pie. "Though it was delicious."

"Aye. Lady Glenda sets a good table, but I must apologize for the company," Lion's squire added. His statement was punctuated by a hoarse shout and a round of drunken cheers.

Wincing, Rowena glanced toward the center of the hall. The tables had been cleared back to allow room for a wrestling match of sorts. Two large men, stripped down to linen drawers, were attempting to squeeze the life out of each other.

"It grows late, and I really must find my brother by marriage to see if he has found us lodging."

Sim frowned. "I did send someone to inquire. Sir Eneas is not within the walls."

"Run off and left me again. Well, I shall have to shift for myself, then." She stood, but Sim barred the way.

"Lion said you were to wait here."

"He does not have the ordering of me."

"Nay, but he is finding a room for you."

"And I can guess where it will be."

Sim flushed. "Nay, my lord is not like that. You can trust him to make honorable arrangements for you."

Once before she'd trusted Lion. No more. "I will see to it myself." She stepped around him and into a burly stranger.

"Well. Lonely, are ye?" He stank worse than the garde-robes. His black-and-purple plaid was stained with food, his eyes bleary with drink. "I can fix that." He reached for her.

Sim shoved between them. "Off with you, John Chisholm. This lady is under my lord of Glenshee's protection."

"Get away, lad," John snarled.

"Nay," Sim said to the brute who towered over him.

Rowena gasped. "Sim, do not—"

"It's ye who'll be moving along, Dank John," said the big redhead who'd materialized beside them.

John glared at the newcomer, but before he could protest, two more men in Sutherland green and blue appeared.

Cursing under his breath, John moved off.

"Thank you," Rowena whispered. Her knees were suddenly so weak she steadied herself on the edge of the table.

"Glad to help." The big man bowed. "I'm Red Will. This here's Naill and that's Lem's Sandie."

The wiry older man grinned at her. Fair-haired Lem's Sandie blushed and bobbed his head.

Rowena managed a smile. "Thank you for noting my plight."

"Oh, we've been keeping an eye on ye," Red Will said.

"Per Lord Lion's orders?" she asked faintly.

"Aye. He doesna want anyone harassing his lady."

"I am not—"

"Lady Rowena?" inquired an imperious voice.

Rowena spun her head, braced for yet another confrontation.

The woman standing before her was of middle age, tall,

thin and horsey looking. Her gown was of costly velvet, but the mustard shade was vastly unbecoming, turning her skin the color of tallow. Still, the crown of wispy brown braids atop her head gave her a regal look, and her eyes held a wary intelligence.

"Ach, 'tis Lady Glenda," Red Will explained.

"My lady." Rowena dropped a hasty curtsy.

"I am sorry not to have come sooner." Her gaze moved from Rowena's untidy hair to her muddy boots and back to her face. "You look as though you've had a long, terrible journey."

Rowena smiled wryly. "My backside can attest to that."

An answering smile curved Lady Glenda's thin lips, making her eyes twinkle and her face seem almost pretty. "Ah. A sense of humor and a bit of wit. How refreshing." She raised her hand, rings winking in the torchlight of the crowded hall.

Donald rushed over. "You have need of me, Lady Glenda?"

"Put the lady Rowena in the green room, Donald."

"But—but when Lady Selena asked to have that chamber, you said it must be held ready for Lady Anne."

Lady Glenda flushed. "That is because I did not want that sly woman entertaining her lovers in my sister's room. She has the morals of a barn cat," she said in an aside to Rowena. "Selena, not my Annie." She glanced about the hall and grimaced. "There's little we can do about yon riffraff being here, Donald, but the earl vowed I would have the arranging of the domestic matters in my own castle."

"Aye, my lady." Donald grinned. "Twill be a pleasure to see Lady Rowena settled in the green room." He cocked his head, surveying her. "You'll be wanting a bath."

Rowena blinked, a bit dazed by the tempting offer. "Oh, but it's so late…so much trouble…"

"Not at all." He bowed. "Shall I show you up now?"

"I'll do it," said his mistress. Her lip curled slightly as she gazed about the hall. "I do wish Alexander would exert more control over his men.'' She sighed. ''Still, I know he has more important things on his mind.'' The lady picked up her skirts and turned in a graceful sweep. ''Come, let us away.''

''Gladly.'' Lifting her muddy skirts, Rowena trailed after her rescuer. The older woman set a brisk pace across the entryway with its impressive display of ancient armaments and into a stone stairwell that spiraled tightly up two floors and opened into a well-lit corridor.

''Drat. I should have thought to bring a candle,'' Lady Glenda grumbled. ''''Tis what comes of acting in haste. Ah well.'' She reached for a torch set in an iron holder in the wall.

''Allow me.'' Rowena lifted the brand free.

''Ah. You are not one of those frail lasses who lets others do all the work.''

''If I were, I'd be home in my bed, not here, alone in a strange place full of louts and brigands.''

''Why aren't you?'' Lady Glenda asked as they walked down the hall. ''Home in your bed instead of here?''

''I've come to ensure my son's inheritance. You see—'' she stepped through the door Lady Glenda had opened ''—my husband died a week ago.''

''Oh. I am sorry.''

''So am I. Both because he was a good and honest man, and because our son is only five.''

''Ah.'' Lady Glenda took the torch and thrust it into a pile of wood lying ready in the small corner hearth. The fire caught quickly, sending flickers of light over the fine furnishings—a tall, canopied bed draped in green velvet, a carved chest, a table and two chairs set beneath the window. ''I know just how much of a challenge it can be, raising a child without a man. My oldest brother was two and ten when our da died. But our clansmen supported William. Is there no one to help you guide your young son into manhood?''

"Aye, there is, but Finlay, my husband's cousin, and Father Cerdic are somewhat old and infirmed."

"Mmm. That is a problem." Lady Glenda plucked a thick candle from the mantel. As she stooped to light the wick from the fire, she groaned. "I am sorry for your loss and your troubles, but at least you loved and were loved in return. And you have your son...a living symbol of that love."

At least you were loved. The pain stabbed through Rowena, quick and deadly as a knife thrust. "Aye," she whispered.

"I—I hope that one day soon I will also know that joy," Glenda said, cheeks flushing.

"You and the earl will wed?"

"He has not yet asked...but he is busy." Her hands fluttered, unnecessarily tidying the bed drapes. "Tell me about your son."

"Paddy is bright and quick and has a sweet disposition. 'Tis a joy to teach him, a thrill to watch him master each new task. But..." Rowena hesitated. Six years of living among the Gunns, of keeping her thoughts and plans to herself, made her cautious. Lady Glenda had befriended her, but if Eneas learned that she intended to have him ousted as Paddy's guardian—

"But...?" Lady Glenda prompted.

A knock at the door spared Rowena from lying. At the lady's command, servants entered with steaming buckets of water. Donald himself ducked behind the screen in one corner and dragged forth a small wooden tub. He set it before the fire with great ceremony, and the servants filled it quickly, then departed.

"Shall I send up a maid to help you?" Donald asked.

Rowena shook her head, dazed by the attention. "I'm used to seeing to myself. Thank you for all you've done."

"Aye, well, I cannot claim all the credit. Before he left on the earl's business, Lion asked me to arrange things thusly," said Lady Glenda.

Rowena's smile faded. "I see."

"Two of the Sutherlands will be outside your door tonight," Donald told her. She did not make the mistake of saying she did not want a guard. "If you need aught else, send one of them down to me in the hall." The steward bowed to her, then to Lady Glenda, and headed for the door.

"A moment, Donald," Lady Glenda called after him. "I've instructions to give you for the morrow." She turned to Rowena. "Enjoy your bath and sleep well. In the morning you can tell me more about the challenge you're facing."

"Thank you, my lady. You have been more than kind."

Glenda smiled wryly. "While I cannot claim to know what lies between you, if anything, I know how it chafes to have your life ordered by a strong man. No matter how well meaning. If it is any comfort, I am exceedingly glad he did, for I've enjoyed meeting you. And I've said that about precious few people these past three months. I look forward to our chat tomorrow." She exited with the grace and dignity of a queen.

Rowena sighed, drained and buffeted by the events of the day. Her emotions had suffered more ups and downs than a skiff on a wind-roughened loch. The quiet of the room wrapped around her like a healing balm. How lucky she was to have this haven.

Lion arranged this, taunted a little voice. Did he think to share this room with her, to take up where they had left off six years ago? Well, he'll soon learn that she was not the foolish, gullible lass she'd been then.

Stiff with determination, Rowena stalked to the tub and shucked off her dirty clothes. "Ah," she sighed as she sank into the hot water. It melted the ache from weary muscles and banished the cold. "This is heaven." There were days on the trail when she'd thought she would never be warm again.

The urge to linger, to steep in the water as she used to

when she was young and carefree, was tempting, but the bath was cooling fast, and if Lion was planning to invade her chamber, she did not want him to catch her thus. She picked up a handful of soft soap, sniffed appreciatively at the sweet scent of heather and began scrubbing her grimy arms.

Working quickly, she moved on to unplait her braids. It was not easy to wet the long, curly hair, harder still to work a lather through it, but her scalp itched fiercely. And she was not climbing dirty into Annie Shaw's bed. As Rowena washed, she tried to keep her mind on meeting the earl, but her thoughts kept straying to Lion.

He'd deserted her six years ago, yet stuck by her side tonight while she tended young Harry.

"There are things you should know," he'd said.

What explanation could he give that would excuse his actions? If his father had changed their plans, Lion could have met her and told her so. Had he feared that she would cry and beg him to stay or to take her with him?

Bah, it did not matter now.

She ladled water from the bucket over her head to rinse away the soap. If only she could be shed of her problems as easily, she thought as she stood and wrapped about her the long linen towel left warming by the fire.

Bundled in a thick bed robe, she crawled into bed and leaned against the pillows. She stared into the fire and drew the wide-toothed wooden comb through her tangled hair, her thoughts on the morrow. She'd arise early, don her best gown and see if she could catch the earl in the hall breaking his fast. With any luck, Eneas would not have had a chance to corner the earl and fill his ears with lies.

Tired as she was, Rowena found sleep elusive, her thoughts haunted by images from the past. Images of Lion.

Had he arranged for her to have this room so he could join her? The notion was terrifying. And thrilling.

"Ah, it feels good to be free of that cursed place, if only for a few hours," Bryce observed as they cantered away from Blantyre and headed into the hills.

"Aye," Lion answered. A slender moon lit their way, the air smelled fresh and clean. It had not been easy for them to leave unobserved by the edgy earl's guards, but soon after coming here, he had secured a copy of the postern gate key. Once away from the castle, he and Bryce had walked down to the village and gotten their horses from Roderick, a Sutherland working there as the blacksmith's helper.

Lion would have been grateful to leave behind the stink of intrigue and corruption, except for his worry about Rowena. The lass had always been headstrong. Though he'd warned her to stay away from Alexander and had left Red Will to watch her, his gut was by no means easy on that score.

It was incredible seeing her again after all this time. The wonder of it had struck him anew as he'd sat beside her in the hall, watching the play of emotion over her face, marveling at the changes the years had made. Rowena was here, free of Padruig, free to take another man. Lion wanted to be that man. He would be that man.

Winning her would not be easy.

Lion grimaced. Somehow he had to overcome her distrust.

"You're worried about the meeting with the MacNabs. Surely Robbie will listen to you. His father and yours are old friends, and you played together as lads."

Lion shook away one problem to shoulder an even larger one, the one that had brought him to Blantyre. "It's not Robbie I'm worried about. Aedh is chief of the clan, and he will have given his son specific orders about what to tell Alexander concerning his barbaric plans."

"Aye, the MacNabs are much like us and most other honorable clans—not eager to make war on their neighbors."

"But I fear the MacNabs are a stubborn lot."

Bryce chuckled. "You are not?"

"At least I know when to bend." Lion's father had taught him that, among other valuable lessons, and he'd never missed Lucais Sutherland's sage advice more than he did now. Lion had fought his way across France, had intrigued with the best—or worst—of them at French Robert's court, yet he'd never felt as inadequate to a task as he did this one. The enormity of trying to protect whole clans of men who resented his interference, while trying to find proof of Alexander's treason, was nearly overwhelming.

"You think Robbie will not bend?"

"I would not have, were I eight and ten and off on an important mission for my old bear of a sire. If you've ever seen Aedh in a rage, you'd hardly blame the lad."

They crested the rise and raced along a high plateau that seemed to stretch endlessly toward the horizon. A rocky outcropping came into view, black against the new grass. Lion headed toward it, slowing so the stallion could maneuver between the boulders. The trail turned sharply, then opened into a tiny meadow. The clearing teemed with horses and with men warming themselves before a few small campfires. Lion was about to complain about the lack of sentries when a wee man sprang from behind a rock.

"We was on the point of sending out a search party," Heckie grumbled, his weathered face cracked by a smile.

"Have the MacNabs arrived?" Lion asked, dismounting and handing the reins to a waiting clansmen.

"A half hour past. 'Twas Robbie who fretted about ye."

Lion nodded and set off in the direction of the largest fire and the group of men in the red-and-black tartan of the MacNabs. "Robbie!" He clapped Aedh's heir on the back.

A lanky lad with the MacNabs' carroty hair and a lean, freckled face, Robbie turned, "You are late."

"Couldn't be helped," Lion said easily. "Have you been offered food and drink?"

"Aye. But we've precious little time for a meal on the

heath. I'm to speak with the Wolf, give him Da's reply and start back for home tonight," Robbie said curtly.

"Come, walk apart with me," Lion said, not wanting to air his plans before a herd of curious MacNabs. The fewer who knew what was afoot, the better. Forcing a smile, Lion led the way to a flat gray rock out of earshot of the others. He leaned a hip on the stone and chose his words with care. "I'll wager your da will not accept the earl's offer to join in the peacemaking."

"Peace?" Robbie snorted. "More like an excuse to murder and pillage and steal the lands of the clans he wipes out."

"Agreed."

"Then why are you with him? Da was that curious."

Lion's smile was natural this time. "I can see him now, storming and fuming and cursing the greedy Sutherlands."

"Well…" Robbie's fair face flushed.

"We want the same thing," Lion said, leaning forward as he spoke. "We want Alexander Stewart gone from the Highlands."

"Then why are you helping him?"

"Because we have little choice if we want to survive. By declaring him viceroy and sending him to subdue the lawless Highlanders, the king has given him leave to do as he will. The clans who oppose him oppose the crown. They can be declared outlaws without ever lifting a sword," he added grimly.

"That is unjust," Robbie growled.

"Aye, but it's the truth of the matter. We must deal with it and find a way to thwart him…within the law."

Robbie's pale eyes narrowed. "What would you have us do?"

"Agree to join his army."

"What?" Robbie slapped his hand against the boulder. "Da would never agree to that—nor would I. 'Tis monstrous."

"I know, but my father and I could come up with no better scheme than to stall for time."

"Till you can assassinate him?" Robbie asked hopefully.

"If only we dared." Lion sighed. "Murder Alexander, and the life of every Highlander involved would be forfeit."

"Better that than to ally ourselves with the fiend."

"Is it? Aye, well, to some I suppose it is." Lion's voice hardened. "William Ross believed that and paid a heavy price."

"We heard he was outlawed for attacking Blair Abbey and killing the priests therein."

"'Tis a lie," Lion said softly. "Will came to Blantyre, just as you have. He refused service in Alexander's army boldly and openly, only to find himself cast into the dungeons to think it over. Still Will held firm. A MacPherson offered to help Will and his lads escape.

"A MacPherson? But—"

"Aye, it was a trap. They were pursued by Georas's men. The Rosses got as far as Blair, where they sought sanctuary. Only Alexander is no great respecter of the church's sanctity."

"Alexander sacked the abbey himself?"

"The MacPherson did, on the earl's orders. They saw to it Will was blamed, and with all of the Rosses who'd been with him dead, who was to say otherwise?"

Robbie swore and sat down on the rock.

"Exactly. And he's not the only one. Padruig Gunn met with Alexander two weeks ago and refused the call to arms. He died on the way home, killed from ambush." Lion scrubbed a hand over his face. "I feel partway responsible. I waylaid Padruig same as I have you, but I could not make him understand that we are not dealing with a sane or honorable man. Alexander is obsessed with raising an army. Any who will not side with him, he eliminates—quickly and without mercy."

"But—but how can this go on? Surely the king must be told what his brother is doing."

"My father and others have been in Edinburgh these past months trying to make Robert understand what terror he has unleashed on us. But Robert is too weak to control his brother. Our only hope lies in finding proof of Alexander's ultimate plans." Lion waited a heartbeat. "Once the Wolf has raised his army, what is to prevent him from conquering all of Scotland?"

"Jesu, do you really think he'd turn on his brother?"

"In an instant. He's mad—mad with the need for power. If we can bring proof before the parliament, they will declare Alexander a traitor and take the matter out of Robert's hands."

"We had not realized…" Robbie swore again. "But Da would skin me alive if I pledged the MacNabs to such a cause."

"It takes time to call up a clan," Lion said. "Time that we can use to find proof of Alexander's treasonous intent."

"What if you don't find this proof? We MacNabs believe a man's word is his bond. We would be honor bound to ride under that madman's banner, to murder our neighbors and—"

"I know." Lion sighed. "My father and I wrestled with that same problem." Lion had argued that an oath sworn under duress should not be binding on the soul, but Lucais was not as flexible. "And found no easy solution. So we must succeed."

Robbie frowned. "Damn me, I do not know what I should do. Da was most specific about my refusing to join the earl."

If Lion had learned one thing in his time away from Scotland, it was when to push and when to retreat. "What harm would there be in waiting a day or two to deliver Aedh's message?" he asked. "Pretend to be undecided. Let Alexander woo you with his ale, his food and his proposals, but when he asks for a commitment, play coy as a virgin before her wedding night. Meanwhile, keep your ears open. The Frasers, MacDonalds and Keiths joined the earl but think as I do. The Cummings, Chisholms and MacPhersons are firmly with Alexander. The Shaws of Blantyre sit the fence. Many of them do not like the earl, but he seduced the Lady Glenda into letting him use Blantyre Castle as the headquarters for his campaigning.''

''But, Glenda is skinny and homely as a horse's—''

''He's using her. And she, poor thing, fancies herself in love. Desperately in love. I fear that Glenda would do anything, sacrifice anyone to keep Alexander.''

''I will remember all you have said.'' Robbie sighed and rose from the rock. ''And I will follow your suggestion…at least till I see how things are at Blantyre. Da has always valued your father's opinions. He'd not want me to disregard this warning out of hand. But I cannot promise that I will swear an oath of fealty to the earl.''

''Your forbearance does you credit.'' Lion clapped the lad on the shoulder, well pleased with the way things had turned out. ''I'll ride on ahead, if you do not mind lingering on the trail a bit. It would not do for us to arrive together, or even to seem overly friendly. Alexander is suspicious enough as it is, seeking for hidden meaning in every man's speech, seeing assassins lurking in every dark corner.''

''Mayhap we'll get lucky and someone will kill him.''

''It will be lucky only if that someone is Georas MacPherson, for 'twould rid us of two mad wolves.''

Chapter Five

Dieu, she was beautiful, Lion thought as he gazed down at the sleeping Rowena.

The sun was just coming up, and he had yet to seek his own bed. His eyes were gritty with fatigue, his nerves wound tight, but the need to see her had transcended all that.

A shaft of pale morning light slanted in through the narrow window, shimmering on the gold in her hair, turning her skin the color of rich cream. She slept on her side, one hand tucked under her chin, her lips curved in a half smile.

Desire caught him, low and swift. Like a punch to the gut, it drove the air from his lungs. He struggled to breathe and drew in the intoxicating scent of soap and Rowena. He wanted to lie down beside her, match his mouth and then his body to hers. He'd known passion and fulfillment, but never had the urge for a woman clawed at him so fiercely.

Because this was not just any lass. It was Rowena. His love. His lady.

He reached out to touch her, hand quivering slightly, then stopped. It was too soon. A raw groan tore from his throat.

She stirred. Her lashes lifted slowly, lazily. Recognition sparked in their hazy blue depths. She started to smile, that

small, cat-in-the-cream smile she'd often worn during those
summer months they'd spent together.

"Ro." He touched her hair, breaking the spell.

"You!" She jerked away, eyes wide and panicked.

"It is all right, Ro," Lion said softly. "I—"

"All right? How can it be? What are you doing here?"
Rowena sat up, flushed and flustered, eyes darting about
for a route of escape. "What are you doing here?" she
asked again.

"Waiting for you to wake up." Lion smiled and sat
down on the edge of the bed. "I sent Sim down for your
breakfast. Will you share it with me, Ro?"

Eyes so dark they were almost black—eyes that had gone
soft as velvet when she'd told him she loved him—glinted
with fury. "I'd sooner dine with a viper. Get out of my
bed and my room."

"It's not your room, exactly. Nor your bed, either,
though I must admit I had no urge to crawl into it when
the occupant was the delicate Lady Anne."

Hurt shimmered briefly below her anger. He was per-
versely glad to see she wasn't as immune to him as he'd
feared. And as she doubtless wanted to be, given her poker-
stiff posture.

"I never slept with Lady Anne," he said gently.

"I could not care less with whom you sleep."

Icy words. Clearly she had more control over her temper
than she used to. Then, she'd been wont to fly at him with
fists and nails when his teasing goaded her.

Pity. He'd have welcomed a physical tussle to ease the
tension in his gut. But if he touched her, he'd lose the slim
measure of control he had over his own emotions. And that
could be the ruin of the plans he'd laid as he'd waited for
her to waken.

So he merely smiled, marveling at the changes the years
had wrought in her. The promise of beauty had been there
when she was fifteen and the bud scarcely open. Now here
she was in full bloom, delectable as a ripe peach. It had

been both pleasure and penance watching her sleep, yearning to touch, to sample, but knowing he must not. Not yet.

"I thought it best we speak alone," he said softly.

"I don't want to speak with you at all. How did you get in here, by the by?"

God, she was enchanting. Keeping his eyes fully on hers, he enjoyed the play of emotions she was not quite capable of hiding. She'd always been more vividly alive than any person he knew. Mayhap that was why his heart had refused to let her go though she'd wed another. "Through the window. You still like to sleep with the shutters open, I see."

"How I sleep is no concern of yours." Her movements were jerky as she tucked the blanket around her shoulders, covering the thin shift she'd worn to bed.

"I've seen you with nothing on," he reminded her.

"Don't start." The words were sharp, cutting, but beneath the anger in her gaze, something else flickered, something small and vulnerable that moved him more deeply than her rage.

Yearning slashed through him, the pain more biting than the assassin's sword that had pierced flesh and bone, nearly ending his life six years ago. "I know I hurt you—"

She lifted her chin, her glare freezing off the rest of his apology. "Aye, I was so hurt I wed scarce two weeks later."

The knife turned, drawing an agony of regrets. "Aye, so you did." Absently he rubbed his hand over the ridge of scar tissue that slashed across his side. He had not yet recovered from that near-mortal wound when he'd received word of Rowena's marriage. The news had nearly done what the assailant's attack hadn't. For days he hadn't wanted to live. "That hurt me, too. As was your intent, I'm sure. Eventually, I forgave you because I knew why you wed Padruig."

"You did?" The flush drained from her cheeks.

"To repay me for leaving you without a word. You al-

ways were a vindictive lass. If you'll let me explain
why—''

"Do you think it matters now?" Her eyes were cool, her
temper well hidden.

When had she learned that? he wondered, wanting back
the turbulent lass whose wayward tongue had often landed
them in trouble. Trouble from which he'd many times ex-
tract them both. And here he was once again coming to her
aid, whether or not she welcomed it.

"Perhaps you are right. The past is gone, but the present
is much in question." He cocked his head. "What are you
doing at Blantyre?"

"I'm minding my own business and suggest you do the
same."

"That I cannot." Leaning back against the bedpost, he
gave her his most charming smile. "Once milady's champion, always milady's champion."

Her eyes narrowed. "I am not in need of a champion.
Now leave, or I'll scream the castle down."

"Nay. You will not." To make certain, he moved to the
head of the bed, sitting beside her and planting a palm on
either side of her hips before she could do more than draw
an outraged breath. "Likely no one would come anyway.
As you saw last night, Alexander Stewart's court is a loose
and lawless place."

She smelled of heather and of woman. He wanted, Jesu,
but he wanted, the need all the sharper and more painful
because he remembered how it had once been between
them. The spark was still there, the pull that had drawn
them together from the first. He saw the knowledge mirrored in her widening eyes.

"Don't," she whispered as he lifted a hand to stroke her
hair. "Don't."

Lion let his hand fall back on the blanket. "Listen to
me, then. I don't know why you've come to Blantyre, but
you must leave. Today. This is no place for someone like
you."

"I will leave when I've concluded my business."

"Which is?"

Her breasts rose and fell against the blanket as she drew a breath and exhaled. "I seek an audience with the earl." She hesitated. "My—my husband died recently."

"I'd heard that. Did you love him?"

"I wedded him," she snapped, but her eyes gave Lion the answer he sought. They held a jumble of emotions, but the sharp-edged pain of loss was not one of them.

He breathed a silent sigh of relief. "I am sorry, then."

"Thank you. Padruig was very special to me. The bond between us was so strong that I will never wed again."

Minx. Did she think to dissuade him with that? "Are you forswearing all men? Or just me?"

"Especially you. Not that I'd expected to see you again." She glared at him. "Why aren't you dead?"

A warning bell tolled in his head. He quelled it. She couldn't have been a party to that long-ago ambush. She'd loved him then. "Did you hear a rumor to that effect?"

"Nay, but I prayed for it...daily after you left me. If I could have found you, I'd—" Rowena clamped her mouth shut, appalled by her outburst, by the rising volume of her voice. She'd not sacrifice her pride by letting him see how badly losing him had hurt her.

"If it's any consolation, I nearly did die," he said to test her reaction.

Fear chased across her face before she mastered it. "Good."

Lion smiled, cheered by her reaction. "You always were a bloodthirsty lass," he teased. "Is that why you've come to Blantyre? To ride with the Wolf as he subdues the clans?"

"Of course not." She frowned. "Is that why you are here?"

Lion shrugged. "More or less. It is a noble mission, subduing the lawless element in the Highlands."

"I suppose a few clans could stand a lesson in leaving

their neighbors' herds alone and not resorting to the sword
to settle every grudge or petty dispute,'' she said absently.
"Now will you go and leave me alone?''

"Not till I know why you are here.''

"Oh, for heaven's sake,'' she grumbled. "To swear fealty to the crown for my son's inheritance.''

Son. The word battered Lion's insides. If things had been
different, she might have had *his* son. Lion shook away the
pain. The longing was harder to ignore. "The king is bound
to be grateful.'' Lion wondered why a Highland lass would
even think of following a Border custom. Beneath her defiance, he sensed fear. Of him? *Dieu,* he had to know.
"There is more. Something you are afraid of,'' he insisted.

She shook her head and looked away. "I .ay.''

"I will not leave till I know the whole of it.'' He settled
back when he wanted badly to take her in his arms, to coax
her into confiding in him as he used to when she'd had
trouble with her family. Family. "Is it your brother by marriage? That Eneas?''

"Eneas.'' The grinding of her teeth was audible. "Aye,
the swearing was his idea. And I accompanied him to make
certain he did not...'' She stopped, appalled at having let
down her guard. But it had always been thus between them.
From the moment Lion had saved her from a group of
bullies, he'd been her friend, her lover, her confidant.

"Did not what?''

Rowena sighed. "Eneas is...'' Hateful. Vindictive. "We
disagree on the raising of Paddy.''

"Your son was named for his father?'' he asked tightly.

Rowena nodded. She should have been pleased by the
flash of hurt in Lion's eyes, but she wasn't. "'Tis nothing
I cannot handle,'' she quickly added. "The Gunns are behind me.'' A few.

"Then why ask the crown to ratify the succession?''

Trust Lion to delve to the heart of the matter.
"I...we...think a neighbor might try to swallow us up,
since Paddy is so young. But if the earl declared Paddy heir

and Finlay and myself his guardians, he would be less inclined to attack.''

"Who is this Finlay?"

She explained that, too.

"'Tis an interesting notion. Very creative, but the timing is not good. Alexander is too busy gathering his army.''

"But the ceremony would take only a short time. An hour at most once the decree is drawn up.''

"Aye." Lion stood, giving her the space she'd craved from the moment she'd awakened to find him camped on the end of her bed. So why did she feel alone and vulnerable? "The earl speaks of nothing that is not related to his mission here. Let me provide you with an escort home and men to guard your lands.''

"I do not want your help, and the Gunns would not want others defending them. Nay. I will see the earl today and plead my cause to him personally." Before Eneas could.

Lion frowned, mindful of Alexander's outburst last night. "I cannot let you do that. Alexander is—''

"Well, you have no say in the matter. I am not tied to you in any way. I—''

"Damn." He sat again, capturing her hands in his large, callused ones. "Must you be so stubborn? I saved your life yesterday, and I have protected you thus far. Can you not admit that I might have your best interests in mind?''

"Ah, just as you did when you left me six years ago?'' She snatched her hands from his.

Lion studied her closed features. "Leaving you was the hardest thing I've ever done. But you are too angry to listen to my explanations," he quickly added. "When you are ready to hear what happened, ask." He stood and stared down at her. "Like it or not, you owe me a debt, Rowena, for saving your life and that of your people. In payment, I ask your promise that you will not ask Alexander about this fealty oath till I can smooth the way.''

Rowena glared at him, then nodded curtly.

"I'll leave you then…unless you'd like to invite me to stay." He waggled his brows suggestively.

"I'd sooner keep a pet snake."

"I'm wounded." He clutched his heart, but his dancing eyes challenged her. "But I'll accede to your wishes…for the moment." Lion crossed to the window, movements lithe and graceful as always. It was impossible not to notice that he'd filled out, his shoulders and chest so wide they blocked the light. "Until later, then." His tone was teasing, his eyes boldly confident. He bowed, then slipped out the window.

Rowena melted against the pillows, her muscles weak as water, her brain in a daze. Damn him. He was back in Scotland. Back in her life, however temporarily.

And she was determined to see it was temporary. Never again would she put herself at a man's mercy—especially Lion's.

"I still think you should stay in your room and let me bring you a tray," Sim said as they started down the stairs.

"So you've told me." Rowena kept her pace slow and steady, in sharp contrast to her racing heart. She longed to stay safely in her room, away from the mocking nobles, away from Eneas's gloating smile. Especially away from Lion.

But she was not a coward. Life had taught her to face her troubles—of which there'd been plenty—head-on. So she'd left the comfort of her chamber for the perils of the hall, armored in her best gown. The blue wool was nowhere near as grand as the silks and velvets worn by the ladies last night, but would have to do. Her hair, at least, looked its best, the braids wrapped in a shiny coronet atop her head.

"What if the earl is in the hall? Lion made me promise I would keep you clear of His Grace."

"I do not see why Lion is so insistent on that. My mission is a harmless one. Why, he'll be glad to know that the Gunns are loyal to him. One less clan to fret over.''

"The earl is not too pleased with the Gunns, since your husband refused to join his army.''

Rowena stopped on the stairs and turned to look up at the squire. "Padruig met with the earl?''

"Aye." Sim shifted uneasily. "Surely you knew.''

"That he was coming, aye—Finlay told me, after the fact. But no one ever said...I'd assumed Padruig was killed on his way to Blantyre." Sweet Mary! Had Padruig and Lion met? The notion was unsettling for some reason. "Did you meet Padruig?''

"Nay, lady. I saw him ride up, though. Lion was surprised he came alone in such perilous times.''

"For which folly he paid...we all paid." She continued on down the stairs, wondering why Lion had not told her of Padruig's visit or the real reason he did not want her to confront the earl. "He is too high-handed by far," she muttered.

"The earl?''

"Lion.''

Sim chuckled. "Bryce says he was born to command and is so often right 'tis a wonder his helmet still fits his head.''

"Annoying man.''

"Aye, well, that may be, my lady, but there is no man I'd rather ride with, and I know the other lads feel the same. You'll find no braver or more honorable man in all the Highlands," he added with youthful fervor.

Rowena snorted. "I do not care if the archangel Gabriel himself came down to vouch for his character. I do not want Lion Sutherland hovering over me and ordering me about.''

"Blantyre is a dangerous place for a lady alone. He is but trying to keep you safe.''

Only because he'd like to help himself into her bed, Rowena thought. She had not missed the flare of desire in

his eyes this morn. "It galls me that I have relied on him
for help."

"We are happy to be of service."

Rowena sighed as she stepped from the stairwell into the
corridor with its vaulted ceiling. Down it drifted the din
from the great hall, a subtle reminder of the bad company
she was forced to keep. Suddenly Sim's presence did not
seem so loathsome. Together they headed for the sickroom.

"Yer Harry is sleeping and there is no sign of fever,"
Felis assured her.

"I will sit with him awhile."

"'Tis not necessary. I've lassies aplenty glad to sit and
wipe the brow of such a handsome fellow."

"I would pay you for your supplies." Rowena fumbled
with the thin purse at her belt.

Felis shook her head. "Lion has taken care of that and
given my lassies a bit of silver, too."

Lion. Again. Rowena fumed silently as she followed Sim
back down the corridor.

"You could return to your room," he said hopefully.

Rowena shook her head. She needed to know what was
going on. Lion claimed the earl was angry with the Gunns,
but she could not take a chance that Eneas would win the
earl over and supplant her as Paddy's guardian. At the doorway to the great hall, she paused, surveying the battle-
ground, as it were.

Despite the fact that it was too late for breakfast and too
early for dinner, the neat rows of trestle tables were packed
with people. Why weren't the men on the training field?
She was relieved not to spot Lion in the crowd. A few
people closest to the door glanced at her, dismissed her and
went back to their conversations. Just as well; she wanted
no undue notice.

"This way, my lady. I think I see an empty spot."

Rowena followed Sim in. As their path took them close
to the head table, a hand shot out, grabbed her sleeve and
tugged.

"Bring us more ale," ordered an imperious female.

Incredulous, Rowena looked from the restraining hand to the beautiful, haughty face of its owner. "Me?"

"Who else would I mean, wench?" She turned to Lady Glenda, who sat beside her. "Really, your servants want manners."

"Lady Selena," Glenda exclaimed, her face crimson with embarrassment. "This is not one of my maids, but Lady Rowena Gunn whom you impugn."

Lady Selena loosed the crumpled sleeve. "Well, how could I know when she goes about dressed like a kitchen slattern?"

"I thought you had seen her last night. She was dining with Lord Lion," Lady Glenda added pointedly.

Lady Selena's exotic emerald eyes moved slowly, corrosively over Rowena's person. "Why are you dressed so meanly? Has your baggage been misplaced, or are the Gunns truly this uncouth?"

"We may not wear velvet," Rowena said coolly, her pride stung. "But our manners are better than some who do."

A collective gasp swept through Lady Selena's gaggle of silly, preening geese.

Lady Glenda chuckled. "Well said." She pushed back her chair. "As it happens, the lady's baggage was stolen, and I'd forgotten I had promised to lend her some clothes. Lady Rowena, if you would be so good as to withdraw with me to yon seat in the window, we need not bore these ladies with the details." She inclined her head to the fuming Lady Selena, then swept from the table, drawing Rowena with her.

"Thank you," Rowena whispered when they reached the curtained alcove.

"My pleasure. There are times when it is difficult to play the gracious hostess." Lady Glenda sat and folded her flowing skirts close so Rowena might join her. Lowering her head, she studied the table they'd left. "I hate her."

"Lady Selena does have a mean mind and a sharp tongue."

"'Tis not only that. She is everything I am not—beautiful, graceful, skillful in attracting a man."

Did Lion find her attractive? Despite her own resolve to hate him, Rowena felt a twinge of jealousy. "She is confident of her allure, I'll grant that, but I wager she has the morals of a she cat. She attracts men, then discards them on a whim."

"But I could not bear it if she took Alexander away from me. Even for one n-night."

Rowena was at a loss to offer advice. Her one affair had ended in disaster. Her husband had not desired her enough to bed her, but had continued to visit his longtime mistress instead. The arrangement had suited Rowena, but had left her with little experience when it came to men. "Do you suspect she has tried to, er, take him away?"

"I suspect everyone." Lady Glenda cast a rueful glance at Rowena. "When I saw you last night, my first thought was that you were young and bonny and he might want you. But then I recalled Lion's face when he asked me to lend you Annie's room." A smile warmed her rawboned features. "I knew I need not worry, for Alexander would never approach the woman of a friend."

"Oh," Rowena said lamely. To shatter Glenda's illusions would be to alarm and alienate her only ally.

"Well, now that that is settled, let us speak of the clothes you will need." She looked Rowena up and down. "Gowns, certainly—"

"What I have is sufficient."

"But before he rode out this forenoon, Lion asked if I had fabric he might buy and if my maids would sew up something for you to wear this evening. Men," she added, shaking her head. "How little even a worldly one like Lion knows of such things. 'Twould take more than a day to measure, cut and sew new clothes for you—"

"I truly do not expect to be here that long. If you would

do me a service, I must speak with the earl." Briefly, Rowena recounted her purpose in coming here, but she did not mention her fears about Eneas. Glenda had befriended her, but if Eneas caught wind of her plans...

"I will do what I can, but Alexander is consumed with his mission. You would not believe the troubles he has had in raising the army he needs to do the king's will. To think that men would refuse their viceroy's summons."

"Lion mentioned as much. He said that the earl might be wroth with me because Padruig refused the summons."

"Oh. I do not recall meeting your Padruig, but so many men come and go, at all hours of the day and night. And too, Alexander keeps his business to himself. He says he does not want to bore me with such things. Not that I'd be bored."

Rowena forced a smile, suspecting, for reasons she could not name, that the earl did not confide in Glenda because he did not much respect women. Mayhap it was the way he had so imperiously summoned Lion the night before.

"The clansmen who *have* joined Alexander become restless and, frankly, something of a problem. Men!" Glenda added ruefully. "They are like lads who must be kept busy or they get into mischief such as befell you yesterday."

"Mischief?" Rowena exclaimed. "My guardsman was gravely wounded, and I was nearly raped."

"Aye. Alexander was most wroth with Georas and his men. He levied a stiff fine and cut their ale rations. Which is good. Too much drink makes matters worse."

"You are chatelaine here. Could you not do something?"

"Nay, Alexander does not like it if anyone questions his decisions." She fingered a faded bruise on her chin. A souvenir of having roused the earl's temper? "He does give me free rein in domestic matters."

How bloody decent of him, considering it was Glenda's castle. Rowena seethed with impotent rage. How could such a canny woman bow down to a brute like Alexander?

Because she loved him. Further proof, if Rowena needed any, of the reasons to steer clear of such entanglements. "If you could point out to me His Grace's scribe, I could ask him about the swearing."

"Alexander does not employ one. He must deal with many sensitive issues, and thus writes his own letters and keeps his own accounts," she said with obvious pride. "He prizes learning most highly, which is one reason he enjoys Lion's company. Did you know he speaks not only French, but Italian and Spanish as well?"

"I doubt he finds much use for them in the Highlands," Rowena snapped.

"Mayhap not, but he sings beautifully and composes the most heavenly verse."

Donald hurried up and bowed before his mistress. "All is in readiness for the weapon shew, my lady. The combat field has been roped off, benches brought out and cook has set up tables to hold the refreshments, as ye ordered."

"Excellent." Lady Glenda smiled at Rowena. "Lion suggested we hold games and tests of skill to keep the men busy till the army marches. Alexander thought it a grand idea. The lairds of old used to do the same when they called up their clansmen to fight. Is His Grace ready?" she asked Donald.

"He left for the training grounds moments ago."

"Without me?" Glenda paled and jumped up. "Drat. I wanted to change, but there's no time. Have my horse brought round." She lifted her skirts and hastened away. Her departure started a flood, as the other women hurried from the hall, calling for their mounts and capes.

Rowena was borne along on the tide, but with no servant to send running for her mare, was forced to walk with the maids and women of lesser rank, some of whom were obviously harlots come to service the clansmen. The trip through the inner bailey to the grassy outer ward was not long, but her boots and hem were muddied by the time she arrived at the arena.

She'd been once to a gathering of Clan Gunn, and this

was very similar. A huge area had been roped off to contain the contestants. The onlookers milled about outside, swilling ale and placing bets on their favorites. Three tiers of benches had been erected to hold the nobles. In the center of the middle row, under a canopy of dark blue Shaw plaid, sat Glenda and the other ladies, their gowns bright splashes of color on the otherwise gloomy day.

Lady Glenda spied her, stood and motioned for Rowena to join her in the stands. Jostled and hemmed in as she was by the crowd, Rowena gave the offer consideration, but noted Lady Selena seated beside Glenda. Nay, she'd had enough of strife.

"I am fine here," Rowena called up.

"So, there you are," snapped a querulous voice.

Rowena whirled and found Eneas at her elbow. It seemed her strife was not over for the day.

"I see you are enjoying the amenities of the castle," he said nastily, scowling at her clean hair and fresh clothes.

She was childishly pleased to see that, though dressed in his best tunic of saffron wool, he still stank of the trail and his hair was greasy. "Where are you staying?"

"I was fortunate to buy a small tent."

"What of the men?"

Eneas shrugged. "They are making do."

Sleeping in the open on the ground. Rowena felt a wave of guilt. It was a chief's duty to provide for his men. She was here to claim that responsibility for her son, yet she'd not given any thought to the rest of the Gunns. That most of them were loyal to Eneas and would like to see her fail did not matter. "I have met the chatelaine of Blantyre," she said. "When the games are over, I'll ask if she can find some room for you all within the walls."

"I do not need your favors." Eneas scowled. "Have you met the earl, too? Have you already used your soft white body to entice from him the guardianship of my nephew?"

Rowena did not like the way he said that. Did Eneas suspect the truth? "I have not met the earl," she said shortly.

"Good, because I intend—"

A blare of horns silenced the crowd.

Alexander galloped into the center of the enclosure. Seen in daylight, his stern visage was daunting. His hooded eyes seemed to pounce from person to person, like an inquisitor looking for wrongdoers. Still, he looked every inch the royal prince, his red-and-black Stewart tartan belted over a tunic of white wool. Three eagle feathers dipped jauntily from a velvet cap as black as his glossy hair. Gemstones winked on his hands as he lifted them in an expansive gesture. "Welcome one and all. I give you the chieftains of the Grand Army of Pacification."

The rope barricade was pulled aside and warriors streamed onto the field, a full two score of them. Some were dressed in gleaming mail; others wore the padded *leine croich*. A few rough men of the far north were bare legged, clad in animal skins and carrying long spears.

Alexander grinned, his teeth white against his beard. "We are met here to test your readiness for battle. What say you, are your clansmen prepared to show me their mettle?"

"Aye!" the chieftains roared back.

Behind the barricades, the clansmen whose fighting skills would be put to the test echoed their leaders' acceptance of his challenge. Waving their swords and spears in the air, they filled the air with a dozen different battle cries.

"The Gunns do not participate?" Rowena asked over the din.

"Did your new friends not tell you we are in disfavor?" Eneas's lip curled. "It seems that my brother did refuse the earl's summons to join the army. Thus we are tainted. Lord Alexander's commander would not even let us show our skills and be judged till His Grace rendered a decision about us." He glared at her. "Did you know Padruig had come here, that he was returning from Blantyre when he was killed?"

"Not at the time," Rowena said weakly. So Lion had spoken the truth. "What of the swearing?"

"I did not ask. If you could have seen the way his Stewarts looked at me, as though I might be a spy or an assassin...." His eyes narrowed. "I am surprised you were lodged in the castle and not tossed out on your arse."

Because of Lion. "Lady Glenda does not know we are in disfavor. She is busy running the castle and not much involved in the earl's business." What would happen when the earl found out? Silently, Rowena moaned, seeing Paddy's future ruined. "What can we do?" she asked of her unexpected ally.

"*I* intend to bide my time and find a chance to prove I am not the coward Padruig was."

"Coward? He was no such thing. He—"

"Was a weak old fool, too shortsighted to see that joining the earl was our one chance to make the Gunns truly important."

"You mean you would join his army?" she asked, aghast.

"If the earl will let me, aye."

"Bastard! Murdering bastard!" someone growled in her ear.

Rowena looked over her shoulder into the twisted face of a youth. Did he mean Eneas? Nay, the lad's hate-filled gaze was fastened on the field beyond her. Before she could puzzle it out, the youth pulled a dirk from his belt and pushed past her.

"I'll kill him. I'll see His Grace pays." The lad ducked under the ropes and started to run toward the earl.

"Stop!" Rowena cried, starting forward.

Eneas was quicker. "Beware! Beware, my lord earl!" he screamed. Vaulting the rope, he scrambled after the assailant.

Alexander turned from his chieftains, who hemmed him in on three sides. Seemingly frozen in place, they stared at the running lad. Comprehension dawned in their faces. The earl shouted something. Men reached for their weapons.

The lad halted and drew back his arm to throw the knife.

"Naaay!" Eneas tackled the boy. They tumbled across the muddy ground, limbs flailing.

Rowena darted forward, saw Eneas snatch the knife from the lad and raise it with deadly intent. "Stop!" She grabbed hold of Eneas's hand and prevented him from striking.

"Damn. Let loose," Eneas shouted.

"He's only a boy. Let us find out what he was do—"

"He was trying to kill me." Alexander pushed Rowena aside, grabbed the youth by the throat and lifted him up. "Who sent you? Who paid you to murder me?"

"No one." Though scratched and covered with filth, the lad's narrow face screamed defiance. He was young, younger than Rowena had thought. No more than ten or eleven, surely. "Ye killed my brother. Murdered him in cold blood."

"Who might he be?"

"Will Ross. I am his brother, Colin."

"Ah." Alexander's lip curled scornfully. "So, the Rosses have bred up another traitor to follow in Will's path."

"Will was no traitor. His only crime was not wanting to be part of yer accursed army. For that, ye sent yer pack of wolves to murder him whilst he did claim sanctuary in Blair Abbey."

An ugly murmur sifted through the crowd.

Alexander ignored them, his black scowl focused on the boy, who hung limp in his grip. "'Tis a lie. But likely the last one you'll utter. Georas, rig me a rope. We'll hang him—"

"Your Grace. Wait, please." Rowena pushed through the crowd. "Please. You cannot hang him. He's just a boy…a child. He cannot fully understand what he was doing. If you—"

"How dare you approach me in such an insolent manner and demand justice for my would-be assassin?" Alexander growled. "Who the hell are you?"

"R-Rowena Gunn. I—"

"Gunn!" It was like throwing oil on a fire. His eyes

blazed with fury. "More traitors. What are you doing here?"

"I...we—" she gestured toward Eneas, who now stood beside her "—came to swear fealty to you for my son."

Alexander's fury mellowed as he looked at Eneas. "You saved my life. And for that I do thank you." His gaze narrowed. "What is this troublesome woman to you?"

"A nuisance," Eneas said quickly.

Rowena gasped. This could not be happening. If some ill befell her, who would raise her Paddy? "I am the mother of Padruig Gunn's heir."

"Do not speak to me of that traitor," Alexander snarled. "Georas, hang the Ross and lock this woman in the dungeon till I can decide how best to deal with her."

"A moment, if you would, Alexander?" called a deep, familiar voice.

Rowena felt an odd surge of relief as she spotted Lion guiding his stallion through the crowd.

"There you are," the earl grumbled. "You picked a damned poor time to go off hunting, Lion. I was nearly killed. By that." He pointed at the youth caught tight in Georas's meaty grasp.

Lion's bland gaze flickered over the lad, then moved to her. "And what has Rowena done?"

"Why do you care?"

"I mentioned last night that I'd long known her. And..." Lion leaned his forearms on his saddle horn. "...we are betrothed."

"Betrothed?" the earl thundered. "I knew naught of this. When did it happen?"

"We discussed it this morn, but I've always known she was the lady for me." He looked straight at her when he spoke, his gaze mocking, daring her to dispute his claim and suffer the consequences.

Chapter Six

If looks could kill, he'd be dead, Lion mused, conscious of the many dark glances cast his way. There was Selena's spiteful envy, Georas's frank loathing and Eneas Gunn's sullen fury.

As for Rowena, she was spitting mad, a hair's breadth from denouncing his claim, despite the danger. He could not afford to care what any of them thought. His mission, and a score of lives—young Colin Ross's included—hung in the balance here. And a delicate balance it was.

Lion concentrated his effort on the man who could tip that balance. "By your leave, of course, Your Grace," he said, pasting on a guileless smile. "It seems a pity to hang the lad before we've found out if there are others involved."

Alexander scowled. "Aye, you are right." He snapped his fingers at the Stewart clansmen lurking behind him. "Take this would-be killer to the dungeons and question him."

Rowena made a small sound of protest and started forward. Lion caught her wrist and whirled her into his embrace. "I am sorry, love. I've not greeted you properly." Crushing her to him, he hissed in her ear, "If you love life, keep silent."

"But—" she said breathlessly.

"Nay. One misstep now and you'll kill us all."

The stiffness left her slender body, and she nodded, but he guessed that her acquiescence was chancy at best. He needed to get her away, but knew they dared not leave. Damn. There was much that needed doing, too many people to protect. Glancing sideways at Heckie Sutherland, he jerked his head toward the party of Stewarts who were leading the terrified Colin away.

Heckie nodded and melted into the crowd on a course parallel to theirs. Small, canny and resourceful, Heckie was just the one to see the lad came to no harm...temporarily.

"I thank you for saving my life, Sir Eneas," Alexander fairly shouted. "Name your reward. Anything I have is yours."

"Nay," Rowena whispered, struggling against Lion's hold.

"Easy." He loosened his grip, but did not free her entirely, keeping one arm around her shoulder. "Wait and see."

"I was glad to be of service, Your Grace," said Eneas, his smile as oily as his manner. "I ask no reward save that I be allowed to join you in your worthy cause."

"Ah." Alexander beamed. "Where do you hail from? How many men do you command?"

"I am Eneas Gunn of Hillbrae."

Alexander's black scowl returned. "Hillbrae...was that not Padruig Gunn's holding?"

"Alas, my brother is dead."

"Mmm. So I had...heard. And you have inherited?"

"Well..." Eneas cast a smug glance at Rowena. "My brother's heir is a lad of five, placed in my guardianship."

Rowena gasped and surged forward.

Lion pulled her back, clamping his arm around her waist. "Speak, and your son will be an orphan," he muttered.

Alexander clapped Eneas on the shoulder with enough force to make him stagger. "Ah. Well, we are happy to have you with us. Come, let us toast our new alliance."

As they wandered off toward the refreshment tables, trailed by the rest of the court, Lion hustled Rowena in the opposite direction, ducking behind the tiers of vacant benches, the only shelter of any sort on the open field.

"Let go of me," Rowena snapped the moment they were private. When he released her, she turned to leave.

"Stay, or I swear I will gag you, truss you up like a goose bound for market and stow you under these seats till the gathering is over."

She turned on him, shaking with fury. "Brute! You awful, hateful brute." She came at him, pounding her fists against his chest, calling him names no lady should know. He let her rail. When the storm was spent, he splayed his hands across her back and held her close while she wept.

At length, she lifted her head. "Why did you let them take Colin away? Why did you not let me speak out for my son?"

"Because Alexander is not a reasonable man. He will not pardon the lad nor heed your pleas for your son. His main aim is to raise an army. Eneas not only saved his life, he offers him more men. At the moment, Eneas holds the upper hand. Only a fool would speak against him."

"Or a coward."

Lion smiled. "You may think me that if it helps."

She hesitated, then shook her head. "Nay, it is just..."

"Hard to stand by and see such injustice prevail. I know, believe me, I know."

She stepped back, and he let her go. "There is no telling what harm may befall Colin in the dungeons."

"Aye, he's in considerable danger."

"Do you think they will hang him?"

Lion was spared telling her a lie when Bryce walked around the corner of the viewing stand, carrying two cups of wine. Lion knew his cousin had not come to offer refreshments, but to receive instructions. Knowing also that time was short, Lion spread his cloak on the grass and bowed to Rowena. "Will you rest and partake of the wine Bryce so thoughtfully brought us?"

She sat, looking dazed, as one who has survived disaster but not come to grips with it.

Lion drew Bryce a few paces away. "Get a message to the lads in the hills," he said in French. Lion had with him thirty men, but another fifty Sutherlands camped secretly in the hills, a reserve force about which the earl knew nothing. "They have three hours to get inside Blantyre and get Colin out."

"Three hours? It'll not be full dark by then."

"I know, but it cannot be helped. We must act quickly. They'll not be looking for anyone to come so soon. And I'd not have the lad spend the night in the dungeon."

"I'll take a few of our lads from here and go now."

"Nay. The MacPhersons will be the first to point the finger in our direction when the lad vanishes. I want every Sutherland visible and accounted for this afternoon. And I want all attention focused here."

"How do you propose to accomplish that? I think the only event left for today is putting the stone. That can be a deadly boring affair and folk are bound to wander off."

"Aye, what we need is something exciting. A challenge." Lion cocked his head, a plan forming. "Send that message to the lads. I'll take care of the entertainments."

Lion's mind was brimming with plans as he sat down beside Rowena and drank from the second cup.

"Why did you claim we were betrothed?" she asked.

"'Twas the only thing I could think of on short notice. I'd no great desire to see you join young Colin Ross in Blantyre's dungeon," Lion said. "And the way things were headed…"

"You cannot hold me to it."

"Not if you do not agree."

"I will not." Her mouth was stubbornly set. "Ever."

It would be interesting to see what won out, her stubbornness or his determination. Because he was not a man who lost easily or often, he began laying his plans. "I'll not force you, Rowena, but you'd best know now that I want you."

Her eyes widened; her face went pale. "Is that what you were whispering with Bryce about? Were you planning to kidnap me and force me to wed you?"

He contrived to look abashed. "Nothing so rash as that, though I may resort to that if my other plans do not work. I did but think a little betrothal gift was in order."

"I do not want any gifts from you."

"Not a ring for your finger or a broach for your cloak?"

"Nay," she said, then her expression turned crafty. "But if you could find some way to free Colin Ross..."

Lion suppressed a smile. Ah, she was a worthy adversary. "It would be too dangerous."

"Could you not at least try?"

He smiled gently. "For you, I would try anything."

"Really? But how...?"

He shook his head. "'Tis best you not know. I wouldn't want you fretting over my safety."

"I gave up doing that years ago."

"Did you, now?" he asked, pleased by the flicker of emotion in her eyes. She was not so immune to him as she'd like to be. "I never stopped worrying about you, lass, even when I heard you'd up and wed another the moment my back was turned."

Anger flamed quick and bright in her cheeks. "'Twas you who left me, without a word or a care."

"Ah, that's where you are wrong. I cared a great deal, but at the time, I had no choice in the matter."

Her eyes filled with emotions that were painful to watch. She opened her mouth, then closed it. "Well, I no longer care why you went." Rising, she twitched the wrinkles from her skirts and turned to leave him.

Not ready to let her go, he hopped up and blocked her retreat. "You do care. That's what sends you running whenever we're together. What was between us once is still here, Rowena. It sizzles and crackles, fierce as a lightning storm on a hot summer night. You remember, same as I do, what it was like.''

''Nay.'' She put her hands over her ears, body shuddering in the grip of the same emotions that sent his own heart racing.

''Aye.'' Impatient, he took her shoulders and gazed deep into the eyes that had haunted his dreams for years. ''Much has changed in six years, but this hasn't.'' He brought his mouth down on hers, hard, demanding a response.

She stiffened, her gasp of shock and, likely, outrage muffled by his kiss. She tried to twist free. He wouldn't let her go. Not yet. Maybe not ever. He tasted anger and defiance on her unyielding lips, but beneath them was a longing he understood only too well. It pierced him to the quick, shattering his ruthless quest to force an admission from her. Rowena might look strong and remote, but she was fragile and needy. Instantly, he gentled the kiss, apologizing, then coaxing, seducing.

She trembled in his grip. Her hands fluttered against his chest, as though trying to decide whether to push or cling. Her lips parted with a soft moan as her body swayed toward his. It was all the invitation he needed. He swept her up, one arm around her waist, the other hand tunneling into her hair, steadying her head as he took the kiss deeper.

Rowena's mind went blank. All her carefully erected barriers crumpled. Desires ruthlessly suppressed over the years swamped her as she responded to the feel of Lion's arms wrapped around her, his strong body pressed against hers as his mouth worked its magic on her senses. Oh, how she wanted him. Now. This instant—

''Ach!'' Lion wrenched his mouth free and buried it in her neck. His breath scorched her skin. His heart thundered to the same clamorous rhythm as hers. ''Oh, lass, I knew—''

''Nay.'' Ashamed and frightened of what she'd almost

done, of the way her body had turned traitor to her mind, she pushed weakly against him. "Let me go."

He loosened his grip, but didn't release her. "Ro?"

"Damn." She pounded his chest. "Why does it have to be you?" She looked up into eyes gone nearly black with passion and a smile that could charm the birds from their nests.

"I guess we are just more fortunate than most." He dipped his head again, searching for her mouth.

"Do not." She pushed, and this time he let her escape. She tottered back one step. "This should never have happened."

"It was inevitable."

She shook her head, as much to clear it as tell him no. "It is not the same. It can never be. I—I could never trust you again. And—and I have duties, responsibilities."

"As do I," Lion said slowly, weighing his next move. "I do not see that they are at odds. You need someone to protect you, and I'd be that man."

"I do not want your protection."

"Aye, but you need it. Have you forgotten what happened a wee bit ago?"

The color returned to her pallid cheeks, and her eyes crackled with intense emotion. "I am not afraid for myself. I've done nothing wrong. But what of young Colin? Surely the earl would not hang a child."

"The Wolf does whatever he likes."

"The Wolf." Her mouth thinned. "Aye, 'tis an apt name for a madman such as he. Can you do nothing to stop him?"

"Alexander is a dangerous man to cross," Lion said, thinking of his own plans.

"I'd not thought to see you afraid," she taunted.

"Afraid, nay, but cautious, aye. Around the earl, I am careful as a man in a pit of vipers."

"Please." She closed the gap between them, hands

clasped over her heart as she looked up at him. "You must do something."

He'd have given her anything just then, had to steel himself to recall that many lives were at stake. "I will speak with Alexander," he said carefully, not daring to confide his plans, lest she somehow betray him.

"Will he listen to you?"

"He has in the past. I do not know if he'll free the lad, but at least I may save his life." Lion cocked his head, needing to steer her away from this dangerous conversation. "As a betrothal gift to you."

"I am not your bet..." She glared at him. "Oh, very well, I will not tell the world that you lied about us, but neither will I sleep with you," she said firmly.

"Not even if I save young Colin?" he asked, half seriously.

"Nay. 'Tis despicable of you even to suggest such a thing."

"I did not. You were the one who brought it up. Could you at least behave toward me as a lass does with a man she fancies?" *The way you used to.* "Smile upon me occasionally. Sit with me at mealtimes."

"I suppose I could to that."

"And afterward...may I sit at your feet and compose verses likening your eyes to stars and your lips to roses?"

That wrung a small, embarrassed smile from her. "You would not be so silly."

"Silly? On the contrary, Alexander requests, nay, demands I sing often. He thinks it lends an air of civility to his crude band." He tilted his head, smiling faintly. "But if I may not bed you or sing to you, what of a walk in the gardens or a ride in the hills?"

"Will you save Colin?"

"I can promise nothing, but I will plead his case. Will you play the part of my loving betrothed?"

"I will," Rowena said grudgingly.

It promised to be an interesting wooing, Lion thought as he took his leave.

The next hour passed in a haze of dread and misery for Rowena. At Lion's insistence, they remained at the games.

"When will you speak with Alexander?" she whispered.

"Later. Alexander is wroth enough with me for being away when disaster fell and with you for trying to save the lad. Best wait till his temper has cooled. Enjoy the games."

How could she keep her eyes or her mind on the men putting the stone when her mind was back at Blantyre with Colin?

A roar from the crowd drew her wandering attention back to the field. Georas MacPherson and a brawny Chisholm stepped up to the line, ready to see who could heave a huge boulder the farthest. The onlookers shifted, some rising to leave.

"I find this boring," Lion said suddenly and loudly.

Rowena started. He'd been so quiet beside her she'd thought him absorbed in the stupid sport. Everyone turned to look at him. A few people looked relieved. Georas looked furious. The earl leaned around Lady Glenda and glared at Lion.

"Are you trying to cause more trouble?" the earl asked.

Lion shrugged, a mocking smile on his lips. "Better that than to sit here while this drags on."

"Will you come down and meet me, then?" Georas shouted.

"Toss a few rocks around?" Lion shook his head. "I'd something a bit more lively in mind."

"Name it. Swords? Dirks?"

"Football," Lion said, grinning.

The word buzzed through the crowd, drawing back those on the point of departure.

"What say you, Alexander?" Lion asked. "Do you not weary of watching instead of playing at sport? Will you lead one team and I the other?"

"Gladly." Alexander leaped to his feet, eyes alight. "I'll have Georas and Eneas Gunn on my team."

"As you will, Your Grace." Lion laughed and bent to kiss Rowena. "Wish me luck," he demanded, before vaulting lightly down the row of benches and hurrying off, a band of hearty, laughing Sutherlands at his back.

"It's a rough, bloody sport." Glenda moved down the bench to Rowena's side. "I do hope Alexander will take care."

It soon became evident that Glenda had cause for worry. There were seemingly few rules to the game, and the men played with little restraint and no concern for life or limb.

"What are they trying to prove?" Rowena asked, staring in horror at the seething mass of men on the field.

"Well, the objective is to carry yon ball—a pig's bladder filled with dried beans—over your opponent's end of the field."

"Aye, I know that," Rowena snapped. "I just do not see why a group of grown men should punish each other so."

Lion was in the thick of things. Face flushed, hair flying out behind him, he carried the ball a few feet down the field before a herd of MacPhersons drove him to the ground.

"Jesu!" Rowena shot to her feet. "They've killed him."

Incredibly, the pile of MacPhersons heaved, and Lion exploded from the center like a trout after a mayfly. He screamed something and tossed the ball to Bryce Sutherland. Bryce caught it and hurtled down the field. The opposition was up off Lion and after Bryce in a flash. Alexander tackled Bryce and scooped up the ball. The Sutherland team leaped on the earl with little regard for his lofty titles.

"Lady Glenda. Lady Glenda." Donald stood on the ground below the benches, looking up at them.

"Not now, Donald, I'm busy."

"We've more guests," the glum-faced steward shouted over the din of the game.

"Tell whoever it is to wait till the match is—" Glenda jumped up. "Look. It's Alexander. He's gotten free. Run! Run!" she screamed, tugging on Rowena's arm in her excitement.

The noise of the crowd rose to an earsplitting roar. The earl lumbered down the field, Georas MacPherson ahead of him, tossing aside would-be tacklers. They crossed the end line a few steps ahead of Lion's men.

The earl danced about, holding the ball aloft while the onlookers roared. Lion was gracious in defeat, clapping the earl on the back and leading the cheers. Eventually, the shouts faded away to an excited babble, and the combatants limped off the field. Good humor had clearly been restored, both winners and losers looking battered, grubby as young lads, but happy.

"Alexander!" Glenda hurtled down from the bleachers and hugged him. "You were wonderful. Are you unhurt?"

"Of course." He shook off her embrace with a cool shrug and turned to accept the hearty congratulations of others.

He tires of her, Rowena thought with a pang. Just as Lion had tired of her. Men.

"Your Grace?" A young man in red-and-black tartan emerged from the ring of well-wishers and inclined his head in greeting. "I am Robert MacNab, sent by my sire to discuss your summons."

"Ah." Alexander's dirt-streaked face brightened. "This is indeed a fortunate day for me. My life is saved by Eneas, I trounce Lion in football and the MacNabs come to join me."

Robert MacNab's expression remained bland. "I've come to talk only, my lord. To hear what you have planned."

"Humph." Alexander's eyes narrowed.

"Well, let us conduct this discussion within the castle,"

Lion said heartily. "It grows dark, and I've worked up a terrific thirst for that ale you promised us to celebrate the earl's win, Lady Glenda."

"Ale and a feast," Glenda said quickly. She gingerly touched Alexander's wet, hairy arm. "Will you lead the victory procession, my lord?"

"Aye." His surly expression faded, and Rowena fancied she could hear many in the assembly draw a breath of relief.

How did these people manage to withstand the uncertainty of the earl's temperament?

"What did you think of the game?" Lion asked, falling into step beside her as they walked back to the castle.

"It was rough and barbaric."

"Just what the lads needed." He grinned at her. "They've grown a mite restless and uncontrollable. An outlet for their energies was called for."

As they neared the inner ward, a soldier pelted out through the gate. "He's gone, my lord."

"Who?" Alexander demanded.

"The lad—Colin Ross."

"What? How could one small boy escape a band of grown men?"

"He—he just vanished. Umfried was guarding him while we readied the rack."

"The rack...oh, my God," Rowena whispered.

Lion put his arm around her. "Shh. He's away."

"When we came back, Umfried was passed out cold in the cell from a blow to the head, and the lad was gone."

"Search the castle. I want him found and—"

"What is amiss?" Robert MacNab inquired.

Rowena leaned closer to Lion. "How did he get away?" she whispered.

"Clearly he is a clever lad," Lion replied.

The odd note in his voice made her look up. His expression, as he listened to the earl rant on about punishment for Colin and rewards for those who found him, was perfectly bland. But there was a twinkle deep in his eyes that made her wonder.

Lion and his men had been at the games all day. Her eyes widened. How had he managed it?

Chapter Seven

"How do you stand this?" Robbie MacNab muttered.

Lion looked around the packed hall. Though the raucous victory celebration was in full swing, darker emotions simmered below the surface of the frivolity, like the hidden eddies of some murky river. The earl's true supporters drank with their usual rapacious greed and disported themselves as crudely as a band of brigands. Those not there of their own free will sipped their ale cautiously and watched their words and their backs.

"It is more bearable than the alternative," Lion said.

"Which would be...?"

"Screaming defiance, making a run for my father's stronghold at Kinduin and waiting behind its walls for this rabble to come and besiege me and mine."

"Mmm."

"What did he say to you, our gracious leader?"

"He asked if my father would call up the MacNabs and fight beneath his banner. I—I took your advice and said I was to gather more information before Da decided." Robbie raked a hand through his hair. "Jesu, after the tales I heard about young Colin, what else could I do? Any man who would throw a lad in the dungeon and threaten to hang him is a fiend of the worst—"

"Easy," Lion murmured. "This is not the place for such

talk." Though they stood in one of the window alcoves, well away from most folk, it was still dangerous.

Instinctively, his eyes sought Rowena. She sat on the dais with Lady Glenda. Safely out of harm's way...for the moment. Despite his pleasure at having her near, he should send her away. Send, ha! She'd given in on the mock betrothal, but he'd seen her wavering when she'd heard that Colin was free. What would she do? Honor her pledge or send him packing?

"Where is the lad?" Robbie whispered.

"Why, I have no idea." Exactly.

"Aye, and I'm the king of Scotland."

"You could not do a worse job."

"Nor you a better one," Robbie said solemnly.

"That's the ale talking, me lad."

"The dozen men who ventured the opinion to me this evening seemed right sober," Robbie replied.

"Daft, they are, then," Lion said, shaking his head. "And they'd best guard their tongues do they want to keep them attached. Our host has little sense of humor when it comes to that subject in particular."

"Mad," the lad murmured. "Mad as a rogue wolf."

"You'd do well to remember that over the next few days, and guard that red-haired temper of yours, for he'll not stop trying to sway you to his side."

"You'd best watch yourself too, my lord. Alexander told me, in confidence, mind, that he was bestowing Westray Tower on Eneas Gunn and putting him in command of his spearmen."

Lion whistled through his teeth and glanced over at Gunn, who stood close by his new lord's elbow like a dog waiting for a bone. "Alexander thinks to show those here how lavish he can be in rewarding one who serves him well."

"Aye. But there's more. Eneas does whisper against you in the earl's ear, saying you must have had something to do with young Colin's disappearance."

Lion's jaw tightened. "He has proof?"

"Nay. Just a healthy hatred, I'd guess, for it was likewise mentioned to me that he was not pleased by your sudden betrothal to his late brother's wife."

"You've learned much in a few short hours," Lion said, masking his unease. "Would you like a job as a spy?"

"I thought I already had one."

Lion chuckled. "I like you, lad. See you come to no harm during your stay here."

"I'd bid you the same, my lord. And now, I'd take my leave, for we've talked overlong for two men who have just met casually at court. And there's a lassie or two who's been glancing my way. 'Twould be rude indeed to ignore such sweet interest." He inclined his head and walked off whistling.

Lion kept the faint smile on his lips as he tilted the cup to drain the last of the watered wine he'd been drinking. The lad had a good point. The piper was playing a lively tune, and Lion had yet to dance with his betrothed. Setting his empty cup on the alcove seat, he threaded his way through the throng to the head table. "Lady Glenda." He bowed low to the lady. "I'd steal my lady away for a reel or two."

"Of course. The night was made for dancing." Glenda cast a wistful glance at Alexander, who stood by the hearth deep in conversation with Georas and Eneas.

An unholy trio if ever there was one, Lion thought. Nor did he like it that the earl ignored Glenda more each day. "Shall I see if Alexander will join us?"

"Nay," Glenda said quickly. Her fingers fluttered nervously to a dark spot below her right ear. A bruise? Surely Alexander would not dare strike the lady. "He—he has more important matters to attend than my amusements."

"I will stay and continue our conversation," Rowena said.

"Nay." Lady Glenda squared her shoulders and stood.

"Go along and dance. I must speak with Donald about the arrangements for tomorrow's games."

Rowena came away with Lion readily enough, but when they reached the small space that had been cleared for dancing, she balked. "I do not feel like dancing." Her features were shuttered, her mouth set in a mulish line he knew well.

"Aye, it's too close in here." He took her arm without waiting for her consent and steered her from the hall.

"Where are we going?"

"Not to my chamber or yours, though I'd prefer that above all things." He led her out into the corridor, then up the tightly winding steps. Three stories they climbed. When he thrust open the door to the battlements, fresh, cool air rushed in to greet them.

"Ah." She slipped past him, flinging back her head as she crossed the parapet to the chest-high wall beyond.

Lion joined her, leaning against the cold stone as they gazed out into the dark night. The breeze was light, scented with damp earth. It chased a few wispy clouds across a wee crescent of a moon. From below them came the gurgle of the burn flowing past the outer walls, punctuated by the cry of night birds on the hunt. "Jesu, but I missed this," he murmured, lifting his face to sample the air again.

"Then why did you go to France and stay so long?"

"You know the answer to that."

"Because your father wished you to be educated in the ways of the world." She faced him, pale and sad. "Was it worth it?"

Lion frowned, considering. He could speak five languages and write a fair hand in three of them. A score of musical instruments did he play, and he'd a repertoire of songs a balladeer might envy. A master swordsmen had honed his skills with a blade. A French marshal had taught him the finer points of taking a castle, or defending one. But to mention all that would be bragging, and Lion had learned that if a man had to blow his own horn it was not worth playing.

"I learned that half the world thinks we Scots are unco' savages," Lion said, mockery deepening his burr.

"Not you, surely," Rowena said. "Your whole family can read and write."

"Aye. Have you found time to keep up your studies?" he asked, remembering the warm summer afternoons he'd spent teaching her her letters...among other things.

"I still have the two books you gave me." She smiled faintly. "Though they're a bit tattered from heavy use."

"I'll have to see if I can find a few more." He recalled the extensive library at Kinduin and wondered how he'd get her there to see it. "My puny education did not impress the French. I was treated like a pig farmer who had wandered into court."

"It must have been a bit dampening to that swaggering ego of yours," she teased.

"Oh, aye, it was that." Lion chuckled. "But there were too many of them for me to fight. 'Twas the first lesson I learned. To get even without raising my sword or my voice."

"How did you do it?" She rested her arms on the wall, her gaze eager and intent as she waited for his answer.

"I became better than them...at everything."

Aye, he had the determination, the will and the intellect to do that, she mused, studying his profile against the night. His features were strong, the heritage from his Viking ancestors. His carriage was proud, unbending, yet it was his eyes that captured her attention when he suddenly turned toward her. They glowed with a life of their own, brilliant as the torch set in the wall a few feet away. That vitality, that power were what had drawn her to him from the first. The magic had not dulled with pain or time.

"What are you thinking, lass?" he asked softly.

"That you are different, yet much the same."

"I suppose that's true enough." He sighed, covering her cold hand with his warm one. "You asked if it was worth it, my tour of France and Italy. In some ways, aye, it was, for I left a selfish, pampered lad and came back a man, better able, I hope, to lead my clansmen." His grip tightened fractionally, and his voice dropped. "But I lost that which was more valuable to me than all I gained. I lost you."

"Don't." She pulled her hand free and turned away. "Don't do this to me." *Don't make me feel again.*

"I must." He pulled her back against his chest and wrapped his arms around her. "I am not one to give up what I want without a fight. And, by God, lass, I do want you."

"Nay." She shook her head, fighting the pull of his words.

"Aye," he whispered. His lips found her ear. "And you want me, too. Only you are too stubborn to admit it."

"It is not stubbornness. I—I have changed. I no longer desire you..." The words trailed off in a moan as he traced the shape of her ear with his tongue.

"This has not changed. I still know what pleases you. I could pleasure you again...if you'd let me."

"Stop," she said, but so weakly she scarcely heard her own words. "Please stop."

"As you will." He loosened his hold on her and turned her to face him, his hands resting lightly on her waist. "But before we go back inside, I would tell you why I left without a word."

"It does not matter," she replied, thinking of Padruig. And Paddy. Explanations would not change what was.

"It does to me. 'Tis a matter of honor, for I'd not have you believe I was so callous as to abandon you."

"I long ago accepted the fact that your father made a change in your departure date and you had not time to get a message to me." She'd accepted, but she hadn't forgiven him for choosing family over her.

"My departure was not speeded up by my father's will, but by a brigand's blade."

"What?"

"I was attacked on the way to meet with you and left for dead in the woods." Lion watched the play of emotions cross her face: shock, fear and something unexpected—wariness.

"When I went to Kinduin, no one mentioned this attack."

"You went to Kinduin? When?"

She lifted her chin. "The next day. I—I was concerned, you see, and feared something had happened to you. Only to be told you'd sailed for France on the very day we were to have met."

"I had not gone anywhere. I was gravely wounded."

"Why would the guards lie to me?"

"Because my father feared another attempt on my life." There was more, but he wasn't ready to share that yet. Not till she believed in him. "No one told me you'd come— not that I was in any shape to go after you." His voice turned bitter. "I was taken with blood fever and out of my head for a week or more. By the time I regained my senses, you were already wed."

She trembled in his grasp, but he resisted the urge to pull her close. "Life is truly cruel at times," she murmured.

"Aye." What was she thinking that made her expression so haunted? "But we've been given a second chance."

Rowena closed her eyes briefly against the wave of pain. When she opened them, he was still watching her. His expression was so like Paddy's when he desperately wanted to make her change her mind about something that the breath caught in her throat. Their son. Lion's son. There could be no second chance. She could not let Lion Sutherland back into her life. Could not let him meet her son and possibly guess the truth.

"I cannot," she whispered.

Lion smiled to hide his disappointment. The anguish in her voice when she refused him had not escaped his notice. There was something going on here, some reason why she denied what lay between them. He meant to find out what it was. Hauling her downstairs and seducing her would have satisfied the ache clawing at his gut, but that small victory might cost him the war. And the ultimate prize.

"Come, I'd best get you back inside," he said lightly. "You're shaking with cold."

She blinked, clearly surprised he'd not pressed. "Aye, there is a sudden chill in the air."

"But not in my heart." He took her arm and led the way, opening the door and then preceding her down the stairs. His mind was on the myriad of problems he must deal with before the morrow. Just short of the landing for the third floor, she suddenly grabbed his shoulder, halting him.

"I—I thought I heard something below," she whispered.

Lion squinted against the gloom. The torch that had burned brightly when they'd come up was out now. Deep shadows pooled about the archway that opened onto the third floor. It contained storage rooms and, farther down the hall, a large chamber where the maids slept. He saw nothing, but heard a faint slither, a foot shifting on the stone floor.

Someone waited there.

In his mind, he saw a likely scene play out. The assailants would wait till he and Rowena had passed, then they'd creep after them to strike from above. Unexpectedly. With deadly intent.

"Take off your slippers and hand them to me," he whispered.

Rowena didn't question; she just did as he'd bid.

Lion had his boots off by the time she gave him her shoes. He tiptoed down to just above the opening and set the footwear on the step. "Ah, Rowena, your kisses set my blood aflame," he said in a hoarse whisper. "Let us hurry to my chamber, for I can wait no longer to sample your sweetness."

He winked at Rowena, drew his knife and flicked the

shoes off the step, one after the other. They made little flopping sounds as they cascaded down the stone slabs.

"It's them. Come on," said a coarse voice. Two dark shapes emerged from the archway, steel glinting in their upraised hands.

Lion debated the wisdom of hand-to-hand combat in close quarters, outnumbered and with Rowena to protect. Safety won out over chivalry. He scampered soundlessly after the men, came up behind them at the next turn of the stairs. The men wore dark tunics, no plaids and, he thought, hoods over their heads.

"Where the hell are they?" one grumbled, bending to peer down the curving flight.

"Here." Lion jammed his fists into the back of the last man and shoved him at his cohort.

A shout of surprise echoed in the stairwell, cut off by the thud of flesh hitting stone as the men tumbled down into the darkness below. They uttered a string of grunts and curses that brought a smile to Lion's lips.

"Lion?" Rowena called softly. "Lion?" She hurtled down the stairs, a dirk glimmering in her hand.

"Here." He caught her to him. "What are you doing? I told you to stay back."

"I thought you might need my help. Oh, Lion, whatever possessed you to follow them instead of raising a cry?"

He laughed. "To which they would likely have responded by slitting our throats ere help could come."

"Of course." She leaned her head against his chest. "I was not thinking. I—I was so frightened."

"They would not have gotten past me to you," Lion said curtly, as though annoyed she'd question his prowess.

"I know," she said faintly. Beneath her ear, his heart thudded strongly. She had been worried about him, dammit. Damn him for making her want things she should not—the comfort and support and closeness of a man. And not just any man.

"It's all right." He stroked her back, then set her from him. "We'd best collect our shoes and—"

"What if they are waiting below?"

"They won't be. Likely they are somewhere nursing their bumps and bruises." And plotting another strike.

"Did you recognize them?"

"Nay."

Rowena sighed. "Wait, will they not limp or have scratches from the stone wall?"

"An excellent notion, but after the football match, most of the men at Blantyre, myself included, are bruised and battered."

"Drat. We must go and tell Lady Glenda—"

"We will tell no one."

"But she should be aware that some in her service are the sort to assault her guests and steal from them."

"I do not think this was a random act of thievery. They were waiting here for us, and the reason I cannot recognize them is that they had hoods over their faces."

"Eneas?" Rowena whispered.

"Or Georas."

"Do you...do you think they will try again?"

"'Tis possible. I want you to leave this to me," he said firmly. "I'll escort you to your room and post a guard outside. I do not want you to go anywhere alone."

"I do not like having some man trail after me."

"As your betrothed, it is my responsibility to guard you," he said silkily.

"The betrothal is a sham," Rowena hissed.

"But you have vowed to make it seem a truth. Come, now. If you do not get your sleep, your eyes will be dark in the morn, and folk will think I did keep you awake all night." Without giving her time to argue, he hustled her back to her chamber. As they approached the door, something moved in the dark at the end of the corridor, just beyond the pale circle of torchlight.

Lion pushed Rowena behind him and drew his sword. "You there, show yourself."

"'Tis only me, my lord." Sim stepped forth. "I was waiting for the lady..." His eyes widened. "My lady, your hair is all tumbled and your gown is dirty."

"We ran into a bit of trouble on our way down from the battlements," Lion said, sheathing his sword.

"We were atta-tacked on the s-stairs," Rowena said. Unaccountably, her teeth were chattering.

"What?" Sim cried. "By whom?"

"Explanations must wait." Lion put his hand on Rowena's shoulder and kneaded gently, the gesture as natural as it was welcome. "We must get you within. Sim, would you run downstairs and see if Mairi would send up a cup of mulled wine?"

Rowena allowed herself to be led into the room. She sat numbly in a chair while Lion rebuilt the fire.

"Shall I help you undress?" he asked in a low voice.

"What?" Rowena sat upright. "Certainly not."

"I just thought your hands might be a mite unsteady."

"And yours are not, I suppose?"

"Well, 'tis not the first time a man's leaped out at me with a dirk." Lion grinned as he came to stand over her. "Not that I relish it, mind, but I'm a bit more used to it than you are." He touched her temple, his expression sober again. "Your pulse is still too quick. Are you certain you are all right?"

"Aye." The hike in her heart rate was caused by his nearness, not any lingering affect of the attack.

"I cannot stand to see you frightened."

Rowena bit her lip. What could she say that would not reveal how close he came to tearing at the barriers she'd so carefully erected? Damn him for making her long and yearn and ache for what could not be.

"It's been a hell of a night, my friend," Lion said to Bryce. They were alone in the large chamber Lady Glenda had assigned to him. Two Sutherlands stood guard outside Rowena's door, but still Lion had hated to leave her. He tossed back the whiskey he'd poured, welcoming the fire it lit in his gut. Slamming the cup down, he told Bryce of Robbie's warning and of the attack in the stairwell. "Damned if I know who they were."

"MacPhersons, do you think?"

"Or Eneas Gunn." He sighed and muttered, "Or, I suppose, I might also take it as a wee warning from Alexander."

"If you really think that, mayhap it's time we left."

A faint scraping sound came from outside. Both men looked at the window, open to let air into the stuffy room. It was on the second floor of the Angus Tower, the oldest part of Blantyre, and had been the master chamber for the first Lord Shaw. The tower's stone face was pitted, providing footholds for climbing. More than once Lion had exited his chamber that way when he wanted to meet in secret with his men. It might also be used by a man who wanted to watch and listen.

Lion laid a cautionary finger over his lips.

Bryce nodded and lowered his voice to a whisper. "We've had word about your sheep." More loudly, he added, "I spent the evening dancing with Mistress Jean Shaw."

"Ah. A right bonny lass. Just passing the time, or has she caught your fancy?" Lion asked, creeping toward the window.

"Oh, she's bonny enough, but not the lass for me. Too young and flighty."

Dirk in hand, Lion whipped into the window opening and looked down. A fat orange cat glared up at him from the narrow ledge just beneath. "It's just a cat."

Twitching its tail in disapproval, the cat continued on its way.

"Even so, we'd best watch our tongues."

Lion nodded and went to pour another whiskey. "What of the *sheep?*" he whispered, with a bit of a wink.

"Arrived safe and sound. Two ewes and one lamb."

The ewes were sheep, in truth. The lamb was Colin Ross. "Whatever possessed the lads to take the sheep?" he muttered.

"Doubtless they're sick of dried meat and oatcakes."

"They had no trouble, then?"

"Nay, the key got them in through the postern gate and back out again with no one the wiser. The fool Stewarts had left only one man guarding the cell. A quick pop on the head and he was out, Colin free and no blood shed. What could be neater?"

"There was talk of the rack. Was the lad badly hurt before our men could get to him?"

"A few bruises. And, of course, he was scared nearly witless by what they'd threatened to do to him. Bastards."

"Aye," Lion said absently, his mind racing ahead to other pitfalls. "What are the plans for tomorrow's games?"

"None. After you left the hall, the earl declared that we would all ride out tomorrow and search for Colin."

Lion gasped softly. His men would have to be warned to move their camp farther into the hills. Or mayhap he should send them back to his holding at Glenshee. Damn, he hated to risk moving them or the lad over open terrain while the earl's search parties ranged though the countryside. "What time do we go?"

"At first light."

Which meant the warning would have to be sent now. It would be risky trying to send a man down to the village, for Alexander had ordered the guard doubled.

"Oh, while we're about it, we can look for Red Will's dog. The thing's gone missing again."

Lion grinned and relaxed. The little terrier was trained to carry messages between the castle and the stables in the village, where Roderick Sutherland worked with the blacksmith. He'd get word to the lads to draw back.

"Well, then, looks like we've a day or so to polish our skills for the remaining games. Georas will likely take the wrestling." The bastard had killed two men already with his bare hands. "See that none of our lads are goaded into entering against him. Spear hurtling is another matter. We'll ride into the hills first chance we get and practice without any of the other clans judging our skills."

Bryce grinned, eyes twinkling with the knowledge that they'd accomplish other things there, as well. "That sounds like a fine idea. I could do with a bit of fresh air."

"We'll see if Lady Rowena cares to ride out with us."

Bryce frowned. "Is that wise?"

"Wise?" Lion cocked his head, remembering their discussion on the battlements and her concern for his safety. "Mayhap not, but I'm beginning to make headway in winning my prickly Rowena. I canna leave off the wooing now. Speaking of which…" He unlocked the chest at the foot of the bed and began rooting through the few personal things he'd brought with him. "Ah." He seized a small leather pouch and upended the contents into his hand—a large cabochon ring, a broach, a set of intertwined gold bracelets. He was not much interested in jewelry, but when he'd seen these in an Italian goldsmith's shop, he'd bought them. Now he knew why. "These should do nicely."

"For what?"

"Betrothal gifts. I intend to shower her with trinkets, ply her with song and honeyed kisses."

Bryce's pale brows rose. Then a wide grin creased his usually somber face. "Given what Sim had to say on the subject of Lady Rowena's opinion of you, I think you've got a long, rough road to travel, my friend."

"What did she say?"

"That she wanted nothing to do with you."

"Mmm." Lion frowned and looked down at the jewelry winking in his hand. "Mayhap I'll give her all three pieces at once."

"They may not be enough. Better see what baubles Lord Alexander has in his strongbox that he might sell you."

Lion's eyes narrowed, his mind shifting from one objective to another. That might work as a ruse. While Alexander showed off the rings and trinkets he had, Lion could get a peek inside the locked box and see if the papers he sought were there. "I may do just that."

"Careful," Bryce whispered.

"Always."

"Well, you can stay up plotting how to win the fair lady. I'm for bed," Bryce said heartily.

"Aye." Lion stowed the jewelry back in the chest and stripped off his tunic.

Come morn, he'd have to find out which way his men had gone so he could steer the search party in the opposite direction.

Chapter Eight

Lion was waiting for her in their special place, the little bower where they'd been meeting every day for a week. Seven days. So short a time, yet it seemed she'd known him a lifetime, been waiting forever for him. Seven days of talking and dreaming and yearning.

He'd been patient with her, gentle and tender and patient in his wooing. Because she was young, he'd said, and delicate and precious to him, he'd not rush her. He'd brought her trinkets—a rose from his mother's garden, a dainty gold chain as fine as a spiderweb to wear around her neck. Presents were a rarity in a household as poor as hers was, but she hadn't wanted the gifting to be one sided, so the day before, she'd baked him cakes sweetened with honey from the hive her mother tended.

They'd eaten the cakes from each other's fingers, washing them down with the wine he'd brought for her because she'd never tasted any. When the cakes were gone, he'd licked the crumbs from her lips and kissed her with a thoroughness that stole her breath. He'd held her close and let her feel what she did to him, his body vibrating, straining against the passion held carefully in check by the force of his will.

Aye, he'd been patient and loving with her.

One look at the light in Lion's eyes as he lifted her from

the saddle today and she knew his patience had reached an end.

So had hers. "Love me," she whispered, wrapping her arms around his neck.

"Ro..." He crushed her to him, his kisses hot, greedy.

She met them eagerly, opening her mouth to him, clinging as her body went liquid with desire.

He lifted his head, groaning when she tried to drag it back down. "Wait. You are so young."

"I'm ten and five. Many my age are wed ere now."

His eyes locked on hers, stripped of the teasing laughter that often lurked there. "I canna wed you till I come back from France," he said quietly. "It may be three years...or four."

"I'd not expected marriage. A noble Sutherland and a dirt-poor MacBean." She shook her head.

"It is not like that." His grip on her shoulders tightened. "I love you, Ro. Jesu, why else do you think I've held back this long time when I've wanted you so badly my innards are strung tight as catgut?"

"I—I thought you were giving me time to know you. I thought you were seducing me." She smiled into his intent, scowling face. "It's been right effective. I love you, too." She touched his jaw, where the muscles bunched. "I want you. Now. Today."

"You would lie with me and no vows spoken between us?"

"I need none, because I love you."

"And I you." Groaning, he dragged her back into his arms and kissed her till they were both breathless.

When her legs gave out, he swept her up, carried her into the heart of the grassy glade and made a bed for them on his cloak. It pleased her that his hands were unsteady as he unlaced her gown and slipped it off.

"Beautiful. So beautiful, my lass." He made her feel she was, his callused hands warm and deft as they raced over

her body, exploring and seducing. Somehow her shift was gone and his clothes, too.

"Aye," she cried, twisting against him, reveling in their differences, the feel of his strong, muscular body flowing over her slender one, possessing, dominating without crushing. She hadn't expected it to be like this, like a swift ride over a high mountain trail.

Her response seemed to inflame him, for he bent to feast on her sensitive nipples. They peaked for him; the heat spiraled through her, tightening the coil low in her belly. She wanted, how she wanted. The innermost core of her bloomed and throbbed. "Please. Please, now," she whispered.

"Aye." He rose above her, face taut with passion. His hands were warm on her thighs, opening her, lifting her....

She arched up, reaching for him, welcoming him....

A muted crash cut through the haze of pleasure.

Rowena opened her eyes. She was surrounded by shadowed velvet hangings, not sun-dappled leaves. Tangled sheets, not her lover's arms, were wrapped damply around her body.

The crash came again, from outside in the courtyard.

A dream. Just a dream.

Dazed, she lay in Annie Shaw's bed and willed her heart to slow. Why had she dreamed of that long-ago day? Because Lion was edging his way back into her life. No matter how hard she tried to hold herself aloof from him, he was the one man to whom she was vulnerable. How beautiful it had been that first time, how pure and unsullied their love. What had gone wrong? If he'd tired of her and simply gone off to France, his interest had certainly picked up again.

Admit it, she thought. It was a bit flattering to have such a lovely man running after her. But she could not afford to give in. She could not risk another broken heart, nor could she risk Paddy's future.

Disgusted with her lack of control where Lion was concerned, she flopped over on her belly. A small pouch slid off the empty pillow and into her hand.

What in the world?

Rowena sat up, undid the leather thong and upended the contents onto the bed. Three bright objects tumbled out on the blanket, old gold gleaming richly in the gloom—a double bracelet, an intricately fashioned broach and a ring with a blue stone winking in its center. A scrap of parchment floated down on top of them.

Rowena didn't need to read it to know the things were from Lion. But she looked anyway, just to see what excuse he'd given for sending them.

Though your beauty far outshines them, I'd have you wear these trinkets I purchased in Italy.

Rowena tossed down the note. So, he expected to woo her with these reminders of the trip that had taken him away from her. "Well, it will not work."

She got up and stumbled around the little screen that hid the washbasins and garderobe. When she returned, she was wide-awake. Plopping down on the bed, she traced the broach with one finger. How had he gotten them in here without awakening her? She glanced at the window and sighed. He'd done it again—climbed into her bedchamber while she slept.

Jennie would doubtless have thought it romantic.

The longer Rowena thought about it, the angrier she became. Tossing back the covers, she leaped out of bed again. "Well, I'll see he gets his jewelry back directly." She dressed in a rush, throwing on the clothes she'd worn to the banquet the night before and not bothering to rebraid her hair. Tossing the jewelry into the pouch, she stalked to the door.

A little man rose from where he'd been crouched against the wall opposite her door. "Where are you off to?"

"Who are you?"

He was not much taller than she was, a wrinkled man

with skin the color of walnut and shrewd black eyes. "Heckie Sutherland, at your service."

"I've business with your lord." It suddenly occurred to Rowena that she did not know where his room was. "If you will kindly lead me to him."

"Well..." Heckie looked down the dim corridor. "Right now, I'd guess our Lion is arse deep in preparing to ride out and a mite short on time for visiting."

"Ride out? Where? It is scarcely light."

"Dawn, aye, that's when himself said they was to send out the search parties."

"Looking for Colin? Oh, my God. Th-they cannot mean to hunt him down."

"That seems to be the plan," Heckie said noncommittally.

"And Lion means to go with them?"

"Everyone's going, except a few who're on guard—"

"We'll see about this." Rowena turned on her heel and marched down the stairs.

Behind her, Heckie scrambled to keep up. "See here, Lion knows what he's doing!"

"I doubt it. I sincerely doubt it. He's so concerned with protecting his standing with the earl that his good judgment and his morals have gone begging." She had to speak with him, change his mind. "He knows these other lairds. If he spoke against going, they'd listen and—and then there'd be no search party."

"Lady," Heckie pleaded.

Rowena plunged ahead. As she rounded the bend toward the first floor, a babble of voices filled the stairwell. Men lined the corridor, she saw when she reached the landing. Men in chain mail and riding leathers, some armed, others just belting on their swords. All were making for the main entrance. She was swept along with them, out the heavy doors and down the covered wooden steps to the courtyard.

Here, chaos truly reigned. Extra torches rimmed the bailey, casting yellow light on the plaids of a dozen different clans. In the harsh glow, men strode about shouting orders. Horses milled and pawed the ground impatiently, while servants scurried to pass out cups of ale and hunks of dark bread.

There was a vitality to the scene that might have stirred her if she hadn't so dreaded the quest that sent them forth. Standing on tiptoe, Rowena scanned the ward and spotted a dark head that rose proudly above the others. Lion stood apart from the swirling mass, talking intently with Bryce, she saw when she finally worked her way through the crowd to them.

She plucked at Lion's sleeve, gasping when he turned on her, one hand on his sword hilt.

"Rowena! What are you doing here?"

"Hoping to persuade you from riding out on this heinous—"

He pressed two fingers across her lips. His other arm went around her waist, lifting her off her feet and hugging her close—a bit too close to be loverlike. "Shh. Are you trying to get yourself hanged?" he whispered hoarsely.

"Nay," she murmured around his fingers. "Just trying to save a lad who—"

"He'll come to no harm."

"How can you say that when this pack of—of fiends is preparing to beat the bushes till they fi—"

"You will have to trust me on this, Rowena." His mouth replaced his fingers. He tasted of strong ale and steely determination. When he raised his head, it gave her slight pleasure to see his own breathing was as ragged as hers. "You found the gifts I left on your pillow."

"Aye." Rowena shook the small pouch under his nose. "I was on my way to return them to you when I learned of this—"

"Why return them?"

"I will not be bought with a few foreign baubles."

"Nor did I seek to do that," he said gently. "I did but

think it wrong that while the other ladies here drip with
gold and gems, the fairest among them goes unadorned.''

Ohhh. Rowena weakened. How kind. How romantic. But
she could not afford to have romantic notions about the
man who had once betrayed her. She was a wise, practical
woman with a son to consider. ''I cannot accept them.''
She thrust the pouch at him.

His hand gripped hers. ''We can discuss it later...when
I return.''

Rowena's anger found a new focus. ''If you ride out with
these child hunters, I will never speak to you again.''

''Ah, you've not lost that fire.'' His free hand went to
her hair, unbound and tumbling about her shoulders. He
stroked it back from her temple, a faint smile warming his
rugged features. ''You've all the colors of autumn in the
Highlands trapped here. Aye, and your eyes are as blue as
a summer sky. But it's your braw spirit that stayed with
me all these years.''

Rowena could not breathe, could barely think when he
set himself to charm. ''You've—you've no right to say
such things to me when I'm angry with you.''

''The truth's never out of place, lass, and the facts are
often not as they seem.'' His eyes, shadowed by the brim
of his helmet, were dark and intent. Hidden meanings
swirled in them, mysterious and elusive as smoke from the
torches.

''What are you saying?'' she whispered.

''Just this.'' He drew her so close her breasts brushed
the cold metal links of his mail. ''That I need you to look
beyond the obvious. The earl rides out, and I must go,
though I'd prefer to stay and while away the day with
you.''

Rowena hesitated, her eyes searching his for answers that
seemed just beyond her reach. Behind her, men prepared
to ride out. Some were friend, others foe. With them might
ride the men who'd attacked them on the stairs last night.
Was this all some elaborate game? A mummers play? Who

were the heroes? The villains? What was the purpose of the piece? And what role did she play? "Too many questions and no answers."

"I'll answer as many as I can when I return. Till then, I'd ask you to trust me and do nothing rash."

Rowena nodded slowly, chilled as much by what he implied as by the cool morning air. "I will await your return, then, but I will not accept these jewels."

"I look forward to debating the matter with you, *madame*." He brought her hand up and kissed her knuckles, his lips lingering over each in turn. That simple touch sent shivers up her arm and down her spine. His smile widened, quick and engaging. "Go back to sleep, Rowena, and dream of me."

Did he know? He couldn't, and yet... Her face heated and she snatched her hand back, but he only laughed and shepherded her inside the castle. The entryway was deserted now, and they were alone for the moment.

"I'm leaving three men behind to watch over you. They'll be along directly after I've given them their orders. This is one matter that's not open to discussion," he added, and kissed her quickly. "Be a good lass till I come back."

He was gone before she could give him the swift kick he so richly deserved.

"Well, your lover is certainly the protective sort," drawled a chillingly familiar voice. Eneas descended from the stairwell that led to the guest chambers. His hair was clean, his face scraped free of whiskers. The mail he wore was new, and the tunic over it was black and red, the earl's colors.

"You look well and prosperous," Rowena said sharply.

Eneas shrugged, but he looked smug. "Saving His Grace's life has had unexpected benefits. A room in the castle, new armaments and horse. And a title. I am now Laird of Westray."

"You are no longer interested in Hillbrae then," Rowena said, feeling a bit giddy with relief.

"I will always have an interest in my home." He paused, eyes hard and malicious. "If only to keep it from the hands of you and that brat you are trying to pass off as my brother's."

Rowena felt the blood drain from her body, leaving her cold and frightened. "Paddy is Padruig's son."

"So you say."

"So Padruig said."

"Aye, he did, but then, Padruig would have claimed the devil's own to keep me from ruling Clan Gunn." Eneas stroked his chin thoughtfully. "I've always wondered how it happened that you bore him a bairn when so many had failed. Or was it his?"

It was her worst nightmare. "Of course Paddy is Padruig's son...and his heir."

"Much you care about the Gunns, you faithless jade. My brother is scarcely cold in his grave and you are spreading your legs for another man."

"That is not true. My betrothal to Lord Lion is—is political. He is a strong man, high in the earl's favor, and he thinks I needed a protector."

Eneas snorted. "Everyone is concerned for your safety. Finlay has sent two men to guard you."

"What do you mean?"

"I dispatched a message to Hillbrae the day we arrived, telling them what had befallen us here, including the unfortunate misunderstanding with the MacPhersons and our rescue by Lion Sutherland. A response came yesterday during the games. Finlay sent two of his men along with the messenger." Eneas's lip curled. "To protect you. He seems to think I am not providing adequate care for his little darling."

"Who did he send? Why did they not come to me last night?"

"Dunmore and Kier came. And they did ask after you, but I told them you were busy with your lover. They quit the hall to bed down with my men, I think," he said offhandedly. "They must still be sleeping off the rigors of their hurried journey here."

Rowena smiled. She could dispense with Lion's men. "I will look for them. What of Paddy? Did anyone send news of him?"

"Aye." From the pouch at his belt, Eneas took a folded scrap of parchment. "A message for you from Father Cerdic."

Rowena clasped the paper to her heart. She'd savor it later, away from Eneas's prying eyes. "Now you stand so high in the earl's favor, will you ask him about the swearing ceremony?"

"Nay. His Grace is a busy man, with no time for such things. And too, I am in no hurry to leave Blantyre. The earl is an important man. I can go far at his side."

"I wish you well of each other," Rowena said. "When he returns from his "hunt," I will ask that the earl confirm me as Paddy's guardian, then I'll go back to Hillbrae and leave you to feather this new nest of yours." She moved past him.

Eneas caught her arm, his grip bruising. "You will do nothing of the sort, you bitch. The earl wants troops, and I mean to offer him as many Gunns as can be mustered."

"I'll not stand by and see any of the Gunns slaughtered in such an unholy cause." Rowena tried to slip free.

His hand tightened. "You will do as I say." His lips drew back in a mocking smile. "Remember your precious lad, left behind at Hillbrae?"

"Paddy? What have you done to him?"

"Nothing…yet. But accidents do happen, especially to active, curious lads."

"Finlay and Father Cerdic—"

"Cannot be everywhere. Do you understand?"

Numb, Rowena nodded.

"Good." He released her arm, smiling as she rubbed at the abused flesh. "I must join the earl in hunting for the assassin. Who knows, I may bring the little bastard to ground and earn myself even greater glory."

The precious note from Father Cerdic clutched tightly in her fist, Rowena made her way to the chapel to pray that young Colin might elude capture. She believed Lion would help Colin if he could. But if he was caught aiding the accused assassin...

Concern for Lion made a mockery of the hatred she thought she bore him. Rowena spent an hour in the chapel on her knees, praying for the safety of her friends and for the strength to resist what she should not want—Lion.

Cleansed, she took a moment to read the brief message from Father Cerdic assuring her Paddy was well, attending to his lessons, and that he sent his love. She was just rising to leave, when Sim rushed in.

"Oh, my lady. I've had them searching everywhere for you. I thought that whoever had tried to harm you last night—"

"I am fine and sorry to have worried you."

"Good. There are two other men looking for you as well. Kier and Dunmore Gunn of Hillbrae."

"We'd best find them and tell them I am all right." She smiled as she led the way from the chapel. "Now that I have my own men, you can return to your normal duties." Odd how such a little thing as having men of her own, men whom she could trust, made her feel stronger, less vulnerable.

"Oh, Lion said I should still stick close to you."

"You mean he knew they were here?"

Sim blinked. "Well, he sent Red Will to the Gunn camp this morn...just to look them over, mind."

"To see if any appeared to have fallen down stairs?"

"Exactly, my lady. Clem Gunn told him two more clansmen had ridden in late yesterday afternoon, sent to serve you."

Yet Lion had failed to tell her she had guards of her own at Blantyre. Annoying man. She tossed the sack of jewels from hand to hand. Lovely as they were, the ornaments were a symbol of Lion's high-handedness. "I think the time has come to show him he cannot bend me to his will."

"What do you mean to do?"

Give back his gift. But if she handed it to him, he would only refuse. If she put the pouch in his room, he'd sneak into hers again—a nasty habit of which she had to break him. "Somehow I must make him see what it feels like to be forced into a corner," she murmured. She must be clever. Very clever, for he was too canny by half. But she was no dullard, as he would soon discover. What a challenge.

Rowena grinned, feeling more alive than she had in years. It would be sweet indeed to make Lion Sutherland back off and eat his condescending... She paused, inspiration dawning. "Of course, the very thing."

"What?" Sim hurried after her. "My lady, where are you going? What are you planning to do?"

"You'll see...and so will he."

It was nearly dark and beginning to rain by the time the earl's party clattered back over the wooden drawbridge—a thoroughly miserable end to a fruitless search.

Lion could not have been happier, though he took pains to mask his joy behind a face as weary and somber as those around him. Alexander, obsessed with finding Colin, had pushed his band relentlessly, ranging farther and traveling faster than Lion had expected. But they'd found no sign of Colin Ross, or of the band of Sutherlands hiding in the hills, thanks be to God.

"Curse the luck," Alexander growled as he dismounted before the keep and flung the reins at a stable hand.

Eneas Gunn vaulted from his mount and attached himself to the earl's side—a position he'd striven to keep all day. It had been somewhat amusing to watch Eneas, the newcomer, vie with Georas MacPherson for Alexander's favor.

Lion supposed it was too much to hope that the two would kill each other off.

"If you like, I can get fresh mounts and set out again." Eneas said, eager as a fawning cur.

Alexander snorted and stomped up the steps. "Waste of time. This bloody rain'll have washed out any tracks."

"He must have had help," Georas said, hurrying after the earl. "Mayhap the villagers saw something. I could go down, seize a few and force them to talk."

"Nay. I doubt they know anything. Besides, I've a better notion." Alexander disappeared into the castle.

"Damn, what's he about now?" Bryce whispered.

"Nothing good, that's sure. See the men are settled, and find Heckie for me," Lion murmured. "I may need to send him out to learn where our sheep have gotten to. Meanwhile, I will find out what diabolical plan Alexander has hatched."

Lion found the earl standing before the fire in the great hall, dripping water into the rushes as he downed a cup of ale. He looked as disagreeable and surly as a wet bear. "I'll tell you what we'll do when I'm good and ready," he snapped at Eneas.

The new laird looked stricken. "I thought I might help—"

"My men and I are at your disposal, day or night," Georas said swiftly. "Only tell me what you'd have done and I—"

"I've not got all the details worked out, and I'm not likely to with the two of you jabbering like a pair of women." The earl caught sight of Lion. "Ah, just the man I need." Thrusting his empty cup into Eneas's hand, he crossed the hall and threw a wet, beefy arm around Lion's shoulders. "Come to my chamber whilst I disarm. I've need of your sharp mind."

Lion caught the furious glances Eneas and Georas sent his way as the earl led him away. The two were cowards and bullies, but they'd bear watching.

When Lion and Alexander reached Blantyre's huge master chamber, Lady Glenda was waiting for them.

"Oh, my lord, you are soaked clear to the skin!" Rushing forward, she began plucking at the earl's wet tunic. "Mairi, Jean," she called to her women. "Fetch the earl's bedrobe and some towels. See the water is hot and—"

He brushed her hands away. "Leave us."

"B-but…" Hurt filled her eyes. "I've water heating in the kitchens for your bath and—"

"I've been drenched in water half the day. I need no bath. Just dry clothes. But I'll see to myself. It sets my teeth on edge to have a pack of silly women fluttering about when I've important matters to think on."

"Wh-who will remove your armor? Who will—"

"Lion will assist me," the earl snapped. "I'd speak privately with him anyway. Get out, the lot of you!"

The servants fled without a backward glance. Lady Glenda lingered, her pain at Alexander's rejection pitiful to witness.

"We've had a long ride in foul weather and are much in need of dry clothes and a hot meal," Lion said gently, as though that excused Alexander's rudeness.

Lady Glenda smiled faintly. "Of course. I—I will go down and make certain all is prepared. Doubtless Lady Rowena will be looking for you, too, Lord Lion. I'd best tell her you are detained here with my lord."

The image of Rowena waiting to greet him with a warm smile and, mayhap, a hot bath was enticing indeed. And about as likely as sheep laying eggs. Still he smiled and thanked Lady Glenda.

"Women," Alexander growled as the door closed behind her. "They've their uses, but most of the time they're a damned nuisance. Now then, see if you can get me out of this."

Though the role of lackey suited him not, Lion expertly pried Alexander out of his mail and the thick, padded gambeson worn beneath. As the earl snatched up a towel and began to dry his large, hairy body, Lion noticed the chain around his neck and the key suspended from it.

The key to the strongbox.

How to get it? Lion mused as he went to pour them each a cup of ale from the pitcher on the table. "You had something to ask me?" he inquired casually.

"Aye." Alexander tossed the wet towels in a heap on the floor and pulled on a long shirt of saffron wool. "We had no luck catching Colin and whoever freed him...." His fist clenched so tight his knuckles turned white. "Damn, when I think of those cheeky bastards, sneaking in here and taking him away in broad daylight. If word of it gets out, my enemies will flock here like flies to honey, thinking to murder me in my bed." His scowl darkened. "I've a mind to kill them all."

"Who?" Damn, had his Sutherlands been found out?

"The Shaws, whose duty it was to patrol the back walls. That must be how they got in, for it wasn't through the front gates past my Stewarts."

You cannot. But Lion knew better than to throw down such a challenge. "You'd kill the Shaws without proof?"

"Lady Glenda will likely weep and wail over their deaths, but I cannot let such laxness go unpunished."

Lion was appalled to have put more men at risk. Damn, would this vicious cycle never be done? "It may be he got out unaided. He could have hit Umfried over the head, hidden in the castle and made good his escape during the confusion while we searched the grounds. One small lad is easy to overlook," he added, lest he doom the other guards.

"I suppose," Alexander said gruffly.

"Why punish the Shaws and deprive yourself of good fighting men when it may be that Colin is already dead?"

Alexander brightened. "You think so?"

"These hills hold many dangers, especially for a lad alone, on foot and unarmed. Boar, wolves, steep ravines..."

"Ah, that is possible," the earl said thoughtfully.

"I do not think the Rosses will cause you more trouble."

Alexander's expression grew cagey. "I will make certain they do not."

"What will you do?" Lion asked, his gut tightening.

"I have not yet decided."

"Is there something I can help you with?"

"Nay. Not yet." The earl's eyes darted about. "And I do sometimes think the walls here have ears."

"Aye, a man cannot be too careful." Damn, he had to know what Alexander was planning so he could prevent it. "Well, if you've no further need of me, my lord, I will get out of these stinking clothes."

Alexander inclined his head in regal permission. "If the weather clears on the morrow, we will resume the games. I would show Robbie MacNab what sort of men have already joined me."

Lion nodded. The games would be part prideful exhibit, part threat. *Join me or face these men on the battlefield.* He'd better warn Robbie to look suitably impressed. As Lion walked to the door, he spotted the strongbox in the shadowy corner.

Were they in there, the papers proving Alexander plotted to usurp his brother's throne? Recalling his earlier conversation with Bryce, Lion turned back to the earl.

"If you can spare me for a few hours tomorrow, I'd go into the village and see if there's a goldsmith of any talent."

"Whatever for?"

"I need a betrothal gift for Lady Rowena. The only things I have at hand are a few baubles I picked up in Italy. She did not care for such foreign-made pieces."

"That's women for you...fickle and ungrateful."

"A knight owes his lady the honor of a gift."

"Particularly when he has not yet caught the lady, eh? Glenda tells me that you two keep separate rooms."

Lion gave the earl a long-suffering, man-to-man grimace. "What can I say? She would wait till we are wed."

"Why give her a choice?"

"It seemed the chivalrous thing to do," Lion said through clenched teeth.

"I suppose." Alexander frowned. "I suppose she is not to blame if her first husband did anger me. Eneas is more reasonable. Gladly will he call up the Gunns to join my army."

Did Rowena know this? Lion wondered. She'd not be pleased. "Well, at any rate, I will visit the village in the morn."

"'Tis a poor place. You are unlikely to find a bauble there that will please her." The earl looked toward the strongbox. "I have a few things I have picked up that I might be willing to sell you."

Stolen from the clans the earl had thus far subdued, Lion thought, sighing inwardly. He inclined his head again. "I am honored you would offer." He only hoped Rowena wouldn't spit upon the stolen jewelry, or him, for suggesting such a thing.

Chapter Nine

Rowena sat at the head table, trying her best not to fidget as she waited for Lion to arrive. Many of the nobles had already entered and taken their seats. What was keeping him? She'd planned for this half the day. Now that the moment was nearly at hand, excitement warred with nervousness.

What would he do when she bested him…and before all these people? Drat, she should have heeded her conscience and waited till she was alone with Lion to have her revenge. She glanced at the cake sitting on a silver plate beside the cup she and Lion would share, along with a trencher of food. She'd made a point of instructing the maids to set it there.

A stir at the doorway heralded Lion's arrival. He'd washed and changed into fresh clothes, his black hair shining wetly in the torchlight as he moved into the hall. She watched as he was detained by first one man, then another. He stopped to speak with each in turn, his expression thoughtful as he listened to their words and spoke in response. Whatever he said eased the frowns and left smiles in their place.

It struck her that Lion had changed from the impatient, carefree youth she'd fallen in love with years ago, into a wise and deliberate man. It was clear that many here respected his opinions, and his own men worshipped him with a fervor few lords could command. Last night, she'd asked him if his time abroad had been well spent. Now she had no doubt it had been. Much as she might hate the fact, his father had been right to send Lion away to be groomed and pruned by others.

"Did you miss me, sweet?" Lion asked as he slid onto the bench beside her.

Rowena glanced up and realized that, too, was a mistake. He sat so close she could feel the heat that radiated from his body into hers, see the flecks of green in his golden eyes. They were focused on her with mesmerizing intensity. Every nerve in her body jangled with awareness. Yet she could not give in to the pull he exerted on her. "I did not," she managed to say.

He grinned and kissed her lightly. "Liar," he whispered. "You've waited for this moment as ardently as I have."

A giggle burst from Rowena. How true. How ironically true. She chuckled again, delighting in the quizzical look he gave her. "You, sir, are far too arrogant for your own good."

"A faint heart never won a fair lassie...especially not one as stubborn as you." He picked up her hand and toyed with her fingers.

That simple touch sent a shivery wave up her arm. "Must you paw me?" She snatched her fingers free.

"Surely a man is allowed to hold his betrothed's hand."

A not so subtle reminder of their loathsome arrangement. "I hear the hunting was unsuccessful."

"It depends on your perspective." His gaze held hers, swirling again with hidden meanings.

"Oh, Lion, do you know where Colin is? Is he safe?"

"Shh. Not here."

Alexander stomped up to the dais and threw himself into the high-backed chair beside Lady Glenda's smaller one. "Where is the food?" he growled. "Do you try to starve me?"

Lady Glenda leaped up, white faced, and clapped her hands. Immediately the door to the kitchens opened and a stream of servants scurried in bearing steaming trays.

Rowena glared at the earl. "Oh, I hate the way—"

"Easy, lass," Lion urged, his hand on her arm.

She sighed, fuming inside. But he was right. Eneas and Georas both had seats at the head table, and the noise in the hall had a way of ebbing at odd moments. "Men can be such pigs."

"I would agree with you, did I not think you meant to include me in that statement."

"Most definitely," she said with a toss of her head.

"Pity. I'd always fancied myself as an eagle, soaring above the common man."

"Arrogance."

"Self-confidence," he countered. "And you...? Ah, you are a fox, I think. A golden vixen with soft fur and—"

"Sharp teeth. Take care, eagle, that you do not stray too close and have your feathers nipped."

"Have no fear," Lion said as he filled their trencher with choice bits of roasted lamb and fresh salmon. "The eagle is far too canny to be caught by a fox."

"Is he now?" Rowena eyed the cake resting on the plate in solitary splendor.

"Wine?" He held the cup for her, his eyes full on hers while she sipped. They kindled with a warm light as he turned the cup and drank from the same spot.

Oh, he was good at this, she mused, her gaze still trapped by his. That much had not changed. Images from this morn's dream flitted through her mind, taunting her with golden memories.

"Aye, Rowena," he whispered. His hand brushed her cheek, slid down her neck to her nape and gently drew her closer. "It can be that way again."

Longing pierced her, sharp as a honeyed blade. But it cut two ways, part pleasure, part pain. She concentrated on the pain. Sweet as their loving had been, nothing could make up for the anguish that had followed his desertion. "There is no going back," she said, wishing her voice was stronger, less wistful.

"Nay." Something in his eyes changed, as though he, too, focused on some distant hurt. "But we can begin again."

Rowena shook her head. "Even if I wished to, which I do not, my duties are to my son and Clan Gunn."

"We could work something out, Rowena. I want you in my life again. I need—"

"You need. Always it is you. That much has not changed. You are still spoiled and self-serving. It happens that my life lies elsewhere, my lord," she said icily. "Circumstances have forced me to endure your company, but I will not be coerced by your soft words or bought with your foreign baubles." She plopped the cake into his outstretched palm. "Here."

Lion frowned down at the offering. "Wroth as you seem to be with me, I wonder…is it poisoned?"

"I'd not be so obvious." Damn, she'd lost her temper and likely the chance to teach him a lesson. "I made it earlier today, to repay you for the jewels you are so determined to foist on me. But if you do not want it…"

"I did not say that." He peered at the cake, sniffed it, then took a wary bite. "Almond," he said, smiling.

"Your favorite, if I recall."

"You remembered."

"I've forgotten nothing." She sat back and watched him as a cat might a mouse.

"It's very good." He held it out. "Would you like some?"

"Nay. When you accepted my gift, you agreed to take all of it." She tried to keep her smile from becoming smug.

He took another bite. Something crunched. "What the hell?" he muttered, spewing crumbs. He spat into his hand, then gingerly poked at his teeth with his tongue.

"Is aught wrong?" Lady Glenda asked anxiously, peering around Rowena to stare at Lion. Nor was she the only one, for suddenly everyone seemed to be looking at him.

Rowena couldn't have been more pleased. Let them all watch and learn that she, at least, could not be bought.

"Shells in the cake, I guess." Lion opened his hand to inspect the discarded bite. He brushed cake crumbs from the foreign lump and held it up. "Why—why it's the ring I gave you."

"I am returning it," Rowena said.

"You do not like it?"

"I do not want it, and so I told you. You refused to heed me, so…" She shrugged. "I chose this way of giving it back."

"She always was addled," Eneas sneered.

"Ingrate," Lady Selena muttered.

Alexander scowled. "That's what comes of coddling women."

Rowena ignored them, her attention focused on Lion, fingers knotted in her lap as she waited for his reaction.

Lion looked from her to the ring and back again. His shoulders began to shake. A chuckle escaped, then another and another till his laughter filled the awkward silence. "I told you she did not like the ring, Alexander," he gasped between spurts of laughter.

Alexander snorted, but his scowl eased. "Well, my offer of a replacement still holds."

"I guess I had best accept." Lion set the ring on the table and brushed off his hands. "Or I'll likely find the broach in my porridge come morn."

Everyone laughed at that.

"I do not want another ring," Rowena said beneath the din.

Lion's smile did not falter, but his gaze sharpened even as his own voice dropped to a whisper. "'Tis vitally important you accept Alexander's offer to choose another piece of jewelry."

"To you, mayhap, but I do not care one wit for a—"

"This is no whim. Lives are at stake."

His anxiety pierced her anger. "What is going on?"

"I cannot tell you."

"Then I will not help. I'm done with secrets and—"

"I must see inside Alexander's strongbox. The ruse of having you select a piece of jewelry was all I could think of."

Rowena frowned, trying to see past his shuttered eyes. "I hate this. You've done nothing but force me into corner after corner from the moment I arrived."

"I am sorry you see it so, lass. What I've done, I've done for your own good," he insisted.

"And for yours."

He smiled and shrugged, looking not the least repentant. "Our needs run in the same track."

"Why must you be so thick skulled?"

"Because I am right."

Alexander stood and stretched. "Lion, come along now if you would get your lady a new bauble. I must be up early and would seek my bed."

"Please, Rowena," Lion whispered. "This is your chance to save hundreds of men, women and bairns."

"How?"

"I will tell you later." Lion rose and extended his hand. "Come along, my sweet. Think of the children," he murmured.

Rowena bared her teeth. "You do not play fair."

"I play to win. Always remember that."

Ignoring his outstretched hand, Rowena stood and stepped down from the dais. "I will do this, but you had better tell me what is going on, else the next cake *will* be poisoned."

He only chuckled and shook his head. "Ah, sweetheart, I've missed you in more ways than I can count."

The papers were there.

Lion glimpsed a roll of parchment sealed with the Campbell crest on top of the pile in the strongbox.

"Ah, here we are." Alexander lifted out a small chest and handed it to Lion.

Lion took a last, quick glance at the sheaf of papers, then turned to where Rowena sat with Lady Glenda. He set the chest on the small table between their two chairs and opened it. "Pick anything…anything at all that strikes your fancy," he said.

Her sharp look said she'd probably like to strike his head. As she bent to examine the jumble of rings, broaches and gold chains, Lion surreptitiously eyed the key Alexander had taken from around his neck. Did he remove the chain when he slept? If only Glenda were not so enamored of Alexander, she might have been persuaded to steal the key so Lion could have a duplicate made. That left picking the lock. Heckie had the best touch for it, but how to get him into Alexander's room?

"This one," Rowena said firmly.

Lion looked at the broach she held, blinked and looked again. It was undoubtedly the largest, ugliest thing he'd ever seen—a huge blob of solid silver shaped like a grotesque bird. "Is it an eagle?" he asked doubtfully.

"I thought it looked a bit like you, my lord." Her smile was sly, appropriate to a crafty vixen bent on revenge.

"A direct hit, my sweet," Lion said. Leaning down to pin it to her bodice, he added, "It's likely the most costly piece."

"It seemed a fair price for you to pay."

He straightened, still grinning. "I can see that you also play to win, my lady."

"I am not your lady," she whispered back.

Not yet, Lion thought, but he was determined she would be. It was not a matter of pride or willfullness. She needed him, whether she would admit it or not.

The fragile peace between them held while he learned how much this ploy was going to cost him. After bidding good-night to Alexander and Lady Glenda, they stepped out into the corridor. Two sets of guards, a pair each of Sutherlands and Gunns, came away from their posts at opposite sides of the door.

"All has been quiet, my lord," Naill Sutherland said.

"Doubtless because we were here," said Kier Gunn, glaring equally at Naill and at Lion.

"Thank you, lads, I'm sure the sight of four of you lurking in this dreary hallway would make anyone think twice about lingering. Come, my lady, I'll see you to your room."

"We can do that, my lord," Kier grumbled. He was a large man, younger and more vocal than his brother, Dunmore. Both had the red-brown hair of the Gunns and fierce expressions. They had made it clear they did not trust him within an arm's length of their lady. Their protectiveness was amusing and reassuring, but they needed to understand that he was not going away.

"I am counting on you to safeguard the lady when I cannot be about," Lion said evenly. "But I'm here now, and I'd not rest easy did I not see her to her door."

Rowena touched his arm. "Really, it is not necessary."

"To me, it is." Lion took her arm and led the way down the gloomy corridor. The crunch of four pairs of booted feet echoed after them. "If we're going to travel about in a pack like this, I'd best engage a piper and a minstrel," Lion murmured.

Rowena chuckled. "It is a bit much, but Finlay meant well and I—I like having them here."

"So you need not rely on my men?"

"It is nothing against them. I like Sim especially, but..."

"I understand." Lion gently squeezed her elbow. "We are much alike in this. Neither of us wants to be controlled by another, no matter how well meaning."

"If you understand that, then why have you forced me into this mock betrothal?" she grumbled.

"You know why, and it does not have to be a sham."

"Aye, it does." She stared straight ahead for several

paces, her expression stark. What inner demons did she wrestle with? he wondered. "Did you find what you needed in the strongbox?"

"Shh. Sounds echo in these hallways, and you cannot tell who is listening at the doors you pass by."

"What a terrible place. What an awful way to live." Rowena shivered, and he instinctively held her closer.

"I will not mind leaving here at all," he confessed.

"When will you go?"

"When my work is done, my ends accomplished."

"What work? What are you trying to do?"

Lion shook his head in silent warning just as they reached her chamber. "Ah, here we are." He opened the door and whisked her inside before she could say a word. As he closed the portal, he cut off Dunmore Gunn's protest.

"What—?" Rowena exclaimed.

Lion pulled her into his arms and covered her mouth with his. She stiffened, then went pliant, her hands sliding around his neck to tangle in his hair. Her lips parted with a sigh that sent his pulse rattling like a minstrel's drum. Groaning, he accepted her invitation to deepen the kiss. Her tongue was as shy as it had been years ago, the first time he'd showed her how far a kiss could take them. That small sign of maidenly resolve tempered his hunger as nothing else could.

Instantly, Lion reined in the greed that surged though him. This was Rowena, his precious one, more fragile than even she realized. He gentled his kisses, coaxing and soothing. He liked the skittishness, the telling mix of eagerness and hesitancy. For whatever reason, she'd not found fulfillment in Padruig Gunn's bed.

But she would in his.

This he vowed as he ran his hands down her back, delighted by her tiny shivers as she pressed herself against him. She felt so good, her shape familiar yet different, the coltish angles of girlhood ripened into womanhood. Beyond the physical, there were other changes, too. She was stronger, wiser, more serious. And even more stubborn. Winning her would not be easy, but it would be worthwhile, he thought as he wooed her with a tenderness he'd not felt in years.

I should be fighting him, Rowena thought dimly as his hands and mouth worked their old magic on her senses. If she resisted, she knew he'd release her. She should kick and scream and bite to keep him at bay, but she couldn't. Even as her defenses crumbled, part of her reveled in the sensations his kisses evoked in her.

It had been like this from the first. He alone roused in her an overwhelming hunger that could be eased only by his touch. When he'd left, she'd rooted out that desire and killed it. Or so she'd thought. But as his kisses turned achingly tender, old needs fought their way past the carefully erected barricades of hatred and mistrust. She wanted him. Oh, how she wanted him. She closed her mind to past deeds and future fears and simply lived in the present. Lived for this moment.

She could feel passion build, her breasts swelling against the hard wall of his chest, her bones melting as the heat swept through her. The exquisite throbbing built in the secret core of her. She shifted, seeking to ease the ache. His hand slid down her spine, lifting her so they fit together. Hard to soft.

Groaning, he lifted his mouth from hers and buried it in the sensitive curve of her neck. "Rowena. Ah, Ro, it is the same. The same as it always was."

She shivered and leaned into him, struggling for breath, for sanity. It was the same...but it wasn't. It could never be. They could never be. "Please go," she whispered. *Go before I give in and am forever damned.*

"Ro?" He lifted her chin and stared down at her, his expression anguished in the faint light from the fire in the hearth. "What is it? Why do you shut me out when I know damned well—"

"You know why. My obligation, my life is with Paddy."

The light faded from his eyes. He dropped his arms and walked toward the hearth, shoulders bowed. Never had she seen him look so dispirited. "We could work this out if you would—"

"Nay. I gave my word to raise Paddy among the Gunns, and that is what I must do."

He braced his hands on the mantel, body trembling as he came to grips with her statement, then he turned. His eyes were narrowed, his jaw square. "I am not giving up."

"You must."

"I lost you once. I'm not doing it again. We will find a way to be together." He knelt and scooped up a basket from beside the hearth. It was small, covered by a gray cloth. "I'd nearly forgotten," he said, smiling in one of those quicksilver mood shifts of his. "I've another gift for you."

"I do not want any more jewels or clothes or—"

He thrust the basket into her hands. "It is none of those things." As he eased off the cover, a small head poked out, ruffled orange fur framing large yellow eyes.

"It's—it's a kitten."

"Aye." He stroked the downy head with one large forefinger. "Four weeks old, Heckie reckons. Way too young to be orphaned."

"Orphaned," Rowena echoed. She lifted the kitten out. Instead of settling in her hand, it clawed at her palm and sank its teeth into her thumb. "Ouch!"

Chuckling, Lion gently pried the teeth from her flesh. "Look here, imp, this is your mama now, and she'll be unlikely to keep you in warm milk if you behave so ungratefully."

The kitten stared at him owlishly.

"She's had a rough life, you see," Lion said. He took the cloth from the basket, draped it over Rowena's hands, then resettled the kitten in the makeshift nest.

"Where did you find her?"

"In the stables, just before dinner. When we rode in from

the search, a MacPherson's horse struck down her mama and her brother. The mother cat was moving her litter, I think. Anyway, I went looking and found this one in a back stall. She's old enough to drink milk from a bowl, but not to fend for herself, especially in such a place as this.''

''Poor thing.'' The kitten had curled up in her palm, and Rowena gently stroked its back.

''There's milk in a pitcher on the windowsill.''

Rowena nodded. Paddy would love the kitten—the only gift he'd ever have from his father. Tears burned the back of her eyes. It wasn't fair. Not fair at all. Lion would have made a wonderful father. If only—

''You aren't thinking of baking her into a cake, are you?''

Rowena chuckled. ''Nay.'' Blinking away her tears, she looked up at Lion. He stood close, too close. Despite the distraction of the kitten, the room still sizzled with tension.

She couldn't give in to it. She couldn't.

Long after the castle had finally quieted for the night, Lion lay awake in bed, thinking of Rowena. And her son.

Padruig Gunn's son.

Though it was surely a sin for which he'd burn in hell, he disliked the lad, sight unseen.

It was not only a sin, it was…dishonorable.

Lion gritted his teeth and stared up at the bed hangings stitched with the proud arms of the Shaws. The crest, and likely these drapes themselves, had been handed down from one generation to another. The Sutherlands, too, had their traditions, their family heirlooms. His father's sword, for instance.

It would come to him one day. And he'd pass it along to his son. Therein lay the crux of the problem. He was jealous, pure and not so simple. Jealous of Padruig's son. The lad should have been his—his and Rowena's.

If, somehow, he managed to win her over and they had

a son, a lad to inherit the Sutherland estates, would he still resent her firstborn?

Lion wanted to believe he was a better man than that. He thought of his parents and the tangled skein of their lives.

Before wedding Lucais Sutherland, Lion's mother, Elspeth, had been wed to Raebert Munro, an abusive brute who had died in a fire. Raebert had sired a bastard child on Lucais's mistress. To save the babe from being ostracized, Lucais had claimed wee Gillie as his own. To this day, few knew that she was not a Sutherland, but the daughter of a man both Elspeth and Lucais had hated. Yet they'd raised the lass with love and devotion.

He could do that, Lion thought. If Rowena would give him a chance to meet the lad and get to know him, he'd get over this ridiculous, unknightly dislike of the boy. Wouldn't he?

Was that why Rowena refused to think they might work this out? Did she sense he was jealous of her son?

Of course she did. Did he not freeze up and change the subject every time the lad's name was mentioned?

Lion clenched his jaw. He would master these stupid, unreasoning feelings. He loved Rowena. He would love her son. Together, they would make a family, a life.

A grating noise dragged him to instant wakefulness.

Was it Bryce coming to bed?

Nay, the sound came from the window—a subtle whisper of rope on rock. Someone was climbing about outside his room.

Lion grabbed the knife from under his pillow and stole out of bed just as a set of grubby hands clasped the windowsill. A dark head slowly rose into view. The eyes were white slits; a sliver of silver shimmered where the mouth should have been. It took Lion a moment to realize the man was masked and carrying a knife between his teeth.

Not a social visit, then.

Lion measured the distance to the sword lying on the

floor beside the bed. Too far. He'd never reach it before the man vaulted over the sill and attacked. Lion wanted to wait till the man had climbed within, then take him prisoner and learn who'd sent him. But if he had not come alone, the accomplice might well enter and overpower Lion.

It took only seconds for these thoughts to crystallize into action. Leaping from the shadows, Lion took a swipe at the hands of the man just as he swung his leg over the sill.

"Bloody hell!" the man exclaimed, the knife clattering to the floor. He leaned back to avoid Lion's stroke, lost his balance and fell. His hoarse scream was cut off by a thud.

When Lion looked out and down, he saw a second man jump down from the rope, grab his fallen companion under the arms and begin to drag him away.

Lion sprinted for the door, snatching up his tunic as he went. As he rushed into the hall, he tripped over Red Will, who slept across the threshold.

"Where are you going?" Will cried, drawing his dirk.

"Outside. Two men tried to climb in the window," Lion said over his shoulder as he hurried to the stairs.

By the time they reached the courtyard, the men were gone. The only clues to their identity was a scrap of Gunn plaid caught on the sill, and the dirk.

At least he now knew who was after him, Lion thought as he retraced his steps to his room.

They were likely the same thugs who attacked him and Rowena on the stairs. His men had wandered through the castle and the makeshift camp in the lower bailey, looking for anyone who bore bruises or walked with a limp. Unfortunately, thanks to the football game and the rigors of training, there were many soldiers in that condition, including some of his Sutherlands. But Lion knew he had wounded this evening's visitor. A fresh cut on the arm should be easier to spot.

Chapter Ten

I must be insane, Rowena thought.

After lying awake half the night telling herself she had to avoid Lion, here she was riding across the drawbridge side by side with him in the soft morning light.

She'd been furious with him when he'd shaken her awake an hour ago.

"I've told you not to creep into my room," she'd snapped, pushing tangled hair from her face with one hand and tugging the blanket up to her chin with the other.

He'd grinned, plopped down on the edge of her bed, casual as you please, and toyed with a lock of her hair. "I had no choice. There's bound to be Gunns guarding your door, and as they do not seem to like me very well, I did not think they'd let me in."

"They have orders to keep you out. You've no right to sneak in here while I'm asleep."

"I had to. It's a grand day, and the lads and I are riding into the hills to get in a wee bit of practice with the spears before tomorrow's games. I said to myself, 'my lady would rather gallop over the heath with the wind in her hair and the sun on her face than stay here cooped up with these harpies.'"

Damn him. Damn him for knowing her so well. "I am not your lady," Rowena grumbled.

"Aye, you are that, lass. You've yet to admit it to yourself, that's all. Now come, you wouldn't want your stubbornness to cheat you of the chance for a lovely ride."

Hateful man. "I'll go, but only for the change of scene and a bit of fresh air, mind."

"Of course," he'd said gravely, but his eyes twinkled.

They were twinkling still, Rowena saw as she glanced at Lion, riding so straight and tall beside her.

He moved his stallion closer. "What say we ride on ahead and leave this pack behind?" His smile was warmer even than the steadily rising sun. Dangerously intimate.

Her insides melted like butter. "My men would not like that," Rowena said, bolstered because Kier and Harry rode with the Sutherlands. Though she'd tried to make Harry stay abed, he'd insisted the wound was healing and he needed exercise. Another stubborn man.

"Ah, you make it deucedly difficult for a man, lass."

"I intend to make it impossible."

"Do you now?" He cocked his head, the warmth spreading to his eyes, igniting a fire that made her own blood heat. "I never saw a lass so set on denying her own true feelings."

"That shows how little you know me." Rowena wrenched her gaze back to the road, but her heart was unsteady. She was tired, that's all. She had slept little the night before, brief snatches of restless slumber punctuated by dreams that had left her sweaty and longing for what she could not have. Lion.

"Have you named the kitten?" Lion asked after a moment.

"Nay. I'm just calling her Cat till I can get home and let Paddy have the fun of naming her."

The hurt that clouded his expression sent a surprising shaft of pain through her chest, making it hard to breathe. By unspoken agreement, they seldom mentioned Paddy. For which she was pitifully grateful. It made the guilt of keeping the truth from Lion easier to bear. *I'm sorry.* But

regret did not change the fact that she and Paddy were tied
to the Gunns.

"How old is he?" Lion asked, the sadness gone.

Rowena started, and her horse shied. Controlling her
mount gave her a moment to gather her thoughts. "Not yet
five," she said, shaving almost a year off his age.

"My parents gave me a dog when I was five," Lion said.
His face was in profile to her, as stark as the mountains
that rimmed the valley. "Rowena, I am sorry that I had to
lea—"

"He'll like the cat," she said quickly, her heart already
breaking. She couldn't listen to him apologize for leaving,
not with her secrets tearing at her.

Fortunately, the trail grew narrower, and they were
forced to ride single file, Lion in the lead. Giant black boulders abutted the path, seeming to hold back the verdant
forest beyond. Birds called out as they flitted from towering
oak to lacy-fringed pine. Somewhere in the brush, small
animals scurried away from the intruders.

Rowena lifted her face to the gentle breeze, smiling as
she inhaled the scents of warm earth and fragrant woods.
As a child, she'd often roamed the countryside near her
home, content to spend hours watching a wren build its
nest or a spider spin its web. Not appropriate pastimes for
a lass who should have been learning to cook and sew, but
the ones she'd preferred.

Lion, too, had shared her love of such things during their
long-ago summer. After their passion had been sated, however temporarily, they would frolic in their glen like bairns.
They'd waded in the burn, spied on a doe and her fawn
and hiked the many animal trails. He'd taught her to fish;
she'd woven garlands of flowers for their hair. While he
climbed trees to pick wild apples, she'd stayed safely on
the ground and collected them.

In all her years at Hillbrae, she'd not once explored the
wild lands thereabouts. Too dangerous for her to go alone,
Padruig had said, and he'd never had time to spend with

her. She had eventually given up asking him for anything for herself. Paddy was another matter. She'd railed at Padruig for ignoring the lad most of the time and growling at him when he did speak to him. "Paddy thinks you do not like him," she'd said.

"I like him well enough. He's canny and braw, or would be if you'd stop coddling him," Padruig had snapped. "He needs to grow up tough and hard if he's to rule the Gunns after me."

The plain truth of the matter was Padruig had not been a loving person, but with him gone she intended to see her son learned tenderness and compassion in addition to swordsmanship. She'd see he grew up to be like his father. If only Lion could—

Do not even think it. Inside her, something cracked, like the shattering of fragile glass. It was an old, familiar pain, this wanting what she could not have, but sharper somehow.

Rowena shook it off. Looking around her again, she tried to find pleasure in what she did have. Oh, but she had missed this. She tipped her head back, letting the sun burn into her cheeks. The day seemed to wrap itself around her, the peace and calm temporarily filling the emptiness that was with her always.

All too soon they reached the crest of the hill and halted on an open plateau bounded on all sides by jagged rocks.

"This will do," Lion called. He swung down from the saddle and walked toward her as the others dismounted.

Rowena tensed when Lion reached for her, but his touch was light and impersonal as he lifted her to the ground. Barely was she settled before he strode off, issuing orders that sent men scrambling to unload the gear they'd brought with them. With little wasted time or motion, they had targets set up at the far end of the open area. Six-foot-long spears were piled at the other end, and the men began choosing sides.

There was nothing quiet or orderly about this process.

The men, some of them with gray in their beards, boasted and taunted each other like a pack of young lads. Wagers and jests flew thick and fast.

"You'll have to excuse the lads," Lion said amiably as he spread a blanket on a flat rock and gestured for her to sit. "They've had a devilish time controlling their tempers while we've been at Blantyre, and I fear their spirits are high."

"Aye, but you can tell it's all done in good fun." Rowena sat and drew her legs up, arms wrapped around them, chin resting on her knees as she watched his Sutherlands.

Like most Highlanders, they wore woolen tunics, with their bright plaids kilted round their waists, the end flung over one shoulder. Yet they looked more civilized than the clansmen left behind at Blantyre, and their speech was more polished. She even caught a few phrases in some foreign tongue.

"Is that French they're speaking?"

"Aye, they picked up a bit of the language while we were away. And a good thing it is you do not understand them, for their words are too rough for delicate ears."

"I'd like to learn. Do you know any decent words?"

"A few," he said absently. Lion stood above her, his hands on his hips, his gaze narrow as he looked beyond his men to the distant peaks.

"What is it? Is something wrong?"

He looked down at her, the sun behind him, hiding his expression in shadow. "Now what could be wrong on such a fine day?" he asked, grinning.

He was waiting for something or someone.

Rowena did not know how she knew, she just did. She thought suddenly of the men who had attacked them on the stairs. Her pulse jumped in alarm. She wanted to ask him if he'd learned anything, he'd been adamant about keeping the incident a secret. Surreptitiously, she glanced about to see who was near.

Harry had wandered over to watch the spearmen, loudly

lamenting the fact that his wounds were not sufficiently
healed to permit him to show the Sutherlands how it was
done. Kier stood at attention behind her rocky perch.

"Join them, if you'd like, Kier. I'll come to no harm in
the midst of so many mighty warriors."

"I'll stay." Kier glared at Lion.

"Kier Gunn, you are making me more nervous hanging
about like some great vulture. And I doubt that was Finlay's
intent. Lord Lion has twice saved my life, for heaven's
sake."

"I'm sure he had his reasons," Kier snapped.

"Enough," Rowena cried. "Go! Go glower at someone
else."

"There's a man who takes his duties seriously," Lion
observed as Kier stomped away. "Where is Dun this fine
morn?"

"Sleeping, Kier said. Dun stood watch at my door last
night and needed to rest."

Lion watched Kier, who stood stiffly to one side of the
contest, yet kept an eye on them. "He does not like me."

"Nay." Rowena sighed. "Kier and Dun were appalled
to learn of our betrothal, and who can blame them, for they
fear I will forswear my duties to Clan Gunn." She pleated
her skirts with clammy fingers. "I have explained the circumstances that led up to your...your declaration."

"Have you indeed? Did you tell them that nothing has
changed between us?" he asked, his voice low and husky.

Rowena gasped, her head whipping up. "Nay, I did not,
because everything has changed."

"Ah, Ro, you can lie to them, and even to me, but you
cannot lie to yourself. This—this fire that burns inside us
is as—"

"Do not." Rowena turned her head away, unable to bear
the intense flame in his eyes, struggling to quell the answering heat that bloomed inside her.

"I am sorry, Ro. I did not mean to frighten you."

"I am not afraid." But she was, terribly afraid that she

would weaken toward him. She stared at the men playing with their spears. "Why have we really come here?"

"So the lads might practice."

She looked up. "Nay, you are waiting for someone."

His dark brows rose, then a smile stole across his face, easing the tense lines. "You are too canny by half, lass." He hunkered down beside her. "There is someone I need to see. In fact, it is the real reason we rode up here, when we could have practiced just as well outside Blantyre's walls. But I cannot have my friend ride in with your Gunns here."

"Why do you distrust my men?"

"Alexander would give much to know where my friend is, and Eneas would delight in ingratiating himself to Alexander by supplying that information."

"Kier and Harry are my men...and Finlay's. They would not tell Eneas anything." She watched Lion closely, studying his shuttered expression. "What is it? What else has happened?"

He shook his head, then one corner of his chiseled mouth lifted in a half smile. "You are sometimes too quick for my own good, lass. I had a visitor last night. A man who crept into my room bent on mischief."

"Lion." She felt her blood drain away, leaving her cold and shaky. "Were you hurt?"

"Nay, I drove him off ere he could strike, but he did leave behind a scrap of his plaid when he fell. Gunn plaid."

Rowena gasped. "Eneas."

"It seems likely," Lion said, shrugging. "There's been ill feeling between us from the first. He may think to climb higher with Alexander by getting rid of me. Or Georas could have paid him to kill me, or—" his eyes glinted with wry humor "—he may take exception to my courting his brother's widow."

"Bah, he does not care what happens to me."

"Even so, I'm a wee bit shy where the Gunns are concerned."

"But you trust me?"

"With my life, lass. Will you come away with me while I meet my friend? I cannot tell you his name, but do think you'll be glad you've seen him."

Rowena stiffened. "If this is some ruse to get me off alone and seduce me in some sylvan glade the way you did before, you—"

"'Tis a charming notion...very charming," he said, drawing out his *r*'s. "But I swear I'm innocent of such plotting, and you know I'd never touch you or force you against your will."

She knew that; she was just afraid that if he touched her, what little willpower she had would evaporate.

"Will you not trust me?" He held out his hand and smiled, his gaze solemn and for once free of teasing or mockery.

"What of Kier and Harry? They will surely follow."

"My lads will see they're entertained while we're gone."

"You'll not hurt them?"

"Not physically, though they may be a bit wroth with me when we get back. Still, it's all in a good cause."

"I do not know why I am doing this," Rowena said. But as she put her hand in his, the feel of his rough, callused palm sliding over her smooth one sent shivers racing up her arm. She knew exactly why she was going with him. Because despite the cold dictates of her mind, there was no place she'd rather be than with Lion.

Light-headed with relief, Lion signaled Red Will to take care of the Gunns, and hustled Rowena off behind the rocks before she could change her mind.

She trusted him, a little at least, and cared for him far more than she'd admit. It was a long way from what he wanted, but he'd learned to take what he could get—and strive for more.

"It's just a short ways." Lion lifted a heavy pine bough

out of the way and drew her into the verge of the forest. It was dark and quiet beneath the canopy of leaves. His confidence fled when she hesitated. "There's no cause for alarm, Rowena."

"I am not afraid." Smiling, she looked around and inhaled deeply. "I was but savoring all this."

"Aye." He relaxed and followed her gaze from tree to tree. "There's naught as sweet as a Highland glen in summer." Out of nowhere came the image of Rowena wading across their burn, her skirts caught up about her thighs, her face flushed with desire. They'd made love on the mossy banks to the sounds of spilling water and humming bees. "Rowena…"

She looked up, eyes filling with memories. The air around them was peaceful no longer, but charged with tension, shimmering with awareness.

He stepped forward; she stepped back.

"Come, we'd best be going." His voice was hoarse with suppressed emotion.

Off to the right, a nightingale sang out. Lion grinned and changed direction, heading toward the sound of a bird that lived a thousand miles away. The thick forest gave way to a small clearing dotted with black boulders. He headed for the nearest one and seated Rowena on it.

"There is no one here," she said warily.

"Yet." Lion settled down beside her.

"Ye're late," said a raspy voice. Wesley Sutherland strode out of the brush, his steps swift but silent.

"Unavoidable." Lion stood and introduced Rowena to his third—or was it fourth?—cousin. "Where's the lad?"

"Nearby." Wes turned and whistled.

"How is he?"

"About as ye might expect."

Rowena gasped, and Lion turned to see Colin Ross enter the clearing, a Sutherland on either side of him. His thin face was ashen, his eyes shadowed and bleak.

"Oh, the poor thing." Rowena started forward, stopped

when Colin whimpered and cringed against one of his guards.

"Give him a moment, lass. The Stewarts roughed him up a bit before we could get to him, and he's frightened."

"Those beasts! Sweet Mary, how did you get him away?" Rowena whispered. "Where has he been all this time?"

"Here with my men," Lion answered. "They took him from the dungeon and have kept him safely hidden from Alexander's search parties, but the time has come to move him." He knelt in the grass. "Do you know who I am, lad?"

Colin nodded.

"Then you'll know I mean you no harm. Have my men been treating you all right? Have you gotten enough to eat?"

"The lad's appetite has been a bit poorly," Wes said.

Colin sniffed. "I want my mama."

"I am sure you do, and I'm sure she wants to see you, too," Lion said gently. "That's what I've come to talk with you about. Will you step closer and sit with me?"

Colin nodded and shuffled across the clearing, his fists clenched tightly at his sides. He stopped in front of Lion.

"'Twas a braw thing you tried to do, Colin Ross," Lion said. "But I wished you'd not put yourself in harm's way."

Colin's childish face hardened. "He killed my brother, and no one else would do anything about it."

"Aye. We'll see he pays, but it may take a bit of time."

"He has not cried, Lion," Wes said in French. "Not out of grief or fear, but you can tell it is eating him up."

Lion nodded. He wanted to hold the boy and ease his agony, but Colin was trying to be a man and he'd not shame him. "Colin, Wes and I have things to discuss. While we're about it, would you sit with my lady?" He glanced sideways at Rowena's pale, compassionate face. "This is Lady Rowena Gunn. She has a lad a wee bit younger than you, and she misses him just as much as your mama must miss you.''

Rowena knelt in a whisper of soft wool. ''It would comfort me if I might hug you, Colin.'' She held out her arms, and Colin's brave facade cracked. With a small, inarticulate sob, he threw himself into her embrace and clung.

Lion's throat closed as he watched Rowena shift Colin onto her lap and begin to rock him, murmuring gentle words. After a moment, Lion stood and looked at his men. Veteran warriors who had faced death without a whimper now had the sheen of tears in their eyes. He swallowed hard himself and led Wes a few paces away. ''My thanks for getting him out of the dungeon.''

'''Twas our pleasure, believe me.'' Wes's eyes narrowed. ''He'd not have lasted the night, I think, for he said they had orders to find out who'd sent him.''

Lion's fists clenched tighter. When he brought Alexander down, he'd settle this score, too. ''I'd wager no one sent Colin. But how the hell did he get to Blantyre?''

''Stole a horse and followed the directions the earl had sent when he summoned William Ross. Colin was furious because his brother Alain did not avenge Will's death.''

''He could not have known how much Alain wanted to. But fortunately, he was wise enough to heed my advice.'' The moment he'd heard of the massacre at the abbey, Lion had sent word to Will's successor, warning him that to attack Alexander would condemn his clansmen to death, also.

''I know he was wrong,'' Wes muttered, ''but I still admire the lad's bravery. To think he rode fifty miles on his own.''

''And nearly succeeded in ridding us of the Wolf. We had word last night from Iain Ross, Colin's uncle. His keep lies twenty miles from here, in Glen Creagan. If we can get the lad to him, he'll make sure no word leaks out that he's there.''

"The lad'll be glad to be with his kin, but he's been asking for his ma."

"Too dangerous. Alexander sent a troop of his Stewarts to watch Styore Castle for any sign of the lad."

"Do you think he'll outlaw the Rosses over this?"

Lion wished he knew. Fergus, chief of Clan Ross, was Colin's distant cousin, and a very powerful man. "Alexander has hopes Old Fergus will join his army. It would be unreasonable for him to alienate Fergus by attacking his kin, but lately Alexander has been none too reasonable. And the MacPherson does not help matters. He is all for moving now, attacking the smaller clans and forcing them to ride with Alexander till his ranks swell and he can take on the larger clans."

"Damn. If that happens, what of your plans?"

"I'd have to leave Blantyre. It's one thing to practice for a war against your friends, quite another to actually take the field and fight them. Nay, I could not do it. We'd have to make a run for Glenshee and hole up there."

"Waiting for Alexander to attack."

"Aye," Lion said gloomily. If Alexander besieged them for no reason, maybe then his father could finally get the king to see how dangerous his brother was and recall him. Of course, by then it would likely be too late to save the inhabitants of Glenshee. Lion raked a hand through his hair and looked over at Rowena. At the first sign of trouble, he'd have to send her back to Hillbrae. No matter how much he hated the notion.

"Lady Rowena has bucked up the lad's spirits," Wes said. Indeed, Colin's crying had ceased, and he sat beside her, talking quietly. "She's bonny and kind, your lady."

"Aye, that she is. You'd best take Colin and get him started for Creagan."

Colin didn't cry, but there were tears in his eyes as he bid Lion and Rowena goodbye. Lion's chest ached as he watched the lad disappear into the forest, surrounded by Sutherlands.

"That was a wonderful thing you did," Rowena murmured, her hand falling lightly onto his bare forearm.

"It was little enough—the life of one lad when dozens, hundreds have died and thousands more will die if Alexander is not stopped."

"How? How can you hope to stop him?"

"By proving he is the traitor." Under Rowena's incredulous gaze, Lion told her what they suspected Alexander was doing. "When we got a peek inside Alexander's strongbox, I saw several parchment rolls bearing the Campbells' boar-head seal. Now all I need is a way to get them," Lion added.

"I could ask to see another piece of his terrible jewelry."

"Nay, it is too risky. I should not have involved you, but the opportunity came up so naturally." He chuckled, shaking his head. "I think I'll leave the cake dough in the ring as a reminder not to force you to accept any gifts you do not want."

She laughed, her face upturned in the dappled light filtering in through the leaves. Lion was suddenly, achingly aware they were alone, truly alone, for the first time since she'd reentered his life. She realized it, too, for her eyes darkened at the exact moment he reached for her.

Their lips met...meshed.

The flare of passion was instantaneous, a firestorm of sensations and emotions that had him lifting her up so their bodies flowed together. He tasted greed and vulnerability as she opened her mouth to his. A heady combination that went to his head faster than Highland whiskey. He felt his needs echoed in the way she twisted against him, giving and taking. His blood burned; his heart pounded so thunderously it seemed the very earth shook beneath his feet.

A sharp squeal burst through the haze of pleasure.

Lion wrenched his head up just in time to see the boar charge across the clearing, its eyes red with fury, its yellow tusks gleaming, sharp and deadly as steel lances.

Chapter Eleven

Rowena gasped as Lion suddenly snatched her off her feet and shoved her behind him.

"Run. Get to that oak and climb," he ordered, his sword hissing from its sheath.

She spied the boar and froze. It was so close she could count the bristles on its ugly snout and see the wicked cleverness in its eyes. "You cannot kill it with a sword."

"Nay, but I can turn it. Now, run! Stay behind me, make for that oak."

Belatedly, she realized her hesitation endangered them both. Turning, she stumbled toward the tree. Its branches dipped invitingly near to the ground. Breathless, she snagged the lowest one and hauled herself up. Even before her bottom settled on the rough branch, she looked back at Lion.

The boar was nearly upon him, tusks lowered, set on a collision course with Lion's legs.

"Sweet Mary, nay," Rowena gasped. "Lion!"

At the last instant, he sidestepped the deadly charge. His sword scored the beast's tough hide, but couldn't penetrate. As the pig squealed, Lion wheeled and ran for the tree.

"Hurry, Lion. Hurry!" Rowena scrambled up to the next branch. But the boar was close. So close.

Lion snagged the branch she had vacated and swung his

long legs up, just as the boar rushed by. It flailed its weapons at the empty air, bellowed in rage and turned.

Snorting furiously, the boar swiveled its head back and forth, as though trying to figure out how it had missed. Finally it looked up and spotted Lion. Tiny red eyes narrowed to angry slits. The boar charged the tree and struck it a few glancing blows, slicing off great hunks of bark and shaking the oak.

Rowena shuddered and closed her eyes, fingers clenched around the limb. "They do not climb trees, do they?"

"Nay, but they're smart enough to wait about beneath for us to come down."

"For—for how long?" Rowena asked weakly. No sooner had one danger been averted than another fear had taken its place. She had always hated high places.

"Hard to say. Are you all right?"

"F-fine." Her teeth were chattering and a cold sweat trickled between her breasts. "I-it is a long way down."

"Damn, I had forgotten how much you dislike heights."

She heard a few scrabbling noises, then the limb on which she sat bent and quivered. Opening her eyes, she found Lion seated on the branch, facing her. "Oh, what are you doing? What if it breaks?"

"It won't. Trust me, sweetheart, I'll keep you safe." A few quick, acrobatic moves later, their positions were reversed. He sat with his back to the trunk, holding her sideways on his lap. "Better?" he murmured.

"Mmm." Rowena kept her face in his chest and her arms locked around him.

"Your fingers are digging holes in my neck."

"Sorry." Rowena eased her grip.

He stroked her back. "I suppose now you'll think I planned all this so I could seduce you."

"What? Nay, why would I..." Her voice trailed off as she realized how loverlike their position was. "Oh!" She sat up straight.

"Oh, indeed." He put his hands on her waist to steady her. "Trust me, Ro, I only want to keep you safe."

Rowena nodded but carefully avoided meeting his gaze. She couldn't afford to be drawn any deeper under his spell.

Below them, the pig grunted, an almost welcome reminder of a more tangible danger.

"How long will it stay, do you think?" she asked softly.

"Longer than we want it to, I'm sure. But don't worry, once Wes finishes seeing young Colin and his escort off to Creagan, he's bound to come looking for us."

Rowena turned toward Lion. "Will Colin be safe there?"

"Safe enough. His kin will not betray him." Because he thought she deserved to know, Lion told her the story of Will Ross and the burning of Blair Abbey.

Rowena sighed. "The earl is truly a horrible monster. What do you think he will do next?"

"I wish I knew." Lion's hands ceased their stroking. "He grows desperate, and that makes him even more dangerous." He drew her closer. "When we return to Blantyre, I want you to go back to Hillbrae where it is safe."

"But what of Paddy's future? I have yet to get the earl to agree that Finlay and I should be his guardians. And with Eneas more in his favor, I fear...I fear for my son's life."

"Shh. I'll send Bryce and the lads with you."

"But what of your plans? Will you not need your men?"

"Heckie and I can do what needs to be done."

Rowena sighed and leaned her head against his chest. She could feel the steady beat of his heart, and had to ask, "Tell me again why you left me without a word."

His hands stilled on her back. His heart lurched, then went on. "It was not by my choice, Ro. I loved you more than anything. I was even prepared to defy my father and remain in Scotland to be near you."

"Really? You'd told him about me?"

"I was never one to keep secrets from my parents. They knew I'd met a lass, fallen in love and wished to wed her."

Rowena raised her head so she could see his face. "It must have displeased them mightily. We MacBeans are so far beneath—"

"My parents are not like that. They wed for love and would see me happy, too. But they wanted me to go to France as planned and wait to marry when I returned."

Doubtless they'd hoped he'd forget her.

"We'd fought about it that very morn. My temper got the better of me, and I swore I'd run away with you. I slammed out of Kinduin in a blind rage and rode straight into an ambush."

"Someone really did attack you, then?"

"Did you not believe me when I told you?"

She shook her head. "I—I was still too angry with you. The story seemed a—a convenient way to make me feel sorry for you."

"Two miles from our glen, six men sprang from the brush. I fought them—Jesu, how I fought—killing two and wounding another before they felled me. I've never felt more alone, more powerless, lying there as they closed in to finish me."

"Oh, Lion…"

"Aye." Lion watched her closely, relieved to see her shock. He'd never thought she'd had any part in the attempt on his life, but the facts were damning. "If you still do not believe me, feel here." He took her hand and ran it down his ribs, over the thick scar tissue.

"Lion." Tears spilled down her cheeks as her fingers splayed over the wound. "How did you survive?"

"One of my father's patrols heard the noise and came to investigate. They drove off the assailants and saved my life."

"But—but why did they say nothing when I came to Kinduin looking for you?"

"I am not surprised. Things were a bit…unsettled. You see, the men who'd attacked me wore Munro plaid."

"Munros! But I thought the Sutherlands' feud with them ended years ago."

"So it had, but Laird Alain Munro had just died, leaving his cousin to rule the clan till his son was old enough. There were rumors that this Seamus was as greedy and ruthless as the old laird for whom he'd been named."

"So, your father had gone to seek revenge on the Munros?"

"Nay, the web is more tangled than that. My attackers wore the Munro plaid, but the two dead men left behind were not of that clan. They were strangers. My father thought someone wished to cause trouble between our two clans, so he held off and waited to see if I had recognized the men who got away."

"Had you?"

Lion nodded, his gaze full on hers, watching her reaction. "The man who led them was your brother."

"John? John tried to kill you? Why?"

"I thought mayhap he opposed our love."

"He did not know. At least, he never said so. Mama knew I had met you at the gathering, and she warned me not to see you or I'd end up getting hurt. So I told no one…" Old Meg had known there was a man in her life, but not Lion's name. Rowena shook her head. "You must have been mistaken. The shock of being ambushed, the fear you were dying…"

Lion shrugged. "I thought it was John."

"Why did your father not attack us, then?"

"Because I kept silent. I was weak from loss of blood and in a great deal of pain, but I did hold my tongue out of fear Papa would do just that if I spoke."

"Oh, Lion." Rowena buried her face in his chest. "All these years I hated you for leaving me, and you were just protecting me and mine."

He stroked her hair. "I told you I was not such a bad fellow," he teased.

Rowena lifted her head. "How can you jest about this?"

"It is in the past, Ro."

"I cannot believe my brother would do such a thing. Mayhap it really was Munros. You were gravely wounded and could have been mistaken about recognizing Johnny."

Lion made a noncommittal sound. He could not actually recall if John had raised a sword against him, but he was certain he'd seen him, watching from the shadows.

"Oh." Rowena framed his face with her hands, her eyes filled with suffering. "When I think you could have died, and I never knew. I thought—"

"Shh." Lion kissed her gently. "I am too stubborn to die." Though it had been a near thing, according to his parents.

"I—I can see why you did not send word to me." Her lower lip trembled. "You doubtless thought I'd—I'd tried to—"

"I never thought that. But my father was concerned the Munros might try again to kill me, so he put it about that I had left for France. Between the blood loss and the fever that came upon me, I was out of my head for nigh three weeks. By the time I regained my senses, you were wed to Padruig and gone to Hillbrae." He searched her eyes for answers. "You wed him just to spite. You must have, because I know you did not love him."

What could she say? Heart aching, Rowena nodded. "I thought you had tired of me and gone off to other adventures, other women. I could not bear to remain in my brother's household, a slave to his wife, who did not like me. So…"

"But Padruig was so old, so cold. How could you bear…?" Lion stopped and shook his head. "Nay, I do not want to discuss your marriage." It nearly killed him to think of her with another man. "It is in the past, sweetheart. We have our future before us." He claimed her mouth in a scorching kiss.

They had no future. Rowena knew that, and it nearly broke her, but she let herself be swept away by the surge of emotions flooding her. It seemed everything inside her had been asleep these past years, and only awakened again at his touch. She had forgotten what it was like to feel this alive, this greedy. Whimpering, she arched against him, tugging at his shirt, hungry for the glide of flesh on flesh.

"Easy." Lion caught her hands in one of his, the other reaching out to steady them on the branch. "Have you forgotten we're up a tree with a boar pacing beneath?"

Rowena drew back, horrified by what she'd almost done. "Oh, Sweet Mary, how could I have been so foolish?"

"'Tis all right." He grinned and kissed the tip of her nose. "I always liked it that you were as hot for me as I for you," he added with supreme male smugness. "But we'll soon be back at Blantyre with the whole night ahead of us, and no matter what Alexander has planned, we'll spend it in bed."

Rowena shook her head. "I cannot do that. I am a widow with a reputation and a son to protect." He winced, and she wondered if she'd hurled the hurtful reminder to push him away. "I'll not give Eneas, or anyone else, cause to claim I'm a loose woman and unfit to guide my Paddy."

"You are right, of course, and I'd not have you think I hold your honor so cheaply. 'Tis just I'd thought it best we not wed till this miserable business of Alexander's army is settled. If things go ill, you'd be better off as Padruig's widow than the wife of an outlaw."

"I cannot wed you," she said slowly, each word caustic as acid on her battered heart. "I thought you understood that."

"You've said so before, but you'll not convince me things are so hopeless. We can work out something so the lad can—"

"Nay, we cannot," Rowena said wildly, the consequences of Lion meeting Paddy too horrible to consider.

"Damn, you are stubborn." But there was more than just temper in her eyes, there was a fear so deep and profound it stopped him. In the silence, he heard the nightingale call.

"Let us hope that is Bryce and the lads." Lion pursed his lips and called thrice, a reply and a warning.

"Are they coming?" Rowena attempted to tug her skirts down. "Drat, whatever will they think we've been doing up here?"

"The lads would not have improper thoughts about my lady."

"I am not your lady." She sounded more sorry than certain, and Lion counted that a good thing. She was weakening. It was only a matter of time till he wore down her objections.

Red Will appeared in the fringe of the forest so silently that the boar standing guard at the base of the oak never heard him. Hand signals sent the others fanning out around the clearing. The spears they'd brought to practice with came in right handy. When the boar belatedly spotted the danger and charged, it was met by a wall of sharpened steel.

Rowena cringed and hid her face.

Lion absently stroked her head. "It had to be, lass, for the boar would not have let us go." And it might yet do them a good turn. Alexander would likely not be pleased that he'd gone off without telling him, but the boar would provide fresh meat, a lively tale to tell at supper and a reason for having lingered so long in the hills.

Eneas watched in growing anger as the people of Blantyre welcomed Lion and his Sutherlands into the castle.

"'Tis like the second coming," he sneered.

"Aye, you'd think folk had never seen a dead boar before," Clem said. "His Grace has even left his chamber."

"Where?" Eneas's eyes narrowed as he followed the earl's progress through the crowded courtyard. Alexander had spent all day in his rooms, or so his bodyguards had claimed. He'd not come to watch the men practice for the remaining events in the games. Not even when a fight had erupted between the MacPhersons and the Grants, and quickly spread to involve the rest of the clansmen. Three men had been killed in the clash and a score wounded, including Dunmore and two other Gunns. Still the earl had not appeared...till now.

"I did not know you planned to ride out," the earl growled, looking vastly displeased, which heartened Eneas.

"I apologize, Your Grace. You were busy this morn when I decided to take my men out for a bit of a practice." Smiling easily, Lion swung down from his horse. "See what we found in the woods." He gestured toward the boar, slung over a long spear pole. "I recalled you had a taste for fresh ham."

"Aye, that I do." Alexander's scowl faded, but his gaze remained cool. "I also like to know what my men are about."

"Next time, I shall remember that."

Eneas's stomach turned as he watched Alexander unbend toward Lion. He himself had saved Alexander's life, yet the man did not show him half the favor he showed Lion. It was not fair.

"I wonder what our hero really did in the hills?" Georas grumbled as he stepped up beside Eneas.

"You do not believe his story?"

"Why should he ride away from Blantyre when there is room aplenty to practice here? And when he knows full well that Alexander does not like his men to go off on their own?"

"What could he be doing?"

"Meeting with Alexander's enemies...the Rosses, mayhap."

Eneas gasped softly. "'Tis too much to hope for."

"Not necessarily." Georas's eyes took on a nasty glint. "Lion's sire is at court now. They say that Lucais is trying to convince the king to recall Alexander and strip him of his viceroyalty. Close as father and son are rumored to be, I thought it strange that Lion came to Blantyre. When I tried to tell the earl this, he brushed aside my warning. He's flattered to have so polished and educated a knight in his tail. He thinks it will persuade others to join us.''

"So…" Eneas studied Lion's chiseled features as he charmed his way back into Alexander's good graces. He jested and smiled, with no hint of the groveling Eneas had seen others resort to when they'd run afoul of the temperamental earl. "We must find out what he is up to."

"Do you think I have not tried?" Georas cursed under his breath. "His men are so bloody loyal they have refused every bribe mine have offered. They do not drink to excess, nor wench nor gamble. And Lion never goes anywhere without a troop of his warriors with him."

"Mmm." As Eneas watched Lion and the earl enter the keep side by side, his gaze fell on another nauseating sight—Padruig's faithless widow fairly drooling over Lion as she walked with him. "I would wager his men are not with him when he beds my brother's widow."

Georas grunted. "I am sure you are right, but no man tells a woman of his plans."

"Nay, but lying with a woman does weaken a man. If she were to ask him what he is about—say, when his mind was clouded with lust—he might say too much."

"Would she help you?"

"She will if she wants her precious son to grow any older."

After a day spent in the fresh air, away from the intrigue, Rowena found the atmosphere at Blantyre even more stifling than usual. For one thing, Kier was most wroth with her for having gone off with Lion.

"I know he was up to no good, for when I noticed you were gone, his men first tried to prevent me from going after you, then sent me searching for you in the wrong direction."

"Let it go, Kier," she said wearily.

"How can I? I come here to protect you and find you betrothed to Glenshee. What of your vow to Padruig?"

"I have explained about that, Kier. It is Lion's way of protecting me from the earl's wrath. My pledge to return to Hillbrae still stands." She would not, could not violate that, for the oath had been sworn on Paddy's soul. To break her word would be to damn her son for all eternity.

"Humph. I do not like the way Glenshee looks at you."

"That is none of your business," she said, temper snapping. "If you do not stop this, I will send you back to Hillbrae." She slammed the door to her chamber and tore off her riding clothes. If she had any sense, she'd use Kier as a bulwark against Lion, but she had always had little sense where Lion was concerned.

Now she had none.

His story of being ambushed and nearly killed had demolished any doubts she'd had about him. The fact that he'd kept silent to save her brother...

Rowena shivered, wrapping her arms about her body as she walked to the high window. Johnny had no reason to wish Lion ill. She tried to recall how her brother had seemed that long-ago day, but her memories were clouded by her own fear, pain and humiliation.

He had acted surprised, then pleased when Padruig announced they were wedding. There had been talk of more horses for John to train, but that was all. Her mother had congratulated her on catching a man above her station, then had gone off to lose herself in ale, as she'd been wont to do since the death of her husband. None of this seemed the least bit ominous.

Rowena shook away her lingering doubts. Lion must have been mistaken, she thought as she went to dress for dinner. The blue wool gown she'd left on the bed was gone, replaced by a velvet one in a lighter shade of blue.

One of Annie Shaw's, no doubt. And more of Lion's doing, she thought as she ran her hand over the soft fabric. After what had happened today, it was hard to be angry with him.

Smiling, she washed, rebraided her hair and slipped on

her borrowed finery. The neckline and edge of the wide, flowing sleeves were embroidered with gold thread depicting fanciful flowers. The hem dragged on the floor till she belted it with a girdle of blue leather, then it draped gently over her body, hugging her breasts and hips. She turned in a slow circle, admiring the swirl of fabric and feeling very feminine.

The glow of appreciation in Lion's eyes when he came to fetch her moments later warmed her to her toes.

"You look lovely." He brushed a kiss on her hand as he executed a courtly bow.

Rowena giggled, her insides aflutter. The mood was dampened by Kier's aggrieved throat clearing. She glared him into a reproachful silence, then accepted Lion's escort to the hall.

Immediately they were the focus of Lady Selena's venomous glances and more than a few curious ones. Drat. Was her reputation already in tatters? Determined to brave things out, she walked resolutely toward the dais, her hand on Lion's arm. Halfway to the high table, she spied Dunmore Gunn at one of the trestle tables, a bandage wrapped around his head, his left arm in a sling.

"Go on without me, please, Lion," she touched Dun's arm. "Whatever happened to you?"

He looked up at her, one side of his face raked with scratches. "There was trouble on the practice field today."

"But I thought you were sleeping."

"I remained abed till just after noon, then went down to see what the other men were doing. I was watching only, when the fight broke out, but—but we were all swept up in it."

"Let me look at your wounds."

"I am sure he is fine," Kier interjected.

"Aye, I am," Dun said. "Felis herself saw to me."

"That should be fine, then, though I'll look at the cuts and dress them again this evening."

Dun's eyes widened, and he drew back. "Nay. I am fine."

Men, Rowena thought, were ever big bairns about such things. She did not press the point, but resolved to check on him before bedtime. "Kier, why do you not stay here with Dun? There are so may pages fluttering about the high table that you would only be in the way."

His stricken look chafed her conscience, but another meal under his baleful eyes was too much to contemplate.

Rowena joined Lion at the head table, but Alexander dominated the conversation. He insisted on hearing about the boar hunt, to which Lion replied with a much revised version of the truth. By the time the long meal was over, Rowena had a pounding headache. She excused herself and made her way from the hall. Kier and Dun both fell into step behind her. She was very glad of the company when she saw who waited in the corridor.

"A moment, Rowena," Eneas demanded.

Her men stayed beside her, as unmovable as stone.

Eneas glowered at him. "I have word from home for Lady Rowena. A private message."

Alarmed, Rowena said, "It is all right." She waited till they had withdrawn a few feet, then asked, "What is wrong?"

"Nothing…yet." Eneas smiled wolfishly. "But if you do not do as I ask, your son will not be at Hillbrae when you return."

"You would not dare to harm your brother's son."

"I said nothing about harming him. I merely said he would not be at Hillbrae. I will send him away and make certain you do not see him again."

Rowena's knees turned to water. "What—what do you want?"

"To know what Lion Sutherland is doing."

The icy chill spread from her hands to her heart. "Doing?" she said blankly, stalling for time, praying for inspiration.

"We think he was involved in Colin Ross's escape. You will find out where the brat is and tell me."

Images of Colin's battered face swam in Rowena's mind. She used them to steady her quivering nerves. "But—but even if this is so, how could I get him to tell me?" she whined, shrinking back and trembling with half-feigned fear.

"In the manner of all whores, you will seduce him into telling you," Eneas hissed. "And if I suspect you have told Lion of my request, Paddy may meet with a fatal accident."

"You would not—"

"For the kind of rewards that lie within my grasp, I would dare anything. Remember that, if you are tempted to cross me."

"I—"

"Rowena!" Lady Glenda called, materializing out of the gloom. "Oh, good. I've saved myself a trip to your room. Alexander will be in conference with his chiefs, and I would like your company in my solar."

Rowena groaned. What she craved now was quiet in which to find some way out of this terrible situation.

"Oh." The lady's plain face contorted with concern. "Lion said your head ached. My maid has a potion she rubs on the temples that works wonders. Come along, do."

Rowena went, both to avoid antagonizing her only friend at Blantyre and to escape from Eneas's piercing stare. She endured having her forehead rubbed with something that smelled worse than boar's breath. Another maid entertained on the harp, and Lady Glenda chattered about a new cream purported to make the skin glow. At the end of an hour, Rowena's head hurt worse than ever and her jaw was so tight her teeth ached, too. Finally, she escaped on the pretext of visiting the jakes.

As she left the master suite, she heard Alexander's voice echoing down the corridor.

Nay, she could not face him at this point. Ducking into the nearest room, she waited for the earl to pass.

"'Tis an excellent plan, Your Grace," she heard Georas say. "If we leave at midnight, we can reach Creagan in good time to rest the men and attack the Rosses at dawn."

The Rosses? Rowena pressed her ear closer to the door.

"Good. You are to storm the keep, kill all within and burn it to the ground."

"I will go and tell the men to make ready," said Georas.

"Nay. Tell no one."

"Not even your Lion?" Georas asked silkily.

"Nay, I have thought on what you said about his frequent disappearances and his alliance with the widow of the man who did call me a butcher to my face. We will keep these plans secret from everyone till it is time to ride out," the earl said tightly. "I want the Rosses taken completely unawares," he continued. "I want them wiped out. Let the other clans see what happens to those who turn against me."

Their heavy footsteps continued on by her hiding place, but Rowena remained where she was, frozen in place. After a moment, she stirred. She had to find Lion and tell him what was going to happen. She peered out, eased from the room and hurried down the hallway. Just as she reached the stairwell, she met Lion and Bryce coming up.

"Lion!" She grabbed hold of his arm, hands trembling.

He reached for his sword. "What is it?"

"He...the earl—"

"Move, Sutherland, you block the steps," said Eneas. He stood below Lion in the stairwell.

Lion swore softly and stepped aside to let Eneas pass. It was as though a cork had been pulled from a bottle, spewing men into the upper corridor, the MacPherson chief and Robbie MacNab among them.

"What is going on?" Rowena asked.

"We are all invited to drink with the earl," Robbie said.

"Come with us, sweetheart." Lion snagged her around the waist and drew her into his arms for a kiss. "What is it?" he whispered against her lips.

Rowena looped her arms around his neck and kissed him back, heedless of the wanton display in her desperation to speak with him. "I overheard the earl tell Georas he will attack the Rosses of Creagan. At dawn tomorrow."

The oath Lion uttered was crude and not at all lover-like. Not that Rowena cared. "There is more," she said hurriedly. "Eneas suspects you helped Colin and has threatened my son's life if I do not find proof for him."

Lion's eyes widened. "What did you tell him?"

"Nothing. I would not betray any of you."

"Sweetheart." He leaned his forehead against hers. "I thank you for the warning, both warnings. I will deal with Eneas."

"Wait." Her confidence faltered. "If Eneas finds out I told you about this, he...he will kill Paddy."

"I swear I'll do naught to endanger your son, but come, we cannot tarry." Breaking off the intimate pose, he escorted her down the hall behind the others.

"What will you do?" she murmured.

"It is better you not know." His expression was grim. "When we get inside the solar," he whispered. "I want you to slap me hard across the mouth, call me an unfeeling brute and leave."

"Leave?"

"Aye. Go to your room and lock yourself within."

"But I want to help."

"You have, first by giving me fair warning and then by giving me an excuse to stay home while the others go raiding."

"What are you going to do?"

"Drink myself sick over you, you fickle jade."

Chapter Twelve

"**D**amn fool thing to do," Red Will grumbled as he and Bryce hauled Lion up the stairs. "I've not seen him get drunk over a wench in nigh on six years."

"Aye, and it was the same lass he lost his wits over then as it was now."

"What do ye suppose she did to set him off?"

"Who knows?" Bryce said wearily.

"Ouch. Watch what you're doing, you louts," Lion hissed as his shoulder bumped stone.

Bryce stopped and stared down at him in the dim stairwell. "I thought you'd passed out."

"Shh. That's what you were supposed to think," Lion whispered. "But I'm not, so mind how you go."

Red Will frowned. "What are ye up to?"

"I'll tell you when we get above. Now quit chattering and be quick about it," Lion said under his breath.

The men nodded and hustled him up the stairs. Bryce shouldered open the door to Lion's chamber, Red Will kicked it shut after them with his heel. Together they pitched Lion onto the bed.

"What is going on?" Bryce demanded.

"Shh." Lion sat up, flinging the hair from his eyes. "Will, see if there's anyone about in the corridor. Bryce, get out my mail and helmet." Lion bolted for the garderobe behind the screen in the corner of the room and rid his belly of as much of the watered ale as he could.

"Jesu, you really are drunk," Bryce said when Lion came back around the screen, wiping his face on a towel.

"Only half. I could not make the act look convincing without swilling a bit more ale than I wanted." He reached for the mail dangling in Bryce's hands.

Bryce held the mesh garment away. "You are in no fit condition for whatever you've got planned."

"I'll do. The air will clear my head." He looked toward the door, where Will stood guard. "Will?"

"I dinna see anyone, but I'll stay here and keep watch."

Lion nodded, went to the window, cracked open the shutters and peered out. The night was dark and moonless, perfect for his needs. Turning away, he quickly appraised Bryce of what Rowena had overheard. "I've got to warn Iain Ross." Colin was at Creagan, and likely the two Sutherlands sent to escort him.

Bryce grabbed his sword hilt. "I'll alert the lads. Do we ride to Creagan and fight with the Rosses or waylay the earl?"

"Neither." Ignoring Bryce's protest, Lion took the chain-mail shirt and drew it on over his shirt. "If we fight Alexander, we ruin everything we've worked for. I'm going to alert Iain and get everyone away before Alexander's army arrives. It is vital that you and the lads ride with the earl, so he'll not suspect we had a hand in warning the Rosses."

"Nay, I will not raise a weapon against—"

"Pray God you will not have to. I intend to have Iain's people in the hills and the keep burning before dawn."

"What if you are caught?"

"Then you'll have the pleasure of rescuing me," Lion teased. He strapped his claymore onto his back and covered it with a ratty cloak. From beneath the bed, he took the coil of rope he'd used when he went visiting Rowena. "I want you to go back downstairs, Bryce, and inform His Grace that I am stinking drunk and dead to the world, unlike to rise before morn, and then with a sore head.''

Bryce frowned but nodded. ''The room smells foul enough that anyone who comes checking will believe you, I suppose.''

''Will, you're to stand guard outside the door to see that no one disturbs my drunken slumbers.''

''Aye. But I'd rather be going with ye.''

''Not this time.''

''Just in case…'' Bryce drew back the blankets, heaped dirty clothes onto the bed and covered the mound again so it resembled a sleeping body.

Grinning, Lion tied one end of the rope to the bedpost and threw the other over the windowsill. ''Enjoy your ride to Creagan, but stay clear of Alexander on the way back. He's bound to be in a foul mood when he discovers his prey has escaped.''

''Take care.''

Lion nodded, then slipped down the rope as quickly and silently as rain water. When he tugged on the rope, Bryce sent the length of hemp tumbling down to him. After hiding the coil beneath a bush to await his return, Lion flitted through the inky shadows in the back garden and thence to the small postern gate in the rear wall. From the pouch at his waist, he took the duplicate key that had come in handy numerous times and thanked his father for having taught him the importance of having an escape route. It paid off now, for he walked out, locking the door behind him so the guard would suspect nothing.

The dusty road from the castle to the village below was edged with large boulders. Keeping low, Lion darted from rock to rock till he reached the bend in the path. Then he stood and trotted the rest of the way to the blacksmith's shop on the fringe of the settlement. He tapped twice on the rough side of the lean-to at the back, where the smith's assistant slept.

''Who the hell's there?'' growled Roderick Sutherland,

whose size and skill with a hammer had gotten him this job under the false name of Rod Shaw. It paid to have a man on the outside, Lion's father had often said.

"The light of your life," Lion whispered.

Roderick opened the door a crack. "Trouble?"

"Isn't there always?" Lion said cheerfully.

In five minutes, he had a swift horse and was headed away from Blantyre. He'd refused Roderick's offer of help, but stopped in the forest glade where Wes and the other Sutherlands were camped. "Sorry to disturb your rest, lads," Lion said as they rolled from their blankets and strapped on their swords. "But the Rosses are bound to need a bit of help getting away."

"'Tis a right fine night for a ride," Wes said, swinging into the saddle. "And I've the instructions Iain sent when he said we should send wee Colin to him."

With Wes in the lead, they raced across the open moor, taking a shortcut Lion hoped Alexander's scouts had not discovered. The air smelled of rain and of the tender grass trampled beneath their horses' hooves. It reminded Lion of other spring nights, other rides filled with danger and adventure.

Not that he'd done much raiding, for his father did not hold with taking what was not theirs. But Lion had often been part of the watch patrolling his clan's far-flung lands. If they did find that someone else had lifted Sutherland cattle, they'd set off on the hot trod. A wild, midnight ride to reclaim the stolen beasts or a wagonload of purloined goods. He'd learned to ride tirelessly over some of the roughest land in all Christendom, then fight with sword, dirk and his fists, if need be, at the end.

If life in the Highlands had honed and tempered him, life at the French court and university had polished those rough edges, just as his father had intended. Grateful as Lion was for the lessons learned abroad, he still bitterly resented those lost years with Rowena. Why would she not give them another chance at happiness?

"There is it," Wes muttered, drawing rein.

Lion shook off his dark thoughts and halted to scan the stern tower hugging the lee of the mountain. The windows were dark, the Rosses sound asleep. Lion's band got within a few hundred yards of the keep before they were challenged.

"Who are ye?" demanded a sleepy voice.

Lion wheeled in the direction of a pile of rocks, over which peered a pale, wary face. "Friends," Lion said curtly. "And you can be glad of it, else you and all within yon tower would be dead now."

"So ye say." The man whistled sharply.

A cry rang out from the left, gravel crunched and another face bobbed up from behind a rock. Ahead, two men dashed onto the path, long spears extended before them.

Fools. Young fools to think they could challenge a troop of thirty men with a few pikes. "I need to speak with Iain Ross right away."

"The laird's asleep in his bed," called one of the spearmen, advancing down the road with his weapon raised.

"Best rouse him quick," Lion called. "The Wolf is coming here...within a few hours. We have come to help—"

"How do we know this is not some trick to get inside?"

Lion gritted his teeth. "We are wasting valuable time. Just send someone to tell Iain that Lion Sutherland is here."

"The same who sent young Colin to us? Why did you not say so in the first place?" The guard shouted orders over his shoulder, then stepped from the path. "Come within, my lord."

By the time they reached the outer wall, lights shone in the tower's second-story windows and torches rimmed the barmkin. A fair-headed man hurried down the wooden steps. "Lion! What's this my cousin says about the Wolf coming here?"

"I fear 'tis true."

The wind sent the torches writhing. In the flickering light, his face was ashen, dazed. "He knows Colin's here?"

"Nay. He's decided to punish Clan Ross, and yours is the closest holding. He means to wipe you out...kill you all and burn the tower."

"Jesu... I'll send word to Fergus."

"Your uncle could not get here quickly enough."

"But he'll not let this attack go unpunished. Fergus will avenge us."

"If he does, Fergie will find himself outlawed." Lion's jaw tightened with frustration. "Alexander is the king's brother. The viceroy of the Highlands."

"Butcher'd be a more apt title."

"Aye, but the fact remains that to raise arms against the king's appointed ruler is an act of treason. The Wolf is counting on you to fight him and give him an excuse to declare the folk of Clan Ross traitors. He'll kill you all as an example to others who refuse to join him."

"We'll not surrender. We'll not—"

"What I'm asking you to do is hard, I know. I want you to get away into the hills and fire the tower. My men and I will help get your people and your livestock to safety."

Iain looked up at the square stone building that likely contained all he held dear in the world. They'd take what they could, but there wasn't time to pack more than the essentials. Filling the bottom of the tower with peat and setting it ablaze would make it impossible for the Wolf's men to get inside, however. With any luck, the raiders would tire of sitting about watching the peat smolder and return to Blantyre. The Rosses could wait a week or so for the fire to burn out completely, then come back, hoe out the ashes and see what they could reclaim.

"Better to fire it than lose lives, I suppose," Iain said. "That's twice ye've helped us, and I do thank you for it."

"Thank me when we've got you and yours safely away."

"How much time do we have?"

"Three or four hours, no more." Lion looked up and saw Colin standing on the step above his uncle.

The lad's eyes were dark and haunted with more misery than one person should have to endure. In a way, Colin was a symbol of all that had happened to Scotland.

Lion was more determined than ever to bring the Wolf down.

Rowena stood in the window of her darkened room and watched the flurry of activity in the courtyard below. Wind-whipped torchlight flickered over the controlled chaos as Georas MacPherson bellowed orders to the milling men. Many of them were still struggling into their leather vests and belting on their huge claymores.

She saw Bryce and the Sutherlands grouped off to one side, armed and ready to ride, though their grim faces contrasted sharply with the avid excitement of the Mac-Phersons, Chisholms and even the Gunns. Eneas was in the thick of things, bullying men and horses into line.

Alexander strode down the side steps, mounted his waiting stallion, then held up his hands for silence. "We ride to avenge the attempt on my life." He wheeled his horse and cantered toward the lowered drawbridge.

"Death to the traitors," someone shouted. It sounded suspiciously like Eneas.

The others took up the cry with resounding fervor, their voices nearly drowned out by the swirl of the pipes. Vaulting into the saddle, the men charged out the gate after the earl.

Rowena's belly cramped with fear. There were so many of them. What if Lion didn't succeed in getting the Rosses away? What if he was captured?

She bowed her head in silent prayer, then turned toward her bed. As she did, her gaze caught a furtive movement below. Two men stood before the stables, heads bent together in a pose that fairly screamed intrigue. They broke apart suddenly, one staying behind to lurk in the shadows cast by the building, the other crossing the courtyard. He looked up as he climbed the stairs to the castle, and she recognized Clem Gunn. Which meant the other man was likely a Gunn, also. Why had they stayed behind?

To trap Lion?

What if Eneas suspected Lion's drunkenness was an act and had left his men here to follow in case Lion left?

She smiled smugly. Lion was already gone, of that Bryce had assured her when she'd cornered him just after he returned from toting Lion off to bed.

Her smile fled.

What if Clem saw Lion return?

Cat snagged the hem of Rowena's bedrobe. Absently, she bent and picked up the kitten. Rubbing her face in the soft fur, she tried to think what to do. Warn Lion, certainly, but how?

Bryce had also said that Red Will would stay to guard Lion's door. She would tell Will what she'd seen.

Rowena tucked Cat into her basket, threw a cloak on over her robe and headed for Lion's room. It was on the floor below hers, which was doubtless why he'd climbed up so easily. If she was not so afraid of heights, she'd have preferred the window route herself, for then she'd not have had to argue with the dour Kier, standing guard outside her door, over her plan to visit Lion Sutherland in the middle of the night.

"Finlay would not like it that ye're putting yerself in danger to check on a drunk."

"The place is virtually deserted, and you'll be with me." Rowena brushed past him and set out. The hallways were dark and ominously silent, and she was actually glad of Kier's company.

Red Will Sutherland and another clansmen she did not know sat before the door playing at dice by the light of a thick candle. Both stood at her approach.

"I've come to see Lord Lion," she said brightly.

Will scowled. "In the middle of the night?"

"I would make amends for our quarrel."

"He's not awake."

Will did not know that she knew what was afoot. "He will be come morn, and then he'll be in a lot of trouble." She fixed him with a hard stare. "He'll have headaches aplenty," she added. "But I've a bit of knowledge that may ease his suffering."

Will's eyes widened as her message reached him. "Oh, well…" He lifted the latch and stood aside for her to enter, slamming the door shut in Kier's face. "What has happened?"

"Eneas Gunn has left men behind. I think they are watching for Lion's return." She peered at the lumpy bed. "He is gone?"

"Aye. Through the window and out the postern gate. He has a key."

"Very foresighted."

"Lion leaves little to chance. He'll come back the same way, with none the wiser."

"Unless Eneas's men see him."

"Mmm." Will scratched at his red beard. "There'll be hell to pay when the earl returns empty-handed."

"And Alexander will be looking for someone to blame."

"How can he accuse Lion when he's been in his room all night?" Will muttered.

"So you say, but you are his man." Rowena frowned, considering. "We must make it seem that Lion is very sick. I will stay with him, of course, but Alexander might not believe me, either. So…so we must create a stir. Involve other people in this play."

Will eyed the bed. "Yon will not bear close scrutiny."

"We will not let anyone in past the doorway. We will send for things…for medicines from Felis, hot water from the kitchen. And clean bed linens, anything that will cause people to think Lion is in here, suffering." She wrinkled her nose. "Indeed, it stinks of the sickroom already."

"Lion rid his belly of most of the ale he'd drunk before he left," Will said.

"How foresighted," Rowena repeated weakly.

For the next few hours, Rowena kept the servants hopping. Maids were dragged from their beds to fetch and carry. Felis's helper brought the herb chest to Rowena, along with a recipe to calm the stomach. Every time the door was closed, Rowena uttered low, anguished moans. When Donald Shaw came to see what the fuss was about, she hinted that Lion's ale might have been tainted.

Donald scurried away to launch an investigation.

As the sun poked up over the castle walls, Rowena flopped onto the bed and closed her eyes. She was exhausted, but triumphant. There could not be a single person at Blantyre who thought Lion Sutherland had spent the night elsewhere.

The loud grinding of the portcullis being raised drew her from her bed to the window. Alexander's army clattered into the courtyard, their sullen expressions a marked contrast to the high spirits with which they'd left. They had not succeeded, then. She hugged herself.

To say that Alexander was out of sorts was to put things mildly. He leaped from his horse, backhanded the stable boy who took the reins and kicked at a curious dog that got too close.

"We will get them when they return," Georas said, but he spoke from several arm lengths away.

Alexander swore, his face purple beneath the helmet he tugged off and hurled to the stones. "Someone warned them of our coming. I want the traitor found."

Eneas, Georas and a dozen other men pressed forward, offering to search.

A slithering noise from behind her had Rowena whirling toward the rear window. A rope sailed in through the opening. The hook at the end caught on the sill, then began to twitch.

She met Lion as he swung his lean body into the room.

"Sweetheart! How nice to find you wait—"

"Never mind that. Get the rope in before someone sees it. The earl has just come, and he is in a terrible temper."

"Good." Lion grinned grimly, but did as she asked, winding the hemp into a neat coil, which he stuck between the mattress and the leather straps that supported it. "Why are you here? Not that I'm complaining, but—"

"Eneas left men to watch the stables and the keep. I think he suspects something." Briefly, she told Lion about the ruse she and his men had enacted.

"Clever lass." He pulled her into his arms and lowered his head. Before he could kiss her, a shout rumbled down the corridor outside the room.

"That sounds like Alexander." Rowena's heart lurched. "Quick, get your clothes off and get into bed."

While he unbuckled his sword belt, Rowena attacked the broach pinning his plaid to the shoulder of his tunic. The six-yard swathe of plaid slid to the floor. Lion wriggled out of the chain mail, opened the trunk and dropped it in.

"At least you do not smell of smoke," she said.

"I washed in the village before coming back here." He bent to tug off his boots.

"Hurry! Hurry!" Rowena cried. The voices in the hall were growing louder, closer. "Get naked and into bed."

Lion stood, grinning wickedly. "Ah, I've dreamed of the moment you'd say those words, lass, but I thought we'd have a bit more privacy."

"Oh, you foolish man. Are you never serious? Do you want them to catch you?" She threw back the blanket, shoved the pile of dirty clothes onto the floor. "Get in."

"See here...ye cannot go in there," Red Will cried.

"I'll go where I damned well please." It was Alexander.

Lion cursed and shucked off his long tunic, giving Rowena a heart-stopping glimpse of his lean, bronzed body an instant before he dove under the covers.

"My lord has been sick all night," Red Will protested from the other side of the door.

"Ha! I've reason to believe he's not in there and never was," Eneas shouted. "Now step aside."

"Lion," Rowena whispered. "What will we do?"

"Brazen it out. You'd best sit down beside me, lass. You look a trifle pale."

Rowena sank down on the edge of the bed, her teeth chattering, her heart galloping. She watched the door, bracing for the moment when the earl would explode into the room and denounce Lion as a spy. What if this ploy didn't work? What if they dragged him away and hanged him? Sweet Mary, how could she bear to lose him a second time?

"Easy, lass. You've done a fine job thus far. We'll get through this, you and I." He took her icy hand and kissed it gently. "Now put your hand on my aching brow and pretend you're offering a wee bit of comfort to your love." He winked at her, then called out, "Who the hell is there?"

For a moment there was silence.

"It's a trick," Eneas said. "It's one of his men."

The door flew open. Eneas stumbled across the threshold, followed by Georas and Alexander. A dozen more men bobbed behind them, craning to see what was going on.

"What is the meaning of this?" Rowena leaned forward, her arm going protectively around Lion.

Alexander frowned. "I thought you said someone saw Lion in the back garden."

"Aye." Eneas turned. "Clem? Get in here."

The man shoved his way through the mob to his master's side. "I saw him creeping about not five minutes ago."

"Really?" Lion raised one black brow and surveyed the thin-faced worm with great disdain. "Now how could that be when I'm here, mending my quarrel with Lady Rowena?"

"My lord was here all night," Red Will insisted. "Powerfully sick, he was. His lady thinks the ale was tainted."

Alexander's fierce expression eased slightly, but the wariness in his eyes remained. "No one else was taken sick."

"No one else drank as deeply as I did."

"You look well enough now," Georas growled.

Lion smiled wanly. "Thanks to my lady's good efforts."

"I am glad you are better," Alexander said tightly. He did not sound pleased.

Lion hoped it was only lingering annoyance over the failed raid and not a sign he was in disfavor. "I am sorry I missed the action. Lady Rowena tells me you rode out to punish—"

"Damn waste of time. Someone warned them. When I find out who it was…" Alexander's gaze turned fiery again, glittering with blood lust. "He'll wish he'd never been born." Turning, he shoved his way out of the room.

Eneas and Georas followed slowly, their gazes more skeptical even than Alexander's had been.

When all save the Sutherlands had clattered down the hall, Red Will sighed and leaned against the doorjamb. "Damn."

"Aye, that was close." Bryce looked pale as new snow.

"Too close." Lion forced a smile as he glanced at the circle of weary, concerned faces. Everyone, himself included, was exhausted. Time enough later for questions and answers, for plotting what to do next. Besides, it might look suspicious if he sequestered himself with his men. "Thanks for all you did this night. Now seek your beds, for you've earned your rest."

"But—" Bryce protested.

Lion shook his head. "Later, my friend," he said softly.

Bryce nodded grimly. "We'll have someone outside your door at all times. Shall I escort Lady Rowena to her chamber?"

"I fear I could not walk so far," Rowena said in a quavering voice.

Chapter Thirteen

Now that the danger was past, Rowena couldn't stop shaking.

"Easy lass." Lion drew her into his arms, her head pillowed in the curve between his neck and shoulder, only the covers and her robe separating them.

They fit perfectly. As they always had. She could have wept for that, for the rightness that filled her as she lay beside him, her senses taunted by the masculine scent of his skin and the sinewy strength of his embrace. For days she'd been tormented by the memory of this, like a madness, it haunted her night and day. Dreams were a pallid substitute for reality, for the measured beat of his heart matched to hers, for the warmth of his breath on her cheek and his hand stroking her hair.

Aye, it was madness to linger where she could not stay. She stirred reluctantly. "I—I must go."

"Nay." He tipped her head back, fingers tunneling through her hair, freed from its braid without her realizing what he'd been about. "All the colors of a Highland autumn," he murmured, sifting the silken strands. "Did you know I dream of you often, your hair tumbled across the dewy grass of our glen?"

"Lion." Her throat ached.

"Do you dream of me? Of us?" His voice was soft, tempting.

"Aye," she whispered before she could stop the word.

"What are we doing in your dream?"

The forbidden fantasies flashed through her mind—dark, erotic things. She could not tell him, but a betraying flush moved up from the V-neck of her robe to heat her face.

She expected him to chuckle or smirk. Instead, his gaze grew hooded. "Aye, it is the same for me. The need for you claws at me till I am near crazy with wanting you. Come to me, Ro, let us give each other what we both want."

"I cannot." Her voice was as weak as her resolve. "I cannot love you." She prayed for the strength to look away, but his glittering eyes held her in thrall.

"You could if you would let yourself. But I am a desperate man. I will take what I can get. You say you cannot love me, but you desire me. Let that be enough."

"What—what are you saying?"

"We are both being torn apart by this unresolved passion between us. For the time we are here, let us take what pleasure and comfort we can in each other."

Rowena hesitated, her heart thundering so against her ears that she could hardly think. A few days ago, she would have rejected what he offered. But that was before she'd realized he had not deserted her. That was before she'd learned what a fine man he'd become—strong, brave, intelligent and, most alluring of all, compassionate. That was before she'd realized how much she wanted him. He made her furious; he made her laugh; he made her think. He made her come alive.

Deep in her heart, she knew that he was her true mate, the other half of her soul. Yet he was denied to her by the pact she'd made to save their son. In a few days, she would leave Blantyre and never see Lion again. The future stretched out before her, bleak and dismal as a Highland winter.

"There can be only this short time together," she whispered. "Eventually I must return to Hillbrae."

Lion saw the acceptance in her eyes, and a nervousness that tempered his impatience. "Only this." With one finger, he traced the shell of her ear, then the curve of her throat, noting the way her breathing quickened. Aye, she wanted him, but she was skittish as a virgin. Nay, more so, for there had been no shyness about her that first time she'd come to him. Reining in his own passions, he set himself to winning her trust. And then her love. Aye, he'd have that too, but it would be freely given.

Anticipation shimmered through Rowena, heightened by the slow progress of his callused fingertip across her cool skin, warming her. His finger brushed over the hollow at the base of her neck, traveled down to flirt with the laces of her robe.

"Shall I undo them?" he murmured.

Rowena's nipples peaked against the thin linen of the shift that was all she wore under the robe. "Aye."

He took his time, feeling her heart pound as he loosened first the tie at her throat, then the next one and the next, till he reached the one that pulled the material taut across her breasts. It excited him unbearably to see the hard points beneath the blue wool. He wanted to rip away the fabric, to gorge himself on the feel and taste of her. Instead, he slipped one finger between the laces and stroked the swell of her breast through her shift. Just that and nothing more.

Rowena gasped as the caress rippled across her skin. Her body heated and tensed, waiting for his next move, the excitement nearly unbearable. He murmured her name, brushing featherlight kisses on her forehead, each eyelid, her cheeks, while her lips parted, hungering. He nipped at the bottom one, then soothed with the tip of his tongue, withdrawing before she could capture it. She whimpered in frustration.

"What is it?" he whispered. His eyes were dark, glittering with sensual promise.

Touch me. Take me. End this torment. But she felt shy and unsure of herself, out of touch with the emotions he'd once roused in her. "Kiss me."

He did, with a thoroughness that left her breathless when his mouth slipped away to tease her ear. "Shall I touch you?"

"Aye."

"Where?"

"Anywhere. Everywhere."

"Here?" His large palm hovered over her breast, so she could feel the heat but not the soothing weight she craved.

"Aye." She put her own hand atop his, pressing it down. Obediently, his fingers flexed, molding her soft flesh, shaping it. Pleasure sliced through her, a fiery ache that spiraled down and coiled tightly in her belly. The raw rush of sensation shocked her. She'd forgotten how potent the loving could be.

"You quiver like a maid," he said, his voice low and husky. "Has it been some time for you, lass?"

"Aye." She managed to smile at the irony of it. Six years and more was, after all, some time.

"I'm glad." His grip tightened fractionally, possessively. "It killed me to think of you with him."

"Then don't." Because she couldn't bear thinking of what those years might have been like if not for some vengeful Munros, she twined her arms around Lion's neck and drew his mouth to hers, groaning when he deepened the kiss. The measured strokes of his tongue, the clever sweep of his hands took away the sting of the past, the bleakness of the future. There was only this dark magic that she dared not call love.

"Come to me," he whispered against her mouth.

She nodded, so weak with longing she could not speak.

"Lie with me, without hesitation or regret."

"Without regret," Rowena echoed, for how could she regret the memories that must last her the rest of her life? "But afterward...when it is done..."

It will never be done.

"...You must let me go."

Lion saw the fear in her eyes and knew he had not won. Not yet, but he would. For her sake, even more than his own. He'd tasted the desperation in her kisses, felt the vulnerability in the tremors that shook her at his touch. Padruig Gunn might have given her a son, but he'd not nurtured her loving spirit. It was dying, as a plant did without sun and water.

Lion intended to restore her with the power of his love. He kissed her again, gently, easing the robe from her shoulders as he did, then divesting her of the thin shift.

Rowena stiffened as the cool air rushed over her heated skin, but instantly he chased it away with the sweeping caress of his large, warm hands.

"Beautiful...you are so beautiful, clothed in nothing save the morning light." He traced deliciously over her arms, down her ribs to the swell of her hip, then up to cup her breasts, weighing them in his callused palms.

"You wax poetical, sir." The nervous words ended in a sharply indrawn breath as he teased her nipples with thumb and forefinger. Pleasure shuddered through her, driving the air from her lungs. She lifted her back off the bed, pressing further into his caress.

"Ah, Ro. How I've dreamed of this, of touching your soft skin and watching your eyes haze with passion." He punctuated each word with a stinging nip, on her neck, her shoulder and lower. "Of listening to your needy cries and tasting your sweetness," he murmured, laving the swell of her breast, coming nearer and nearer to the crest.

She waited, nerves screaming in anticipation of what would come next. His tongue touched her nipple, sending a shock wave cascading through her, drawing a ragged moan from her.

"Do you still like that?" he asked in a heated whisper.

"Aye. Oh, aye."

He swirled his tongue over her once more, then drew the

sensitive peak into his mouth, sipping erotically. Each tug
was like a little lick of lightning. Whimpering, she threaded
her fingers into his thick hair and held on to anchor her
spinning world. "Nay. Don't leave," she said when he
lifted his head.

"I won't. Never again." Lion took the other nipple so
insistently offered up, sucking more greedily as passion
clawed at his tightly held control. She writhed against him,
the fire he'd so carefully tended burning hotter and hotter.
He could end the torment now and bury himself in her
sweetness, but he wanted the moment to last. He wanted
to take her to such heights that she'd not be able to look
at him without remembering how it had been between
them.

Because he knew, that, despite her assurances, a part of
her would regret this. When passion cooled and reason prevailed, her mind would turn to duty and the son who stood
between them. Lion wanted to convince her that they belonged together, too.

So he kept the blanket between them to preserve his sanity and feasted on her breasts with a delicacy that made her
cling and cry out his name. His fingers slid past the dip of
her narrow waist to the enticing swell of her hips. He
stroked her thighs and her belly, glorying in the way her
slender body tensed and quivered in anticipation.

Rowena moaned softly as his fingers at last touched the
nest of curls at the juncture of her thighs. Deftly, they found
the tiny nub that was the focus of her need. One stroke,
one lovely, rapturous stroke and the coil began to splinter.
She sobbed his name as her body went wild and her mind
hazed, clutched him with desperate fingers as she soared
out of herself. As she drifted down from that dizzy height,
her first thought was that she did not want it to be over.

"It is not...not by a long sight," Lion growled, making
her aware she'd spoken the plea aloud. He whipped the
woolen blanket from between them and drew her against
his body. It was like standing too close to a smith's forge.

Desire speared through her, sparked by the feel of his smooth chest crushing her breasts and his arousal filling the empty cradle between her thighs. "Nay, it is not over."

But it would be, one day soon. Fear mixed with passion, agony with the joy of their reunion. Blinking back bitter tears, she framed his dear face with her hands and kissed him greedily, desperately.

Her urgency fed his hunger, which leaped along his nerves like sharp talons, clawing at his control. His hands slipped down her back, molding her to him, close as two people can be, and still it wasn't enough. Wrenching his lips from hers, he sought the haven of her breast, pleasuring her till she arched off the bed. Her legs thrashed and tangled with his; her nails dug into his shoulders, urging him on.

"Lion," she whispered, her voice so hoarse and urgent she did not recognize it. "Please, I can stand no more."

He lifted his head from her breast, his features taut with suppressed passion, his eyes so dark they were nearly black. "Do you want me as much as I want you?"

"Aye. I do." She'd hoped, prayed the need for him would pass, but it was greater than ever, greater even than her self-control. "Please, I'm so empty without you." Her thighs parted instinctively to offer him sanctuary, and a small sigh escaped her as he accepted the invitation. The weight of him, the scent of his skin and the rasp of his muscular legs moving between smooth ones were so achingly familiar that her throat tightened.

"Rowena. Look at me, love." He hovered over her, sparing her his weight. The sun chose that moment to spill into the room, gilding his fierce features so that he resembled the Vikings from whom he'd sprung—proud, powerful warrior princes. "I want to see your face when we become one," he said softly. One arm slid under her bottom, lifting her. "I want you to look deep into my eyes." They shimmered, more brilliant and searing than the sunlight. "I want you to remember this moment forever."

"Forever," she whispered.

"Forever." Slowly, so slowly and tenderly it was almost a torment, he began to fill her.

Rowena whimpered his name, lifting her hips as her body stretched to accommodate his size. It felt good, so good she could not suppress the small moans that escaped her lips. She wanted to close her eyes, to savor the moment, but his own commanded hers in a joining that was almost deeper than their physical one.

"Aye, just so was it meant to be," Lion whispered. She was hot and tight, a small silken glove entrapping him, drawing him deeper and deeper till it seemed he'd found the core of her. Giving and taking, they moved together in a rite as old as time, a rhythm of life and renewal. Each thrust took them higher, made the fire burn brighter. They rode to the crest together, their cries of completion filling the sun-drenched chamber.

"It was him I saw," Clem Gunn insisted.

Eneas swore and slammed his fist against the sill of the window in Blantyre's great hall. "If only we could prove it! But Alexander will hear no word spoken against his favorite."

"That favor is a slippery thing these days." Georas turned his crafty eyes across the hall.

There the earl slumped in his great chair, staring broodily into a cheerless fire. He'd been there all day, refusing rest or food or drink. Lady Glenda hovered at his elbow, her expression strained, a bruise marring her left cheek. Alexander had backhanded her for asking how the raid had gone and then again when she'd tried to offer solace.

"The lady may soon find herself out on her arse, no matter that she is chatelaine of this castle. And if that can happen, then Lion Sutherland's star may wane, too."

"How?" Eneas demanded. "Alexander would not let us question the bastard. He comes and goes as he pleases, does not lift a weapon to aid the cause and beds my brother's widow with poor Padruig scarce cold in his grave.''

''Not a very fine example for her young son and the next chief of your clan, is it?''

''Bah, I do not care if the whole army has access to her bed. Oh, I see.'' Eneas's eyes narrowed. ''I might use that to convince Alexander to name me the lad's guardian.'' But that plum no longer seemed as juicy, not when he wanted his pick from a larger, more fruitful tree.

''Then you could call up Clan Gunn to fight with us.''

''Aye, I could.'' Eneas rubbed his gritty eyes. He had not sought his bed, either, staying near in case the earl needed him. ''But even if Alexander declared me chief, many of the Gunns would stay at home, for they are loyal to Finlay.''

''Then they would suffer the Wolf's wrath.''

Eneas's eyes widened. ''Shh, he may hear you, and you know how he hates that byname.''

''Well earned though it is.'' Georas smiled thinly. ''The more fearful he becomes that his plan will not succeed, the more he resembles a wolf. A desperate wolf. And they are the most dangerous. The most likely to turn on their own kind.'' His smile turned evil. ''Do you know that he has twice asked Lion to raise Clan Sutherland to fight with us? Lion has managed to avoid that by clever side steps. He claims he can vouch only for the clansmen of Glenshee, his holding, as the rest of the Sutherlands are under his father's control. He hints that he may bring his sire around to Alexander's side, but that has not happened. I say the time is right to force Lion to make good on his promises.''

Eneas grinned. ''And if he cannot…''

''Or will not—'' Georas lifted a scarred brow ''—we will have him where we want him.''

''Swinging from a gibbet.''

''Exactly. Are you with me?''

''Aye,'' Eneas answered. *So long as it suits me.*

Georas nodded, left the window and crossed to Alexander with a deliberate stride. "Your Grace?" he said softly. "I think the time has come to act."

"Act?" Alexander's head came up. His blurry eyes fought to focus on Georas's face. "On what? It'll be days before the Rosses return to the tower. We've men there watching, but—"

"Iain Ross is only the top of the barrel," Georas said. "The rot goes deep, I think, for someone within your ranks did warn them and betray you." He looked over his shoulder at the clan chiefs idling in the hall. "There are men here who have broken bread with you, drunk your wine, yet not committed themselves to your cause."

"You are right." Alexander straightened, his own gaze flicking from face to face. It narrowed as it lit on Robbie MacNab. "Georas is right," he continued more loudly. "The time of decision is upon us. Tomorrow, each of you will swear fealty to me as viceroy of the Highlands. You will send word to your clansmen and tenants, demanding they come to serve in my army."

Eneas was the first to step forward. "A messenger will leave for Hillbrae today, Your Grace."

One by one, the others added their agreement. Some, like the MacPhersons and Chisholms, did so quickly. The Keiths were slower to respond. The Sutherlands said nothing at all, and Robbie MacNab looked shocked.

Eneas studied each man, wondering who had betrayed their raid on the Rosses. If he could uncover the culprit, he'd sit that much closer to the earl's right hand.

With a sigh of supreme contentment, Lion rolled onto his side, taking his weight from her, but keeping Rowena in the curve of his body.

So sated she was boneless, Rowena lay there, dimly aware he'd twitched the blanket over their cooling bodies. How often had they lain like this, savoring the sweet aftermath of their loving, still connected in body and in spirit.

Nay, it could not go on.

She tried to sit up; he anchored her in place.

"No regrets," he said, voice hazy with lingering passion.

"I do not regret what we did. Only that—that you may get the wrong impression."

"You made it clear you think we have no future."

"Because we have none."

"So you've said." Why could she not see she could be mother to the chief of one clan and wife to the chief of another? Lion thought angrily. "But we are very good together."

"Aye," she said in a small voice. Because she couldn't help herself, she trailed her fingers over his strong chest. He was magnificent, her lion, his tawny hide stretched taut over finely honed muscles. Her body still hummed with pleasure, yet she wanted him again. "The fire always burned fiercely between us."

"Fire be damned." He grabbed her hand and held it to the thunder of his heart. "Do you think that is all this is?" he growled. "Passion? Sex? Nay, I have tasted of that fruit, and know that what we give each other is finer, sweeter, purer. A pearl without price."

His words brought tears to her eyes. "Please, I'd not spoil the moment with arguing."

Lion spat out a low, frustrated oath. Damn her stubbornness. He wanted to shout and rail, but that would only drive her further into her shell.

"Tell me about your son," Lion said at last.

She leaped like a scalded cat. "I…there is little to tell. He…he is a lad like any other."

"Nay, he is special, for he is yours." And Padruig's, but Lion had to get over that, look beyond it. "I would apologize, for I am guilty of a grave sin where he is concerned."

"You?" she said faintly.

"Aye." He drew in a breath, held it, then released it with a sigh. "It pains me to admit this, but I am jealous of

him and let that taint my actions. Small wonder you refuse
to think of wedding me when I have ignored your son.''

"Wed you? But I thought you understood—"

"You are naturally wary," Lion continued, holding her
stiff body against his, trying to soften it. "Clod-wit that I
am, I thought only of myself. I was too overwhelmed with
the joy of seeing you again and never realized that by not
speaking of the lad, I made you think I would not be a
good father to him.''

"Father? You? But—"

"Second father," Lion amended, warming to the subject.
He felt better already, just having it out in the open. "I
have little experience at the task, but I would pattern my
behavior after my own sire." He looked down to find her
regarding him with openmouthed shock. Well, it was pref-
erable to the stubbornness. "You may not know this," he
added, toying with the fingers resting on his chest, "but
my eldest sister, Gillie, is not really a blood relative." He
went on to unravel for Rowena the tangled web of his
mother's disastrous first marriage and his parents's tempes-
tuous courtship after she was widowed.

When Elspeth Carmichael had initially turned down Lucais Sutherland's marriage proposal, Lucais had taken a
mistress, a woman who resembled the one he couldn't have.
"Poor Jean was raped by Raebert Munro, Elspeth's husband. Gillie was the result of that assault, and because he
felt responsible for Jean, my father claimed that Gillie was
his. To this day, few people know the truth, for my parents
raised her as a Sutherland. So you see, with them as my
model, I know I can be as good a father to your Paddy as
Papa was to—"

Rowena's composure shattered. Burying her face in his
chest, she let the bitter, hopeless tears flow.

"Ach, Ro, there's no need to weep." He patted her
shoulder awkwardly. With his other hand, he soothed the
line of her spine as misery shuddered through her.

His gentleness and compassion made Rowena cry all the

harder, but eventually the well ran dry, and the sobs trickled off to a few wet snuffles. Wiping her face on the sheet, she looked up into his dear, dear face. "I—I am certain you w-would make a fine father, but…" *Sweet Mary, give me the strength to get through this.* "But Paddy and I are tied to Clan Gunn. I swore an oath, on Paddy's soul, that even if something should happen to Padruig, I would live out my life at Hillbrae, and Paddy would be trained to take his place as the next chief."

Lion's face went stiff, a pale mask of anguish from which his eyes stared, flat and lifeless as yellow stone. "Why…why would he require such an oath?"

"Because he was so much older than I, and he feared that if he died defending us before Paddy was of age, I might wed another and take my son away."

"Why would you agree to such a thing?"

To save our son, to give him a name and a far, far better heritage than he'd have had as the bastard son of a penniless woman from a poor clan. "I did not think it would matter. I thought I would be content to stay at Hillbrae."

A spark kindled in his eyes. "And now you do not?"

She realized her mistake instantly and tried to retrench. "It is a moot point." She sprang up, reaching for her robe, needing to put distance between them before she caved in again.

He grabbed hold of her shoulders, forcing her gaze to meet his. "We can find a way."

"Oh, would you give up Glenshee and *your* heritage to live with us at Hillbrae?" she asked, hotly.

"I do not know." He released her, dragging both hands through his tangled mane. "Damn, Ro, I—"

A fist thudded on the door.

"Lion! Lion, it is Bryce!"

"Aye. Coming." Lion leaped from the bed. "There must be trouble," he said to Rowena as he headed for the door, wrapping his plaid about his hips as he went.

Rowena had barely gotten her robe tugged around her

when he opened the door. Outside stood a ring of anxious men—Sutherlands and two of her guards.

Kier's expression darkened, and she could almost read his censure as his eyes moved from her disordered hair to her rumpled robe and the tangled sheets. The glare he directed at Lion was lethal.

Drat, another confrontation, Rowena thought.

Lion swore ripely and shut the door on their rapt audience. "Bloody hell," he muttered as he stomped across the room. "The world has gone mad. Nay, *he* has gone mad."

"Who?"

"Alexander." Lion bent to rummage in his clothes chest. "He wants us to swear an oath of fealty to him—as viceroy."

"That is his title," Rowena said.

"By the king's proclamation. But if we are forced to swear to Alexander, we acknowledge his authority over us. Thus far, I'd managed to convince him he was not strong enough to ask that of the chiefs. I had hoped I'd have proof enough to thwart him before he pressed the issue. I see Georas's hand in this." Lion tugged out a fresh shirt. "That is only half of it. We're to call up our clansmen to fight." He wheeled on her. "Bryce says Eneas will ride out to summon the Gunns."

Rowena gasped.

"Will they come, do you think?"

"Some will," she said past the lump in her throat. "But not Finlay. He'll refuse." She went to Lion, needing his strength, his advice. "What will happen? Will Alexander attack Hillbrae?"

"I do not know. He is desperate," Lion replied, taking her in his arms.

"What of Paddy...and Jennie and Finlay and—and Father Cerdic? Oh, I must go to them."

His embrace tightened. "It is too dangerous. Alexander is having us watched. I'll send Wes and the other lads, for no one knows of them. They'll get your kin to safety."

Chapter Fourteen

"What the hell are we going to do?" Robbie MacNab cried.

"Keep your voice down, for one thing," Lion replied. They stood on verge of the grassy field outside the castle walls, ostensibly watching the MacNabs and Sutherlands at sword practice. The wooden bleachers and other evidence of the harmless games Lion had hoped would keep the earl's mind occupied had been torn down. In their place, groups of men charged about, filling the air with hoarse shouts and the clash of arms as they readied themselves for battle.

Robbie braced his hip on a bale of straw used for spear practice and leaned closer. "My da will think I've turned traitor when he receives the message the Wolf forced me to send. With the castle priest writing out the words, there was no way I could explain your plan."

Lion nodded grimly. He'd sent word to his father, too, telling him of recent developments and his failure to get the papers. "All is not lost yet. It will take several weeks for men to answer the earl's summons. And longer still for him to train them and plan a march on his first victims."

"Mmm." Robbie drew the dirk from his belt and pretended to show it to Lion. "Who will that be?"

"The Rosses, mayhap." Lion toyed with the knife, letting the sunlight play over the jeweled handle. "I've sent a man to your father, telling him what we are about and begging him to bide his time, neither refusing nor accepting the summons. Another rode to warn Fergus Ross to stay quietly at home."

"And what of us? Are we to stay here and do nothing while the Wolf grows stronger and stronger?"

"Sometimes the safest offense is none at all," Lion said. He knew where the documents were, and he'd soon take steps to get them. "Meanwhile, we will stealthily amass our own forces. If worst comes to worst, and The Wolf strikes, we will have the means to either get the victims away or protect them."

"You'll fight him, then? What of the risks?"

"When all is said and done, I'd rather be branded a traitor and put to the horn than stand by doing nothing while innocent people are slaughtered."

"Amen to that," Robbie said tightly. He sidestepped as a pair of MacPhersons brushed by, swords clashing. "Whatever you plan, count me and my lads in on the fight."

"I appreciate that," Lion said absently, staring across the way to Alexander, who sat atop his black warhorse, watching them. "But I think it best we not be seen often in each other's company. He's suspicious of me and not at all sure of you."

Robbie nodded. "'Tis time I joined my men, anyway, for I see yours are giving them a drubbing." He inclined his head politely and turned to walk away.

"Your dirk." Lion took two quick strides toward him. Behind him, he heard a hiss and a thunk.

"Jesu," Robbie exclaimed.

Lion turned and saw an arrow sticking out of the straw, chest high, in the place he'd just vacated. "Damn." He whirled, drawing his blade and crouching low.

"Someone tried to kill you." Robbie was beside him, his own sword out.

"Aye." Lion's narrowed gaze scanned the crowded field, stopped to account for the Gunns at the far side.

Eneas was readying his men for the ride to Hillbrae. Clem stood beside him. Dunmore watched from the fringe of the group, for he would not be going. Kier and Harry were likely with Rowena. None of the Gunns was carrying a bow, nor even looking in Lion's direction. But it would have taken only seconds to shoot the arrow, then drop the weapon in the grass.

Bryce rushed up, Red Will and a dozen Sutherlands behind him. "What happened?"

"Your lord was nearly killed." Robbie straightened and pointed to the arrow buried in the straw. "It could have been an accident, I suppose, what with all this confusion."

"Nay," Bryce said, glaring at the mass of men. "'Tis the third time someone has attacked him. I told you you should not have come out here where we cannot protect you."

Lion snorted. "'Twas likely as Robbie said, an accident."

Heckie pulled out the arrow and studied the shaft. "'Tis one of our own, by God."

"Damn," Lion said softly.

Bryce growled a curse. "Someone planned this beforehand, to shift blame from themselves."

"Eneas is more clever than I had supposed," Lion said.

"Is he that opposed to you wedding his brother's widow?" Robbie asked.

"He has other reasons to wish me ill, as well, but I do not have sufficient proof to accuse him openly."

"Lion, a word with you." Alexander had ridden across the field on horseback and sat glaring down at him.

"I am at your disposal."

Alexander sniffed, then swung down from the saddle and handed the reins to Bryce. "Walk apart with me."

Nerves tingling with apprehension, Lion matched his

stride to the earl's impatient one. It ate up the distance to the rim of the plateau on which Blantyre had been built.

Stopping, the earl turned on Lion. "Did you warn Iain Ross that we were coming for him?" he asked.

Only years of honing his self-control kept Lion's features impassive as he replied, "How could I, Your Grace, when I was here the entire night, abed and sick unto death."

"Your men, then?"

"Were with you, or so they did tell me."

"Aye." Alexander turned his stern gaze on the rugged land below, a wild sweep of rocks and bracken, bounded by a thin line of green where trees grew along the burn. "There are those who think you are not truly committed to my cause."

"Georas and I have ever been at odds," Lion replied.

"Mmm. When you came to Blantyre, you pledged your Sutherlands to this mission. Yet you've thus far not brought more than the thirty in your personal guard. I'd have you make good on that vow."

Lion's blood froze. "I promised my men and I would ride with you, but my father's—"

"I want them!" Alexander roared. He turned on Lion, face purple to the roots of his hair. "I must have them. If the Sutherlands fight under my banner, so will lesser men. I will have what you promised me," he thundered.

Lion held himself very still, though part of him wanted to flee from the rage glittering in the earl's eyes. Wild eyes. Mad eyes. "I have written to my father asking—"

"Ask, be damned. Am I not viceroy of the Highlands? Do men not owe me their allegiance?" Spittle flew from his lips, and his fists pounded the air. "By God, I will have my due."

"I will do everything in my power to see you get what is coming to you," Lion muttered. "But I cannot force my father—"

"If your life hung in the balance, would your sire send me the men I want?" Alexander snarled.

Lion's gut twisted. "Does it hang in the balance?"

Alexander scowled. "Not yet...but it may if I do not get what I want. Those who are not with me are mine enemies."

"I will remember that, Your Grace, but I hope that you do still see me as a friend and valued supporter."

"Humph." Alexander's fists unclenched, but his expression remained guarded. "We shall see. Come, it grows late and I am hungry. Return with me to my chamber, and we will speak of what words might persuade your father to join us."

Shaken, Lion followed after the earl. He'd had a narrow escape, but the danger was in no way past. Alexander would not take nay for an answer. If he did not get the men he wanted, Lion might well pay with his life...and others, as well. He had a few days at most to try and steal the Campbell papers, then he must get his men and Rowena away from Blantyre.

Seated on a stool before the hearth in Lady Glenda's room, Rowena finished the last passage of *The Green Knight* and closed the book. "'Tis a fine story, is it not?"

"Aye." Lady Glenda's smile was marred by her split lip and bruised jaw. "Thank you for reading to me. It did ease my heart and make me forget..." She brushed a hand over her puffy mouth.

Rowena slipped from the stool and knelt at the lady's feet. "Why do you stay with him when he hurts you so?"

"He—he did not mean to. It was my fault, really. I did nag at him about getting more rest when he is so busy."

"That is no excuse for him hitting you."

Lady Glenda shrugged. "It is the way of men, is it not? My da loved Mama very much, but he sometimes raised his fist to her when beset by weighty problems."

Well, her father had never once beaten his family. Rowena gritted her teeth. She'd been at this for hours, ever since noon, when Lady Glenda had not appeared to eat and Donald had admitted that she was indisposed. Indisposed, ha! Rowena had found her sobbing her heart out, her lips bloody, her eyes tragic. "Well, if this war of his is going to make him so cross, why do you not come and stay with me in Annie's room?"

"Oh, I could not leave him. He needs me to take care of the little things...his food and drink, his clothes."

"You've maids aplenty to do that. Come and stay with me."

Glenda shook her head, eyes filling with tears again. "You are dear to care for me." Extracting a linen square from her belt, she wiped her eyes. "We met only a few days ago, yet in that short time I've come to know and value you as a friend. I know you wish me well, but Alexander..." She sighed and looked down at her hands, twisting the handkerchief. "He is so handsome, so—so much the knight. I—I never thought such a man would want me, skinny and ugly as I am."

It's your castle he wants, Rowena thought, but she did not have the heart to say so. "Many a man here would be honored to court you, were you not already involved with the earl."

Glenda snorted. "You say that because you like me."

"It is true. Sir Bryce Sutherland, for one, is—"

"You are mistaken. Sir Bryce is young and handsome."

And a man who saw beneath surface plainness to Glenda's beautiful soul. "I've seen him watching you."

"And doubtless wondering—as is everyone—why one ugly as I has captured Alexander's interest."

Rowena rolled her eyes. "My lady—"

"I'd speak of it no more." Glenda rose and began to pace. When she came to the earl's strongbox, she paused. "It was kind of Lord Lion to buy a bit of my lord's jewelry for you."

"I did not need anything, but when he gets a notion in his head..." Rowena's voice trailed off as an idea struck her. If she could get inside the box, mayhap she could take the letters. "I, er, find that he was right in this, however, and do like the broach very much. Do you think the earl has another piece of the same metal and design? A ring or necklace?"

"Oh, I do not know. He has never shown me what is within, but we could ask."

"Well, I hate to bother him for such a trifle, especially when his temper is so uncertain. Mayhap we could peek inside."

"He wears the key about his neck."

"Even when he sleeps?"

"Aye, he says there are spies and thieves about."

"Too bad." Rowena bent down and peered at the lock. It was small and intricately fashioned, but if she could get the tip of her dirk into it, she might—

The door burst open and the earl strode in.

"What the hell?" he roared. Charging across the room, he grabbed Rowena by the arm and shook her. "Bitch! How dare ye try to break into my strongbox?"

"I wasn't," Rowena cried. "I—"

"Hold!" Lion stepped between them. "Release her. I am certain there is a logical explanation—"

Alexander's eyes glinted red with fury. "What excuse could she possible have for trying to open my strongbox?"

"My lord." Lady Glenda tugged on his sleeve. "She did not touch your box. I—I dropped my handkerchief, and she was but picking it up for me because my arm is sore."

Alexander glared at the rumpled linen on the floor, then at Glenda. "What were ye doing standing so near my box?"

"We were walking about to ease the stiffness in her ladyship's body," Rowena said coldly.

"Humph." Alexander said, but he had the grace to flush. "Clumsy wench. She tripped on a stool this morn."

Liar. Rowena struggled to hide her loathing. No one spoke. The air hummed with raw tension as the three of them waited to see what Alexander would do next. It was much like being caged with a mad beast, Rowena thought, her knees so weak the only thing keeping her upright was Lion's arm around her waist.

"Humph," Alexander said again. Wheeling around, he stalked to the table by the hearth and poured a cup of ale. For a moment, he stared into the cheerless fire, then he looked back at them over his shoulder. "Well, do not stand about like a dumb sheep, Glenda. Can you not see that Lion and I have business to discuss? Get you gone...and take her with you."

Lion hugged Rowena gently, and under cover of kissing her temple, whispered, "Go to your room, pack what you can in one saddle pouch and be ready to leave in an hour...two at most."

"But what of Paddy's guardianship?"

"I doubt the earl will grant you anything. Get ready, and leave Paddy's safety to me."

"All right, but—"

"What are you whispering about?" Alexander demanded, crossing to them, his expression hard and suspicious.

"A few gentle words to ease her fright," Lion said lightly, giving Rowena a final squeeze and nudging her toward the door.

"I will stay, my lord," Glenda said. "In case you need—"

"Nay!" Alexander snatched her arm and shook her so sharply her head snapped back. "You will get out and leave me alone. If I see you creeping about, I'll—I'll blacken both yer eyes." He released her so abruptly she staggered into Rowena.

"Come." Rowena wrapped an arm around the shivering lady and hustled her out of the room.

The quartet of Stewart guardsmen at their posts outside the door came to attention as they exited. Bryce and Kier also waited in the corridor. They took one look at Glenda's battered face and leaped forward.

"What has happened?" Bryce demanded. "Has that whor—"

"'Tis nothing," Rowena said quickly, fearing the earl's guards would kill Bryce on the spot. "Lady Glenda did...did trip on a stool and hit her head. I am taking her to my room."

Bryce's eyes flared with fury. "I will kill—"

"You must carry her, Sir Bryce," Rowena said in a firm voice, "for her legs are weak." Indeed, Glenda leaned so heavily on her, Rowena feared they'd both fall over.

Muttering a string of curses, Bryce lifted Lady Glenda into his arms. She lay there limply, her eyes open but unfocused. "Is she badly hurt?" he asked.

"That is what I must determine. Kier, if you will lead the way," Rowena said, fearing at any moment that the earl would burst out and kill them all. They reached her chamber in record time, but none of them relaxed till the door was shut and Lady Glenda deposited on the bed.

While Kier stood watch at the door, Bryce drew Rowena aside. "What the hell is going on?" he whispered.

"The earl had gone mad."

Bryce tensed. "Lion. I must go back for him."

"He seemed to be in that beast's good graces," Rowena whispered. "Lion bade me pack and be ready to leave Blantyre in an hour or two."

"About damned time." Bryce looked at Glenda. "Is she hurt?"

"A few bruises and a broken heart."

Bryce's features tightened. "We must take her with us when we leave this place."

"He needs me," Glenda roused herself enough to whisper.

"That filth is not—"

"Gently," Rowena said. She sat down beside Glenda and took her hand. "It might be best if you stayed away till the earl's temper cooled."

"But Blantyre is my home. Who will run the castle?"

"Donald will," Rowena said, shaken by the earl's fury and his unrepentant abuse of the lady. Next time she made him angry, he might kill Glenda. "Think of this as a wee holiday."

"Where are we going?" Glenda asked.

Rowena looked at Bryce, who shook his head. "On a glorious ride into the Highlands. Sir Bryce, why do you not leave Kier here with us and make certain my lord's men are ready to leave when he is?"

Bryce inclined his head. "Lion was right, you are indeed a wise and brave lass." He cast a final, concerned glance at Glenda before hurrying off to see to the Sutherlands.

"I cannot go," Glenda said faintly. "What will Alex think if I desert him when he is so busy?"

Rowena wanted to scream, but schooled herself to patience. "His mind is much occupied with the battles yet to be fought. Men are often unreasonable at such times and look upon even well-meaning attempts to aid them as a distraction."

"You mean he is not snappish because he tires of me, but because he is so busy."

"Exactly. Think how much more he will value your company and your help if he has been deprived of it for a few days."

"I suppose that is true," Glenda said doubtfully. "But..." She tossed her head. "I do not think I could bear to leave him."

Fool! Certain that if Glenda stayed, she'd end up dead, Rowena ground her teeth in frustration. She could hardly bash her friend on the head or truss her up like a piglet bound for market. Inspiration struck when she spotted the medicine chest Felis had loaned her when Lion was ill.

"At least let me give you something for your headache and stiff muscles," Rowena said. And what could be better than getting away from here? She rose and poked about in the chest. Selecting a packet of poppy powder, she mixed it with a bit of watered wine and helped Glenda to down the concoction.

The lady was sound asleep before Rowena had finished rinsing and drying the cup.

Sighing, she tucked the covers under her friend's chin, then set about packing her few clothes. Unwilling to leave Cat to fend for herself, she fashioned a pouch from the pillowcase. She had just set the last stitch when Lion arrived.

Rowena rushed to him. "Oh, Lion. I was so worried about you." She wrapped her arms around him and held on tight.

"And I about you." He hugged her so close she could scarcely breathe. "Are you packed?"

"Aye." She leaned back, studying his face in the candlelight. "But will he let us go?"

Lion nodded, his expression closed and hard. "He thinks I go to Kinduin to gather my father's men."

"We aren't going there?"

"Nay. We go to Glenshee. The tower is smaller, but nearly inaccessible. Once inside, we'll be safe enough till Papa and I can decide what to do next."

Rowena stepped back, shaking her head. "I cannot go with you. I must return to Hillbrae and my son."

"I've already sent Wes and the lads who were in the hills to warn them about the summons."

"But Paddy will be frightened. I must be with him."

"It's too dangerous. You'll have to trust me to do what is right for everyone."

She nodded, but she didn't like it.

Chapter Fifteen

Near nightfall of the fourth day out from Blantyre, Lion led his little cavalcade through a narrow glen, abutted on two sides by sheer cliffs.

"See, there is Glenshee." He leaned toward Rowena, pointing ahead to the summit of the mountain.

"Where? I see nothing but stone and sky."

"As you were meant to. Glenshee's twin towers are nearly invisible, blending in with the stark gray stone from which the keep was hewn many generations ago by my ancestors."

"It is wild country," Rowena said, but the words held awe, not fear as she gazed about them.

"Aye." Lion scanned her wind-pinked face, her ruffled hair and bright eyes. She'd never looked more beautiful, his Highland lady. "And I've dragged you too quickly through it, but—"

"That you did." She smiled wryly. "Truth to tell, despite the fact that Alexander's wolves may be on our trail, I've enjoyed our journey. It's been some time since I've ridden out like this, felt the sun on my face and the wind in my hair. I liked camping under the stars and dining on partridge cooked over an open fire."

"Aye, Heckie does have a way with a bird."

"Mmm. The only thing I had to complain about was the sleeping accommodations." She waggled her brows at him.

"Aye, well..." Lion felt his face heat. "I was not best pleased the Lady Glenda shared your bedroll instead of me, but it didna seem right, somehow, to—to..."

Rowena giggled. "There's always tonight."

"Aye." He glanced back at the tired men and worn mounts. "That is one reason I'm glad we've reached home and shelter."

"Will Alexander follow us such a great distance?" she asked as they began to ascend a narrow, winding trail, which appeared to be little more than an animal path.

"It depends on how angry he becomes when he realizes I am not coming back to him with a thousand Sutherlands."

"What of the papers? The ones in the strongbox?"

Lion shrugged. "To stay longer searching for them would only have endangered all our lives." He did not say that when everyone was settled at Glenshee, he planned to ride back, slip inside Blantyre and try his luck at finding them.

"How soon can we expect word from Hillbrae?"

"Tomorrow, at the earliest."

Rowena sighed and tried to relax. Wesley and his lads had skillfully extracted Colin from a fortified castle; surely they could safeguard her family.

Alerted by an outrider, the folk of Glenshee were expecting their arrival. The drawbridge was down over the deep chasm separating the keep from intruders. The portcullis was up and the far gate swung open. As they entered the inner bailey, people poured out of the keep, laughing and cheering.

"Lion! Lion!"

Grinning, Lion swung down from his stallion and went to lift Rowena from her saddle. "Gently, gently," he shouted above the din of happy voices and wailing pipes. "You will give our visitors a fright. I would bid you welcome Lady Rowena and Lady Glenda, lately of Blantyre Castle.''

Rowena smiled in response to the rousing cheer raised for her, but Glenda only glared down at the Sutherlands from atop her horse. She'd worn that scowl the whole trip.

"We should have left her at Blantyre," Lion growled.

"You'd not say that if you could have seen the earl's expression when he hit her. I fear he had murder in his eyes." Rowena sighed. "Glenda is a good person, only misguided in her blind love for the first man to show any interest in her."

"In her castle and her men, you mean."

"I know, I know, but she doesn't see that. She considers herself lucky Alexander courted a lady as plain as she is."

"She has caught Bryce's eye."

"Aye, he's been most attentive."

"For all the good it has done him," Lion muttered, watching Bryce look at Glenda with the wistful expression of the lovelorn.

"Now that we have arrived, mayhap I can cajole her back into her usual gentle temper."

"You could charm the birds from the trees, my lady." Proud of the way she'd borne up on the trail, Lion took her hand and led her up the wooden steps to the keep. The hall was ablaze with lights. A simple supper of roasted meat, oat bread and ale was served as soon as they were seated. Lion sated his hunger and thirst, then settled back, his gaze drifting from Rowena's delicate profile to the faces of his kinsmen. Contentment filled him, more satisfying than a full belly. Long ago he'd dreamed of sitting here, ruling Glenshee, with Rowena beside him.

"Are you happy here?" he leaned close to ask.

"Happy?" She looked around, lips curving up as she scanned the hall. "It is unexpectedly neat and clean for the home of a bachelor knight who's been much absent."

Lion nodded. Woolen hangings brightened the white-washed walls. The trestle tables were in excellent repair, the hearth clear of ashes and the rushes on the floors reasonably fresh. "Micheil has been an excellent castellan in my stead and Ailsa, his wife, an exemplary chatelaine. But that is not exactly what I meant when I asked the question. I wondered if you could be happy here...with me?"

Rowena's smile fled. "Lion, I thought you understood that I must return to the Gunns."

Nay, he didn't understand why she refused to speak of compromise, to try and find a way for them to be together. But now was not the time to press. "You must be tired," he said, drawing her to her feet. "Let me see you to your chamber."

"Lion." She touched his cheek, eyes dark with remorse. "I wish things could be different, but I'd not imperil my son's immortal soul by going back on that vow."

Lion nodded despite the ache in his chest. He was not giving up. He'd find a way to make it work out.

Could you be happy here?

The question haunted Rowena through the evening, while she saw Glenda settled in a fine wall chamber, and even coaxed from her a small smile.

"Aye, it is like being in an eagle's nest," Glenda said as they gazed out her window to the glen far, far below. "Still you should not have taken me away by guile."

"I feared for your safety. Though he may not have meant to hurt you, the earl is a brutal man with a hasty temper."

"I provoked him."

Rowena ground her teeth together. "It is late, and we are both tired. I bid you good sleep and will see you in the morn."

"Wait." Glenda clasped her hand. "I am sorry to seem so ungrateful. You've done what you thought right."

"Well, I suppose I'd not be too happy if I'd been dragged away from my home with only the clothes on my back."

Glenda flushed. "Sir Bryce says there are bolts of cloth

in the storerooms. I have only to choose what suits me, and Ailsa's women will stitch gowns to replace what I left behind.''

"He is most thoughtful," Rowena said carefully.

"Aye." Glenda looked wistful, then shook her head. "I am committed to Alexander. Sir Bryce is likely only being kind."

"The Sutherland men are like that," Rowena said as she moved to the door. "They are kind and honorable." The notion haunted her as she readied for bed in the room down the hall from Glenda's. Rowena had been surprised and a little hurt when Lion had indicated she'd be sleeping here.

"Is this your room?" she'd asked, looking at the small bed, with a delicately carved chest at the foot of it, and the single high-backed chair before the newly made fire.

"Nay. The master chamber is on the floor above."

"But—"

He'd kissed her quickly, lightly. "You are tired from the long journey, and I thought it might ease Lady Glenda to have you nearby. And—and I did not want you to feel constrained." With that, he'd fled the room.

Constrained? After pursuing her with the relentlessness of a charging herd, he did not wish to pressure her?

Men, Rowena thought as she climbed into her cold, lonely bed, could be obtuse at times. She did not make the mistake of thinking he'd lost interest, not after the declaration in the hall. His kindness made everything so much harder to bear. The knowledge that they could not be together churned like bitter acid, eating at her heart. Better she had never gone to Blantyre and seen him again. Better she had gone on hating him for having deserted her, than to learn he was the most wonderful of men. The only man she'd ever love.

Hot tears filled her eyes, slipping down her cheeks to wet the pillow. She loved him, yet she'd betrayed him most horribly. She'd kept from him the truth about Paddy.

How could she do anything else? If he knew he had a

son, Lion would doubtless want to claim Paddy, despite her oath to Padruig. Damn Padruig for having tied her hands with that vow. She could not doom Paddy's soul to eternal hell, even if it meant lying to Lion and giving up what she wanted most—his love.

Rowena turned her face into the damp pillow and wept for all of them, but mostly for Paddy, who would never have the joy of knowing his father's love. When the storm was spent, she lay awake, exhausted but still unable to sleep. The need to be with Lion gnawed at her till she could no longer stand the emptiness.

Rising, she threw her cloak on over her night shift, opened her door and tripped over something on the threshold.

Harry cursed and sat up, rubbing his eyes.

"Harry? What are you doing here?"

"Kier said we must not relax our vigil."

"Oh, of all the ridiculous..." She stepped over her guardsman. "I am going to Lord Lion's chamber."

Harry hurried after her. "Kier say we cannot trust the lord. He says—"

"Hush. You'll wake the whole tower." Holding her hem up with one hand, Rowena climbed the tight, circular stairway. She was not annoyed to find Harry on her heels when she reached the upper story. "Go down and sleep in the hall. I neither need nor want your protection."

Harry shrugged and did as he was bid. Feeling victorious, Rowena hurried down the short, gloomy corridor. As she neared the wooden door at the far end, she was perplexed to see someone hunched over, peering through the lock.

"Who goes there?" she demanded.

Kier jerked upright, his shoulder thudding against the door. "L-Lady Rowena. What are ye doing here?"

The door flew open. Lion stood in the aperture, wearing his shirt and a furious expression, his sword upraised. "What the hell is going on?" he growled.

"It is just us." Rowena stepped into the wedge of faint

light spilling from the room. "I, er, came to talk with you about an important matter. I am not certain why Kier is here."

Lion's gaze narrowed and shifted to Kier. "Explain."

"I do not answer to ye," Kier snarled. "I thought my lady might be with ye, and I'm charged with seeing to her safety."

Rowena frowned. Surely Kier must have known she was in her room with Harry on guard outside. Tomorrow she would speak to Kier again. "I will come to no harm here at Glenshee." She crossed the threshold to stand beside Lion. "Now, be off and seek your own bed."

"While ye warm his?" Kier snarled.

"Silence, damn you." Lion started forward.

Rowena restrained him with a gentle hand. "Kier, you do forget yourself. Go below, now."

Kier growled something under his breath, then stalked off.

"What is this all about?" Lion asked as he settled the bar over the door.

Rowena spun away and walked toward the hearth, feeling unaccountably shy suddenly. "I...I needed to speak with you."

Instantly he was beside her. "What is wrong?" His hands were warm, reassuring on her shoulders.

"Nothing. Everything." She turned toward him, sliding her arms around his neck. "I missed you most terribly."

"Ach, sweetheart." He drew her into his embrace, the hard planes of his body scorching her through the layers of cloth separating them. "And I you. I didn't want you to feel you *had* to share my bed."

"I don't. I'm here because I want to be." More sure of herself—and him—she trailed her fingers over the solid muscles of his chest, around to his back and down his spine. His bottom was lean and tight from years in the saddle. She inched the hem of his shirt up till she could stroke the warm, taut flesh.

Lion groaned and shuddered beneath her touch. Always before he'd been the instigator of their love play. Being the focus of her female aggression had him hard and aching in a single heartbeat. "Ro. Ah, Ro." He ground his teeth together, struggling against the need to bury himself in her sweetness.

"You do purr like Cat," she whispered, scoring him lightly with her nails, glorying at the heady sense of power that rippled through her as his big body trembled. "Lion. My Lion." She twisted slowly, brushing her peaking nipples over the warm wall of his chest.

"And you are my lioness...my lady." Lion lifted her off her feet and molded their bodies together. It felt so good, so right. He gloried in the way she clung to him, her mouth opening beneath his, inviting the joining that was a prelude of what was to come. Hunger nearly overwhelmed him, tearing at his restraint. He tempered it with love. Aye, he loved her, totally and without reservation. If only he could make her understand. Desperate, he set out to show her the only way he could.

Rowena shivered with excitement as he carried her the few steps to the large, curtained bed. The cool sheets did not dull the passion running hot in her veins. "Come to me," she whispered, reaching for him.

He knelt beside her, but evaded her grasp. "Easy, love. You are not ready yet."

"I am," she said, pouting.

"Patience, lass." He brushed a kiss over her mouth, her nose, her eyes, his hands tracing lazy circles on her ribs, drugging her till her eyes drifted shut.

As he drew the shift over her head, she whimpered softly, quivering in anticipation of that first sweet touch of his hands on her bare skin.

"Open your eyes, love," he whispered. "I want to watch you. I want to see passion heat them to blue smoke."

Rowena lifted her lashes, her vision filled with his face

poised above her in shadow and light, rugged features softened with emotions she feared to read. "Touch me, Lion."

"Aye." He cupped her breasts, sending fiery shivers racing across her skin. As he teased the nipples into aching
points, she gasped, arching up and pressing herself into his
hands. "You are so sensitive, so responsive, love." His
mouth closed over her flesh, drawing so tenderly on first
one breast, then the other, that she cried out his name.

"Lion." Her hands tangled in his hair, clutching at him
as the fires built inside her. The throbbing at the center of
her womanhood was almost unbearable. Her legs shifted
restlessly as she sought to ease the pressure, the empty
yearning. When at last he lifted his head, she sighed and
reached for him.

"Not yet, love. Let me pleasure you." He dropped a line
of stinging kisses along her ribs. His hands raced down her
spine, cupping her bottom and kneading gently. He dipped
his tongue into her belly button, chuckling when she
gasped. Drowning in the scent of her skin, the openness of
her response, he moved on, lower, lower....

"Lion. What are you doing?" she asked, stiffening.

"You will like this, I promise." He parted her thighs
and kissed her where she'd least expected it.

"But...oh," she breathed. The word ended in a moan of
pure bliss as he worked his magic on her. Indescribable
sensations rippled through her. The pleasure turned and
coiled, tightening as he took her higher and higher. All
restraint melted before the ravenous, gliding strokes. His
name falling like a litany from her lips, she surrendered to
the wonder of it, crying softly as she fell off the sensual
peak.

"I love you, Ro." Lion's voice was husky and low in
her ear, repeating the words over and over as he rekindled
the fire in her with greedy hands and fevered kisses.

Where moments ago she'd been sated, now she was hungry. Reaching between their slick bodies, she took his heat

and guided it to hers. "I love you," she cried as he slipped inside her, filling her, completing her.

"Oh, Ro." He clasped her close and together they raced toward that shattering ecstasy, losing themselves, finding each other. Two halves of one whole.

They made love through the night, dozing lightly, then rousing to join again. Twice Lion tried to evade her marauding fingers. "You need your sleep, love."

"Nay. I need you," she said, trying to keep the desperation from her voice, for she knew that this night might be all they would ever have. Tomorrow or the next day she must set out for Hillbrae and Paddy. "Love me."

"I do," he whispered, and her heart broke again.

When she awoke the next time, sunlight spilled into the chamber and she was alone in bed. "Lion?"

"Here." He strode to her, just pinning the end of his plaid to his shoulder.

"Where are you going?" she asked sleepily.

"Below. The men just rode in."

Sleep vanished. "Word from Hillbrae?"

"Likely, but you do not have to get up."

Rowena was already out of bed and rummaging through the things on the floor. Hastily she pulled on her shift and tied the cloak over it, then ran to peer down from the high window. "Is there any sign of wounded?"

"Not that I could tell. Why do you not stay till—"

"Nay." Rowena headed for the door. "I've been too long without news of my son as it is. I must know where he is so I may go to him and—"

Lion gripped her shoulders and dragged her against him. "Did last night mean so little that you could leave me?"

"Last night meant everything to me, but—"

"You said you loved me. Was that just passion speaking?"

Rowena stiffened. "Better for both of us if it were, for though I do love you, I cannot live with you." She slipped from his grasp, unable to bear the pain she'd put in his eyes, and struggled to lift the bar from the door.

Lion removed it, opened the door and stepped aside. "This is not over, Ro," he warned as he followed her down the hallway.

The courtyard was filled with milling men, shifting horses and barking dogs. Standing on tiptoe, Rowena attempted to find Wes so that she might ask him how things had gone. Instead, her gaze fell on someone she'd not expected to see.

"Finlay!" Rowena raced down the wooden steps and into the courtyard, pushing people from her path until she was standing beside his horse. "Finlay, what do you here?"

He looked down at her and smiled wearily, pain etched into every line of his face. "It seemed the only safe place."

"Oh, my God. What has happened?"

"Eneas brought with him such a large army that Wesley feared we could not withstand their assault, so we fled into the hills and came here."

"Paddy?" Rowena cried. "Where is—"

"Mama," replied a voice she knew well.

Spinning, she spotted her son bouncing up and down in the arms of a Sutherland trooper.

"Mama, I rided like the wind to you."

"Oh, Paddy." She was beside him in an instant, her fears not eased till he'd slid down into her arms. "Oh, Paddy, I was so worried." She hugged his sturdy body as tightly as she could and buried her face in his sweaty neck.

"Mama." He wriggled. "You're squashing me."

She eased her grip, but kept him secure in her arms. "I've missed you, lambie."

"Not a lambie," he said indignantly. "I'm a trooper."

"Oh." Was it her imagination, or had he grown in these few weeks? "Well, I—"

"So, you have him with you," Lion said from behind her.

Rowena felt the blood drain from her body. She prayed

for the earth to swallow her up. But of course, that did not happen. She slowly set Paddy on the ground and turned, trying to keep him tucked behind her. Would anyone else notice the similarity between man and child? "Aye," she said shakily, unable to meet Lion's gaze. "He's exhausted, though. And filthy." Her laugh was as hollow as her heart. "I had best get him inside." She bent to shepherd Paddy ahead of her.

He slipped under her arm and smiled up at Lion. "Hello. You didn't ride with us. Who are you?" he asked brightly.

Around them, the swirl of activity seemed suddenly muted, drowned out by the thud of her pulse as she waited for Lion to answer. When he didn't, when the silence spun out, tricky and deadly, she knew...

Sweet Mary, give me strength.

Rowena looked up, saw Lion's shocked expression, and all hope of getting through this vanished. *Please, please do not hurt him,* she silently begged as his startled eyes met hers.

Lion's jaw tightened. His eyes widened with a shock that went beyond pain, beyond words, then he looked away from her.

"He—he is Lion Sutherland," Rowena said.

"Oh." Paddy's smile dimmed. "Sir Wes did tell me of you. He says you are lord of Glenshee. I—I didn't mean to frighten the horses and make us lose time this morn," he said faintly.

"I am sure you did not." Lion's throat sounded as full as her own. "Such things happen."

"They won't when I'm bigger and can have my own pony. Then he'll know me, you ken, and he won't shy when I bounce."

"Indeed." Lion knelt down, his eyes intent on Paddy's face, as though he could scarcely believe what he was seeing. "Do you bounce a lot when you ride?"

"I fear so. Da beat me for it more than once." Paddy inched forward. "Do you have any ponies here?"

"One or two."

"Can I see them?"

Rowena could stand no more of this. "Come, Paddy. We'd best get you cleaned up, and I'm sure you are tired. And hungry." She reached for his hand, was hurt when he pulled back.

"Sir Wesley says you have the biggest sword in all the Highlands," Paddy said brightly. "May I see it?"

"Later, you can see Avenger, mayhap," Lion replied. He pulled his gaze from Paddy to her. "When you have finished settling your son, I would see you in my chamber, *madame*."

"I may be quite some time," she said faintly.

"You'd prefer now?" Gone was the gentle lover, the man who'd coaxed her into believing in him and in their love. In his place was a warrior, cool and furious.

She shook her head. "I—I will come as soon as I can."

Chapter Sixteen

"Finlay is gone, you say? Gone where?" Eneas roared, raking Hillbrae's steward with furious eyes.

Wat swallowed hard. "That I could not say. Some men rode in two days ago with a message—"

"From who?"

"I could not say, for he spoke privately with Lord Finlay."

Eneas cursed, the ball of rage inside him tightening. "Glenshee. It had to have been him." Somehow the meddling bastard must have known he was coming here to force Finlay to accept the earl's summons. Aye, Eneas had relished the thought of marching the Gunns off under his banner. Two hundred men he'd pledged to bring, but as his eyes swept the hall, he saw only a few frightened servants and those of his men he'd left here. Fifty at most. Damn, Alexander would have his head. "How many went with Finlay?"

"Well, there was Father Cerdic, of course, and Gowain and—"

"I do not want their names, you daft fool. How many?"

"A good hundred, I'd wager...and the lad, too. I told Finlay as how ye'd left strict orders the lad was to stay here, but—"

"Idiot!" Eneas backhanded the steward into the trestle

tables stacked against the wall. The crunch of bone and
cracking wood did not ease the fury in his gut. "They'll
have taken him to his whore of a mother. Where?" He
lifted Wat by the shirtfront and shook him. "Where did
they go?"

"I—do—not—know," the steward stammered, blood
running from his nose and mouth. "They—they rode
north."

"North. I have to get them back." Eneas dropped Wat
and whirled on the other servants. They huddled together
like sheep, eyes round with fear. "A generous reward to
the man who shows me the path they took."

No one moved.

"Want I should break a few heads?" Clem asked hopefully.

Eneas glared at them, his mind whirling. Rowena had
left Blantyre with Lion, but the Sutherland castle at Kinduin
lay west and south of Hillbrae. Were they trying to throw
him off the track, or had they gone someplace other than
Kinduin? Time was short; he needed answers. "Aye, start
with Wat and work your way through the lot till I know
where they went."

His son. He had a son.

The words rang over and over in Lion's head as he paced
in his chamber, waiting for Rowena.

"Do we increase the patrols?"

Lion whirled to find Bryce leaning against the closed
door. "Patrols? What patrols?" he asked.

"In case Eneas Gunn tries to follow his kinsmen here."
Bryce's eyes reflected grave concern.

"Jesu, I'd forgotten." Lion raked a hand through his
tangled hair and glanced out the window. Clouds crowded
the sky, covering the sun, which had shone so brightly this
morn. An ill omen? Nay, he did not want to think so, not
now when things were finally going his way. Rowena loved
him, and they had a son together. Still...

Sighing, he dragged his gaze back to his friend. "We'd best be on our guard. What better way for Eneas to bring me down than by proving I'm holed up here, when I should be at Kinduin raising troops for the earl's army?"

"I'll set the patrols, then," Bryce said.

"Have them range as far south as the loch. Oh, and best have the herdsmen bring the sheep in from the summer pasture. We can pen them in the lower bailey and pitch tents there to shelter the crofters, as well. At the first sign that Eneas, or anyone else, approaches, we'll strip the fields of crops and bring everyone inside."

"You think it will be that bad?" Bryce asked softly.

"A wolf crossed is a ruthless enemy. If Alexander has reason to believe I betrayed him and comes looking for revenge, he'll ravage the countryside hereabouts. We'd best be prepared to withstand a siege." Lion grinned. "It may be a shorter one if there is nothing for his men to forage."

"What of your father? Surely he'll come to our aid."

"He will want to, but Edinburgh is a long way off. It could take a week for my message to reach him, several more for him to gather troops and come to help us. And too, he must think of the rest of the clan. Besides, Glenshee is unassailable and has a deep well. We can hold out as long as the food does."

"Pray God it does not come to that." Bryce reached for the door latch, then turned back. "He is your son, is he not?"

"Aye." Lion's heart beat raggedly in his chest. "Is it that evident, do you think?"

"I suppose it would not be did I not know your family so well. His eyes are like yours, only more brown. In all else, he is your father."

Lion nodded. He'd realized it the instant he'd seen the lad. Paddy was Lucais Sutherland all over again—dark red hair, crooked smile and that beak-like nose his mother said it had taken Lucais years to grow into. "He is my son."

"What will you do about it?"

"Claim him, of course. Why?" Lion asked in surprise.

Bryce scowled. "From the look on your face when you beheld the lad, I take it the lady had not told you you had a son."

"Nay," Lion said slowly. "It could be she feared I'd not believe he was mine. And too, she had promised Padruig Gunn that Paddy would be the next chief of the clan. But of course, that will not happen now," he added hastily. A niggle of fear intruded as he recalled how adamant Rowena had been about honoring the vow Padruig had wrung from her.

"Will you wed her?"

"Aye." Surely his rights as Paddy's father would negate Rowena's oath. The church could not hold her to so unnatural a pledge, foisted on her by a tyrannical old man when she was alone, afraid and vulnerable. "Imagine how pleased Mama and Papa will be to find there is already another Sutherland to come after me." He frowned. "The lad must be declared legitimate. It is possible, I think. Father Simon at Kinduin will know what must be done about that." *And what must be done to absolve her from this damned oath.* "I will write to him tomorrow."

"It still strikes me as odd she did not tell you, especially after you convinced her you had not deserted her."

"Not so strange when you know Rowena. She was ever a secretive little thing, afraid to reveal too much of herself and chance being hurt. Things happened so quickly and have been so unsettled, what with Alexander's schemes to be thwarted and all. Doubtless she was waiting for the right moment."

"I suppose that could be."

"Should she not have him abed by now?" Lion asked, scowling at the door.

"I've heard tell it takes time to settle a bairn in a new place," Bryce said. "And they've been apart some time."

Lion understood, for he found the separation from Rowena unbearable. "I hope she does not stay away apurpose, fearing to face me in case I deny the lad.'' The instinctive need to be with her propelled him toward the door. ''I had better go and reassure her.'' He grinned. ''And I've much to learn about this fathering business.''

Lion ran lightly down the stairs to the floor below. Even the sight of Kier standing guard outside the room did not dull his good spirits. Nodding to the glowering soldier, he gently pushed the door open.

Paddy had removed his tunic and sat on the bed wearing only his hose. His mother knelt before him, pulling off a muddy boot. ''I missed you, Mama,'' he said.

''Not half as much as I missed you.'' Rowena reached up and drew him into her arms, rocking him gently.

The poignant tableau brought the sting of tears to Lion's eyes. His lady. His son.

''Hello,'' Paddy said, peering at him over her shoulder.

Rowena started and turned. ''L-Lion. I thought I would come to you later.''

''I could not wait.'' Aching to join the family group, Lion crossed the room and hunkered down beside them. ''You've a pound of mud on you, lad.'' Needing to touch, he grazed the grimy cheek, so soft, so warm. ''And you're shedding it everywhere.''

Paddy looked down at the dirt on the floor and the blanket. ''I—I did not mean to.'' He looked stricken.

''It is all right,'' Lion said. Damn, was the lad timid?

''Da says a chief must set a good example always. I should have rinsed in the stable yard as he used to. Only—only I was tired and I missed Mama.''

Far too serious for one so young, Lion thought. ''That is true, but trail dirt clings to laird and trooper alike. There's no harm done.'' He smiled and indulged himself by ruffling the lad's sweaty hair. ''And I can well understand your being anxious to see this fair lady. She's a favorite of mine, too.'' He glanced at Rowena, hurt by her wary expression.

''She is?'' Paddy looked at his mother, then back at Lion. ''Why?''

"Because I lo-"

"Laird Lion and I are old friends," Rowena said quickly.

"Very old friends." Lion brushed his fingertips over her cheek, finding it as soft as her son's. Their son's.

She batted his hand away and glared at him. "Jennie is on her way up with wash water for Paddy. I'm sure you will find the process of getting him clean lengthy and tedious. Why do I not find you later, and we can—can talk."

"We can talk whenever you like, Rowena," Lion said gently. "But I'd stay and watch Paddy's bath...I've missed so many."

"You do not have to take baths?" Paddy asked.

"Aye." Lion grinned at him. "I've a big tub in my chamber with room aplenty for a lad and a fleet of wooden ships."

"You have ships in your bath?"

"I did when I was your age. Now I'd rather have your mama."

"Lion!" Rowena exclaimed.

"Mama! Mama, what's that?" The boy pointed toward the hearth, where Cat's ruffled head peered over the top of her basket.

"It is a kitten."

Paddy wriggled down from the bed. "A kitten?" He charged toward the hearth, skidding to a halt on his knees beside the basket. "What is it doing here? Whose is it?"

"Yours, if you like," Lion said, joining him.

"Mine? Really, Mama?" Paddy was already reaching to lift the kitten out of the covers.

Rowena nodded, unable to speak past the lump in her throat. She wasn't ready for this. Might never be. "I—I thought you were going to wait for me," she said to Lion.

"I've waited long enough."

"I—I do not want to leave him alone in a strange place," Rowena said, though Paddy was so wrapped up in fondling the kitten that she doubted he knew she was there.

"I understand." Lion tucked a strand of hair behind her

ear. "But I did think you might fear I'd deny the lad was mine, so I came straight away to disabuse you of that notion." He cupped her cheek, desperate to ease the pain in her eyes. "He is the very image of my father."

"Oh." She looked like a cornered rabbit.

"All will be well, Ro," he murmured. "I will claim the lad and wed you...today if—"

"Nay, Lion, it is not possible."

"Of course it is."

"Lion, you do not understand." Nor could she explain, not while he looked at her with such wonder in his eyes. Not while her own guilt tore at her like sharp claws. "Please, just leave us and I will come when I'm done here. We can discuss it then."

"There is nothing to discuss, nothing to fear," he said with that pigheaded firmness she so detested at times. "I will take care of everything. We will be wed as soon as—"

"Nay, Lion, you must listen," she whispered frantically. The door creaked open, drawing their attention.

Jennie stepped into the room, bearing a tray of food and a furious expression. "Unhand her, you...you—"

"Jennie!" Rowena leaped up, glad of the interruption, but fearing yet another unpleasant scene. "We are guests in Lord Lion's keep. Where is the bathwater?"

Still glaring at Lion, Jennie jerked her chin over her shoulder. "The menservants are bringing it." Indeed, a trio of burly men entered, one carrying a pair of steaming buckets, the others dragging a small wooden tub. "Put it there by the fire," Jennie ordered. She set the tray on the table, then rounded on her mistress. "Are you all right?"

"Fine. I—"

"Jennie, see the kitten his lordship gave me?" Paddy held up the ball of purring fur.

"Very nice indeed. Now put it in its basket while we see about getting ye shed of all this dirt."

Paddy sighed, but did as he was told, settling the kitten

into its nest, then wriggling out of his hose while Jennie filled the tub and dismissed the servants.

Like a man in thrall, Lion watched Paddy at these mundane tasks, marveling at each gesture, each flicker of light on the features that echoed his father's. But even as he soaked up the details, he was conscious of Rowena's tension. Despite his reassurances, she was still as anxious as a doe facing a hunter.

"Much as I'd like to stay for this, mayhap we had best go and have that talk," he said softly.

She bowed her head, then nodded stiffly. "Jennie, if you could see to Paddy's bath, I'll be back to tuck him in."

Anger flared in Jennie's eyes. "As if I'd let ye go off alone with this—this despoiler of—"

"Jennie, I'm going of my own will, and I'll thank you to mind your manners."

The maid sniffed. "I will...providing ye take Kier along in case ye've need of help."

"I do not need protecting." Rowena kissed Paddy's grubby cheek, bade him behave and promised to return soon. Not that he seemed to care, his immediate attentions were focused on watching his new pet climb out of the basket.

The walk up to Lion's chamber was the longest of her life. The moment the door was shut on Kier's glowering face, Lion drew her over to the window and into his arms.

"Ach, lass, he's that bonny. You've done a fine job raising him." He hugged her tighter, his heartbeat slow and measured in counterpoint to her racing one. "I'm only sorry I wasn't there to take a part. Was it difficult?"

"Raising him?" She shook her head. "He's always been a bright bairn, loving and eager to please."

"Carrying him. Birthing him." He trembled. "Women die in childbed. I could have lost you and never known."

"I was scarcely sick a day except in the beginning. That's how old Meg knew." With his arms wrapped securely around her, she answered his questions, told him when she'd first realized their loving would bear fruit.

"Jesu, when I think of you waiting there for me. What must you have thought when I didn't come? Oh, love, if only I could have spared you that."

"It was not your fault—I know that now."

"But at the time, you must have been furious, thinking I'd run off to France." He shifted them to the bed, settling her on his lap. "Is that why you wed Padruig so quickly?"

"Nay. Well, only partly. Mostly, I wed him because he would give my child a name and a future."

"He knew you were pregnant?"

"Aye. He'd overheard old Meg and me talking. If he was the answer to my problems, I was also the answer to his. He did not want Eneas to inherit the lairdship of Clan Gunn, but he'd had no luck fathering a bairn on any of his women."

"Was he good to you?"

Rowena sighed and considered her answer. "Padruig was not a gentle or loving man, though I suppose he may have been different with his mistress."

"He was wed to you and kept another woman?"

"Aye. It chafed on my pride some, especially when Eneas or one of his cronies would rub my nose in it, but actually, I was grateful, for it meant Padruig did not seek my bed."

Lion tipped her chin up so their eyes met. "Never?" When she nodded, his eyes twinkled. "Ah, and that's a relief, for here I was eaten up by jealousy every time I thought of you in his bed." His smile dimmed. "For a time, I was even jealous that you'd borne him a son, and I fear I resented Paddy."

"I can understand that." She only hoped he'd understand the rest of what she'd done. "Lion…"

"Shh. None of that matters. We are together again, more in love than ever and the parents of a healthy lad." He fitted his mouth to hers, kissing her till the stiffness left her body and she was pliant in his arms, her hands and mouth clinging to him. Her response eased the doubts that had plagued him earlier. "I love you—" he whispered against her slick lips "—so much."

"And I love you." But when she opened her eyes, they were filled with pain, not pleasure. "But we cannot be together."

"What?"

She struggled upright. "I told you of the oath I swore—that Paddy would be the next chief of the Gunns and we would stay—"

"Paddy is my son."

"I know. I know, but..." She scrambled off his lap, unable to stay and feel the emotions quivering through him. "But I swore on holy relics—and Paddy's soul. Would you damn his soul?"

"Nay, but I would damn Padruig for forcing such a heinous bargain on you."

"I swore of my own free will." She blinked back bitter tears. "I did not think to ever see you again."

"Well, you've done more than see me, you've made me fall in love with you." He surged off the bed and grabbed her by the shoulders. "Dammit, I will not give you up. I'll not let you doom us both to a lifetime of unhappiness for some oath—"

"You must." She placed her hands on his chest. "Padruig took us in, gave Paddy a name and a future so his clan would have a decent leader when he died. Much as I want to be with you, I cannot let him down."

Lion stared at her intently, eyes burning. "I will not give you up, Ro. Not you or the lad. You are mine."

"We are not things to be owned, like a horse or a sword." Frustration fueled her anger. "I made a bargain, and however much either of us may wish it was not so, I will uphold it."

"Well, I intend to fight for you and the lad, Ro."

"Nay, you will not. However much it hurts, you will let

us go, for you are a man who believes in honor.'' She walked to the door, her knees shaking, her heart breaking.

"This is not over,'' Lion said.

She turned and faced him. "It must be.''

Damn, if he wasn't going to get drunk and stay that way till the pain passed, Lion thought, having sought refuge in his counting room with a pitcher of Glenshee's finest.

He gulped down his fifth, or mayhap it was his sixth, cup of ale. The brew that had tasted smooth as fairy nectar the night before was bitter as gall today. And he, alas, was still stone sober. Sober and miserable, his gut rolling with a deadly mix of frustration and impotent rage.

Her oath be damned! He was not giving them up.

He'd...he'd hold them prisoner here, he'd—

"Ah, here ye are,'' snapped a voice as coarse as gravel. A leathery old man glowered at him from the doorway.

"Get you gone, Finlay Gunn, I'm in no fit mood to play host to you right now.''

"This isna a social call. I've a piece of business to discuss.'' Finlay limped in, settled his bulk in the chair across the desk and eyed the puddles of spilled ale on the polished surface. "Ye've been at this quite a spell.''

"So?'' Lion said belligerently. Here, at least, was a focus for his anger. "If you've come to tell me you are leaving, I'll tell you straight out that Rowena and Paddy stay.''

Finlay's shoulders slumped. "When I heard ye were at Blantyre, I feared she'd take up with ye again.''

"What do you mean?'' The moment he spoke, Lion knew that Finlay was privy to the truth. "You know about the lad?''

Finlay nodded. "I'm the only one at Hillbrae who does, excepting for Rowena and her maid. Damn, I knew this would happen.'' He poured himself a cup of ale and downed it in two swallows. "I knew that if I didn't do something, you'd ruin everything Padruig worked so hard to build.''

Lion stared at him, mind whirling. "So you sent Kier and Dunmore to watch over Lady Rowena."

"Aye." Finlay poured more ale, sipped it slowly.

"And mayhap gave them orders to get rid of me, as well?" It fit. It fit too horribly well.

Finlay's head came up, eyes narrowing. "Never."

"Ha! The night they arrived, two men tried to shove me down the tower steps and ended up falling themselves. Next day, both your lads had stiff backs...supposedly from the journey." Lion told him about the scrap of Gunn plaid left behind by the person who tried to creep in through his bedroom window. "I cut the man, and next day Dunmore claimed to have been wounded in a fight on the training grounds."

"Coincidence."

"Shall I put them to the test?"

Finlay snorted. "Aye, ask away. We've nothing to hide. Look to Eneas if ye search for a murderous Gunn."

"I suppose," Lion muttered. "You've nothing to fear in any case," he added bitterly. "She says she'll return to Hillbrae as soon as it's safe."

"Because of the oath she swore to Padruig."

"Aye, because of the damned oath." Lion stood and began to pace. "I love her, dammit, and she loves me, but because she gave her word to your cousin, she'll throw all that away."

"We'd none of us love her quite so well if she wasn't that sort of person," Finlay said quietly.

"Small comfort that will be to me," Lion snapped.

"Mayhap when Paddy's grown..."

"Aye, if I haven't died of a broken heart by then."

Finlay stood and approached him warily. "Ye said ye'd not let them go."

Lion braced his hands on either side of the arrow slit that served as a window. Through the narrow opening he could see the rugged green hills and the sky beyond—the lands he'd one day pass on to his son. "I could no more keep her here against her will than—than she could stay against her honor.''

"I'm sorry for that," Finlay said gently. "Padruig knew that he might die before the lad was of age, and wanted to ensure the clan was in good hands." He patted Lion's shoulder. "He never meant to hurt any of ye, only to save the Gunns."

Lion nodded morosely. "I've met Eneas. If he was next in line for my title, I'd likely do as Padruig did."

"Would ye?" Finlay looked away quickly. "I doubt that, but it's too late to change anything now." He limped toward the door. "We've kin at Chilton, three days west of here. Under the circumstances, I think it might be best if we went there till the danger's past and we can return to Hillbrae."

"Nay."

"I ken it's hard, but if you keep them here a few more days, it will only make the parting that much harder."

Lion shook his head. These few days might be the only time he'd ever have with them. "It is not safe for you to travel."

As if to punctuate his statement, a horn blast sounded from the gatehouse below the keep. Seconds later, Bryce pounded into the room.

"An army's been sighted."

"Eneas?" Lion demanded.

"And Alexander, if we've read the banners rightly."

Lion groaned. He spared one moment to send a prayer winging skyward, then began to issue orders for the defense of Glenshee.

Chapter Seventeen

"**Y**ou mean Lord Lion was attacked and that is why he never met you that day?" Jennie asked in a hushed voice.

Rowena nodded and looked across the chamber to the bed where Paddy slept. "How different our lives might have been if not for that ambush."

"Do you think he would have wed you?"

"Aye," Rowena said without hesitation. "He asked me to wed him today. Not asked, demanded." She smiled faintly. "He is like that—forceful and honorable. Aye, no matter his father's grand plans for him, Lion would have wed me in an instant."

"But how can you wed him and keep your pledge to Padruig?"

"I cannot," Rowena said. But she wanted to. "Padruig upheld his part of the bargain when he wed me and named Paddy his heir. I could not let him down or imperil Paddy's soul."

Jennie sighed, reaching over to pat Rowena's tightly clasped hands. "I wish there was some way to change things."

"Well, there is not." Rowena blinked back more tears.

"I admire your strength, my lady."

"Strong, ha! 'Tis all a facade, Jennie. On the inside, I

am weak as water where Lion is concerned, which is why we must leave Glenshee as soon as we may."

"Finlay will not argue with that. He was beside himself when Eneas sent word that Lion was with you at Blantyre. He sent Kier and Dunmore there posthaste with instructions to guard you as the king might his virgin daughter."

Rowena smiled grimly. "They followed his orders with such zeal I wanted to bash their heads." But their presence could not stem the tide of true love. Her smile faded and the ache in her chest grew. If only...

"And when the Sutherlands came to warn us of Eneas's plans, well, Finlay wanted to reject their suggestion that we seek safety here. 'Twas only his fear for Paddy's life and those of the people loyal to you that convinced him otherwise."

"Poor Finlay. I—"

A clamor of voices suddenly arose, coming in through the narrow arrow slit that served as a window.

Rowena ran to look out, Jennie at her heels. The courtyard was filled with people. The gates to the outer bailey stood open, and the grassy field beyond was crowded with sheep.

"Something has happened," Rowena said, alarmed. "I am going to go down and find out what. Stay and keep Paddy here."

Dunmore stood outside her door, his left arm still bound with a thick bandage. Naturally, he insisted on accompanying her. Down the stairs they went, and through the hall, where a group of servants frantically set up trestle tables while others laid out platters of bread and cheese.

Unexpected company Rowena thought as she raced through the gloomy entryway and out into the pallid afternoon light. Pausing at the top of the stairs, she swept the courtyard with a quick glance. The place resembled a giant hive, with armed men swarming back and forth, horses anxiously pawing the ground and dogs running about in circles. The chaos was punctuated by the wail of pipes.

She immediately looked for Lion, found him sitting atop his warhorse, issuing orders in a calm, clear voice. Even from this distance, she could feel his strength, his steadiness. Whatever calamity had occurred, he was coping with it, doing what must be done to salvage the situation.

A man edged past her on the stairs. She caught at his sleeve and demanded news.

"The earl's army's been sighted coming down the glen. We're bringing everyone inside," he said before dashing off.

"The earl." Rowena raised stricken eyes to the sheltering mountains visible over the walls. Unassailable, Lion had called Glenshee, but Alexander would doubtless be ruthless in his quest to avenge himself on the lord he'd once trusted.

How much food and water did they have? How many crofters and herdsmen would seek shelter inside Glenshee. Needing answers, Rowena picked up her skirts and moved down the stairs.

"See here," Dun grumbled. "This is no place for ye."

"There must be something we can do to help." She plunged into the crowd and worked her way to Lion, growing worried when she saw the gleam of mail beneath his shirt and the battle targe strapped onto his horse. "Lion, is it so desperate?"

The sternness in his face melted when he saw her. "You should not be here," he said gently.

She drank in every nuance of his appearance—the fatigue bracketing his mouth, the worry lines fanning out from his eyes and the pain in their golden depths. The pain she had put there. "I heard that the earl comes, I thought there might be something I could do."

"There is one thing," he said, his voice harsh.

"I would if I could," she said in a raw whisper.

He glanced away, then quickly back, his expression shuttered. "It isna fair of me to tear at you over it when..." He sighed. "Ah, well, there's no sense in beating that beast, is there. Aye, there's more than enough to do—supplies to be counted, nigh on fifty people to be settled in a strange place.''

"I will see to it." She laid a hand on his thigh, felt his muscles bunch beneath the warm plaid. "Do you go to fight him?"

"Not if I can help it. We ride the hills to bring in any stray Sutherlands, gather the livestock and what crops we can. The rest we'll burn. Let us see how long Alexander and his men care to dine on thistles and roots."

"How long can we hold out?"

"It depends. Months, perhaps. More if we ration our supplies."

"Surely someone will come...."

Lion doubted it. He'd sent messages to the Rosses and the Frasers letting them know what was happening, but urging them to stay clear. And his father could not arrive in time. "The good news is—" he gave her that cocky grin "—if Alexander is busy here, he'll not be off plaguing other folk. Ah, here are the first of your charges."

She turned to see a line of dusty people walk in through the open gate—men carrying packs on their backs, women with bairns in their arms. All looked frightened and harried. "I'd best make them welcome. God keep you, Lion," she said softly.

"And you." He raised her hand and brushed a kiss across her knuckles before guiding his horse toward his waiting men.

"Ye've an odd way of keeping your vow," Finlay growled.

Rowena whirled on him, the hand Lion had kissed curled protectively. "I said I'd raise Paddy to be chief of the Gunns. I did not make any promises regarding my heart."

"So it's love, is it?" Finlay glared at the departing men.

"It was always love," she snapped. "And if Lion had not been attacked and nearly killed six years ago—" She broke off. "Never mind. I've work to do, if you will excuse me."

Rowena had expected a certain reluctance on the part of the Sutherlands to take orders from a stranger, but when she approached Ailsa, the housekeeper greeted her with a smile.

"There's a lot to do, that's sure, trying to cram so many inside Glenshee."

"The first priority is sleeping places for everyone."

"The hall is already full," Ailsa told her.

"Mmm." Rowena studied the neat outbuildings that rimmed the inner court. "What of the stables? If we put the horses in the lower bailey and swept the stables, they might hold everyone."

After a quick consultation with the head stable man, it was agreed. Everyone from Ailsa to the pot boys in the kitchen lent a hand at clearing sufficient space. Rowena finished settling the first group of refugees into their new living quarters and walked outside for a breath of air.

"Rowena, there you are." Glenda pounced on her, eyes wild with excitement. "Someone told me Alexander had come."

"His army marches down the glen."

"Oh." Glenda released her and hugged herself. "I should have known he'd follow me."

Rowena sighed and led her friend around the side of the building to a more private spot. "I do not think that is entirely why he is here."

"What other reason could there be?" Glenda peered toward the open gate, as though expecting Alexander to ride in.

"He...he wishes to punish Lion."

"Nonsense, he values Lion's opinion and respects his intelligence." All smiles, Glenda walked toward the gate.

Rowena followed. "That was before he learned that Lion would not call up his father's men. Now Lion fears Alexander will attack and kill us all for failing to join his army."

"That's ridiculous."

"Nay, it is not. Glenda, Alexander had my husband and countless others killed for refusing his summons."

"I do not believe you," Glenda said stubbornly. "You do not like Alexander and are making up lies to turn me against him."

"Oh, how can you be so blind to..."

She spoke to empty space. Glenda had picked up her skirts and was hurrying down the road that cut across the outer bailey.

"Wait!" Rowena dashed after her, tripped over a rock and turned her ankle. Down she went, hitting her knees and scuffing her hands. "Of all the clumsy..." She picked herself up, dusting off her stinging hands, and limped on in pursuit.

Glenda had a head start and two sound ankles, which soon put her far ahead. Rowena passed a horse tethered to a rope line, but knew she'd have trouble mounting without help, so moved on. Now she rued having sent her three guards to help build a temporary stockade for the horses.

"Stop her," Rowena called to the first group of people she met—a crofter, his wife and six bairns—staggering under the burden of what was likely all they owned in the world.

"Who?" the man asked dully.

"Never mind." Rowena hurried on, confident that Glenda would not be able to get past the outer gate.

The road cut sharply downward, bounded on both sides by steep rocks, like the narrow neck of a funnel. Men in Sutherland plaid stood guard atop the rocks. Small wonder Lion had praised Glenshee's defenses, for an attacking army would have to run this gauntlet if it managed to get past the main gate.

"Did you see a woman come through here?" she called.

"Aye," one of them shouted down at her.

Rowena sighed in exasperation. Obviously their orders were to keep folk from coming in, not getting out. The road made an abrupt turn, and she was at the entrance. The stout wooden gates stood open to admit another party of farmers. Beyond them, Rowena saw Glenda striding down the dusty trail.

"Of all the stupid…"

"Lady Rowena, what are you doing here?"

She looked up at the score of guards and found a familiar face. "Sim, thank heavens. We must stop Lady Glenda from leaving." She pointed toward her fleeing friend.

"I'm sorry, my lady. I was distracted and did not recognize the lady. I saw her rush by and thought it was someone going back for a dropped bundle."

"It doesn't matter. Let me borrow a horse to go after her."

"I'll get her."

Rowena debated for only an instant. Glenda was not likely to come willingly, even for her. "It might be better if I went."

Sim gave her his horse, and helped her to mount.

She caught up with Glenda at the base of the mountain, where the road verged on a stand of pine. Her quarry, however, refused to cooperate.

"I am not going back. I am going to find Alexander."

"Glenda, you are making a mistake. The earl is no longer interested in you, and you will only end up looking the fool."

Glenda's lower lip trembled. "What a cruel thing to say."

"The truth oftimes hurts."

"Alexander loves me," Glenda insisted. "He—"

"Well, well, what have we here?" Georas MacPherson's ugly face peered out at them from the brush.

Glenda gasped.

"Ambush!" Rowena cried, and tried to turn her mount.

Too late. The MacPhersons swarmed onto the trail. Georas pulled her from the saddle, covered her mouth with his filthy hand and pinned her against his burly body.

"Let her go at once," Glenda ordered.

"Hell I will."

Glenda's mouth gaped in surprise. "We've done you no harm. I insist you take me to Alexan—"

"Shut up, ye stupid bitch," Georas snarled. "I'll take ye to the earl, right enough. And I've no doubt he'll be pleased to see what valuable hostages I've brought him."

"Hostages?" Glenda repeated, turning confused eyes on Rowena. "What do you mean?"

Georas mashed Rowena closer. "Should be an easy matter of getting inside now we've got ye to bargain with."

"This is ridiculous," Glenda said. "Take me to the earl, and we will straighten out this—this misunderstanding."

Georas grinned. "Aye, that's just what we mean to do, though I doubt he'll be too pleased to see ye, now that he's got my sister waiting back at Blantyre to warm his bed."

"Nay." Glenda's eyes filled with tears. "Oh, Rowena, what have I done?"

Doomed us all.

But Rowena had no time to dwell on the matter. A shout rang down from Glenshee, warning that they'd been spotted.

"Mount and ride," Georas snarled, dragging her away.

It was nearly suppertime when Lion returned to Glenshee, triumphantly shepherding twenty crofters and a small flock of sheep. The news that awaited him was grim.

"How did such a thing happen?" he demanded of Red Will.

"Near as I can piece together, the lady Glenda thought Alexander had come for her and went out to greet him. Lady Rowena went after her and the pair of them were captured by a MacPherson scouting party."

"And where were our patrols?" Lion snarled.

Red Will sighed. "Out watching the enemy camp. We had no notion they'd come so close so quickly."

"Well, you should have." Lion turned on the ashen-faced Gunn guards. "What were you three idiots doing while your lady was being kidnapped?"

Harry hung his head and said nothing.

"She sent us to help with the horses," Kier growled.

Dun shrugged. "At least Paddy wasn't with her."

"Dunmore Gunn," Finlay gasped. "That's a callous—"

"Well, none of this would have happened if *he* hadn't seduced her and brought her here."

Lion snarled a curse and reached for the sullen Gunn, the perfect target for his simmering rage and frustration.

"Easy," Bryce admonished, coming between them, though his own expression was as grim as Lion's. "The question is, what happens now? Do you...do you think he will harm them?"

"God alone knows." Lion shook off Bryce's restraining hand and began to pace. "Damn, why could Rowena not have let the fool woman go?" But he knew the answer to that. She was not one to let a friend face danger alone.

"Lion?" Heckie trotted up, his features grooved with concern. "There's a messenger below, hailing the keep."

Lion raced out of the keep, to find his horse saddled at the foot of the steps. The short ride to the main gate seemed to take hours. He was barely aware of Bryce and the others galloping along in his dust. Nerves ajangle, he mounted the battlements and stared down at the trio of men waiting outside, their white flag fluttering in the evening breeze.

"MacPhersons under a flag of truce...how ironic," Lion muttered. "What do you want?" he shouted down to them.

Georas looked up, his brutish face split by a malicious grin. "Surrender the keep or we kill the women."

"They would not dare," Bryce whispered, and behind them, many men echoed the sentiment. "King Robert is a decent man. If Alexander murders two women in cold blood, we'd not have to find proof of his treason, the king would have his head."

"I'd not test that theory too far. Alexander is a master at twisting the truth to suit himself. He'd have Rowena and

Glenda branded witches or some such, to justify his actions. The important thing is we cannot let them die, and Alexander knows it.''

''Will you surrender?'' Bryce asked.

Lion looked around at the circle of grim faces—Bryce, Red Will, Wes and Heckie. They'd been through a lot together, he and this cadre of brave, loyal men. He looked beyond them to the worried Gunns. He thought about his son asleep in the tower and the hundreds of other innocent women and bairns huddled under his roof. If he gave in to Alexander's demands, they might all be killed. ''Nay, that I cannot do, even to save Rowena.''

Bryce scowled. ''What then?''

''I'll give the Wolf what he really wants—me.''

''Nay!'' the men shouted in unison. ''You cannot.''

''I must. For Rowena, for Glenshee...'' And for his son. Lion shivered, thinking of the lad he'd never had the chance to hold, to know, to laugh with, to watch grow into a man. One day, when Paddy was older, mayhap Rowena would tell him about his real father.

''What are we going to do?'' Glenda asked for the hundredth time since they'd ridden into the Wolf's camp.

''We are going to find a way out of here.'' Rowena stomped up and down in their prison, the Wolf's luxurious tent. Furious with herself and with Glenda, she kicked a camp stool out of her way, then turned and faced the woman huddled on a pallet of furs. ''We are going to escape from here, because if we do not, we will be the instrument of hundreds of deaths.''

''Oh, Rowena, I am so sorry.'' Glenda rose and tottered over to her. ''I—I can only say that love made me blind.''

Rowena sniffed. ''Aye, it did.''

''I misjudged him terribly. I let him use me and my clansmen.'' She shivered, squeezing her eyes shut. ''Did you see the...the bodies pinned to the tree when we rode in?''

"Aye." Rowena swallowed hard and tried not to remember the poor, mutilated remnants of what had been men.

"When I asked Georas about them, he said they were Shaws, punished by Alexander for deserting his army. To think that I—I lay with a man who would do such a thing." Glenda bowed her head, her body trembling.

Rowena sighed and enfolded Glenda in a healing embrace. "You must put it behind you."

"Aye." Glenda stepped back, her eyes blazing with righteous fury. "I want to make him pay. Not just for what he did to me and mine, but for your husband and for all the other horrible things you say he's done."

"He does not only need to pay, he needs to be stopped. If we could just... Wait." Rowena spun in a circle, scanning the chaotic disarray, the jumble of blankets and chests and soiled clothes. "Where is that strongbox of his?" she whispered.

"Taking his jewels would surely annoy him, but—"

"I don't want his precious baubles. I want his papers." Rowena pushed aside the armor piled in one corner, gingerly kicked through dirty clothes and plates caked with old food. "You'd think he'd been here months instead of two days."

"Here...here it is." Glenda pointed to the small trunk concealed under a large folding bed. "But it's locked, and he always keeps the key around his neck."

Rowena bent to examine the lock. She retrieved a food-encrusted eating knife from the ground and stuck it in the lock. "Trying to pick this is probably hopeless. Do you know if there is another key?"

"I do not think so." Glenda slumped down beside her. "What sort of papers are in here? How can they help us thwart him?"

While she worked on the lock, Rowena explained about the Wolf's treasonous scheme. "Lion says Alexander has made a pact with some of the more powerful clans, the

Campbells and MacKays among them, promising them land when he has the throne."

"Campbells?" Glenda tapped her lip gingerly. The cut had healed, but it was still puffy. "A Campbell did come calling on him late one night. I thought it odd at the time."

"Do you know what was said?" Rowena asked eagerly.

"Nay. Alexander took him into my solar, but when he returned, he did open the strongbox and put something inside."

"Ah." Rowena attacked the lock with renewed vigor. "Look around and see what you can find. Any man who is this untidy may have left something lying about."

They worked until it grew dark, then lit a brace of candles and looked some more. Glenda unearthed lists of men and supplies and even a draft of a letter to the king declaring the Rosses outlaws for attacking the viceroy, but no incriminating note from the Campbells.

Rowena's fingers grew raw from working the knife in the lock, but she could not open it. Depressed, she sank down on the bed beside her friend.

"What now?" Glenda asked glumly.

Before Rowena could reply, the tent flap was flung aside and Alexander strode in, still clad in his mail. His glittering eyes passed over Glenda and pounced on Rowena. "Ah, Georas said he'd captured you. Good. Good. It seems we will take that bastard traitor sooner than I'd hoped." He shucked off his leather gauntlets and tossed them onto a pile of dirty dishes. "You there." He snapped his fingers at Glenda. "Make yourself useful and get me out of this cursed mail."

Glenda stood at once.

Rowena grabbed hold of her hand. "You do not have to."

"But I want to." Glenda's muddy brown eyes held an odd, almost triumphant light. Smiling, she went to the earl. "If you will bend, sir." As he leaned over from the waist, she took hold of the collar of his mail shirt and tugged.

The garment of interlocked metal links slid slowly off over his head.

Like a snake shedding its skin, Rowena thought.

Glenda deftly caught it before it hit the ground. Turning, she deposited the mail on the bed beside Rowena. "We will see this cleaned for you."

Not I, Rowena was about to say, but the intensity of her friend's expression stopped her. What was Glenda about?

The earl, clad in his long saffron shirt and padded gambeson, flexed his shoulders. "Mmm. Better." Turning his back on them, he snatched up a crumpled length of Stewart plaid and kilted it around his body.

"Do you sup with us, my lord?" Glenda inquired sweetly.

"What?" Alexander's eyes narrowed. "Nay. I thought I made it plain that what was between us is ended. You and Lady Rowena will stay here the night. Come morn, you'll be exchanged for Lion Sutherland."

"Nay!" Rowena surged off the cot. "I will not let him make such a sacrifice."

"You? You have no say in the matter," the earl snapped.

Rowena started forward; Glenda barred her way. "Nay, Rowena, there is nothing you can do."

"For once the ugly ninny makes sense." He pushed the tent flap aside. "Stay within and cause no trouble. The exchange will take place whether you're the worse for a few bruises or not."

As soon as Alexander left, Rowena sank back on the cot, burying her face in her hands. "Oh, Lion. I cannot live with this. I cannot."

Glenda knelt and shook her gently. "Rowena, cease your weeping," she whispered. "I have the key."

"What? Where?"

Grinning, Glenda picked through the folds of the mail and withdrew the key, still suspended on its gold chain. "When he demanded I disarm him, I snagged this, as well."

"Oh, you are the cleverest of women."

"If I was clever, I'd not have landed us in this mess."

Rowena sighed, for it was true enough. "Come, we must open the box and take out the letters. If he notices the chain is missing and returns, it must be back with his clothes."

It took only seconds to unlock the box. Inside was a jumble of plunder, including parchment missives, some rolled, others folded and crumpled. They bore a variety of wax seals.

"The Campbells' badge is a boar's head," Rowena said.

"But how will we know what is in these messages?"

"Lion taught me to read years ago." Rowena ruffled through the correspondence, sorting out the ones bearing the boar's head. The chief of Clan Campbell wrote a fair hand; still it took awhile to find the ones she wanted—six damning messages in all. "You take three and I'll take three." They hid them in their clothing, then replaced the other things in the box and relocked it.

Glenda tucked the key and chain inside the pile of mail and collapsed in a heap on the bed. "Ah, I feel wonderful."

Rowena sat beside her, fingering the eagle broach pinned to her shoulder. "The task is only begun. We have the means to bring him down, but we must get the letters into the hands of the king and, most important of all, save Lion."

"What do you think Alexander will do to him?"

Rowena shivered, thinking of the two dead Shaws. "I think we must come up with a plan to get away before tomorrow."

Someone scratched at the tent flap.

"Who—who is it?" Rowena called out, nervously patting the paper concealed beneath her belt.

"I've brought ye food and drink," a rough voice replied. At her bidding, a man entered bearing a tray. He wore a coarse tunic, his face obscured by the cowl of his short cloak.

Rowena set the earl's chain mail on the floor and patted the end of the cot. "Please set it here."

As the man bent to follow her instructions, Rowena caught a glimpse of a familiar freckled face and shock of red hair. "Who are you?" she whispered.

"It's Robbie MacNab," he muttered. "We heard you'd been taken, and I had to make certain you were all right."

"Aye, we are." Rowena hesitated. "Tomorrow Lion will exchange himself for us."

Robbie's expression hardened. "Aye. The lads and I have racked our brains for a way to save him, but the Wolf's men outnumber us, and we are watched, for he trusts no one."

"We...we have information that will bring the earl down, but it would take time for it to reach the king, and I fear Lion will be killed the moment he is in the earl's hands."

"You've found the Campbell letters, then," Robbie murmured. "Lion said they would be our salvation."

Rowena smiled for the first time in hours. If Lion had confided in Robbie, then he must trust the MacNab. "Shall I give them to you? Can you get them to Edinburgh?"

"Nay. I think the earl is less likely to search you ladies than he is me. As to getting them away..." He frowned. "MacPhersons and Stewarts guard the perimeter of the camp. They are so numerous and so vigilant, no one can enter or leave without being challenged. The few who have been caught..."

"We saw them," Glenda said wretchedly.

"Then we must act tomorrow," Rowena said. "When Lion comes to exchange himself for us, we must turn the tables on Alexander by threatening to expose him if he does not free us all."

Robbie nodded. "It would require careful timing. Likely Lion will bring with him men to see you back to Glenshee. You and the letters must be safely in their hands before the revelation is made."

"Aye, but what of Lion? If Alexander has him, he would demand the letters for Lion's life."

"I told you it would be tricky." Robbie pursed his lips thoughtfully. "A diversion, mayhap, at the moment the exchange is being made…"

"What kind of diversion?"

"Leave that to me." Robbie stood and pulled the cowl back up. "Be alert tomorrow, ready to run when I call to you."

Arethusa Bay

"Are you ready, Lion?" Ilsa asked. His face, he would remind the hunter for Lucas's life.

"I bid you, I would be brave." Redric pressed his fist to his mouth. "I'd rather anything at the moment, the exchange is being made."

What kind of a brave—

"Leave their money where I can reach both of the coins, pick up the..." so I know what I call to you.

Chapter Eighteen

Dawn was just lighting the sky when Lion stood beside his son's bed, filled with a sense of wonder.

His son.

It awed him still that he and Rowena had together created this sunny, witty bairn with such lively eyes and avid curiosity. Paddy slept much as his mother did, on his side, with one hand tucked under his willful little chin.

This might be the last time Lion saw his son.

The pain pierced him, sharp and jagged as a lance. It sent him to his knees beside the bed. His hand trembled as he reached out to touch the lad's cheek—so soft, warm and full of life.

"Mmm." Paddy stirred, eyes opening sleepily. "Hello."

"Hello yourself." He wanted to seize the lad, to enfold him in his arms and hug him tightly. He wanted to weep and wail and gnash his teeth. But that would only frighten Paddy, so instead he ruffled the mane of tousled red hair. "I did not mean to wake you, lad." *Dieu,* he wished his father could see Paddy.

"Did you bring my mother back?"

Lion shook his head. "Not yet," he said hoarsely.

"Today, you said. You promised."

"Aye." Well Lion recalled the vow. Last evening, after making what plans he could to ensure that today's exchange was a success, he had gone to the great hall. There he'd found Paddy surrounded by wary Gunns and anxious Sutherlands.

Seemingly oblivious to the adults' tension, the lad had been playing by the hearth with his kitten. The moment he'd spotted Lion, though, he had jumped up and run to him.

"Is my mama back?" he'd asked.

"Nay." Lion sank down before him. "She—she…"

"Finlay said she and Lady Glenda had gone visiting."

Lion had looked up into the old man's gray face, grateful that the lad had been spared the terrifying truth. "Aye. That she has, so you'll just have to make do with us."

"Will you play with me?"

Lion had nodded, his throat so full he couldn't speak. For the rest of the night, he'd been entertained by his son. They'd gone out to visit Lion's warhorse and the new foal Turval had sired. Then Paddy wanted to see Lion's sword.

"I'm going to have a sword like this when I'm growed up."

"Aye, you will." Lion had vowed then that he'd leave Avenger behind for Paddy to have when he was older.

That was only part of the reason he'd come here this morn. He'd come for one last look at his son.

"What's wrong?" Paddy sat up, brow furrowing.

"Nothing." Everything.

"You look like you have the stomachache."

Nay. Lion's heart hurt so he was amazed it still beat. "I came to bid you goodbye. I am riding out to fetch your mama."

Paddy smiled. "Good, 'cause I wanna show her Turval and the foal and the mews where the hawks sleep. Can I?"

"Of course."

"You can come, too. I like you, 'cause you smile and laugh and are not always telling me to mind my manners."

"I am glad, because I like you, too." Lion hesitated. "I—I may not be back for a while."

Paddy frowned, then his eyes widened. "Are you going off to slay evildoers like the knights in Mama's stories?"

"Aye, that I am," Lion said, smiling faintly. "There are plenty of them abroad these days."

Paddy scooted onto his knees. "Can I come and help you?"

"Not this time. I need you to stay here and look after your mama." Lion stood, tears prickling against the backs of his lids. He reached out one last time and stroked his son's cheek. "Take care of her for me."

"I will," Paddy said cheerfully.

Lion paused at the door, imprinting on his mind the sight of Paddy in the bed that had been his as a child. Then he fled, taking the stairs to the ground floor at a reckless pace, the tightness in his chest unbearable.

When Lion reached the courtyard, he found Bryce waiting with fifty mounted men, veterans of the French campaigns. The light from the nearby torches flickered over their grimly determined faces, glinted off the polished armor they wore beneath their dark blue and green Sutherland plaids.

"Alexander said I was to bring only two men to act as escort for Rowena and Glenda," Lion said.

Bryce grunted. "I do not trust the earl. Red Will and the rest of the lads will stay back from the meeting site, within calling distance in case there's trouble."

Lion sighed. "All right, but take no unnecessary chances."

"I might caution you with the same."

"I will do what I must to get Rowena free." Lion mounted and wheeled toward the gates.

Though last night he'd told Bryce he wanted none to know of his mission, word had spread. The baileys, inner and outer, were filled with Sutherlands, a somber, watchful throng come to bid their lord farewell.

"Lion! Lion!" Micheil shouted, breaking the tension.

Others called out to him, raising their arms and cheering.

The wail of the pipes picked up the beat, notes swirling and crashing off the old stone walls.

Lion's heart swelled, and his spirits lifted. It could not end here. Somehow, some way, he was coming back to them. He lifted his hand in acknowledgment of their faith in him, then spurred toward the gatehouse.

As they rode out across the drawbridge, he looked back over his shoulder. The sun was just poking its head over the mountains behind the keep, bathing the stern gray fortress in soft pink light. He would survive.

When he saw Alexander's army drawn up around the clearing picked for the exchange, however, his courage faltered. The Stewart red and black and the MacPherson red and blue were everywhere, swamping the plaids of the MacNabs and Frasers. Even if his friends had been foolish enough to try and help him, they were surrounded and hopelessly outnumbered.

The circle of MacPhersons was thickest around Rowena and Glenda, whose hands were bound at the wrists. Sword drawn, Georas himself stood behind the women, clearly ready to strike at the first wrong move. Alexander, flanked by Eneas and a dozen bodyguards, was in front and to the left of the hostages.

"I do not like this," Bryce murmured. "What if Alexander does not honor the white flag we carry?"

"I am trusting you and Red Will to get the women safely away," Lion answered. At the first sign of treachery, the Sutherlands waiting on the road had orders to move in. "Best get this over with." He urged forward the Highland pony he'd chosen to ride, leaving Turval safely behind at Glenshee.

As they drew nearer, Rowena's features became more distinct. She was pale, her eyes dark and haunted, but a faint smile played over her mouth.

Lion's own lips curved in response. *Dieu,* but she was brave and beautiful, his lady. *I love you,* he said with his eyes, and her own answered back. Then Lion transferred his gaze to the man he'd come to best.

Alexander glared at him, his face shadowed by an elaborate helmet topped by golden eagle wings. "You came," he growled as Lion drew rein a short distance away.

"I could, in honor, do nothing else." He hoped to subtly remind Alexander that he, too, had an obligation to honor the flag of truce and his promise to release the women.

"Humph. Dismount and bid your men stay back."

"I will when the women are brought closer to my men."

"Do you not trust me?" Alexander snapped.

Lion smiled thinly. "As much as you do me."

Alexander grunted. With a wave of his gloved hand, he motioned Georas to bring Rowena and Glenda a step nearer.

"I fear a trap," Bryce whispered.

"Aye." Casual as a man watching a feast-day play, Lion glanced around. His gut tightened as he marked the sly look Georas sent the nearby MacPhersons, and the surreptitious way Dickie MacPherson slipped the dirk from his belt. From the corner of his eye, Lion saw Eneas Gunn's grin broaden, and the hair at his nape prickled. "Be ready," he muttered to Bryce.

Lion swung down from the saddle, keeping the sturdy pony between himself and Dickie. "Let the women go to my men."

"I will say what is to be done," Alexander snarled. Over his shoulder, he called, "Bring them forward."

Georas prodded the women with the flat of his sword. They stumbled along before him, clinging to each other for support. It killed Lion to remain still when he wanted to rush over and snatch them away from the MacPherson. His breath caught, his heart stopped as he watched Bryce take a step toward them. Another few yards and they would be safe—

"Seize him," Alexander suddenly roared. "Kill the traitor. Kill them all!"

The frozen tableau of men came to life. Georas shoved the women to the ground and raised his sword.

"Nay," Lion cried, surging forward.

Robbie MacNab was quicker. His knife cut through the air, striking Georas's arm. The man screamed and dropped his weapon.

"Bryce! To me!" Even as Lion opened his hand to receive the sword Bryce handed him, he saw the MacNabs leap into action.

Swinging blades from beneath the concealment of their cloaks, they fell on the MacPhersons and Stewarts. The Frasers and Keiths were making war on the Chisholms. Alexander screamed threats and orders, while the Sutherlands joined the fray. Lion's men and his allies fought with a vengeance, but they were outnumbered by the earl's forces.

Red Will had best hurry, Lion thought as he darted through the melee toward Rowena. She and Glenda were still sprawled on the ground. He reached them just as Georas wrenched the knife from his arm and lifted his sword again. Blood dripping from his hand, he prepared to strike.

"Nay!" Lion went in low, countering the blow a foot from Rowena's body.

Georas parried and regrouped. Teeth bared in a curse, he swung at Lion, driving him back with a punishing fury. But Lion knew his opponent's weakness. He thrust, feinted, found the opening and sank his blade in Georas's chest.

Georas gasped, his own sword clattering to the ground an instant before he slid down to join it.

"Rowena. Are you all right?" Lion knelt and sliced through her bonds with his dirk.

"Aye. Terrified, but unhurt. I..." Her eyes widened. "Look out! Behind you!"

Lion rose and wheeled, sword coming up to counter the downward thrust of Eneas's blade.

"Bastard!" Eneas fought with less finesse than Georas, but he was not alone. Clem stood with him, shoulder to shoulder, forcing Lion to divide his blows between the two of them.

Lion danced back, poking and parrying, spinning to counter first one man, then the other. He pricked Clem's arm and drew blood, then took a slice from Eneas's shoulder.

"Bloody hell," Eneas growled.

"That is to repay you for trying to have me killed."

Eneas grunted, his face contorted with pain and hatred. "I wish I had thought of it. Slip behind him," he shouted to Clem. "He cannot cover his back, too."

"Nay!" Rowena leapt up and drew her eating knife.

"Ro, for the love of God, stay back," Lion cried as he parried the pair of swords. "Take Glenda and get clear of the fighting before you are injured." He had no time to see if she complied, for the Gunns fought with desperate fury. Their blows reverberated up his arm, numbing it. Sweat dripped into his eyes, his lungs burned. Still he fought on, dimly aware of the clang of steel and hoarse shouts of those around him.

Finally he managed to get in under Clem's guard, hook his blade and send it spinning away. One quick lunge ended the man's life.

Growling a curse, Eneas came at Lion's unprotected side, but his deadly swing was brought up short by Bryce's sword. The stroke cleaved Eneas's sword in half and ripped open his chest. Eneas stared at the bloody wound for half a second, then fell to his knees, begging for mercy.

"Why should we spare you?" Bryce muttered. "You tried time and again to murder Lion."

"I did not, I tell you," Eneas said wildly.

"Then who did?" Lion demanded.

"I do not know." Spittle flew from Eneas's mouth as he gasped for air. "I wanted you in disfavor, but—I never tried—" The word ended on an ominous gurgle. Eneas stiffened, then breathed his last.

"Glenshee!" Alexander roared. He and his followers, a

hundred strong at least, had regrouped on the far side of the clearing. "Surrender, you whore's son traitor."

Lion scanned the clearing. It was littered with fallen men, some allies, some enemies. Robbie MacNab was still on his feet, bleeding from a shoulder wound. No more than fifty of his men and Lion's were in condition to fight. Rowena and Glenda had taken refuge at the base of an oak, huddling together for protection. His first thought was to get them away, but the only horses left standing were the earl's.

"Let us fall back to the road," Bryce said. "We can form a rear guard while the others make for the keep. Mayhap the guards will see us and send out reinforcements."

"There aren't enough men at Glenshee to aid us." Lion straightened, his eyes locking on the earl's glittering ones. "I am still prepared to offer the same exchange. My life for those of my people."

"Nay!" Rowena's cry was echoed by a dozen others.

Lion glanced at her and shook his head. He must do this, for his clansmen, for his lady and for his son. "What say you?" he shouted at Alexander.

"Why should I spare any of you when I have the superior force?" Alexander sneered. His expression made Lion's blood run cold, devoid as it was of decency and mercy. "I'll see you all hang for having defied me," he continued. "But you—" his lips curled back over yellowed teeth "—you, Lion, will roast over a slow fire. I'll..." He went on to describe tortures so horrible that even his own men squirmed.

"Lion, for the love of God, let us run," Bryce whispered.

Lion wanted to. But the thought of what such a madman might do to the women and bairns hardened his determination. "We'd not get far before he caught us, and his fury would be the worse for the chase. Nay, I must—"

"Take them," Alexander shouted.

His men started forward, weapons raised.

"Halt!" roared a voice as rough as gravel.

Lion spun just as an old man rode into the clearing. His hair was snowy white, his face lined and weathered, but he sat erect in the saddle, his blazing gaze fixed on the earl.

"Fergus Ross," Bryce whispered.

Lion swore. "Damn, I told him to stay away."

"Who the hell are you?" Alexander snarled.

"Fergie Ross of Clan Ross. I've come to see young Lion comes to no harm at your hands, Wolf of Badenoch."

Alexander stiffened as though he'd been struck. "How dare you call me that, you old fool? Seize him."

"Oh, I dinna think ye'll be doing that." Fergie raised a large, gnarled hand, and the clearing was suddenly filled with men wearing the Rosses distinctive red-and-black check. There were easily two hundred Ross clansmen, Iain among them. They were armed with spears and long pikes, their faces painted for war.

Alexander's eyes widened, and some of his men edged backward, but he was not cowed. "I'll have you put to the horn for this, Fergus, and every man by the name of Ross will be hunted down and killed like vermin."

"That's providing ye get away from here alive, Your Grace."

"Kill me, and my brother will hang you for treason."

"He's right, Fergie." Lion started toward the Rosses, but Rowena caught hold of his arm.

"Lion, I must speak with you."

"Not now, sweetheart. Get back where it's sa—"

"Nay." Her grip on him tightened. "We have the proof."

"What?" He started, then leaned closer.

"The letters. You were right, they do contain the promises he made to Archie Campbell and Donald MacKay. I have them." She patted her belly, where the parchment was bound beneath her clothes by a length of towel. "Glenda and I found a way to open his strongbox and take them. With him none the wiser."

Lion grinned and kissed her quickly. "Ach, I do love you, lassie."

Tempted though he was to tip his hand, to shout across the meadow that the earl and his horrendous schemes were doomed, Lion realized none of them would be safe until the letters were in the king's hands. And admitting he had them would be like waving a bit of choice meat under a hungry wolf's nose.

"A word, Fergie." He strode over to the Ross. "I know it's tempting to end it here and now, but he's right when he says Robert would hunt us down. I have a better way." Quickly he told the chief about the letters and Alexander's promises.

"After what he's done to me and mine, I'd rather sink my blade in his gut," the old man grumbled.

"I know. The dead cry out to me, too, but what good is it to avenge them and die ourselves? Better to hit the Wolf where it will hurt him most. And believe me, I do think he would prefer death to the disgrace that will be heaped on him when Robert sees proof that his brother plotted to take his throne."

"I suppose," Fergie said grudgingly.

Lion walked back over to where Bryce and Rowena waited. "My lord earl," he called out. "I do give you leave to depart my lands in peace."

"What?" exclaimed Bryce. "But—but after all he's done—"

Rowena poked him in the ribs. "Oh, he will pay. Lion will make certain of that. And knowing our illustrious earl, I do think that being stripped of power and titles will be a worse punishment than any death we could devise."

"Amen to that," Glenda said, coming over to join them. Her triumphant smile transformed her face, making her almost pretty.

"You will all regret this," Alexander warned. Dragging his horse's head around, he thundered down the road, away from the clearing and, hopefully, out of their lives for good.

Lion grinned and drew Rowena into the circle of his arms. "Aye, Bryce, we've very likely won. And the very best part of it is that the earl was bested by two very clever ladies."

Chapter Nineteen

"When will we go back to Hillbrae?" Dun asked.

Rowena paused outside Glenshee's stables and sighed. "Not till Lion returns."

"What of yer vow to Laird Padruig?"

"I've told you, over and over again, that I will honor it." She stepped into the building and waited a moment for her eyes to adjust from the brilliance of the afternoon sun. The cool darkness wrapped around her, the familiar scents and sounds of the animals oddly calming to her frazzled nerves. Lion had been gone for nearly two weeks and not a day had passed without Dun or Finlay or Kier asking when they'd leave.

"At least let us take Paddy back where he belongs," Dun pressed, his deep voice more gravelly than usual.

"I will not be parted from my son." Twitching her skirts, Rowena hurried down the aisle between the stalls, past Lion's great warhorse to the enclosure where her mare dozed.

"Nor, it seems, from your lover."

"Aye, I do love Lion." Rowena whirled, glaring at Dun. "But I will keep my word. However, I will not go till he is back from Edinburgh and I know all is well. If parliament and the king do not believe Lion's proof, if they do not declare the earl guilty of treason, we will all be in grave danger."

"With Eneas dead, we'd be as safe at Hillbrae as here."

"That may be, but I am not going till I'm ready." She would see Lion one last time, for once she returned to Hillbrae, she would never leave again. And Paddy deserved this chance to know his Sutherland kin and his father's home. She reached for her mare's saddle.

"I will do that."

Rowena frowned. "If you are going to pick at me about this, I will ride out alone."

"Nay. The Sutherlands say the land hereabout is safe, but I'm sworn to guard you, my lady." Dun proceeded to saddle two horses. "Does he know?" he asked as he tightened a cinch.

"Does who know what?"

Dun's eyes met hers over the mare's back. "Does Lion know that Paddy is his son?"

Rowena gasped. "Who...who told you that?"

"Laird Padruig himself...years ago."

"You never said anything," Rowena whispered, trying to read the older man's expression in the gloom.

Dun shrugged. "When I saw *him* with the lad, I marked the resemblance, though I don't think most folk would. Paddy's coloring is lighter, but there's something about his eyes and mannerisms...if you know to look."

"Aye," Rowena said faintly.

"Does Lion know?"

Rowena nodded. "Apparently Paddy looks like Lion's father, Lord Lucais."

"What will he do about it?"

"Nothing," Rowena said quickly, hoping to stem another flood of scowls and scorn. "He...he understands about the vow."

"Mmm." Dun turned his attention back to the horses, checking the tack before offering her a hand up.

Rowena sighed wearily. The castle was still crammed

with crofters whose huts had been burned by the earl when he retreated from Glenshee. Her every waking hour was filled with the hundred tasks necessary to help Ailsa run the keep. The activity helped keep her mind from the eventual parting with Lion, but she needed a few moments to herself. Ailsa had suggested she ride down to the loch. "I'm riding out for a bit of peace. If you are going to plague me, you can stay behind."

"I'll not mention it again."

Rowena nodded, accepted his help in mounting and guided her horse from the stables. "I am surprised you do not require a troop of men," she observed as they headed out the inner gate. "Where are Kier and Harry?"

"Busy," Dun curtly replied, his hard face in profile to her.

Paddy crept from the foal's stall and stared after his mother and Dun. His excitement at having eluded Harry and sneaked in here to play paled alongside what he'd just heard.

Lion was his da? How could that be when they'd only just met him? A bit of memory flitted through his mind, elusive as a wispy cloud. Lion. Sometime long ago Paddy remembered Jennie saying that name, and his mother hushing her.

His eyes narrowed as he tried to catch hold of the memory, but all he could recall was the sadness in his mother's face. He thought he understood, because he felt sad himself. Sad and a little confused, as though he'd eaten butterflies for supper.

How could he have two fathers?

Finlay would know. Finlay was old and couldn't run and play, but Finlay knew things.

Sighing, Rowena cantered beside Dun down the dusty road. Her happiness at this outing was considerably dimmed by his dour countenance. If there'd been any Sutherlands to spare, she'd have begged one of them to accompany her. But Lion had taken Red Will and Sim with him, leaving Heckie in charge of the keep's defenses. Bryce was not yet back from escorting Glenda to Blantyre, which was not surprising, because the two of them had become so wrapped up in each other Rowena would not be surprised to hear there was a wedding in the offing.

Rowena tried to feel happy for her friend, but a wee bit of jealousy crept in. Here she was, yearning to marry the man she'd always loved, and yet she'd never be free.

As they thudded across the wooden drawbridge, Rowena looked back over her shoulder at the stalwart castle. In a few short weeks, it had become more like home to her than Hillbrae, where she'd dwelt for six whole years. She supposed it was the Sutherlands' doing, for they were warm, friendly and caring.

Paddy had positively thrived at Glenshee. He'd made friends with several lads his own age, and together they roamed the grounds, stealing cakes from the kitchen, chasing sheep in the wide outer bailey and climbing the trees in the small orchard behind the keep. Most often, however, he could be found in the stables petting Turval's foal.

Before he left, Lion had told her he would send the horse to Paddy when he was old enough to ride it. The prospect of seeing her son—*their* son—mounted on his father's horse, carrying the huge Sutherland claymore that would also be his someday, brought tears to her eyes.

They belonged together, Lion and Paddy.

Just last night, Paddy had asked her, "When is Lion coming back? I miss him. He laughs with me, and he shows me things, and he doesna yell if I make a mistake. He's my bestest friend...next to Flame." The orange cat.

Rowena had smiled with him, then cried bitter tears into her pillow. The Gunns were right to fear she'd not keep her vow, because she did not want to. She did not want to at all. But she had no choice. Glenshee's priest had told

her, glumly, that such an oath was binding unless the
church lifted it. Which it would be unlikely to do just because she had now been reunited with her son's father and
wished to be absolved of the vow.

Rowena sighed and looked up in time to catch Dun's
intent stare, so piercing and scathing it seemed he must
guess her thoughts. If so, he'd know how anguished she
felt. A heavy, leaden weight seemed permanently lodged in
her chest. The only thing that gave her joy was Paddy. Not
even today's bright sunshine, or the feel of the soft breeze
on her face, or the cheerful sounds of the birds winging
through the meadow they passed could lift her spirits. "We
might as well go back," she said glumly.

"I thought ye wanted to see the loch," Dun exclaimed,
sounding oddly alarmed.

She shrugged. "It doesn't much matter."

"Well, I've a notion to look at it, and it might ease ye
to walk along the water," he added.

They rode in silence, past the field where ten days ago
the earl had been brought low by his own sins. Had he not
made an enemy of the Rosses and Lion not befriended
them, Fergie Ross wouldn't have arrived in time to save
the Sutherlands.

"When I received word that the Wolf was marching on
Glenshee, I called up every Ross I had to hand," the old
man had later explained, sprawled in a chair beside Glenshee's hearth. "I ken ye told me to stay at home and keep
safe, but had ye done that, Iain and wee Colin would have
been lost to me, too. I couldn't let ye face that madman
alone."

Lion's grin had lit up the great hall. "'Tis glad I am you
are a stubborn man, Fergie Ross, else I'd not be here today."

The memory of that triumph made Rowena smile. Lion
had refused to take any credit at all, insisting that they had
been saved by two brave, canny ladies. She and Glenda
had been the heroes of the feast that evening, not Lion and

not the men who had fought so gallantly against the earl's troops. His generosity of spirit had amazed Glenda, but not Rowena.

Lion was a man among men.

If only she had not heeded Padruig's offer six years ago. If only she'd been brave enough to face her mother's scolding and her kinsmen's scorn. If only she'd waited, Lion would have regained his senses and sought her out. They would have wed.

"We are here," Dun grumbled.

Rowena blinked. Sure enough, the horses had stopped at the edge of the loch. It stretched out before her, a huge expanse of water reflecting the deep blue of the sky, bounded on all sides by steep mountains. The only signs of habitation were a huddle of cottages at the crest of the nearby hill and the five fishing skiffs pulled up on the beach.

"It—it is breathtaking." Rowena slid from the saddle without waiting for Dun's help. Slowly she picked her way among the rocks to sit on one at the loch's edge. The water lapped against the shore, a gentle, calming slurp. She bent to dip her fingers in. "Oh, it's as cold as winter's snow."

"Aye." Dun came to stand behind her. Arms crossed over his chest, thick legs braced among the stones, he stared out over the loch. "A body'd not last ten minutes in such cold."

"I suppose not." She gazed up at him, feeling a bit more in charity with her solemn guard. He was only doing his best to protect his clan's interests. "Thinking of taking a swim?"

"Nay," he muttered, his expression even more foreboding. Truly he was a man who hid his thoughts well. Imagine having known about Paddy all these years and given no hint of it.

Rowena slanted him a wry smile. "Will you not at least sit, Dunmore? It is hard to relax with you hovering over me like a great, scowling giant."

Remorse flickered across his weathered face. Bending, he picked up a large rock. She supposed he meant to toss it in the water, as Paddy might. "I am sorry for this, my lady. Ye've always treated me decent like, but I know of no other way to make sure the old laird's wishes are carried out."

Rowena grunted as the stone collided with her head. She tried to cry out, to shy away. But the pain exploded inside her, and the darkness sucked her down...down....

It was just past noon when Lion rode in through Glenshee's massive gates. The road to the keep was lined with cheering Sutherlands, soldiers and crofters alike.

"Lion! Lion!" they chanted.

"Ach, there's something about coming home a hero that makes all the fighting worthwhile," Red Will said, his left arm still in a sling from catching a Stewart blade.

"That it does," Lion's smile dimmed as they rode into the courtyard and he did not see the one person he craved above all others. Had Rowena gone back to Hillbrae? She'd said she would remain till he returned from delivering the Campbell letters, but he'd guessed Finlay would try to persuade her otherwise. It looked as though the old man had prevailed.

Well, he would just have to go after her, Lion thought. He'd not come so far or gone through so much to lose her now. His parents were prepared for the fact that their son might be dividing his time between Hillbrae and Glenshee. They were not well pleased with the idea, but the bitter was tempered by the very sweet notion that they had a wee grandson. In fact, they would have returned with Lion had Lucais not feared to leave Edinburgh till parliament's warrants against Alexander were signed, sealed and sent off.

"Did they put the Wolf to the horn?" Micheil called out.

"Aye. The king was aghast at his brother's perfidy, but it was parliament that insisted the earl be brought in for

trial," Lion replied. Dismounting to the cheers of his clansmen, he handed his horse's reins to a stable lad. Though
he doubted the king's brother would hang, at least Alexander was no longer in a position to wreak harm on the
Highlands.

"Let us broach a keg of ale to celebrate," Lion shouted.
That was greeted by a roar of excitement, and the throng
surged up the steps into the keep. Micheil had the ale open
by the time they reached the hall. Cups were filled and
toasts drunk to Lion, the clan and Fergie Ross.

"So ye've won," Finlay Gunn said, cup in hand.

Lion blinked. "I—I thought you'd returned to Hillbrae."

"Nay. Rowena insisted we wait till ye came back."

"Then where is she?" Lion turned, rising up on his toes
as he tried to see over the heads of the cavorting Sutherlands.

"Gone for a ride." It was Kier, his expression sour as
ever.

"Alone?" Lion exclaimed.

"Nay. Dun went with her. I can show ye where they
went."

"Just tell me. I know the land hereabouts right well."

"I'd rather show ye," Kier muttered.

The hair at Lion's nape prickled. "What is going on?"
he demanded, oblivious to the celebrating around him.

"Naught."

"Liar." Lion caught Kier by the front of his tunic and
shook him. "Tell me what you and your brother are up to.
Where has he taken Rowena?"

"Easy," Finlay, said, laying a restraining hand on Lion's
arm. "I am sure she is fine."

Lion shook Finlay off. "Well, I am not. Someone has
thrice tried to kill me...once when Rowena was with me.
I suspected it was Gunns, but now—"

Something tugged at the bottom of Lion's kilt.

Swearing under his breath, he looked down—into

Paddy's pale face and round, frightened eyes. "Paddy, what—"

"Are you my da?" the lad asked softly.

"Paddy." At a loss for words, Lion let go of Kier and knelt before his son. "Where did you get such a notion?"

"From Dun. I heard him and Mama talking. He—he said 'twas so." Paddy's chin was thrust out, but his lip trembled. "Is it?"

Not now. Not like this. Lion looked up at Finlay for guidance, for inspiration.

"It isn't true," Kier snarled. "It's a lie. A damned, filthy lie, for which ye'll pay, Lion Sutherland."

"Look out! He's got a knife," someone shouted.

Kier's blade flashed in the crowded, sunlight hall, arching toward Lion's neck.

Lion leaned away from the slashing blow and saw Kier whip the weapon around for a hacking backstroke. There wasn't room for Lion to draw his sword, nor time to get the knife from his belt. He lashed out with his foot, catching his opponent in the leg.

"Bloody hell!" Kier's knee buckled. He fell sideways, right into Lion's sweeping uppercut. Bone crunched, blood spurted. Kier groaned and collapsed in a heap on the floor, his dirk spinning from his hand as he passed out.

"Lion!" Heckie charged through the crowd, his knife drawn. "What happened? Are you all right?"

"Aye." Lion stood, his legs shaky.

"Seize them! Get the Gunns," someone cried.

"Nay." Lion held up a hand to forestall his clansmen. "Disarm them, nothing more," he said to Heckie. "They are our guests till we determine otherwise."

"L-Lion?" A small hand tugged at his. "Why did Kier try to hurt you?"

He reached down to pat Paddy's shoulder. "It is all right, lad. Just a—a misunderstanding." He fixed Finlay with a hard stare. "One we are going to get to the bottom of right now."

"Did Mama and Dun have a mis-misstanding, too? Is that why they were arguing about going home to Hillbrae?" Paddy asked.

Dread chilled Lion's blood. Kneeling, he placed his hands on Paddy's shoulders. "Where did your mama and Dun go?"

"To the loch." Tears filled his eyes. "Is she all right?"

"Aye," Lion said with a conviction he didn't feel. "I'm going out to get her, right now."

"Can I come, too?"

"Not this time, lad."

"But you will bring her back safe, just like last time."

Lion nodded, incapable of speaking. He left the hall in a rush, barely conscious of being followed till he reached the stables and found himself surrounded by Sutherlands.

"Dinna be thinking to leave us behind," Heckie said.

"All right, but you'd best keep up, for I'm not waiting." A few frantic minutes later, Lion galloped out of Glenshee with thirty men scrambling to keep up.

Bypassing the road, they cut across the high moor and came upon the loch from the rocky hills to the east. Rather than ride straight down to the water, Lion dismounted and snaked up the rise on his belly. His nerves sizzling with apprehension, he scanned the shoreline for some sign of Rowena and Dun.

"It's possible he means her no harm," Heckie whispered. "We should have waited for Kier to come around, and questioned him."

"Nay, if she is in danger, every second is precious. Look there!" He nodded toward the solitary figure sitting on a rock at the water's edge. "There's Dun."

Heckie shielded his eyes. "I do not see yer lady."

"Nor do I, but do you see something in that fisherman's boat? The one nearest to Dun?"

"A bundle of cloth in the bottom."

"Cloth? Or my lass?"

"Mmm. Could be Dun is waiting for Kier to show up

with ye, then the bastards think to pitch ye both in the water.''

''Aye.'' Lion studied the scene and the problem for a moment. ''Heckie, I want you to take half of the lads, go around and come down the road, slowly like, as though nothing was amiss. The rest of us will work our way to the shore.''

Crawling from rock to rock, Lion and his band reached the water's edge without arousing Dun's suspicions. His attention was focused on the road, though from time to time he walked over and glanced into the boat. Knowing Rowena must be in it made waiting hell for Lion. Every nerve in his body vibrated with the urge to run and snatch her from harm's way.

''She must still be alive,'' Naill whispered. ''Else he'd not keep checking on her.''

Lion nodded. It was small consolation.

''Here they come.''

Lion's gut tightened as he watched Heckie and the troop meander toward the loch.

Dun stood, shielding his eyes from the sun. Something must have alarmed him, for he suddenly spun, grabbed the prow of the boat and shoved it into the water.

''Nay!'' Lion jumped up and ran toward the launch site, but it was too late. Dun had the boat in the water and was pulling on the oars for all he was worth. What Dun lacked in experience he made up for in strength, sending the boat spurting out into the loch. ''Come back.'' Lion waded in.

''Wait!'' Naill tugged him back. ''Ye'll drown with all that mail on,'' he reminded Lion.

Lion ran for one of the other boats, but all four had gaping holes in them. He cursed and threw his helmet onto the rocks. ''Bloody hell!'' He ground his teeth in impotent fury as he watched Dun's boat draw farther and farther out of reach.

By the time Heckie and the other lads thundered up, the

boat was near the center of the loch. "What now?" Heckie asked, dismounting.

Lion's eyes narrowed as he gauged the distance to the boat. "If you kept him busy, I could swim out and take him unawares."

"Ye'd freeze yer arse off," Heckie grumbled. "Let us put a ring of men around the loch and wait for him to come in."

"What if he throws Rowena in the water first?" Lion shook his head. "Go ahead and string yourselves out around the loch," he said. "Make a show of it. Talk to him. If he asks where I am, say I've gone back for more men."

Lion stalked off over the hill from whence he'd come and stripped down to bare skin. Using a small ravine to shield his movements, he sneaked back to the shore. Along the way, he spotted a large log and dragged it with him. When he entered the water, he kept the log between himself and the boat.

The threats Dun shouted across the water at Heckie were nearly as chilling as the water Lion surreptitiously lowered himself into. Nearly. After only a few moments, his arms and legs were numb from the cold. Still he persevered, clinging to the log with one hand as he propelled himself slowly toward the center of the loch.

Dun's voice grew louder. "If Lion Sutherland does not show himself, I'll cast his whore into the loch."

"He's gone back to Glenshee, I tell ye," Heckie shouted. "He said I was to inform ye that if ye brought the boat in with his lady unharmed, he'd spare yer life."

"Ha! As if I believe that." Dun was silent a moment, and Lion paddled closer, hoping against hope that Rowena was all right. "I'll never get him now," Dun said, his voice lower. "I don't suppose it matters. With her dead, we'll take Paddy home."

"I doubt Lion'll let his son leave," Heckie retorted.

"What? How—how do ye know that?"

"Kier blurted it out in the hall before he attacked Lion."

"Attacked? But he was supposed to lure him here."

"Lion was too smart for him. He knew something evil was afoot, and he—"

"What of Kier? Is my brother dead?"

"Nay, but the both of ye will hang if any harm comes to Lion's lady," Heckie warned.

Lion peered around the edge of the log. He was still a good distance from the boat, but he didn't dare risk taking it closer for fear Dun, who presently sat facing the far shore, would turn around and guess what was up. Drawing a deep breath, Lion ducked under the icy water and stroked toward the boat.

The water was clear, but his arms and legs were so numb they barely obeyed his commands. He moved sluggishly, slowly. Fear that he'd drown ere he reached them sent a burst of strength through his flagging muscles. At last he arrived at the boat. Keeping close to the far side, he poked his head up and soundlessly drew in much-needed air. The moment he tried to enter the bark, Dun would attack so he must move quickly.

Rising out of the water, Lion grabbed hold of the edge of the boat and leaned his weight on it. The craft tipped toward him and he spied Rowena slumped in the bottom. Her eyes were closed. A bloody gash marred her forehead.

"What the hell?" Dun turned. "Glenshee!" He stood, drawing the sword from its sheath. The sudden movement sent the boat bobbing like a leaf in a tempest. Dun cursed, stumbling over a seat as he lunged forward, murder in his eyes.

Lion heaved on the side of the boat again. Water poured in over the edge. The boat shuddered, then flopped over, dumping Dun and Rowena into the icy water with Lion.

As her limp body floated by, Lion snagged Rowena around the waist, kicked out with his legs and cut away from the boat toward the shore. Dun thrashed around beside the capsized hull, cursing and calling for help.

Lion had his hands full trying to keep her face above water. "Rowena! Ro!" Treading water, he shook her a little.

Blessedly, she coughed, then opened her eyes. "Lion?"

"Easy, love, I've got you." He put his arm around her and began to tow her again toward shore.

"Dun?" she gasped, arms flailing a bit.

"Do not worry about him. Let me get you to safety. Relax, love. Let me do the work."

Naill and a dozen men, none of whom could swim, waded out to help haul them from the water. Warm, rough blankets were wrapped around them, and someone pressed a flask of whiskey to Lion's lips. He drank deep, letting the fiery liquid burn away the cold. Then he passed it to Rowena, still held secure in his arms. She took a sip, coughed and lay trembling against him.

"Dun?" he asked when he'd gotten his breath back.

Heckie shook his head. "Could be the weight of his armor dragged him down. We none of us can swim a stroke, so..."

"He tried to kill me," Rowena whispered. "All this time he pretended to be my protector, and he wished me dead."

"Shh. It's over now," Lion said.

But when the little cavalcade returned to Glenshee, they were greeted by a somber-faced Finlay Gunn.

"Rowena?" he asked anxiously.

"I—I am fine," she replied, teeth chattering. Lion had carried her into the hall, but still held her in his arms, as though he'd never let her go. Nor did she want him to. "Finlay, I do not know why Dun would try to kill me."

"I do." The old man sighed heavily and sat back down in the chair before the fire roaring in the hearth. "It pains me to say this, Lion, but my cousin did take extraordinary measures to ensure he had an heir."

Lion sat, too, his arms tightening around Rowena. "Go on."

"While Ailsa was bandaging Kier's side, he confessed

the whole sorry tale. Six years ago, Dun accompanied Padruig when he went to fetch his horses from yer brother, Johnny,'' Finlay said to Rowena. "Padruig immediately suspected ye were breeding, and set Dun to follow you when ye went off to meet young Lion.''

Despite her recent dunking in the loch, Rowena's face heated. Drat, what must he have seen? "He spied on us?''

"That I dinna know. When Padruig realized 'twas Lion's child ye carried, he became obsessed with having it. He learned a bit about the Sutherlands' feud with the Munros—''

"And sent his men to ambush me, dressed in Monroe plaids,'' Lion said grimly.

Finlay nodded. "Aye.''

"That—that bastard. He acted so noble, offering me a marriage to save my honor and give my son a name, and the truth was he had tried to have Lion killed.''

"Aye.'' Finlay looked at his hands.

"Was…was my brother involved?'' Rowena asked.

Once again, Finlay nodded. "Padruig threatened him with ruin if he did not guide Dun to the ambush spot. I gather he did not take part in the attack, but ye can question Kier further. There is more,'' Finlay added. "When Padruig learned Lion had not died in that attack, he feared someday ye and Lion might meet again. So he pressed upon ye that oath to tie ye to Hillbrae.''

Rowena was so angry she couldn't speak.

"But Dun and Kier thought the oath might not be enough to keep us apart, so they tried to kill me,'' Lion muttered.

"Dun felt he had a sacred duty to see his laird's wishes carried out…no matter what,'' Finlay said.

Lion cursed again. "What of Harry?''

"Oh, he was not involved,'' Finlay said quickly. "Harry's a good lad, the son of another of my cousins.'' His frown deepened. "I suppose it's too much to ask that ye spare Kier's life.''

"I might,'' Lion said, heartily sick of killing. "On condition he leave Glenshee and never bother us again." He drew Rowena a bit closer. "Rowena and Paddy will be staying here."

"I know how ye must feel, but what of the oath?" Finlay asked. "She did swear it on holy relics."

"Well, I do not see why I should be bound by a vow to a—a murderer," Rowena exclaimed.

Lion squeezed her hand. "We will try to absolve you of the oath. I'll set Father Simon to work on it."

"I will stay with you no matter what," Rowena said, but her eyes were dark with the same fear that clouded Lion's happiness. They had thwarted Alexander and overcome the tragedies that had tainted their past, but could they imperil their son's immortal soul in order to remain together?

Epilogue

Hillbrae, November, 1390

"He still has not returned?" Rowena glanced at the messenger she'd dispatched to Glenshee a week ago.

Rob Gunn, the young clansman she'd entrusted with the errand, sighed and shook his head. "Nay, the guards said they've had no word from Lord Lion since he departed for Italy."

"But that was nearly five months ago." Rowena knees went weak, and she sank back into her chair at the high table, conscious of the whispering among the Gunns assembled for the evening meal. Lion was gone, just when she needed him most. History came so close to repeating itself that she might have laughed...if she hadn't felt so like crying. Or throwing up. She'd been doing a lot of both recently. "How long can it take to sail to Italy and return?"

Finlay reached over and patted her hand. "It is no easy thing to arrange an interview with the pope."

"Why did he have to go in person? He could have sent a letter along with my petition," she muttered.

"'Twould not have the same impact as pleading your case himself," Harry reminded her. "Lion must make the pope see how vital it is that you be freed from that damned oath."

Harry now sat in Padruig's chair, having won the right to be chief three months ago by besting Padruig's other blood cousins in a test of battle skills. Still, Harry's hold on the clan was by no means assured. Many questioned whether Rowena's oath to Padruig was binding on the Gunns, as well. Did they imperil Paddy's soul if they accepted another as chief?

"I know why he went, I just did not think it would take so long," Rowena snapped.

In mid-July, she and Lion had reluctantly concluded that until they could settle the matter of the oath, she and Paddy had best return to Hillbrae. Lion had escorted them here, then set off for Italy, vowing he'd not rest till he'd obtained a dispensation for her. It was not until a month later that she'd realized they had another problem.

She was pregnant with Lion's babe. Again.

"Is Papa coming to get us?" Paddy asked from her other side. His face was alight with joy for the first time since he'd been forced to part from his adored father.

"Not yet, dearling."

"Oh." Paddy's smile faded, replaced by the lost look he'd worn ever since their return to Hillbrae. "Did he die like my other papa?" he asked in a small voice.

"Nay." Rowena cuddled her son close. "He is not dead." Fate would not be so cruel. "He'll come home to us."

Finlay glanced at her burgeoning belly and sighed. "Robert the Bruce waited a long while for his dispensation from Rome."

"Years," Harry added glumly.

Rowena's stomach rolled. She might well have two bastard children by the time the pope acted.

Finlay whispered, "My offer to wed ye still holds, lass."

Her eyes filled with tears, but she blinked them back. "Nay, I've traveled that road before. I will wait."

A Gunn clansmen streaked into the hall. "Visitors, my lord," he said to Harry, but his eyes strayed to Rowena.

She straightened. "Lion? Could you tell if it was Lion?"

"Nay, 'tis a lady...a very grand lady."

Indeed, the woman was just entering the hall. Her riding cloak flung back to reveal a peacock blue gown, her carriage proud as a queen's, she advanced on the high table. Eyes a startling shade of violet latched onto Rowena's. "You must be Lady Rowena. I am Elspeth Sutherland."

"Oh," Rowena said faintly. Lady Elspeth looked as polished and intimidating as she'd feared.

Finlay rose. "Will ye sit and refresh yerself?"

"In a moment." Elspeth smiled, deepening the wrinkles around her mouth and eyes, the only signs she was no longer young. "First I'd like a private word with Rowena. If I may."

"Of course." Rowena stood, her knees going weaker when the lady's eyes strayed to her mountainous belly. Grimly, Rowena led the way to a small window alcove and sank onto the stone seat.

"Well, I see my son has left you in a bit of a fix," the lady said as she sat beside Rowena.

"He did not know when he left." Rowena stiffened. "Sweet Mary, has something happened to him? Is that why you've come?"

"Nay." She clasped Rowena's cold hands in her warm ones. "The steward of Kinduin wrote me in Edinburgh saying you've sent messengers looking for Lion. I feared something might be amiss."

"It is." Rowena placed a protective hand over her unborn child, starting as the babe kicked.

"Oh, may I?" Elspeth gingerly touched Rowena's belly, her composed features warming with wonder. "How I envy you."

"Me? But..."

"Ah, well, the circumstances may not be perfect, but

there's no greater joy than carrying your love's child." The woman's gaze sharpened. "I assume you love my son."

"With all my heart." Rowena's eyes filled with tears.

"Go away," exclaimed a childish voice. Paddy stood beside them, his expression fierce. "Dinna make my mama cry."

"You must be Paddy." Lady Elspeth slipped from the bench to kneel before the lad. "You are the very image of my Lucais."

"Wh-who is he?"

"Lion's father...your grandfather," Elspeth said softly. Her hands brushed lightly over Paddy's hair and tweaked his nose. "Even to this beak... You'll grow into it when you are older."

"I never had a grandfather before," Paddy said warily.

"Or a grandmother, either." Lady Elspeth opened the purse at her waist and pulled out a small packet. "Well, it's a grandparent's job to spoil bairns." She opened the oiled parchment, extracted a sweetmeat and handed it to Paddy.

He glanced at his mother, then popped the sugared treat into his mouth. "I like you," he decided, chewing happily.

"And I you." Elspeth settled on the bench with Paddy in her lap. "I can tell you stories about when your papa was a lad."

"Do you have more sweetmeats?" cagey Paddy asked.

"Mmm." Elspeth grinned at Rowena. "He also inherited Lucais's deviously clever mind." Dropping her voice, she added, "Lucais is certain Lion will succeed in his petition."

"Really? How can he know what the pope will do?"

"Lucais gave Lion a letter from the king to present to the pope, asking for a speedy resolution of the situation...along with a hefty chest of gold."

"He would bribe the pope?" Rowena asked, aghast.

"Boniface is pressed for funds just now, and His Holiness is none too saintly when it comes to such matters. He has been known to sell priories to the highest bidder, and believe me, the fortune Lion will offer would buy two priories.''

Rowena blinked. ''You would beggar yourselves for me?''

''You are family, my dear. We Sutherlands would do anything for our kin, but do not fear we will go hungry.'' She frowned. ''I do not understand why Lion did not wed you before he left.''

''He wanted to. I did not wish him to tie himself to me if he could not get the oath rescinded.''

''A noble gesture, my dear, but—''

''Can you tell me a story?'' Paddy asked.

''Of course.'' Settling back, Elspeth began to weave a tale of Lion's first hunt. The hero of the story, however, was Lucais, who saved his son from a charging wild boar.

Rowena left them only long enough to fetch a cup of wine and a plate of bread and cheese for their guest. Paddy, however, left his grandmother little time to eat or drink, for he demanded story after story from her. Listening to the events that had shaped Lion's life, Rowena felt relaxed for the first time in months, and closer to him than ever before. When Paddy finally drifted off to sleep, she handed Lady Elspeth a fresh cup of wine. ''I am so happy you came.''

''And I, too.'' Lady Elspeth brushed a kiss on Paddy's head. ''We regret missing so much of his youth, and do vow that we'll spend as much time as we can with your other babes.''

''Babes. You do not think they are twins, do you?'' Rowena exclaimed. ''I am larger than I was with Paddy, but—''

''Nay…that is, I do not think so, but Daibidh—you know he is our second son and the soothsayer of Clan Sutherland?'' At Rowena's nod, she continued. ''Daibidh says you and Lion will have six bairns.''

''Six!'' Rowena blinked, trying to take it in.

''In fact, Daibidh sent you a gift.'' Elspeth shifted Paddy

slightly and took from her purse a small sack. Upending it into her palm, she showed off six small hunks of amber, each suspended from a thin gold chain. "You are to keep them and give them to each babe on its naming day."

"Six," Rowena repeated. As the babe inside her kicked, she winced. "Now is not the time to tell me I must go through this four more times."

Elspeth chuckled. "Well, I recall the—"

The door to the hall flew open. Lion stood silhouetted in the light flooding into the room. "Rowena!" he shouted.

"Here." She struggled to her feet, fearful that his dark scowl as he ran to her boded ill for his mission.

"Oh, Rowena!" Lion swept her into a fierce embrace. "I—"

The babe kicked and squirmed.

"How—how did this happen?"

Conscious of their avid audience, Rowena felt her face heat. "I should think you'd know full well the how of it."

"Aye, but…" Lion looked around wildly. "Where's the priest? We must be wed at once before you…you burst."

His mother laughed. "You've several months till the babe is born, my son." She wrapped her arm around the waist of a tall man who had entered with Lion, a man with glowing eyes and silver lacing his dark red hair. "Let me introduce to you your future father by marriage. Lucais—"

"Grandpa?" Clutching his grandmother's hand, Paddy looked up at the laird. "Do you have any sweetmeats?"

Lucais smiled, but his eyes looked suspiciously moist as he bent down. "Nay, but I've a wooden sword made specially for you, and I'll teach you to wield it."

"Really?" Paddy let go of his grandmother's fingers and tugged on Lucais's. "Can we get it now?"

Elspeth chuckled. "I can see I'll have to come up with a better bribe if I want to compete with you. Before you go anywhere, tell us what news from Italy?"

Lion hugged Rowena closer. "The best. His Holiness—upon due consideration, and after having our gold twice counted—has granted you a dispensation from that damned oath.''

''Oh, Lion.'' Rowena buried her face in his dusty tunic, smiling as a cheer swept through the hall.

''Boniface agreed that since Padruig lied to you, the vow he pressured you into swearing was null and void. And—'' he glanced down at Paddy, holding tight to his grandfather's hand ''—his Holiness further agreed that Paddy is my legal issue, since I would have wed you before his birth had Padruig not tried to murder me.''

Rowena blinked back happy tears. ''So we can be together?''

''Always.'' Lion turned to Harry. ''If you've a priest, we will wed this afternoon.'' His expression sobered as it strayed to her belly. ''Just in case. And we need to baptize Paddy again, as well, with the Sutherland name.''

''I get a grandmother, a grandfather and a new name?'' Paddy frowned as he considered this.

''Aye.'' Lion let go of Rowena long enough to lift his son into his arms. ''From now on, you are Paddy Sutherland.''

''Paddy is my old name,'' he said, sticking his lip out. ''I want a new one. I want to be called Avenger, for your sword.''

''Avenger?'' Rowena said weakly. ''Why not Lion or Lucais?''

''Well…'' Paddy glanced from one man to the other.

Rowena took one look at the wonder chasing across Lucais Sutherland's rugged features and made a decision. ''You already have your grandsire's nose and hair, love. Why not his name?'' There'd apparently be plenty of bairns to name after Lion.

''Mmm.'' Paddy—the former Paddy—eyed Lucais slyly. ''If I'm called Lucais, will you take me hunting and save me from a boar?''

His grandfather ruffled his hair. ''Your father is right. You are too canny for your own good—or our peace of mind. Aye, I'll take you hunting, but I cannot promise a boar, young Luc.''

Still it was agreed. So anxious was Lion to make them his that Rowena barely had time to change into a fresh gown and see Luc attired in his best tunic before the event began. The ceremonies were conducted in Hillbrae's courtyard, the chapel being too small to hold all the Gunns and Sutherlands.

There were tears of joy in Father Cerdic's eyes as he proclaimed them man and wife. With the huzzahs of the crowd ringing off the old stone walls, Lion enfolded Rowena in his arms and claimed her mouth. His kiss of peace was so passionate it curled her toes inside her leather slippers.

"Come, we've a fine supper laid in the hall," Harry called out, bubbling over with happiness and relief himself, for now the way was clear for him to rule the Gunns.

Up the steps they went and into the keep, but at the entryway, Lion turned Rowena away from the doors to the great hall. "I've had enough of crowds," he whispered, drawing her instead up the stairs that led to the sleeping rooms.

"But the feast?"

"They can get drunk without us." He hustled her into her chamber, barred the door and leaned against it, heaving a sigh. "Do you mind? Five months is a long time away from you."

"Aye, it is, and nay, I do not, but..." Rowena hesitated, feeling fat and frumpy.

"Good." Lion crossed to her and attacked the laces down the front of her gown.

"Lion, wait, I—"

He cut off her protest with a long, hot kiss. "I've been dying to get you out of this damned thing," he murmured.

Cool air rushed over her warm skin as he parted the front of her gown. She raised a protective hand.

"Nay, let me see you." His expression reverent, he

slipped a hand inside and cupped one swollen breast. "You are so beautiful." He lowered his mouth, covering the aching peak and sucking gently. "Are you tender?" he whispered.

She nodded, swallowing hard. "Tender and—and fat."

"Fat?" He looked up at her through his lashes, eyes brimming with love. "You cannot know how seeing you like this makes me feel, or you'd not say that." His gaze holding hers, he eased the gown off her shoulders to pool on the floor.

When the shift followed, leaving her naked and vulnerable to his steady gaze, she shivered.

"None of that." He soothed away the gooseflesh. "I love seeing you, all rosy and glowing..." his hands moved over her belly, stroking softly "...filled with our babe." He went down on one knee and kissed the swollen curve. "I missed this the first time, and I intend to savor every moment." Straightening, he swept her into his arms and carried her to the bed.

There, on the counterpane where she'd cried bitter tears, he made slow, healing love to her. In the sweet aftermath, cradled close in his embrace, Rowena felt contentment seep through her, chasing out the pain of the past.

"I love you, my lady," Lion whispered. "And I do thank God that we've a long, happy life ahead of us."

"Not to mention fruitful," Rowena said, chuckling.

* * * * *